FICTION

BLACK

SIMON BESTWICK

MOUNTAIN

NOVEL

ISBN: 979-12-80713-13-1
NOVEMBER 2021
COPYRIGHT (EDITION) ©2021 INDEPENDENT LEGIONS PUBLISHING
COPYRIGHT (WORK) ©2021 SIMON BESTWICK
COVER ART: JUMALASIKA LTD
PROOFREADING: KAREN RUNGE

HWA SPECIALTY PRESS AWARD RECIPIENT

BLACK

SIMON BESTWICK

MOUNTAIN

PART 1

WARE

1: THE GHOSTS OF HAFAN DEG

SALFORD QUAYS, SEPTEMBER 2013

One of the best things about being a freelance writer is that you can randomly browse the internet, checking out any site that takes your fancy, and still claim you're working. One of the worst things is that you actually *are*, so if you're not careful, everything becomes potential copy—a payday of one kind or another.

My name's Rob Markland. I make a bitty, scrappy sort of living: some of it's copywriting, some of it's editing and proofing and some of it's from journalism—mostly feature articles of one kind or another. I had a go at writing fiction back in the 1990s, but I was rubbish at it. In the early 2000s, I still dreamt of becoming an investigative journalist or war correspondent, but it turned out I was far better suited to sitting on my backside doing random Google searches than I was dodging bullets in a combat zone. I've made my peace with that. It provides me with a living.

Or I *had*. It *did*.

I: POKER93

I was trawling urbex sites in search of material for an article—that's urban exploration, for those not in the know. People who go sneaking into abandoned buildings and structures, looking around and taking pictures. Old lunatic asylums used to be popular targets, although they've pretty much all been demolished now. There are still no end of railway stations, factories and underground tunnels though, to name but three. A lot of urbexing is borderline or outright illegal as it usually involves trespassing on private property, but that doesn't stop the urbexers from either doing it or posting a skip-load of photos to these forums.

One of the sites I looked at was called Forgotten Spaces. At first glance there wasn't much going on; no new posts on any of the existing threads. But there *was* one brand new thread, showing half a dozen posts, created by a user called Poker93. It was titled HAFAN DEG.

Poker93 had pasted most of the pictures into a single long post. *Found this place in North Wales, nr. Bala,* he or she had written at the top. *Built in 70s I think. Freeky lookin place.*

The first pictures showed a lake surrounded by heavy woodland, and a cluster of odd-looking buildings on the far shore. They were made up of circular, pill-shaped units, each with four thin metal legs and a row of circular windows, like portholes, around the edges. They put me in mind of flying saucers. There were a couple of single units, but most were bolted on top of one another in stacks of two or three.

More shots followed, at closer range. The units were made of plastic or fibreglass; they'd once been a variety of bright colours but had faded over the years. Most of their windows were cracked or missing.

Closer in, I could make out a flight of steps running up the side of each stack. The main entrance to each structure had a sort of extruded porchway you could step into. Some of the doors were firmly shut; others gaped open.

Like little plastic pods, said Poker93. *Well mad!*

Another post showed the inside of one of the pods. The door and most of the windows were gone; the dim interior was awash with stagnant water, with mould and moss crawling up the walls.

Check this, said the next post. A photograph of one of the few intact pods, focused on the porchway and a neighbouring window. Then a blow-up of the window. A pallid blur showed behind the glass; it looked a little like a face. *Think it's a ghost? ;-) That WELL shat me up.*

There were a couple of questions from other users about access and security, but after that the thread petered out.

It was enough, though. This was weird, and different. I printed off the thread.

*

Typing *Hafan Deg* into Google didn't give me any joy; turns out the name means 'Bright Haven' or 'Fair Haven', which meant I found a succession of care homes, cottages and B&Bs. Nearly an hour later, I'd reached the conclusion that—other than Forgotten Spaces—there was no mention of the place online.

I already had an account on the site. Some posts could only be viewed by members, and since it was free to join I'd done so—but until then I'd only used it to lurk. Now I put it to another use, and sent a direct message to Poker93.

Hi – that Hafan Deg place is great! Where did you find out about it? Can't find anything online.

Poker93 must have had time on his or her (I never found out which) hands, because in less than five minutes I had a reply.

Yeh I know. Mad innit? My dad had a box of old mags in the garage – i was having a flick through and read about it there.

I asked if there was any chance they could scan the article for me.

No probs. Already done it so I could put it on my phone. What's your email?

Five minutes later, I was printing off a PDF marked *Hafan Deg*.

II: THE SILENCE OF HAFAN DEG

THE SILENCE OF HAFAN DEG
By Russell Ware
Unexplained Magazine, Issue 4, 1978

Llyn Daioni, in North Wales, is a lake about a hundred feet long by fifty wide. Hidden in a pine forest away from the outside world, it is, to look at, as tranquil and picturesque a scene as you could hope to find in Britain.

But when you go to Llyn Daioni, what strikes you most of all is the silence. Not a single bird sings, as if they know not to come near.

Beside the lake is a cluster of strange-looking buildings, their bright colours already fading, symbols of a future that will never come to pass; they are the only surviving monument to a story of greed and ambition that ended in ruin and death.

It all began with an architect from London by the name of Harry Yelland. Young, handsome and smooth-talking, Yelland was determined to make both his name and his fortune before he was thirty, and had few scruples as to how he did it; at twenty-three, rumours of past shady dealings already dogged his career.

Yelland had designed a prefabricated home he called the ESCAPE house (Enclosed Self-Contained All-Purpose Environment), that he claimed could be set up on any landscape, in any climate. He set about trying to attract investors, touting it as the home of the future, but without success.

Forty-two-year-old Bill Lewis was a would-be property developer who'd inherited the land around Llyn Daioni. Yelland wooed him with a bold proposal; an exclusive holiday resort for a select—and wealthy—clientele. Peace, quiet, solitude, a private lake for boating and fishing, undisturbed woodland—the land Lewis owned even included a mountain.

And to cap it all, a new and unique kind of home to live in: one offering all mod cons and creature comforts, but which their customers could site and position at their whim. The ESCAPE houses could be set up singly or stacked on top of one another, bunched close together or set far apart. Residents could have their homes hidden away in the woods, perched on the shore of the lake—wherever they wanted them.

Lewis was won over, and the two men went into partnership. By early 1973 a prospectus was being circulated to potential clients for Hafan Deg Executive Village, to open the following year.

Lewis and Yelland decided to build a marina on Llyn Daioni, for boating on the lake. It was a much more conventional construction project than Yelland's houses, and should have been a straightforward undertaking. But there were problems from the start; delays getting the building materials to the site, then a strike and, later on, an outbreak of food poisoning that laid up nearly the entire workforce.

Finally the building work started—but then came the first death. A worker called David Lloyd, apparently drunk, fell in the lake and drowned. The disturbing part was that this happened in broad daylight, during a lunch break. The rest of his colleagues were eating their lunch no more than thirty yards away, but none of them heard a sound—even though marks on the steep earth bank beside the lake indicated Lloyd had been scrabbling at it for several minutes, trying to get out.

Meanwhile, the first prototype ESCAPE houses were coming off the production line. But they turned out to be riddled with problems; roofs leaked, faulty heating caused fire hazards or released toxic fumes, and problems with the adjustable legs made the houses prone to collapse. Production was delayed while Yelland struggled to iron out the bugs. It was not until May 1974, a month after Hafan Deg had been due to open, that the first ESCAPE houses were installed.

And at the planned marina, things only got worse. Equipment and materials either disappeared or failed to work properly; a section of bank collapsed, throwing a cement mixer and air compressor into the lake along with two workers, one of whom suffered a crushed leg. Then one of the pilings for the marina collapsed, and workers Martyn Rees and Hughie Evans were killed. Four others fell ill with an unidentified virus that left them unable to work for months. Heavy rains caused flooding, destroying more equipment and causing the rest of the marina to collapse.

"Everything that could go wrong, went wrong," one former worker on the site, John Davies, 33, said. "There's always the chance of accidents in this line of work, but this went above and beyond that. And it never felt right, that place. Always felt like someone was watching."

Costs overran and time slipped by. Rumours circulated that Bill Lewis had borrowed heavily to keep the project afloat, throwing good money after bad, and that in his desperation he'd now ended up owing money to organised criminals.

At last the ESCAPE houses were installed at Llyn Daioni, but the problems that had supposedly been ironed out of them still turned out to be very much there: they were leaky death-traps that would either gas their occupants or burn them to death. From that moment, Hafan Deg was doomed. The money to build new houses, even ones of more conventional design, simply wasn't there.

And that was when Harry Yelland vanished, taking with him the last of the partnership's funds and leaving Lewis facing bankruptcy. Two weeks later Bill Lewis's body was found floating in nearby Bala Lake, with a bottle of Scotch and another of barbiturates in his system. Officially the cause of death was suicide, although others said his shadier creditors had helped him on his way. Harry Yelland was never seen again; opinion was divided as to whether he'd made a clean getaway or if Lewis' creditors had caught up with him too.

Whatever the truth, Hafan Deg was abandoned. Virtually nothing is left of the planned marina; only the ESCAPE houses remain —abandoned, faded monuments to Harry Yelland's greed and ambition, standing isolated and uninhabited. Or are they? Locals report seeing mysterious lights on the shores of Llyn Daioni, or even glimmering inside the houses themselves, while others claim to have heard strange, eerie music coming from Hafan Deg. There could be natural explanations for all of these, of course.

Or perhaps there's a good reason that Llyn Daioni is little-known, and largely shunned by those who live nearby. Perhaps Harry Yelland or Bill Lewis knew why, but that knowledge has gone with them—to the grave in Lewis' case, and to parts unknown in Yelland's.

Whether the silence of Hafan Deg will ever be broken remains to be seen. But as we'll see in our next issue, it's not our only clue as to why the people who live near Llyn Daioni give it and its surroundings a wide berth.

III: Colmore

Sometimes you can't find everything you're looking for on the internet: now and again, what you need is down somewhere in cold print.

Luckily, I have my contacts—whatever you write, you always end up with some of those—one of whom is a second-hand book dealer by the name of Paddy Colmore. He runs a shop down in Hay-on-Wye and is one of the world's biggest SF and Fantasy geeks. The enthusiasm extends into non-fiction too: UFOlogy, cryptozoology, Forteana, anything like that. The perfect person to contact.

I emailed Paddy and asked him about *Unexplained* magazine—if anyone could tell me, it would be him. And he didn't disappoint.

Unexplained magazine had been published by Greenvale Publications between 1977 and 1979, when Greenvale went bankrupt. It didn't have enough in the way of a circulation or advertising revenue to interest anyone else in picking it up, so that was that. Folded after a grand total of eight issues. So there was a good chance there was more on the story.

Any second-hand copies floating around? I asked Paddy. I'd already searched on Amazon and eBay without success.

Leave it with me, came the reply, and a couple of days later another email informed me that he'd traced a complete set of *Unexplained* via a dealer he knew in Plymouth. Copies of obscure short-lived publications can either be insanely expensive because they have a cult following, or dirt cheap because nobody gives a toss. Thankfully *Unexplained* was in the second category: twenty pounds for the full set.

Sold.

*

I paid Paddy to have them express-delivered by courier: I had the bit between my teeth and couldn't wait. Sometimes you can just *tell* when there's a story to be found.

When the package arrived, I tore off the wrapping, dropped everything else and read through every issue while drinking endless cups of coffee. First I went through Issue 4, just to make sure there wasn't more on the story that Poker93 might have missed. There wasn't, so I moved on to Issue 5, and the follow-up article.

Except there wasn't one.

I read and re-read the issue two or three times, practically using a magnifying glass on the last attempt, but there was nothing. Same story with Issue 6.

Finally, halfway through issue 7, the words *Hafan Deg* leapt out at me: not from an article, but the letters page. Looked like I hadn't been the only one who wanted to read more.

> *Dear Sir,*
> *I read with great interest Russell Ware's article on Hafan Deg in North Wales (Issue 4). The article, however, ended with the promise of further revelations about the area around Llyn Daioni, which I have been eagerly awaiting, but to no avail. Can you tell us when Mr Ware's next article is to grace your august pages?*
> *Yours, etc,*
> *Colonel V.I. Paxton (Retd.)*
> *Salisbury*
> **EDITOR:** *Russell is hard at work on a full-length book about the area surrounding Llyn Daioni, and we hope to publish an extract in our ninth issue.*

Bugger.

*

Still, now I had another lead: Russell Ware's book. I typed the name into Google, and found a stub article on Wikipedia and two or three Amazon listings. Those made my heart jump briefly, but they were science fiction novels and a short story collection—no non-fiction books, not about North Wales or anywhere else.

I dug further down the results, and finally found an obituary on an SF fan site, scanned from some long-ago 1980s fanzine. There was even a photograph: it showed a lean, handsome black man in his thirties, with neatly barbered hair and a trimmed moustache.

> *Russell Ware, 1938-1981. West Indian/British science-fiction author. Born Kingston, Jamaica. Came to Britain in 1954, aged sixteen. Published his first short story, 'The Gaudy, Blabbing and Remorseful Day', later that year in Carnell's* Amazing Stories. *Published another dozen or so over the next few years. Married Sidonie Palmer in 1966, earning a living partly from fiction but*

mostly from a wide variety of journalistic articles. Two published novels: Out of the Fire *(Mayflower, 1967) and* The Wind Dancer *(Sphere, 1970), but major success continued to elude him.*

Ware destroyed the manuscript of his third novel, The Sand Ghosts, *after repeated rejections convinced him it was unpublishable; he began and abandoned several subsequent novels and found it increasingly difficult to place his shorter works. Ware claimed he was a victim of racial discrimination, while others pointed to his increasing drinking and its effect on his work. Nonetheless, he produced a high volume of successful journalism during the 1970s for a variety of markets, earning a living but again falling short of the wider success he felt he deserved.*

Ware's only posthumous book was the hard-to-find short story collection, *Weapons of* Grass—the copy listed on Amazon had an asking price of nearly a hundred quid. According to the obit he *had* been working on a non-fiction book at the time of his death, but it appeared to never have been completed, let alone published.

There were a couple of other obits, but none provided any more details. I was on the point of dropping the whole thing, but I had that niggling feeling still: there was a story here.

If Ware had been working on a book, there would have been notes, maybe even a completed draft. They might still exist— bequeathed to a newspaper or a library, something like that. Writers often did that.

I emailed Paddy Colmore and asked if he could give me any information. *What did your last slave die of?* was his initial reply, but it had piqued his interest, too. You never knew when an unpublished novel or story might turn up, and if that saw the light of day it would be one to brag about. *I'll see what I can do, in between more important stuff. Like flossing.*

Only ten days later, he emailed again. *Ware's papers weren't bequeathed anywhere. Turns out his widow's still alive in Liverpool, and she's still got them all. The old dear's over the moon someone even remembers who her husband was—she'd love to hear from you.*

IV: SIDONIE WARE

There are a few phrases that might describe Sidonie Ware, but *old dear* definitely isn't one of them. I have the photographs to prove it.

I took a few when I visited her at her large detached house in Aigburth. She was a tall woman with silver-touched blonde hair and a handsome, leonine face, who chain-smoked Sobranie Black Russians, looked me in the eye without blinking, and let out a huge and surprisingly dirty laugh when something amused her. Assuming she'd been of an age with her husband, she had to be in her seventies, but could easily have passed for twenty years younger. One photo shows her, in jeans and sweater, holding up a copy of *The Wind Dancer;* another caught her with her head thrown back in laughter, which made her look younger still. She put me in mind of a cross between Lauren Bacall and Charlotte Rampling: grace, intelligence and poise.

She was also a joy to interview: articulate, eloquent, often funny and needing little prompting to speak at length; more than likely, she'd been waiting to say a lot of this for decades. Either way, it gave me a wealth of information for minimal effort.

*

EDITED TRANSCRIPT OF INTERVIEW WITH SIDONIE WARE:
Russell wasn't always the easiest man in the world to live with, but I understood why. He was a very talented writer, but never achieved the success he felt was his due. He felt he'd been overlooked because he was black.

Personally, I felt—and feel—that it was more complex than that. That is, I don't believe publishers deliberately shunned him because of his race. There was a lot of that about, of course—as you can imagine, I experienced my share at first hand for marrying him. 'Nigger lover', that sort of thing. Or on one memorable occasion, 'race traitor', by some weedy lackwit in leather shorts and a brown shirt. I remember poor Russell was quite put out that I kicked the little swine smartly in the goolies before he had a chance to defend my honour.

But publishers back then ate up science fiction and fantasy. Ate it up. A writer of Russell's talent should have had no trouble making a success of himself. But the way he saw the world, and its expression in his fiction, was very much rooted in his background— particularly in his faith.

Russell was very religious. Strict Baptist upbringing. I was a Christian myself—I was very well-brought-up, don't you know. My father was an Anglican vicar. I rebelled, of course, but under it all the acorn hadn't fallen very far from the oak. These days I call myself more of an agnostic. But anyway, you aren't here to listen to me prattle on about my 'journey'. So—yes, I think that might have been a problem. This was the free-wheeling free-loving sixties, after all. Russell could be very traditional about many things—but at the same time, he was very sharp about things like race and colonialism. And he did smoke grass quite often, so some of his work tended towards the psychedelic. What I'm saying, I suppose, is that he was too conservative for the hippy crowd but not very comfortable reading for white English conservatives either. And that was reflected in his sales.

Of course, it didn't help that I was having quite a successful career of my own. I'd opened a small shop, selling good quality second-hand clothes, then new material. Once I could afford better premises, I started a small boutique. It eventually grew into a chain. Did very well throughout the seventies, which unfortunately was just as Russell's career was losing momentum. That was when he started drinking, really, which didn't help his work—especially the novel he was trying to write. That's right, dear, *The Sand Ghosts.* Bless you for remembering.

Yes, he destroyed the manuscript, and I'm sorry to say that it was no great loss. I still think it was a brilliant idea—the kind of story that only Russell could have written and conceived—and it should have been his masterpiece. But the execution was the most appalling mess. Lazily plotted, cardboard characters and these great... diatribes... on racism and religion throughout. I was as kind as I could be, but he knew I thought it was terrible. I think he knew that it was, too. He sent it out anyway, and all and sundry rejected it, so he burned it. And that was that. He stuck quite firmly with non-fiction from that point on. Oh, he wrote another two or three short stories, and every so often—usually when we took a summer holiday—he'd try to write a new novel, or to begin again with *The Sand Ghosts*, but come what may they all foundered within ten or twenty pages. Excuse me... just a moment....

It's just so sad to remember now—all that potential that he never realised. I never remarried, you know. No-one could replace him. All I've got left of him is his writing. We couldn't have children. I've tried to interest publishers in reissuing his work, but—no joy.

Yes, he wrote a great deal of non-fiction. Well, one might call it non-fiction. There was a rather eager market for anything that savoured of the paranormal in those days. You know the sort of thing. Ghosts, the Bermuda Triangle, UFOs. Bigfoot, the Yeti, the Loch Ness Monster. Mysteries of the unexplained. There were a lot of stories published as unquestioned fact that were either grossly exaggerated, embellished to the point of being unrecognisable, or just flat-out made up on the spot. In a way, he took to that. It was another way of telling stories, even though he hated himself for it. Hackwork, he called it. He made more money, but I'm afraid he drank most of it. It was a very bad time for us both, the only time I actually contemplated leaving him. But—funny, really. If he hadn't spent so much time in the pub, he'd never have met that chap. What was his name? Something very ordinary. Smith? Brown? No, it was something Welsh. Jones? Evans? No. Wait. Tip of my tongue. Ah, that was it—Davies.

This Mr Davies was a construction worker. He'd worked on that place—the village with those funny buildings. He told Russell all about what had gone on, and Russell decided there was a story there. Around the same time, I had it out with him about his drinking. He was very angry, but he said we'd talk when he got back. He wanted to go up to Bala and photograph this place— *Hafan Deg*, that was it.

Traditionally-minded or not, I honestly thought that was it, I really did. The end of our marriage. But he came back from there and it was as if a different man had walked in through the door. He was like the Russell I'd married again—confident, fired-up, very purposeful. He'd already written the Hafan Deg article and sent it to *Unexplained*. He was actually *enthusiastic* about what he was doing, and that hadn't happened in a very long time,

When I asked what had brought this change on, he said there were two reasons. One, he didn't want to lose his marriage on top of everything else. And two, he'd realised that he was still a very lucky man—he got to do what he loved for a living. So he was going to use that to write a new book. One that, by rights, ought to make us a decent bit of money.

He'd originally planned on doing a series of articles for *Unexplained*, but after he'd sent them the first article he decided this was too good a project to waste on them. He'd give them some excerpts, some abridged chapters, get extra money and free publicity, but he decided this should be a book.

I know what you're thinking—a whole book about Hafan Deg? But apparently that whole area around the lake had something of a *reputation*. And Russell felt with a little embellishment, he could turn *that* into a book. Just the sort of pot of message everybody would want to read. *The Bala Triangle*, he wanted to call it. I wasn't at all convinced by the title, but that hardly mattered.

But no, he never finished it. He ended up taking the project far more seriously than he'd originally intended. He compiled extensive notes, but he was very secretive about them, didn't want to show them to me—and after he died, I couldn't bring myself to read them. I tried to interest a couple of other writers in completing the project, but I didn't have any more success than when I tried to get his books reprinted.

Anyway, I'll happily give you access to the notes. It would be good to see something come of the project. It meant a lot to him.

V: THE FACE IN THE WINDOW GLASS

Sidonie's enthusiasm didn't quite extend to letting me take the notes away with me, but she'd had them all scanned at an earlier date—just in case anything had happened to the originals—and she emailed them to me in a zip folder. I thanked her for her help and said my goodbyes.

"No problem," she said, surprising herself as much as me, I think, with the quick hug she gave. "I hope it's of use to you. But if it is—please remember to credit Russell, won't you?"

"Of course," I said. Or both of them.

Once I was home, I brewed coffee and started printing off the notes. It took the rest of the evening to do so; the following morning I sorted them into some rough order. Ware had, at least, jotted rough headings on the various pages of notes in red biro, presumably in an effort to impose order on a rapidly expanding project, and also numbered the pages to give a rough running order. I sorted the notes into piles based on this system, then bound them into bundles with rubber bands.

I started with the original notes on Hafan Deg. They matched Sidonie's version of events; Ware had interviewed John Davies and got the bones of the story he'd write for *Unexplained*. He'd tried contacting other people who'd worked at the site, but none of the ones he found wanted to talk. Yelland and Lewis, of course, were respectively missing and dead.

Ware went out to Llyn Daioni himself, near the North Wales town of Bala, armed with notepad and camera. He made a rough sketch map of the area and filled a couple of pages with notes and impressions of Hafan Deg and the lake.

Brilliant, he wrote, *it's bloody perfect. This place is as creepy as hell. If I'm honest, I was actually glad to get away. Next step's to get some corroboration on what happened. That means talking to the local fuzz. That should be fun. Give Dave Trent* [a police contact of Ware's] *a call, see if he knows anyone on the force out here.*

Apparently, Trent did: the name *Sergeant Huw Llewellyn* was scribbled underneath that paragraph, along with a phone number. And it looked as if the sergeant had been pretty helpful; Ware had scribbled a number of bullet points underneath.

Multiple on-site accidents – three dead, half a dozen serious injuries
 Hafan Deg – site supposedly haunted!!
 Deaths and disappearances in area
 Beast of Maes Carnedd?!
And underneath that: *Bloody hell. There's a* book *here.*
Under that: *THE BALA TRIANGLE?*

*

There was one last document in the first bundle of notes. It was a photograph—one of the original set, I guessed—that Ware had taken at Hafan Deg.

He must have turned the camera on its side to fully frame the tallest stack of ESCAPE houses. There were four of them, looming like a tower, sunlight glinting off their portholes.

I rummaged in a drawer until I found an old magnifying glass, and peered at the photograph through it.

It wasn't sunlight. The pale smudges against the glass were too uniform in shape, too exactly duplicated on each window, to be that.

Even through the magnifying glass they were indistinct, but it was the same shape each time: a blurred white oval with two dark stains side by side, and a third, wider one below. I remembered Poker93 mentioning something about this. They looked like faces, screaming. Or maybe laughing. And below them—were those hands, pressed against the glass?

I shook my head and put down the magnifier. Most likely it was a flaw in the window glass; given the catalogue of weaknesses and failures in Harry Yelland's design, one more was hardly a surprise. I wondered if the view was the same from the inside, looking out. It wouldn't have been a pleasant sight when all that was around you was the night, and the woods, and the silent lake.

Row on row of white, howling faces.

*

Or perhaps I was wrong. Perhaps they weren't screaming, or howling, or even laughing.

Perhaps they were calling instead.

Perhaps, even then, they'd been calling Russell Ware. And kept on calling him, until the Black Mountain claimed him, too.

2: THE STRANGE DEATH OF BRITT NORDENSTAM

I had paid work to do, which my amateur detective work had left me behindhand on, so it was another three days before I had time to look at Ware's next bundle of notes.

The first item in it was an article from a magazine called *UNSOLVED*. It was a short piece, copiously illustrated, written to fill the gaps between meatier features on Lord Lucan and Marilyn Monroe. The first page had a photograph of the lake itself, a picture of police officers gathered around a sheeted body, and inset portraits of three people. *Professor Robert Thurlow*: a grey-haired, bespectacled man in his fifties. *Craig Stowe*: a dark-haired boy in a rugby shirt, grinning for the camera. And a flinty-looking man in his forties, with salt and pepper hair, a clenched jaw and cold, weary eyes: *Detective Inspector Clifford Thomas*.

Another photograph took up most of the second page: a laughing, blonde-haired girl wearing jeans and a white sweater.

The text read *Britt Nordenstam, a week before she disappeared*.

I. The Dig at Capel Teg

At around 7a.m. on 3rd May, 1969, the police were called to Heol Capel farmhouse, about a mile and a half from Bala in North Wales. The farmer and his wife took them to the kitchen, where two young people sat clutching mugs of hot sweet tea.

In their statement to Police Constables Rodgers and Foulkes, the youths gave their names as Craig Stowe and Fiona Patterson, students at the University of Manchester. They'd walked from Llyn Daioni, where they and a dozen of their fellow students were camped, as soon as it became light, in order to fetch help. The night before, Britt Nordenstam, one of their fellow students, had left her tent (apparently to use the latrine) and hadn't come back.

Rodgers and Foulkes were from Bala, which only boasted a small police station, and so they'd called divisional headquarters for assistance in searching the area around the encampment. This meant the marshes around the westerly end of the lake, the thick pine woods surrounding the area, and requesting boats in order to drag the lake itself.

The initial supposition was that Britt had got lost in the woods—although she was known to be an experienced outdoorswoman—or met with an accident. As long as she hadn't drowned in the lake or the marshes, there was a good chance that she'd be found alive, given the time of year. But when the searchers failed to find any sign of her, concerns arose that something else might have happened.

At which point the CID were contacted, and Detective Inspector Clifford Thomas enters the story. Russell Ware obtained a copy of the case file through his contact in the Welsh police, DS Llewellyn, who also probably provided the brief sketch of DI Thomas in Ware's notes. Thomas was a local man who'd worked his way up through the ranks. He came from a poor background with little formal education, but had a solid reputation as a detective. He was a devout Methodist, a teetotaller, and insisted on the highest standards of rectitude and sobriety from his men. Perhaps not the most congenial company then, but by reputation he was tough while fair, and known to get results. And this, of course, was at a time when the rules governing interrogations were nowhere near as stringent as today.

So he, too, would play his part in the tragedy set to unfold.

*

A DMV, any historian or archaeologist will tell you, is a deserted mediaeval village site. Between the massacres of the Norman Conquest that nearly depopulated the North; the mediaeval 'Little Ice Age' that rendered numerous settlements uninhabitable; and the clearing of villagers off the land to build monasteries, create deer parks or graze sheep, England is full of them.

Wales has its share of deserted settlements, of course: villages drowned to create reservoirs, like Capel Celyn or Llanwyddan; expropriated to serve as firing ranges like Mynydd Epynt; or—by far the biggest single category—abandoned mining villages such as Porth y Nant, near Llithfaen, on the Llyn Peninsula. One of those, Maes Carnedd, lay a few miles north of Llyn Daioni, and judging by what I'd glimpsed while sorting Ware's notes into order, that was a story in itself. But those are all comparatively recent: DMVs are few and far between, and mostly in the south of the country.

But Robert Thurlow, Professor of Archaeology at Manchester University, had found traces of one near the marsh at the lake's west end, during a walking holiday in North Wales in 1967.

"I found evidence of earthworks," he later told DI Thomas, "and patterns of vegetational growth, such as nettles and thistles, suggesting prior cultivation. Although the growths were nowhere near as lush as they should have been, for that time of year. At that time, I didn't have an explanation for it. But yes, I was sure I'd stumbled across a former settlement."

Thurlow had a solid reputation in archaeological circles. He was intelligent, observant—he'd never have picked up on those clues otherwise—but above all, methodical. As a result, when time permitted, he'd visited the site on two other occasions, where he'd found potsherds and the remains of further earthworks. Meanwhile, he'd searched for evidence of a settlement in the area. The records were pretty sketchy, but eventually he found a reference to a village called Capel Teg, which had apparently ceased to exist at some point in the 1400s. Doubtless this was where the both the nearby farmhouse and the woods surrounding Llyn Daioni—Coed Capel— had got their names.

It was enough to convince Thurlow he'd found something worth serious investigation. But that was too big a job for one man; the time had come to call for volunteers. His students were the logical place to look: Thurlow was a popular tutor with an infectious sense of humour and an enthusiasm that belied his years.

And so, on the 29th April, 1969, he and a dozen students arrived at Llyn Daioni, and set up camp on the south shore. At that time the easterly end, where Hafan Deg would be built a few years later, was heavily wooded. The lake's west end was surrounded by a marshy area, leaving only a small clear space where the trees hadn't encroached—the space occupied by the Capel Teg site.

Based on the earthworks he'd traced thus far, Thurlow had sketched a rough map of the village's layout; over the next few days, his team investigated and marked out the area, then began to dig.

*

EXTRACT FROM 1ST INTERVIEW WITH PROFESSOR THURLOW, 3RD MAY, 1969:

(CT: DI Thomas, RT: Prof. Thurlow)

CT: And did you find anything, Professor?

RT: Oh, yes. We very quickly started turning up more pottery fragments, and what appear to be the remains of middens—that is, rubbish heaps. There were animal bones—sheep, principally, and small game—but fishbones as well, suggesting they lived mainly by farming but also trapped wild animals and fished the lake. And we found the remains of tools that corroborated that hypothesis. An implement, very badly rusted, but we think it was a hoe, and a number of bone and iron hooks—for the fishing, of course.

(PAUSE.)

CT: You seem a little ill at ease, Professor. What aren't you telling us?

RT: Well, it's nothing to do with the case.

CT: I think I should be the judge of that, Professor, don't you?

RT: Very well. We also found fragments of weapons. Arrowheads—about a dozen of those. Two axe heads, and a number of blade fragments—both short ones and long. We also found charcoal. A great deal of charcoal.

CT: Meaning?

RT: Meaning a fire, Inspector. And quite an extensive one.

CT: And the weapons?

RT: Would not have been native to a farming village, Inspector. It bears all the hallmarks of an attack—a massacre, even—following which the village was razed to the ground.

CT: I see. That's very interesting, Professor. However, I'm interested in events of rather more recent a date.

*

So who was Britt Nordenstam?

'Little Miss Perfect' was one student's slightly bitchy term for her, but that was the closest to hostility anyone expressed. The envy was understandable: classically beautiful, athletic, intelligent and funny, Britt was an object of desire to most of the male students, and the female ones would have probably hated her if she hadn't been so good-natured as to make that impossible.

As well as being one of Thurlow's best students, Britt was used to the outdoors and an experienced camper, so she'd been invaluable on the dig. She'd been as adept at the physical work as any of the lads, methodical and sharp-eyed.

For all that, Fiona Patterson, who'd shared Britt's tent and worked closely with her on the dig, had noted some changes in her behaviour as their work progressed.

*

EXTRACT FROM 1ST INTERVIEW WITH FIONA PATTERSON, 3RD MAY, 1969:

Well, there were quite a few things. Just little things. I mean, it was hard to put your finger on exactly what. She seemed a little… distracted, I suppose.

And that wasn't like her; it really wasn't. Don't get me wrong, Britt had a great sense of fun. She was a real laugh, nice girl, and my god, she could drink, but—it was like she kept everything in compartments. Do you know what I mean? When she was working, she was working, and nothing—I mean *nothing*—got in the way of that.

A boy? I don't think so. There were a lot of lads who liked her, but no-one in particular who stands out. I don't think she was seeing anybody right then. I don't know about any boys she had been out with. I mean—we didn't mix much. I'm not really much of a party girl, you know?

Aye, I got the impression there was something on her mind—but not necessarily in a bad way. The opposite, really. She'd be off in these little reveries, bit of a smile on her face in fact, and you'd almost have to shout to get her to snap out of it. It only really started once we got underway with the dig—happened more and more as the dig went on.

Okay, that night.... We'd had the evening meal and turned straight in—read a bit, then sleep. That was the idea, anyway. I'd actually nodded off, but then I got woken up by Britt. All of a sudden she was really chatty. You ken the way people do sometimes, when they're trying to keep their minds off something? She was telling me all about Sweden, this farm her grandfather owned—think she even said I must come and visit her there. I was half-asleep, though—she'd already woken me up once, if you remember. Anyway, she suddenly broke off and said she had to go for a—to go to the toilet. She unzipped the tent and climbed out, zipped it back up again, and... and that's about it, sir. I was asleep straight after.

Next thing I knew, someone was tapping at the tent door. I pulled the zip down and it was Professor Thurlow. He was asking if anyone had seen Britt. This would have been about eleven o'clock. So she'd been gone about three hours—I looked at my watch when she left, and it was about twenty past eight.

How did Professor Thurlow know Britt was missing? I've no idea.

*

Extract from 2ND interview with Professor Thurlow 3RD May, 1969:

EXTRACT FROM 2ND INTERVIEW WITH PROFESSOR THURLOW 3RD MAY, 1969:

Britt had asked to speak with me, as everyone else was turning in that evening. She didn't say what it was in connection with; she gave me to understand it was a private matter. She said she would come to my tent at about half past ten—I'm presuming she wanted to make sure the others were asleep. But she didn't show up.

I went to her tent at about quarter past eleven. I was concerned something serious might be troubling her—that she might be contemplating doing something foolish, if you follow. However, she wasn't in the tent. Fiona—her tent-mate—said she'd gone out to use the latrine a little after eight.

At this point I became concerned. I think you'd agree that I had cause to. So I organised the students into pairs, with torches, and we did our best to find Britt. Without success. In the end, I had to call a halt to it because there was a danger of other students getting lost or injured. Also, there were other lights in the woods around us. I'm not sure what. Torches, perhaps. Yes, that must have been it—I can't see what else they could have been.

In the end, I had to balance my responsibility to Britt with my responsibilities towards the rest of the student body. So we returned to the camp, and I did a head count to make sure everyone else was present and correct. And then at first light, Fiona and Mr Stowe volunteered to go and look for help.

*

Extensive searches of Llyn Daioni, Coed Capel and the surrounding area continued over the next two days, with diminishing hopes of finding the student alive. They found nothing, not even an item of clothing. Nothing at all. DI Thomas widened the search area, co-opting local volunteers to help, but still without success.

By then Capel Teg, the dig, had been abandoned, and the students had returned to Manchester. Britt Nordenstam's parents were notified, and they made arrangements to fly into Britain. Meanwhile, Professor Thurlow's head of department began receiving calls from irate parents, demanding to know how the University could have exposed their children to such danger.

A couple of newspaper clippings from the time dwelt on the possibility that a local youth or youths might have abducted the pretty young student for what the old-fashioned would have called 'a fate worse than death', before murdering her and disposing of the body. It didn't help that another student, Rachel Morris, had gone missing in the area four years earlier, leading to speculations that she and Britt had both fallen victim to the same attackers.

That probably didn't do wonders for Detective Inspector Thomas' mood either, as the newspaper coverage—limited though it was—took a general tone of presenting the rural Welsh as a bunch of inbred rapists (one article just about stopped short of claiming her abductors had compounded rape and murder with cannibalism) and the region's police as incompetent buffoons. Nonetheless, he persevered; not least because something interesting had finally turned up.

Thomas had only a Detective Sergeant at his disposal at the time, which made thorough interviews a slower process than they otherwise might have been, but he'd finally spoken to Craig Stowe who, along with Fiona Patterson, had first reported Britt's disappearance.

*

EXTRACT FROM 2ND INTERVIEW WITH CRAIG STOWE, 5TH MAY, 1969:

(CT: DI Thomas, CS: Craig Stowe)

CS: It was Professor Thurlow.

CT: What was?

CS: He killed her.

CT: Stop there. Go back. What do you mean?

CS: They were—she was—he was having an affair with Britt.

CT: Professor Thurlow and Miss Nordenstam were having an affair? For the record, Mr Stowe is nodding.

CS: Yes, that's right. Lot of people knew.

CT: Did they now?

CS: Not everyone. But a lot of the students. He was sleeping with her. His student. It was common knowledge.

CT: So why do you think that Professor Thurlow killed Britt?

CS: Isn't it obvious? She was in love with him, but he only wanted her for—you know.

CT: You mean sex?

CS: Yes.

CT: All right. Go on.

CS: She wanted him to leave his wife for her. Correction: she thought he was going to leave his wife for her.

CT: She told you that?

CS: Yeah.

CT: She confided in you?

CS: We talked a few times. She was a nice girl. I knew it would end badly, so I tried to talk her out of it, make her see. She thought I was funny. 'Cute', she called me. And now look. She must have threatened to tell someone. His wife, or someone at the university. So he killed her.

*

EXTRACT FROM 3RD INTERVIEW WITH PROFESSOR THURLOW, 6TH MAY, 1969.

(CT: DI Thomas, RT: Prof Thurlow)

CT: Let's talk about your relationship with Miss Nordenstam, Professor.

RT: She was my student.

CT: That's right. Which would put you in—what's the Latin phrase? *In loco parentis*, isn't that right?

RT: To a degree.

CT: A degree? What degree?

RT: A student isn't a child anymore, Inspector. They're young adults with minds of their own. Legally speaking—

CT: What about morally, Professor Thurlow?

RT: Morally?

CT: The term's unfamiliar to you?

RT: Of course not.

CT: It isn't? I'll ask you again, Professor Thurlow: what was your relationship with Britt Nordenstam?

RT: I've already told you; she was my student.

CT: Nothing more?

(PAUSE)

RT: No.

CT: Isn't it true, Professor, that you and Britt Nordenstam were having an affair?

(SILENCE)

CT: Professor Thurlow? Is it or is it not true?

RT: Who's saying that—

CT: I'm asking the questions, Professor Thurlow. Were you and Britt Nordenstam lovers?

RT: We had—an understanding.

CT: An understanding? Is that the sophisticated term for it now?

RT: There was no illegality—

CT: She was your student!

RT: She was twenty-one years old! An adult!

CT: You were old enough to be her father, for God's sake. In a position of trust!

RT: She initiated the relationship!

CT: So, it was a relationship now? Infatuated with her tutor, was she? Just because she threw herself at you—you could still have said no. You had a *responsibility* to say no! I put it to you,

Professor, that Miss Nordenstam had expectations of you that you were unwilling to fulfil. Indeed, that you never had the slightest intention of fulfilling, no matter what you may have promised her at the outset.

RT: I must protest—I must—

CT: I put it to you, Professor Thurlow, that you seduced Britt Nordenstam, that you promised to leave your wife for her without any intention of doing so.

RT: You know nothing—nothing of what you're talking about.

CT: And I put it to you that when Miss Nordenstam pressed you to fulfil those expectations, when she threatened to expose your conduct to your superiors, that you panicked and killed her, and concealed her body in the woods.

RT: No! No! No!

CT: After all, isn't it true that you know the area almost as well as any local? Who could be better placed to dispose of the body where it couldn't be found?

RT: This is outrageous!

CT: Where is Britt Nordenstam's body, Professor?

RT: I did not kill her!

CT: Where did you conceal the body?

(PAUSE)

RT: I want my solicitor. Now.

*

Robert Thurlow was arrested on suspicion of murder, but his solicitor quickly had him released on bail as Thomas had no conclusive evidence. Thurlow was lucky he was a well-off university lecturer, otherwise after a few hours in the cells away from prying eyes, DI Thomas could have had a signed confession of him by the morning. This was 1969, remember—long before the Guildford Four, the Birmingham Six or PACE.

But with or without proof, the damage was done. Word soon spread of Thurlow's affair with Britt. 'CORRUPTER OF YOUTH' screamed one headline from the *Manchester Evening News*, above the most sinister-looking picture of Thurlow they'd been able to find. There was a fresh outcry from parents, and within the week Thurlow was dismissed from his post.

A few days later, Thurlow drove out to the woodlands near his house, took an overdose of barbiturates, and led a hosepipe from his exhaust pipe to the inside of his car. Luckily (or not) he was found in time. Sort of. He survived, but with severe brain damage, unable to even feed himself or keep himself clean.

Many took this as a tacit admission of guilt, but there was no point in prosecuting what was left of Robert Thurlow. And that was where the whole business might have ended, had it not been for the professor's wife, Margaret—his widow now, in all but name.

The press descended like vultures on Mrs Thurlow, hoping to wring some fresh headlines out of the scandal. They did, too. But not the ones they were expecting.

Mrs Thurlow, as it turned out, was more than happy to be interviewed, but was less grief-stricken than outraged. She insisted that her husband could not possibly have killed Britt Nordenstam. An expected response, perhaps, but the reasoning behind it was enough to give the reporters pause.

According to Mrs Thurlow, she and her husband had been leading separate lives for the best part of a decade. There was, she specified, no animosity involved; they'd simply grown apart.

"Yes, I knew of his affair," she told the newspaper. "In fact, I even met Britt. I rather liked her. She was a sensible, pleasant, very mature girl. She certainly wasn't expecting to marry my husband."

And before long, Mrs Thurlow's story was corroborated by an unexpected source: the Nordenstam family themselves.

Britt's parents had by now flown in from Stockholm. Bengt Nordenstam was a successful psychologist, while Astrid Nordenstam lectured in Economics at a major university. Both had an open, liberated attitude to sex that they'd passed on to Britt, and produced over a dozen very frank letters from their daughter in which she'd discussed her love life, including her affair with Thurlow, whom she'd described as 'kind, mature and a good lover'.

It was clear from the letters that she didn't see the relationship as long-term in any way, nor even as an end to a better grade. Britt planned on working towards a doctorate—perhaps in the UK, or perhaps back in Sweden—before finding a suitable husband to raise a family with whilst juggling an academic career. In the meantime, her relationship with Thurlow gave her pleasure and companionship; the professor had got the same, but could still look forward to a carefree single life when his divorce came through.

These revelations generated some salacious hoo-hah—on the front pages of the relevant local papers and halfway down page four or five of the national ones—about the ways of the liberated/decadent Swedes/intelligentsia/middle classes/all of the above, but before long the papers performed a shameless U-turn and rounded on the police. Detective Inspector Thomas, in particular, came off badly. He went from being the hero of the hour to a bigoted fanatic who'd ruined an innocent man's life.

Whatever else he might have been, however, Thomas was a capable and methodical investigator. While this new storm raged, he looked again at the evidence.

Interrogations of local men with histories of sexual assault yielded no fruit. It was always possible that Britt had fallen victim to a stranger passing through the area, but Thomas thought that unlikely. The Capel Teg site was far from any main road, and some distance even from the narrow dirt track that led to Llyn Daioni from the Heol Capel farm.

Thomas also dismissed the possibility that Britt might have met with an accident in the woods. 'The latrine area was close to the camp,' his report read, 'probably to prevent any of the team becoming lost at night. Even if Miss Nordenstam had wandered further afield and met with an accident, a body would have been found by now. There are abandoned mine workings around Maes Carnedd and overgrown well shafts in or around Mynydd Du, but these are several miles away and on the opposite side of the lake. It hardly seems likely that Miss Nordenstam, who was used to the outdoors, would have wandered so far afield.'

*

EXTRACT FROM 2ND INTERVIEW WITH FIONA PATTERSON, 2ND JUNE, 1969:
(CT: DI Thomas, FP: Fiona Patterson)
CT: I'd just like you to go back and think about any boys who might have been interested in Britt.
FP: Really? I mean, as I said, pretty much all the boys liked her.
CT: Anyone particularly stand out? Martin Stevenson?
FP: They went out a couple of times.
CT: Joseph Strickland?
FP: I think he asked her out but she said no.
CT: What about Craig Stowe?
(PAUSE)
FP: No, I don't think he was interested.
CT: No? Why do you say that?

FP: Well, it's not as if he couldn't have his pick.

CT: Lot of girlfriends, has he? Puts himself around?

FP: No, not at all. Craig's very—I mean, he's a Christian. Doesn't believe in that sort of thing. Wants to wait for the right girl and get married and that. But I mean, he's very handsome.

CT: What's your relationship with Craig?

FP: Relationship? I don't have a relationship with him!

CT: Not even as friends?

FP: Oh. Oh, I see. I mean, aye, we're friends.

CT: Do you ever get the feeling he'd like it to be more than that?

(SILENCE)

CT: Fiona?

(FP STARTS CRYING)

CT: Fiona?

FP: No.

CT: Would you like it to be more than that?

FP (ALMOST INAUDIBLE): Yes.

CT: So why hasn't that happened?

(SILENCE)

CT: Is there someone else? For Craig, I mean?

(SILENCE)

CT: Or *was* there someone else?

(SILENCE)

CT: You're in love with him, aren't you?

FP: (CRYING) Yes.

CT: Who was Craig in love with?

FP: You know who. You know.

CT: I need you to tell me, Fiona. Come on.

FP: Britt. All right? It was Britt.

Transcript ends.

*

EXTRACT FROM 3ᴿᴰ INTERVIEW WITH CRAIG STOWE, 4ᵀᴴ JUNE, 1969:

(CT: DI Thomas, CS: Craig Stowe)

CT: How close were you to Miss Nordenstam?

CS: We knew each other.

CT: You knew each other. Could you go into a little more detail for me?

CS: What sort of detail?

CT: How well did you know each other? Are we talking about knowledge in the biblical sense here?

CS: No! No, there was nothing like that.

CT: Would you have liked that to be the case?

CS: No.

CT: You're sure?

CS: Yes, I'm sure. Sir.

CT: I mean, she was a very pretty girl. Some men would go so far as to call her beautiful.

CS: She was pretty, yes. But so are a lot of girls.

CT: Fair enough. So you weren't seeing each other, and you didn't have any designs on her. Is that fair to say?

CS: That's right.

CT: But you and her were close. Yes?

CS: Not particularly.

CT: Not particularly? And yet she confided in you.

(SILENCE)

CT: Didn't she, Craig?

CS: What do you mean, confided?

CT: I mean, she told you that she was in a relationship with Professor Thurlow.

CS: Everyone knew that.

CT: Not everyone. Fiona Patterson had no idea, for one.

CS: Fiona's very shy. She doesn't go out much.

CT: Misses all the gossip, you mean.

CS: Yeah.

CT: She doesn't miss as much as you'd think.

CS: What do you mean?

CT: You said in a previous interview that Miss Nordenstam told you the professor was going to leave his wife for her. Yes?

(PAUSE)

CS: Yes.

CT: Which is interesting, since the professor's wife and Miss Nordenstam's family both say differently. And they both knew of the relationship and had no objection to it. Unlike you.

CS: Me?

CT: You did object, didn't you, Craig? You regarded it as sinful.

CS: It was, wasn't it? He was a married man and she was his student. You can't get much more immoral than that.

34

CT: Be that as it may, it wasn't illegal. And Professor Thurlow didn't kill her. No, Craig, I've been right and wrong all at the same time.

CS: How do you mean?

CT: Now, what I thought at first was that Britt was murdered by someone at Capel Teg and her body was dumped somewhere nearby. And do you know what? I still think that's what happened. I think I was right about that bit. I just went after the wrong man.

CS: What are you talking about, Inspector? I don't understand what—

CT: They were both adults, Craig. Neither of them was hiding the truth from their families, and certainly neither of them had anything as serious as marriage in mind. They may have been lovers, but they weren't in love. But you were, weren't you?

CS: Me? What are you trying to say?

CT: Miss Patterson tells me that you were in love with Miss Nordenstam.

CS: Fiona? What? No! She's jealous. She's got a crush on me.

CT: I also spoke to Angelica Markham.

CS: Who?

CT: Miss Nordenstam's flatmate.

(PAUSE)

CT: According to Miss Markham, you'd pestered Miss Nordenstam on several occasions. Both to go out with you, and to end her relationship with the professor.

CS: I may have done the second. I told you, it was sinful. Immoral. You should understand that, Inspector. You're a Christian, too.

CT: I'm also a police officer, so just now I'm concerned with the law, Mr Stowe, not morality. Do you deny that you were infatuated with Britt Nordenstam, that you pursued her, without success?

CS: She was… she was….

CT: What was she, Mr Stowe?

CS: You're trying to make this dirty. It wasn't. It was pure. Yes, all right, I loved her. I wanted her to stop her goings-on with the professor. Because I wanted what was best for her. I knew I could be good for her. A husband.

CT: But she didn't want that, did she?

CS: No. It was her parents, you know. They're godless, and they brought her up to be godless, too. No sense of right or wrong. If she's damned, then it's their fault. You should arrest them.

CT: Why should she be damned?

CS: Because she didn't believe in God, because she was an adulteress, because—

CT: Because she's dead?

CS: What?

CT: Hell's for the dead, right, Craig? She wouldn't be there if she was still alive.

CS: She's not been seen in two weeks. How could she still be alive?

CT: You tell me. Start by telling me what really happened that night. Why was she going to see Thurlow? Were you still trying to get her to see the error of her ways?

CS: I might have spoken to her.

CT: So she was going to complain about you?

CS: No. No. She was just planning on having another of her little—*trysts*—with the professor. Late at night, when she thought nobody would know.

CT: But you knew.

CS: Everyone knew. Nearly everyone knew, anyway. She was shameless. Dragging her reputation through the mud, and she didn't even care.

CT: And you decided to make her care?

CS: I tried to speak to her—when she left her tent, to go to the woods.

CT: But she wouldn't listen.

CS: No.

CT: And so you killed her.

CS: No!

CT: Explain it to me, Craig. I want to understand what happened. Did you rape her?

CS: *No!*

CT: So what did happen? She insulted you? You lost control? Hit her? You fought, and she fell and hit her head? Was that it?

CS: No!

CT: And then you panicked, didn't you, Craig? You panicked and you hid the body—hid it where?

CS: No! No! No! The devil! The devil took her! The devil!

*

A search of Craig Stowe's digs turned up a bracelet belonging to Britt Nordenstam. There were traces of blood on it.

Craig Stowe was arrested and formally charged with Britt's murder. He maintained his innocence to the last. No body was found, but he was convicted anyway. A plea of insanity was rejected, and he was sentenced to life imprisonment.

There was an inquiry into the events leading to Thurlow's suicide attempt, but Thomas emerged with no more than a reprimand. Having brought the case to a successful conclusion—as it seemed at the time—probably helped his case.

The case was closed. Little more than a nine-day wonder to begin with, it was soon forgotten. Just another ugly little murder, a juicy little scandal now squeezed dry, all grist to the reporters' mill.

II. THE BODY IN THE MARSH

During the May Day Bank Holiday in 1971—almost two years to the day since Britt's disappearance—Arthur Ward, a widowed electrician from Birmingham, visited North Wales and rented a room at the hotel in Bala where he and his late wife had honeymooned.

"We were married nearly twenty years," he told the police later. "Haven't known what to do with meself since Ida passed on. Thought it'd be nice to retrace our steps, like."

Mr Ward spent several days traipsing through the hills around Bala, ranging farther and farther from his base in the town as he refamiliarised himself with the area. On the fifth day of his holiday, he walked up a small side road that branched off from the A494 between Bala and Llanfor. About a mile and a half along, he came to a farmhouse with a FOR SALE sign above its door, shortly beyond which the side road petered out. However, he found a dirt track leading off into the pine woods beyond the farm grounds. As the day was unseasonably hot, he decided he'd be glad of the shade, so he followed the path.

"Really bloody still," he said later, "that's what I noticed. Couldn't hear any birds, any animals, anything. You don't expect a place to be so still."

Mr Ward pottered along the trail for nearly half an hour before emerging into the light. He shaded his eyes against the sun, registering as he did the yeasty smell of fresh water. When his eyes had adjusted to the glare, he saw he'd emerged beside a small lake, about a hundred feet long by fifty feet wide. At last there was some sign of life, too; there was a *plop* as a fish jumped at a fly, and two ducks scattered from the surface, quacking furiously and flapping their wings.

Mr Ward sat on a fallen tree and unpacked his lunch, contemplating the peaceful waters. It was clearly rarely visited— there was a pleasing dearth of litter, the pathways were almost completely overgrown, and he found the sense of discovery an agreeable one. Once he'd eaten, he carried on along the lake's shoreline, but as he went he felt the stillness he'd encountered in the woods return. The ducks hadn't returned to the water; no fish now disturbed its surface. There was no sound at all. Before long the place felt less tranquil than oppressive, and Mr Ward began to seriously contemplate turning back. When he reached the marshes at the west end of the lake, he decided it was time to do so. But as he began to turn, something in the marsh caught his eye.

Something was floating in the water, something large and bedraggled-looking. A clump of weeds, perhaps, or an animal—a dog, a sheep—that had drowned. But then Mr Ward looked more closely, and found himself venturing into the marsh, wincing as the chill, stagnant water seeped into his boots. By then he really wanted to turn back, but a combination of civic duty and morbid fascination drew him on. And soon he was close enough to be certain that what had appeared to be tangled vegetation was in fact hair, and that what he'd taken for a sheep's fleece was in fact a stained and sodden white sweater.

It was a body, all right—a woman's, he thought. It lay face-down in the marsh, and the long blonde hair wafting in the water around its head thankfully concealed its face. Now, suddenly, he could hear animal sounds: the buzzing of flies around the corpse. The stench of decay reached him a second later.

Mr Ward twisted away from the body just before the packed lunch he'd eaten came back up, at speed. After that he turned and stumbled through the marsh, then broke into a run along the lakeshore, heading back up the dirt path through the woods towards the farmhouse he'd seen for sale.

And so, for the second time, the police were called out to Heol Capel farm on account of Britt Nordenstam.

*

The body was badly decomposed, and DNA testing in 1971 was the stuff of science fiction rather than standard police procedure— but the dead woman's teeth were intact, and when compared to Britt's dental records, the impressions taken were an exact match. The waterlogged remains of personal effects in the jeans pockets, also identified as the missing student's property, confirmed the findings.

For all that, the discovery raised more questions than it solved. The shallow marsh had been searched repeatedly during the original investigation and yielded nothing, and the body was too badly decayed to determine the cause of death. But the pathologists were able to state roughly how long Britt had been dead for.

Where she'd been in the interim was yet another unanswered question, but several second opinions—each sought with greater desperation than the one before—all returned the same answer. Britt Nordenstam had died no more than two or three months ago, twenty-one or twenty-two months after she'd last been seen, apparently wearing the same clothes she'd been in at that time. However she'd died—accident, suicide or murder—Craig Stowe couldn't have killed her; he had the entire population of HMP Walton as an alibi for the time of her death.

The police might well have wanted to hush that part of things up, but they weren't given the chance. No-one ever determined who leaked copies of the pathologists' reports to the Stowe family, but while Craig's parents were poor, they weren't foolish. The reports were sent on to several newspapers, and a prominent barrister offered to take on an appeal *pro bono*. Very shortly afterwards, Craig Stowe's sentence was quashed and he was released from prison with several thousand pounds in compensation.

As for Detective Inspector Thomas—now Detective Chief Inspector—he was persuaded to take early retirement, and shortly thereafter retired with his wife to Spain. He died there in 1996, of a heart attack.

Within a year of the body being found, the lake's peace was disturbed again when Harry Yelland approached Bill Lewis with plans to build an executive village at the east end of the lake. When the Hafan Deg venture ended in failure, Llyn Daioni and Coed Capel were left once more to their silence, and their secrets.

III. THE LOST OF MYNYDD DU

At which point, enter Russell Ware—or rather, dozens of pages of his handwritten notes, interspersed with photocopied official documents.

When Ware came to the Bala area in 1978 to research the Hafan Deg affair, he made contact with a Detective Sergeant called Huw Llewellyn. In 1969, Llewellyn (then a uniformed constable) had taken part in the search for Britt Nordenstam, and the experience—along with the circumstances surrounding the discovery of her body—had stayed in his memory.

More importantly, Llewellyn knew the people on his beat, and the stories that surrounded Llyn Daioni and its environs: the pine woods of Coed Capel, the deserted mining town of Maes Carnedd, and the mountain three miles north of the lake, Mynydd Du.

Maes Carnedd, Ware wrote in his notes, *has been deserted for nearly eighty years—long before Llewellyn's time, but he thinks he can find a few old timers who might remember what happened. Meanwhile, there's the Britt Nordenstam business—very weird, and it's got all the makings of a great article for* Unexplained. *Actually, maybe a lot more than that. Maes Carnedd, from what he's said, could make a good story as well, but if Llewellyn's on the level with some of the other things he's talking about, then sod* Unexplained *magazine and all who sail in her! There's an honest-to-God* book *here.*

Ware had sketched a rough map of the area. Here was Bala and the lake; to the north were Llyn Daioni and Coed Capel, with the sites of Hafan Deg, Capel Teg, and the marshes where Britt's body had been found all marked with a cross. Two miles north of it was Mynydd Du itself, a clump of straggling contour lines. About the same distance to the north of the mountain, another cross marked the location of Maes Carnedd. Five crudely-sketched houses—*Heol Capel, Cairnfield Farm, Tŷ Mynwent, The Roberts Farm* and *Plas Gwynedd*—denoted farmsteads in the vicinity.

There were five other crosses on the sketch-map—each an event, I assumed, which Ware had thought would serve as material for his book. There was a number beside each cross, and after the sketch-map were five sets of copied police reports, with a number clearly printed in ballpoint on the top page and with accompanying notes by Ware.

1) JOHN ROGERS, 1932

A photograph of a gaunt-looking man with greying hair. His name was John Rogers, aged thirty-six, a farm labourer by occupation, who lived in Llangwm, a tiny village several miles north-east of Mynydd Du. A First World War veteran, Rogers was well-known in the area. An outgoing, affable youth before the Great War, he was now largely silent, moody, irritable and prematurely grey. For all that, he was hard-working and reliable, which ensured he remained in steady employment.

On 5th October, 1932, Rogers was seen by several acquaintances on a road not far from his house, looking southward in the direction of Mynydd Du, apparently in something of a reverie. When one of them called out to him, he started, and briefly engaged them in conversation. One of his friends offered around a packet of cigarettes; as the day was windy, the men gathered round to shield the light. When they turned round, Rogers was nowhere in sight; the cap he'd been wearing was lying on top of a nearby wall, but there was no sign of him. He was never seen again.

A penknife, house keys and other personal belongings were found wrapped in a handkerchief beside a stream a mile south of Llangwm two months after his disappearance. The police concluded it was most likely that Rogers had committed suicide in the woods, or by drowning himself in a lake or river. But his body was never found.

2) MARGARET JONES, 1942

The next picture showed a round-faced, capable-looking woman with light hair done up in a bun. Margaret Jones, a housewife from Ty-Nant, to the north-east of the mountain, had been fifty-four years of age when she vanished in 1942. Her husband, an RAF Flight Sergeant on home leave, left the house with their young son for a walk while his wife prepared lunch. On returning to the house, he found the table set, the kettle whistling on the hob, and the sandwiches Margaret had been making abandoned.

There was no sign of violence, or any struggle. Nor was there any reason to believe Mrs Jones likely to harm herself. But, like John Rogers, she was never seen again.

3) Richard Herbert, 1948

In August 1948, Richard Herbert, a retired house painter from Margate, Kent, disappeared while on a walking holiday in North Wales. A keen watercolourist since his retirement, he'd been in the process of sketching and painting a number of landscapes in the vicinity of Bala, where he was staying. He was last seen by a motorist near Fron-Goch, a small hamlet two miles west of Mynydd Du, heading in the direction of the mountain.

Locals reported him asking about the best approach to Mynydd Du. Police opinion was that as there were several long-abandoned farmsteads in the vicinity of the mountain, Herbert had likely fallen down an overgrown well shaft. He was a tall, thin man with long white hair and a Van Dyke beard.

4) Katherine Owen, 1953

Eight-year-old Katherine Owen, of Llandrillo (several miles east of Mynydd Du), disappeared in February 1953. A small, solemn-looking girl with fair hair and prominent front teeth. In the week before her disappearance, she'd become fascinated with Mynydd Du and kept begging her parents (who ran a shop in the town) to take her there, without success. One morning they woke up and found her gone. All the house doors and windows were locked.

5) Rachel Morris, 1964

In December 1964, twenty-year-old Rachel Morris, an English Literature student at the University of Aberystwyth, got off a bus in Bala. She was on her way home to spend Christmas with her family in Wrexham, but had decided to visit an old friend of hers, Dorothy Price, who had recently married and moved to Bala. She brought a Christmas card and present for Price and her husband.

She stayed for two hours before leaving. While there, she confided in Price that she was deeply unhappy at university. Rachel was the first person in her family to pursue higher education and had done so in the face of considerable opposition from her father, although Price said that Rachel's mother—and Price herself—admired her for her determination. Rachel was finding the workload and pressures of her college work hard to cope with and was afraid she'd made a mistake—perhaps in her choice of subject, perhaps in studying at all. At the same time she didn't want to quit, especially after all the conflicts with her father on the subject, and was struggling to make a decision as to what to do.

The two women discussed the subject at length; no definite resolution was reached, but Price was adamant that Rachel seemed in good spirits when they parted. As the day was fairly mild and there were still several hours before nightfall, Rachel decided she would walk for a couple of miles before getting the bus. "I haven't stopped once in the last few months," she told Price. "Haven't just looked around me and taken stock. Bit of a walk and some fresh air might clear my head."

Rachel was described as petite, with short dark hair and blue eyes, wearing jeans and a red coat and carrying a knapsack. Three motorists reported seeing Rachel on the road between Bala and Sarnau; a farm labourer in Sarnau reported seeing her passing through the village before she stopped and turned back.

That was the last sighting of her. Despite extensive searches, no trace of Rachel Morris ever came to light. The case file was reviewed four years later in connection with the disappearance of Britt Nordenstam , but no new leads were unearthed and the cases were not felt to be connected.

IV. THE DEVIL IN THE WOODS

Ware attempted to trace the other participants in Britt's tragedy, but with little success. Robert Thurlow had died in 1977 without ever regaining his faculties, and his widow, now remarried, had no interest in revisiting the incident. Arthur Ward, unable to bear the loss of his wife, had hanged himself in 1974. Most of Britt's fellow students didn't want to discuss what had happened, or could add very little to what they'd told the police. An attempt to make a long-distance call to DCI Thomas had ended with a two-word instruction (the second being 'off') before the phone was slammed down.

Ware *did*, however, track down Craig Stowe, so that the final piece of the Britt Nordenstam file was his interview with the man who'd served two years in prison for her murder.

It hadn't been easy. Ware prefaced the interview with a few paragraphs describing Stowe's experiences following his conviction. His time in prison had been, frankly, brutal. He was more or less automatically assumed to be a rapist as well as a killer, and his protestations of innocence had cut no ice with his fellow convicts— half the prison's inmates claimed to be victims of bent coppers or incompetent lawyers.

As such, he'd been treated as the lowest of the low while inside, receiving countless beatings and narrowly escaping worse. He bore ugly facial scarring courtesy of a man who'd been about to castrate him before prison officers intervened. In addition. Stowe was believed to have been raped repeatedly while incarcerated.[1]

The man who emerged from Walton Prison only two years after Britt Nordenstam's death was a near-wreck, drinking a bottle of whisky a day and smoking incessantly, while also using an eclectic variety of illicit substances, including marijuana, amphetamines, LSD and heroin.

Craig had received a substantial sum in compensation, but most of it was quickly frittered away on alcohol and drugs, together with visits to local prostitutes. Initially he moved back in with his parents, but they'd found themselves unable to cope with who their child had become. They'd clearly expected him to put his

---

[1] Although this passage in Ware's notes is underlined with *CUT??? No-one wants to know that* written beside it. Ah, the joyous days of the 1970s. RM

experiences behind him and go back to university, or find a job. Craig Stowe was, by now, capable of none of these.

After a final bitter row, Craig had moved out and rented a flat. He'd moved a couple of times more due to dwindling funds and eviction by outraged or disgusted landlords. Finally, his money ran out and his various addictions reduced him to a state where even if he'd had the money, no-one would have rented him a place.

There were a couple of photographs of Stowe—one in colour, one black and white—but he was barely recognisable as the grinning young man in the rugby shirt. His face was almost skeletal, deeply lined around the eyes and mouth, the corner of which was twisted up by a gnarled, ugly scar on his left cheek, and his nose was askew. The eyes were deeply sunken and looked bloodshot, and his long hair, held back by a sweatband, was streaked with grey. He was smiling, or trying to, but he shouldn't have. Two or three teeth were missing, and those that remained were yellow and brown.

This was the man Russell Ware finally caught up with, one freezing cold January night in 1979, sleeping rough in Liverpool. Nearly a decade on from the events at Capel Teg, he was a week short of his thirty-first birthday and looked nearly twice his age. He had no future worth picturing and no past that he wanted to recall—but to achieve the second aim, he'd need something to drink, smoke or inject, which was how Ware got him to talk.

And so they sat, on a freezing, derelict dockside, a tape-recorder running as Craig Stowe took gulps from the bottle of Scotch Ware had brought along, and talked about the last night Britt Nordenstam was seen alive.

*

Excerpt from Russell Ware's interview with Craig Stowe (11TH **January, 1979):**
(RW: Russell Ware, CS: Craig Stowe)
CS: So what do you want to know?
RW: I want to know what happened that night.
CS: What I told that fucking twat of a Welsh copper...
(PAUSE, HEAVY BREATHING)
CS: Sorry. Every time I think of that bastard my blood boils. What he did to me. Okay. What was I saying?
RW: What you told Inspector Thomas...

CS: Yeah. That. Well, it was true. I didn't kill Britt. The devil took her.

RW: What do you mean, the devil?

CS: Don't need to spell it out, do I? You know who the devil is. You a Christian?

RW: Yes.

CS: Me too. Not much of one. Not anymore. Every night I ask God to forgive me, but I don't know if He will. I sin with drink and drugs, beg forgiveness, and then I do it again. And the one time I was called on to do God's work, I failed. I ran. I was weak. But there's a devil all right, and he was in the woods that night. I... was up that night, watching Britt's tent. I knew she was going to—to be with Thurlow again, sooner or later, and... I wanted to try and talk her out of it. Christ, I wish I hadn't. But I did. And so I ended up telling Thomas about Thurlow. Thought it would shift attention away from me, but in the end it did the opposite.

(PAUSE)

RW: Go on.

CS: I tried talking to her, but she ignored me. Didn't even look at me. That hurt, but I thought, right, I'm going to persevere. So I went after her. Thought she was going to Thurlow's tent at first. Then I thought she was going to the latrine trench, but she didn't go near that either. She went up into the woods. Faster—I had to jog to keep up. She didn't even take her torch with her. I could see her, though. It was as if she glowed. (CRYING) She was so, so beautiful.

(PAUSE)

CS: I didn't know what to do, but it seemed weird, her going off like that, without a light. I thought that maybe—maybe the guilt was getting to her at last, over the things she was doing with Thurlow. Thought she was planning on harming herself. And I wasn't having that. And so I went after her, into the trees. I tried to grab her arm, but when I caught that bracelet of hers it snapped off. Cut her, I think, 'cos it still had her blood on it. I should have thrown it away, chucked it in the lake or something, but I didn't. Hid it. All I had left of her. So of course when they found it, they were sure they'd got their man.

RW: So you followed her into the trees, caught her bracelet... what happened then?

(SILENCE.)

RW: Craig?

CS: There's no point. You won't believe me. No-one does.

RW: I'll listen, Craig. And I won't dismiss it out of hand. Something happened that night, I know that—something strange. What was it? Tell me.

(CS BEGINS SHAKING HIS HEAD. PUTS HIS HANDS OVER HIS EARS AND ROCKS BACK AND FORTH, MOANING AND HUMMING.)

RW: Craig?

CS: I can hear him. I can still hear him.

RW: Hear what?

CS: The devil.

RW: What?

CS: I could hear him. Not one voice, but dozens. Hundreds. You know your Bible, Mr Ware? 'Call him Legion, for we are many'? Many voices, but all one. It was a call and it was beautiful but I could never quite hear it, and I *had* to. I wanted to follow it. Same as Britt. But it was worse for her, because it was her the devil wanted. He was calling her and she had to go. And I was put there—God brought me to that place to save Britt's soul. And I failed. She was lost. Because I could hear it too, and it was calling me up into the pines. Because, you see, Mr Ware, that wood—Coed Capel—it isn't always as small as it looks. There are places where the pines stretch out and out forever, and the paths through them coil around so you can never find your way back. And the devil's waiting there for you in them. I saw them there.

RW: Saw who?

CS: The dancers. The dancers in the pines. When I held back, when I ran rather than go after Britt and pull her back, I looked back once and I saw them. Just a glimpse, as the ways through the pines coiled in on her and took her away. I saw them and... (MOANS) No. No. Stop it, stop it, stop it...

RW: Craig? Craig?

(CS PUTS HIS HANDS OVER HIS EARS AND ROCKS BACK AND FORTH, MOANING AND HUMMING AGAIN. CONTINUES TO DO SO DESPITE REPEATED ATTEMPTS TO RESUME DISCUSSION.)

*

Ware had gone back the next night with a fresh bottle of whisky, hoping to get more information, but Craig Stowe was nowhere to be found. None of his fellow rough sleepers knew where he'd gone. One mumbled vaguely about him hitching a lift somewhere, but didn't know where to. London, perhaps. Or Scotland, or Leeds.

He was never seen again. Most likely he disappeared into the subterranean community of drinkers and addicts in one big city or another and never emerged, finishing up in a nameless grave somewhere. A couple of unconfirmed sightings did surface: one at King's Cross Station in London, and the other in Chester, waiting for a bus bound for somewhere in Wales.

This concluded Russell Ware's notes on the case of Britt Nordenstam. There were a few further jottings about the other missing persons, mostly ideas for unearthing more material about them or their disappearance. But before he could put them into practice, Russell Ware was dead — another, perhaps, of the lost of Mynydd Du.

3: THE BEAST OF MAES CARNEDD

Work took my time up for most of the following week, but finally I was able to get back to Ware's notes. There were two bundles left: a small bunch of notes, suggesting other aspects of the Bala Triangle worth investigating (leads that Russell Ware had never had time to follow up) and a larger, thicker bundle covering the last case Ware had covered before his death in 1981.

*

The North Wales countryside is sparsely populated at the best of times—small towns and tiny villages separated by empty hills, woods and lakes—but the Bala Triangle has grown progressively *less* populated as the years have gone by, despite the UK's swelling population and Wales' perennial appeal as a quiet place to retire, settle or holiday.

As recently as the early 1970s, there were five working farms in the immediate area: all of these now lie abandoned. And while there are no villages within the Bala Triangle today, that wasn't always true.

North of Mynydd Du, you'll find an area choked with tall weeds and brambles. The woods are encroaching on it, but if you look closely you'll find the overgrown remains of a number of small stone cottages beneath the brambles' shroud.

Not far away you'll find some remnants of the mine workings, and the tumbledown ruins of the chapel. There might even be a few gravestones left, but the inscriptions are probably too worn and overgrown with moss and lichen to decipher the names of the men, women and children buried there. The lost, forgotten generations of a lost, forgotten village, crumbling steadily away.

Not that I've ever been there, but I don't need to. I have the photographs Russell Ware took in 1979, more than seventy years after the mining village of Maes Carnedd was abandoned by its inhabitants.

*

Among Ware's notes I found a clipping from a guidebook, *Gwynedd's Hidden Delights,* where Maes Carnedd was listed as a deserted village. In a few short paragraphs, it laid out the tale of the village's rise and fall.

Up until the end of the nineteenth century, Maes Carnedd had been a tiny hamlet with a declining population. There were about thirty souls there, forty or fifty if you counted the two or three farmsteads just outside it. The young people were moving away, drawn to the big cities of the Industrial Revolution. Within another generation or so, there'd be no-one left.

But in 1901, Isaiah Milne, who owned one of the nearby farms, saw something gleaming yellow on the bed of Nant Coch, the small stream that ran past the edge of his property. Looking closer, he found what appeared to be a lump of gold the size of a walnut. He took it to a jeweller in Bala who confirmed it was indeed gold, and bought it from him for a handsome sum.

There are two big seams of gold in Wales: one near Dolaucothi in the south of the country, and another in the north—a band stretching from Barmouth, past Dolgellau and up towards the Snowdonia range. Maes Carnedd lay just outside it, and it occurred to the jeweller there might be a deposit under or near the village.

At this point, Charles Richmond enters the picture. A Yorkshireman, he'd made money from coal mining, but branched into other areas of the industry. He was also a friend of the Bala jeweller, who wrote advising him of Milne's find. Richmond sent company representatives up to the area and they soon confirmed the presence of a rich deposit of gold near Mynyddd Du.

Richmond bought land from the locals and hired men from the area. Maes Carnedd expanded quickly from a sleepy hamlet to a bustling village with a population of nearly two hundred, and enjoyed a short-lived boom.

But sometimes things seem at their strongest before they collapse, and that turned out to be the case with Maes Carnedd. The mine quickly proved itself prone to accidents. Tunnels caved in or flooded, killing a number of miners and maiming more. Of course mining was dangerous work, and such risks came with the job—but even so, rumours spread that the Maes Carnedd mine was unlucky, jinxed, cursed.

And then there were the murders: a family was slaughtered in their home, and the killer was never caught. Ware had scribbled in the margin, *Other murders too*, but the clipping gave no information on that.

Rumours of the curse spread, and people began to leave. No-one wanted to work at Maes Carnedd any longer, not if they could help it. Coupled with that, the cost of the workings kept climbing due to cave-ins, floods and equipment malfunctions. And then finally, Richmond and Sons began experiencing financial difficulties. Soon it became impossible to keep the mine going.

In a way, it paralleled Hafan Deg's collapse seventy-odd years later: accidents, deaths, financial crises, all mounting to the point where the project had to be abandoned. By early 1904 the mine had closed and the village was all but empty, with only a handful of die-hards from the old pre-mining days hanging on. By the time of the 1911 census, the village was completely empty.

Maes Carnedd was left to the grass and the brambles, the encroaching woods, and to the wind and the rain. That, and whatever else lay in the shadow of Mynydd Du.

*

Ware had also found references to 'the Beast' in three different books of Welsh folklore, of the kind that get written with the tourists in mind. All agreed that there was, or had been, a creature that had lived in, or haunted, Maes Carnedd—but they agreed on almost nothing else.

One book described it as a manlike creature covered with fur, while another said the animal was four-legged and wolflike. The third spoke of a creature that lived in water, haunting the streams and pools around the village.

Two agreed that it had terrorised the village's population till Maes Carnedd was abandoned, but one of those claimed the events took place in 1830. The third account didn't specify when the Beast had flourished, but described it as 'preying on the unwary' back 'in olden days'.

Two of the stories were illustrated. One depicted the manlike version of the Beast, complete with fangs and taloned fingers, and the other showed a wolflike creature with webbed paws. Rereading the articles, I saw they agreed on one other point: in all the accounts, the Beast had glowing red eyes.

Nothing about Maes Carnedd's desertion needed a weird or supernatural explanation. The mine had always struggled to make a profit, and when you added a company in financial difficulties, there was no mystery. As for the Beast itself—when you couldn't find two accounts that agreed on what it looked like or even when it had been active, it was hard to take the story seriously.

On the other hand, by now I'd gained a healthy respect for Russell Ware. He might have planned *The Bala Triangle* as another piece of lurid 1970s sensationalism, but he'd shown himself to be a careful, thorough investigator. There had to be more to the story.

And there was.

*

EDITED TRANSCRIPT OF INTERVIEW WITH SIDONIE WARE:

Russell was sure he was onto something—something real, I mean. So he began sifting through newspaper clippings, books of folktales, writing to or telephoning this police officer he knew— Huw, his name was, Huw Llewellyn—looking for more cases, more stories.

And he found this abandoned village—what did you say it was called? Bear in mind, I never read the book. There were stories about some sort of werewolf, I think, but he wasn't sure of the details. So he contacted this Welsh policeman, who helped him try and track down any former villagers still alive. There weren't many, of course, because the village had been abandoned around the turn of the last century.

In the event, he traced three people who'd lived in thiswhat was the place called? Mice Cardiff?—and wrote to them to ask if he could interview them. Unfortunately they all turned him down flat. Very sharply, too. Wouldn't see him, told him never to write or try and get in touch again.

That had a profound effect on Russell. On the one hand, he felt almost vindicated. He was sure he'd hit on something, something that frightened these people so much, even after all those years, that they clammed straight up. But at the same time he was frustrated, because he was baffled as to how to take things any further.

He tried writing to them again. One never replied, and another one's daughter sent an absolutely *scathing* letter back to him, threatening to involve the police if Russell kept 'harassing' her grandmother. The third letter he got back was actually from the man's solicitors.

So there he was, nowhere to go. Oh, he spent a couple of months digging around on other aspects of the area, but if he found anything as meaty as this village, he struggled just as much to make any headway.

It was a very bitter blow to him. He'd begun this thing as a money-spinner, remember, and to an extent he still saw it that way—but he'd ended up taking it very seriously as well. By May 1979, he had no idea as to how to take the project any further.

He made an attempt to resuscitate his third novel—yes, *The Sand Ghosts,* that's the one, darling. Bless you for remembering. He'd destroyed his earlier attempts, but went back to the original concept and tried to begin again from scratch. No luck, though. Eventually he gave up and turned his attention back to shorter fiction. Actually managed to write three or four novelettes, two of which, I think, are among his finest work. They both appeared in *Weapons Of Grass*[2]—but he only sold one of them.

It was a very black time for him, and I'm afraid he was drinking very heavily. I was getting close to my limit, I don't mind saying— but in March 1980, Russell received a letter.

He was in bed when the post came, I recall—at ten o'clock in the morning! This was a man who used to think nothing of rising at five to begin work. I gave him this letter and went out again. By this point, I was feeling quite depressed myself, what with the state of him—and the next thing I know, there was this unholy *whoop* and Russell came tearing out of the bedroom in his underwear, grinning from ear to ear. Kissed me full on the lips, raced downstairs and made some strong coffee, dashed into his study and that was it for the rest of the morning. He was running back and forth between his study and the telephone all that day.

As you've probably guessed, the letter was from one of the former villagers—it was the one whose solicitor had come after Russell, in fact. He said he'd changed his mind, and he'd talk about it after all. So a few days later, Russell went off to North Wales again, to interview him.

*

That phone call led to the longest document in the Maes Carnedd file.

---

[2] *Weapons Of Grass: The Great Short Fiction of Russell Ware.* Posthumous short story collection, Sphere Books, 1983. RM

Ware's correspondent, Owen Lloyd, had been born in Betws-y-Coed in 1878 and had come to work in the Maes Carnedd mine when it opened in 1902. Now 102 years old, his health was declining and he knew he didn't have long left—which had prompted his change of heart.

'Someone ought to know what happened,' he told Ware in his letter. 'The truth shouldn't be forgotten.'

Lloyd was in the Geriatrics Ward of the hospital at Dolgellau, and Ware drove out to see him. The doctors told him that the old man had about a month left. But he was still hanging on and in good spirits, and more importantly he was lucid. Given his condition, and his determination to tell his tale, the nurses allowed Ware to see him outside visiting hours, although only for an hour or so at a time. Ware took a room at a nearby hotel and interviewed Lloyd over several days, recording their conversations before returning to his room to type them up. As he went, he compiled a list of points to corroborate, and made several calls to Sergeant Llewellyn in search of information.

The last, and biggest chunk of the file, consisted of the interview with Lloyd, which Ware had interleaved with copies of police reports from the early 1900s—God knew how Llewellyn had laid hands on them for him.

At any rate, this was the tale they told; the true history, according to Owen Lloyd, of the Beast of Maes Carnedd.

*

FROM WARE'S INTERVIEW WITH OWEN LLOYD, MARCH 1980:

I'll tell you about the Beast, boyo. Oh, yes, it was real all right, and, yes, it killed. And it was killed in its turn, but it finished Maes Carnedd, even so. Oh, you're right about the accidents and the deaths, there were those too. And the company bloody near went bankrupt, and all of that helped put the lid on the coffin. But it was the Beast that put the nails in.

Besides, I think it was all part of the same thing—the Beast, the accidents, the company's troubles. Haven't you understood it yet, Mr Ware? You've been digging into the things that have happened around Mynydd Du. Haven't you? I can always tell. So you must have understood by now, or else you're on your way to it.

There's something there, boyo. Something on Mynydd Du, or in it. Maybe even the mountain itself. And it wants to be left alone.

*

The chain of events that led to Maes Carnedd's desertion began in May 1903, when a tunnel collapsed.

It wasn't the first such incident, of course—mining is a dangerous trade—but for Owen, at least, it had great personal significance: his younger brother Dewi was one of the victims.

"A couple of miners were injured in the rockfall," he told Ware. "But three lads were buried alive—trapped in a little part of the tunnel. Dewi was one of them. The others were Gwyn Davis and Tom Jones."[3]

The three men were uninjured—save for Jones, who may have broken his leg—and at first, as their comrades set to work digging them out, it seemed they'd been lucky. But it quickly proved not to be the case, as every attempt to clear the rubble brought about a fresh fall of rock, and threatened to collapse the remaining roof on the rescuers.

To make matters worse, the trapped section was beginning to flood. The land around Mynydd Du was honeycombed with caves and underground streams, many of which broke spontaneously out above ground and ran down to fill Llyn Daioni. As a result, the miners ran a constant risk of accidentally crossing the path of one of these watercourses. Lives had been lost in the past when tunnels flooded.

In the case of Dewi Lloyd and the rest, the section was filling slowly but steadily; they and the rescuers at least had time. But it did no good; the rubble proved impossible to shift.

They kept trying, though—for all three of the days it took for the trapped section to flood completely. They couldn't get through to the men, couldn't even see them, but they could hear one another well enough. Which meant Owen heard his younger brother's terrified screams as the water rose to fill the last of the space.

"Went a little bit mad myself, around then," he told Ware. "They had to drag me away."

According to Ware's transcription, there were a couple of minutes' silence after that, before the old man began to speak again.

---

[3] Yes. Really. RM

A day or so after the voices had fallen silent, water began seeping through the rubble that choked the tunnel. The water level finally stopped rising when the tunnel was thigh-deep in murky water; they fenced the tunnel off, and carried on digging elsewhere.

Owen Lloyd grieved for his brother, and comforted his mother and sister — his father, a fisherman, had drowned off the coast near Fairbourne two years earlier, which had eventually driven the family inland in search of work—but otherwise, life went on. There was work to do, bread to earn, and one less of the family left to earn it.

*

The deaths of Dewi Lloyd and the others seemed to mark a turning point. Over the month that followed the incident, a series of tremors shook the mine. There were several more cave-ins and two floodings, although the death toll was comparatively light— only six men actually died, and only four were maimed for life. It could have been a lot worse. But for all that, the rumours started to spread: people began saying that the mine was cursed.

"One family actually left," Owen Lloyd told Ware. "Just packed up one night and were gone by morning. But they had relatives who took them in. Most families there didn't. They just had to stick it out. Besides, they were tough folk, all of them."

But in the second month following the deaths of Dewi, Tom and Gwyn, the Beast of Maes Carnedd came.

*

It began on a small scale, with the deaths of animals.

Most of the mining families kept a dog or cat, or both. The family of a miner called John Rees owned a big lurcher they called Gelert, after Prince Llywellyn's legendary hound. On the 2nd July,1903, the dog was let out of the house and didn't return.

When Rees came home from his shift at the pit the following day, he found his wife white-faced and his two children still in hysterics. They'd gone out to play in the woods near the mine, and Lily—the youngest child, five years old—had seen something red. She and her seven-year-old brother, Tom, had gone to investigate, and found the remains of their family pet.

Mary Rees had managed to bring Gelert home, wrapped in a sheet. She put the body in the yard—if what was left of the poor animal could still be called that. Rees went outside, lifted the sheet, and nearly vomited. The dog had been, quite literally, torn to pieces. Its legs had been broken and wrenched from their sockets, its eyes gouged out and its belly ripped open. The body cavity was almost completely empty; the dog had been gutted. The ripped-out limbs had been chewed and gnawed, as had the tattered remains of its innards.

Rees dug a hole and buried Gelert. His shock and nausea—and grief too, because he'd loved the dog—gave way to anger, and he went from house to house, spreading the word. Whatever had killed his dog, he wanted it dead, too. And not just out of vengeance: anything this savage—especially if it had been strong enough to overcome the lurcher—wasn't just a danger to animals. Rees forbade his children to play far from the house. Other parents followed his lead.

Over the next three weeks, more animals died: three dogs, four cats and four sheep from an outlying farm were all butchered in the same way: ripped apart, gutted, eaten. The torn and tattered remains of about a dozen wild rabbits were found scattered about as well. Those who owned shotguns took to keeping them loaded and close at hand.

Meanwhile, locals argued over the killer's identity. The most popular theory was that a big dog of some kind had gone rogue. Others reckoned a wild animal (part of a travelling zoo, or some wealthy man's pet) had escaped and was running loose, although they were divided among themselves as to whether it was a wolf, a bear or a lion.

And others still—among them John Rees, who'd seen for himself how his dog's limbs had been torn from their sockets, the way a man might wrench and twist the leg off a roast chicken—thought the killer wasn't an animal at all, but a man.

The police, though, found nothing. No madmen had escaped their keepers lately, there'd been no travelling zoos in the area and there was no evidence of any local eccentrics whose taste in pets ran to the larger carnivora.

On July 26th, a miner shot a mongrel dog on the outskirts of the village. It was mangy and slat-ribbed, but a big animal all the same—big enough, perhaps, to take on a lurcher and win. But if that was the case, John Rees wondered, why did it look so hungry and thin? It should have fed well over the past weeks. And there were no scars from fighting on it, no marks from bites or scratches.

But no-one listened; no-one wanted to. The miners and their families began to breathe easy again, and two weeks passed almost without incident.

Almost, but not quite. On one night the peace of the village was shattered when two young lovers came running out of the woods at speed, screaming and in a state of partial undress. They insisted they'd seen something in the trees—a naked man covered in hair, with a snarling face, long fangs and bloodred eyes.

Unfortunately, no-one believed them. It was assumed the man had pressed his suit too eagerly, only to be rebuffed, and the resulting lover's quarrel had spilled out into the open and the gaze of witnesses. Although it was interesting how the couple seemed to come up with such consistent accounts on the spur of the moment.

Anyhow, in the face of fairly non-stop mockery on the part of their peers, they shut up about the man in the woods. And the incident would have been forgotten—if the Beast hadn't killed again.

*

Inserted into this part of the interview—according to Ware's method of page-numbering, anyway—was a copy of a police report. Unusually (given that the area would have been something of a backwater at the time), they included photos. I'd love to tell you that I took one look at them and put them aside, but I stared at them long and hard. At first because I wasn't sure what I was looking at, and then out of appalled fascination.

Remember Isaiah Milne, the farmer whose chance discovery had turned Maes Carnedd into a mining village in the first place? His farm still remained, on the outskirts of the village. He was a stubborn man, albeit now a rich one, and refused to move.

On the morning of the 10th August, 1903, Samuel Roberts, a labourer who assisted Isaiah, arrived at the Milne farm. Oddly, there was nobody in sight; the farmer was usually up and about by the time Roberts arrived. Roberts called out, but there was no answer. And then he noticed the front door was ajar. Entering the building, he found the hallway in disarray, strewn with broken china and the splintered remains of a wooden chair. There was also blood on the floor, and on the walls. The blood on the floor led into the farmhouse kitchen. Roberts followed the trail—then, after staring in appalled disbelief at what lay at the end of it, he fled the house screaming.

That was the gist of his statement, in any case. The police report itself, and those bloody (in both senses) photographs told the rest of the story.

The Milne household consisted of Isaiah, his wife Sarah, and three children: Martyn (aged sixteen), David (ten) and Blodwen (six). They also owned a dog and two cats. All but the dog were in the kitchen, and all of them were dead.

The dog had apparently tried to fight the attacker, and paid with its life. It had been smashed to a pulp against the wall of the hallway—hence the bloodstains there—and its throat torn out before being flung upwards onto the staircase. The cats' heads had been wrenched off.

Isaiah Milne had been propped against the kitchen wall, his arms and legs smashed, and had been completely eviscerated. The remains of his wife and children were heaped in a bloody pile on the floor before him, so mangled it was barely possible to distinguish one corpse from another, or even where one body ended and another began. Thankfully the pictures were in black and white, and not the best quality.

I finally turned them over and tried to forget I'd seen them, but nothing would erase the image of Isaiah Milne's face: his eyes huge, his mouth agape in a silent scream. He was believed to have outlived his family by some time: his limbs had been shattered several hours before his death.

The bodies had been part-eaten and dismembered by a combination of teeth, claws and main force, all of which pointed to some sort of animal, but the treatment of Milne's body suggested an all-too-human cruelty and sadism.

The reign of the Beast had begun.

*

FROM WARE'S INTERVIEW WITH OWEN LLOYD, MARCH 1980:
The worst part after that was the waiting. For the next two or three weeks, there wasn't so much as a dead rabbit. It was as if everything that had gone before had been... building up, you know? Just working to get our attention. And now the Beast had it.

So it started taunting us. Letting us know it was there, but not striking yet. Letting us wait and wonder and fear and dread who'd be next, where it would come from.

You'd hear this… howling. I don't know what else to call it. Wasn't like the cry of any creature I've heard of. You'd hear it in the woods, in the village itself. Or even in the mine. That's what no-one could understand—how the thing could get down there.

Yes, there were sightings of it. People kept as clear of the woods as they could, but you couldn't avoid them completely. And they'd see it there, watching them through the trees. Ran like hell when they did, and thought themselves lucky to get out alive. They saw it in the village too, slinking down the street. Even saw a face at the window myself one night, looking in.

And what did it look like? That's your next question, isn't it, boyo? I'll bet you've seen a few different pictures. And I'll bet you something else—that no two of them were alike. Well, don't worry. That was par for the course.

What I saw was something like a man, but covered in thick black fur and with long sharp teeth and claws. It had glowing red eyes, too—they were red all the way through. No white or iris or pupil, just red, and glowing. That was the one thing that never changed.

See, John Rees saw it too, only it was running on all fours and he swore it had a tail, and he was sure it had a snout, like a dog or a wolf. But it had the glowing eyes all right. And a fellow called Ieuan Griffiths saw something in one of the pools by Nant Coch. It swam and it was black and shiny, he reckoned, with webbed hands—like a big newt or something. But the same eyes: glowing and red. So we were all arguing over what it was, but the one thing we did agree on was that the Beast was real.

What was done about it? What could be? The police decided they were looking for a madman and the company agreed. They certainly weren't having any nonsense about a monster or a werewolf or whatever it was. After all, I suppose, we couldn't even agree among ourselves what the thing looked like.

The company weren't happy either. Mr Newell, the manager—he was a big hard bastard, him, from Birmingham—said he'd sack the next one he heard talking about any Beast. Bloody stupid, of course, but what else was he going to do? He was just like the rest of us, deep down. Scared to bloody death.

And then the Beast killed again. This time right down in the mine itself.

Give me a moment here. It's not an easy one, this. Bill Probert was a good friend of mine. That was one of the men who died. The others were Bert Williams and Jack Griffiths. Good lads, both of them, but I didn't know them well. Bill and Jack... look, all right, here's how it happened.

First thing we heard was the howling. We were all down the pit, chipping away, and we heard the thing howl. No mistaking that noise for anything else. Then it came again, a minute or two later. And then again. And each time it got closer and closer. I grabbed my pick and got ready to use it. But Bill and the others all had their picks too, and much good it did them. We found one of the picks later—the handle'd been snapped clean in half.

Screaming started a minute or so later. I couldn't move at first, not even when I realised it was coming from where Bill had been working. But then one of the other lads started running towards it, and the rest of us went after him. God....

The screaming was still going on when we reached the place they'd been working, but it was getting farther away. See, Bill and Jack were still there—what was left of them, anyway, but Bert Williams, the poor sod....

We could all hear his screams, fading away as it dragged him off. And we could have gone after him, but we didn't. No point. We'd have been dead, too. You didn't see what it did to those men. They were torn to pieces. I mean literally. Limb from limb. Like you'd pull a roast chicken apart—rip off the drumsticks, gouge and tear off the breasts. Strip the carcass. We could recognise the faces, just— and by Christ, I wish I hadn't—but as for the rest? You couldn't tell which bits were Bill's and which were Jack's.

As for Bert Williams? No-one ever saw him again, living or dead.

*

More clippings: an article from a local paper saying the three men had been lost when a shaft flooded, with comments from Newell, the manager. And, just for a moment, I could believe that the Beast of Maes Carnedd hadn't existed anywhere but Owen Lloyd's imagination.

But either on his own initiative or by orders of his paymasters, Newell had lied—because the clippings were followed by another police report. And more photographs. One look at those told me I'd seen all I wanted to, and I turned them face-down. The report itself bore out everything Owen Lloyd had told Ware.

The Isaiah Milne murder, you could explain as the act of a lone madman. But this? It couldn't have been any of the other miners— they were all accounted for, and whoever had killed Probert and Griffiths would have been bloody from head to toe. But no-one could understand how the killer had entered the mine. Or got out again. If it had left at all.

*

"What happened in the mine was the beginning of the end," Owen told Ware. "Two families packed up and left that very night. And they weren't the last."

Over the next few nights, sightings of the Beast multiplied, now in the village itself (not, as Owen pointed out, that anyone would have been stupid enough to go wandering in the woods by that point). The Beast was seen moving down the main street—even standing there, still, in the open, its eyes glowing.

*

FROM WARE'S INTERVIEW WITH OWEN LLOYD, MARCH 1980.

And the thing came looking in through my back window before long. And not just mine. Oh, I wasn't the only one in Maes Carnedd to have seen that face peering in at me, but after what happened in the mine? By Christ, it was the rule, not the exception, after that. That bloody, damned thing went prowling round Maes Carnedd by night—slinking round the backs of houses, looking in through the windows... and of course, if you didn't see it looking in on you, that was only the start of the fear. Because now you wondered where else it might be. Like at your door, trying to find a way in.

There were no more deaths, though. Not until that last day, and I'll tell you about that in a minute. But it wasn't for lack of trying. I heard it scratching at my door one night—when I looked the next morning, it had clawed the hell out of the wood. Just toying with me, of course. I'd seen what it'd done to grown men; if it had wanted to, it could have come through my door as if it was a paper hoop.

It did smash into two houses that I know of, but they drove it off. In one house they had a shotgun and in the other they threw a pan of boiling water at it. But even then, we all knew it could have killed if it had wanted to. We all agreed on that, even though we were still arguing about what it bloody looked like.

Well, Mr Newell was at his wits' end. He couldn't say it was all wild stories any more—and besides, he had problems of his own. All of a sudden there was trouble at head office. Looked as if the company was going bust. More people were packing up and leaving, and what could he do now to stop them? Threaten them with the sack? From a company that mightn't even be there much longer? But, you know, he was a loyal company man, whether you call that a virtue or not. That's why he was there at the end.

It was John Rees' idea. He called us all together in the chapel. First thing in the morning, as soon as it got light. We should have been down the pit, of course, but no-one cared about that now. Risking your life for the company down the mine was one thing when all you had to worry about was floods and rockfalls—but this? We were scared and we were angry, and it was an ugly mood. Even more so when Newell and a couple of the other company men turned up. I don't like to think how it might have gone, to be honest, if he'd tried to throw his weight around. But he had more sense than that. Besides, he was frightened too. He was a big man—stout, yes, but very strong as well—with a great square face and a walrus moustache, but he looked almost shrunken that day.

Pretty much the whole village was there, crowded into the chapel. The minister, Mr Powell, didn't look too happy, but he could see the best thing was to stand back and let us get on with it.

Even though it was light, everyone was armed. Those who had shotguns had brought them, and the rest had picks and shovels or anything else they could lay hands on. Mr Newell had a revolver with him, though we didn't know it at the time. I don't know if that was for the Beast, or for us.

Anyway, John Rees spoke. Said we had to make our minds up what to do—either to leave, or to put a stop to the Beast once and for all.

That set off an argument. There were some stubborn men who didn't want to be driven off. Most others favoured going—said the mine would be closing anyway, so why hang around and risk being torn apart by that thing? I could see Newell—I was keeping an eye on him, if truth be told, just in case he was about to try something daft—and I couldn't help but feel sorry for him. You could see he wanted to say something, or that he felt he should, but at the same time you could see he agreed with Rees—and, probably, with the people who wanted to get the hell out of Maes Carnedd.

And then there was this scream, from near the main doors. And that was when it all broke loose.

There was a young girl—Bryony Pritchard, her name was, a pretty little thing, about eleven years old—who'd been standing by the main doors, which were standing open. She was shrieking her head off. Her mother was too, grabbing the child to wrench her away from the thing that had hold of her and was trying to drag her outside.

It was the Beast, all right. The same face I'd seen glaring in through my window. A man's, sort of, but covered in fur and with sharp fangs for teeth, and eyes glowing red.

Bryony's father was on-hand, too, which was lucky for her. He hadn't a shotgun with him, but he had a great thick pick-handle in his hands and he smashed the Beast in the face with it, again and again. It howled that howl we'd all got to know over the past months and let the child go. Then it tore the pick-handle from Pritchard's hands and snapped it like a twig, raking him across the face with its claws as he staggered off-balance.

It nearly made it into the chapel then, and God alone knows what would have happened if it had. But one of the other men ran forward, one of the ones that'd brought his shotgun, and he gave the Beast both barrels. He didn't hit it full on, much less kill it, but it went reeling backwards through the doors, long enough for the rest of us to slam them shut and bar them. They were good thick doors, maybe—*maybe*—thick enough to keep even that thing out.

It was madness in the chapel then. Panic, screaming, men as well as women. They'd thought they were safe in the daylight. But no, here it was. Anyway, there was a rush now towards the back of the chapel, towards the back door. With the Reverend Powell in the lead, no less. More was the pity for him.

Because, you see, he got the door wide open, and what should leap through but this thing - looked like a great, sleek wolf to me. But I wasn't the closest. Another man, who got a damned good look at it, said it was like a wolf or a big dog but with a shorter, thicker snout. And its paws—its paws were webbed, with long sharp claws, like an otter's.

It landed on Powell, tearing and clutching at him with those claws, pinning him down as he thrashed and bled and begged and screamed. And then it glared at us with the same glowing red eyes the thing at the other door had, and it howled the same howl—and then it dragged the minister outside. I didn't see what it was doing to him, but I could hear the screams. The man nearest the door took one look, and then he slammed it shut and we were all hunting round for things to keep it that way.

There were more screams from the chapel, and when we ran back through, we saw a face at the window. Something was clinging to the wall and glaring through the glass. It smashed a hand—more like a claw—through the window. And we could see it clearly. This one was man-shaped, but with great webbed claws for hands, and its head was like that of the wolf-otter thing. But it had the glowing eyes, too. And it made the same howl when John Rees shot at it and made it drop away.

So there you have it—why all the descriptions of the Beast are so different. There was never *a* Beast of Maes Carnedd. There were three of the buggers. Three at the least.

Well, we'd kept them out of the chapel for now, but we were trapped in there. Outside we could still hear Powell screaming—went on for a while, that did. They didn't like to kill too quickly, those things. Someone helped Pritchard to a pew. His wife and daughter were in hysterics, and his face—Christ alive, that thing had nearly torn it off. He lost an eye, as I recall.

John Rees reloaded his shotgun and took charge. A good man, he was. Split the men with the guns up so some were covering each door and the rest were watching the windows. But there weren't enough guns. We all knew that.

Powell finally stopped screaming, and after that there was just silence. I remember it getting brighter in the chapel as the sun came up, watching the shadows move across the floor. It was strange to be out of doors at that hour. We couldn't hear anything. I remember hoping they'd gone away, that they couldn't stand the sun, but I wasn't going to be the one who took the risk. I think we must have passed an hour, maybe two, just waiting.

I heard the noise and saw the shadow on the floor at the same time, and I turned and looked. When I saw it, I couldn't speak for a second: one of the Beasts, the one that looked the most like a man, had climbed up and was crouched in one of the chapel windows. I managed to get out a shout—nearly a bloody scream, if truth be told—just as it jumped.

It smashed through the glass and landed in the chapel, and by God there was such a screaming and a panic as you've never heard before. It ran straight at me and I got my pick ready to hit at it, but I knew if it was on me I wouldn't stand a chance.

Luckily, one of the lads with a shotgun was near me and he was on the ball—do you know, though? For the life of me, I can't recall his name. I'm ashamed to say. He saved my life, and it's only right to remember a man's name if he does that for you, isn't it?

But anyway, yes—he gave that ungodly thing both barrels, right in the chest, and it went flying backwards. And then… then it got right up again.

Oh, it was damaged all right. There was a big ugly wound in its chest and blood in its thick black fur, and you could tell it was hurt and in pain, but it was a long way from done. It howled its howl at us, and it sprang again.

We both got out of its way and it landed in a crouch, looking from me to the other man. We'd gone in different directions, see, so it had to make up its mind which of us to go for. And that probably saved us both.

See, while it was hesitating, I could hear John Rees' voice shouting, sounding like he was calling from a long way away. But there were people moving, running in. Men with guns. They opened fire on it, slammed barrel-load after barrel-load of shot into the Beast. It kept trying to come at us, but they kept firing, knocking it backwards till it was pinned up against the wall.

The chapel seemed to be full of smoke. I remember that. Stank of it. If you've ever smelt gun smoke you know it has a bit of a sulphur smell, doesn't it? So if I say the whole place stank like Hell… my ears were ringing, too. This bloody humming sound.

The guns were all empty and the men were reloading, fast and in a near-panic in case it came at them again, but the Beast was done. It was struggling to stay stood up, and as we watched we could see it lose that fight as well. It slid down the wall—left a bloody trail as it did—and then that red glow went slowly out of its eyes, and I knew. Knew it was gone.

But there were still two of the bastards left out there, and they chose that second to attack.

They must have both come round to the main door and waited to throw themselves at it together. There was a crash and the door shifted in its frame, and we could hear it splintering. And then it came again, and the doors just flew apart, smashed bits of wood flying all ways.

The other two came tearing in, the wolf one in the lead. It was heading right for the little Pritchard girl, who was knelt down by her poor father bawling her eyes out. She wouldn't have had a chance, but Newell stepped in front of it. Yes, him, of all people. Folk can surprise you sometimes.

Remember how I told you he had a pistol? Well, he had it out and aimed at the wolf-thing, but it leapt at him instead and brought him down. I heard him screaming as it tore at him, and then I heard the gun firing, again and again and again.

The men with the shotguns were trying to get reloaded in time as the other animal came barrelling down the aisle—and here I was again, right in its path. Must be a bloody gift or something. Anyway, I swung at it with my pick, and I got it. Right through the chest. More bloody luck than judgement, that was.

I was already ducking down to try and avoid those claws, which I managed to do. They passed over my head, and then it banged into me and sent me flying into the pews while it went sprawling in the aisle.

It got up, painfully, my pick still stuck in its chest. I could see the sharp point sticking out of the thing's back—and beyond it, I could see John Rees and the others, taking aim with their shotguns.

The Beast turned and ran, faster than I'd thought anything could with a wound like that. But then they'd had to shoot that first one God alone knows how many times before it died.

The third Beast leapt over its pal, which was lying tangled up with Newell in a big dark pool of blood, ran out through the chapel doors and outside. Rees and the others followed, and I heard more shots.

Newell was dead. The wolf-thing had its jaws locked on his throat, and had damn near bitten it out. But the wolf- Beast was dead, too. When it brought him down, he must have shoved his gun's muzzle up under its chin and started firing. Kept on going, too—emptied the gun before he died. The top of its head was blown clean off.

As for the third Beast—it ran Rees and the others a good race, I'm told. They hit it as it tried to run away, but it kept going. They lost sight of it, but they followed the blood trail, and they realised it was heading towards the Milne farm.

The trail led across Milne's land, and at first they didn't know where it could be making for. And then someone remembered how the Beast had been seen in Nant Coch, and they realised it must be making for the stream.

They caught up with it on the banks of Nant Coch, near the spring where the stream comes out of the ground. The last Beast had collapsed to the ground and was trying to pull the pick out of its chest. When it saw them, it seemed to panic—it flailed about and fell into the water.

They ran to the bank, but all they saw was the pick, lying in the shallows. Then one of them yelled and pointed, and they saw the Beast swimming upstream, towards the source of the spring. Its fur was all slick and glistening and smooth-looking, like bare, slimy skin, and they could see why it'd looked to Ieuan Griffiths like a great big newt. They ran towards it, took aim, and….

Well, this is what they told me. The hole that the water came out of was narrow—seven or eight inches wide at most—but when the Beast reached it, it just… squeezed through somehow, as if it was boneless, or a jelly. Squeezed through and was gone.

But I didn't learn that till later. Right at that moment, in the church, I was staring at something. Something that had caught my eye.

I was looking down at the wolf- Beast, collapsed across Newell's body with the top of its head gone, and saw something gleam gold. I looked closer and I could see something on its left—paw? Hand? Claw? I'm not sure what the best word for it would be. It wasn't like a wolf's paw, I know that. Can still see it now. As I said, it was webbed, with long digits, each with a sharp claw on the tip. On one of them—where the wedding finger would be on a man—there was a gold ring.

That wasn't all, either. It looked familiar, this one. I know, one wedding ring looks much the same as another, but this had a pattern etched on it, a sort of zig-zag. And I knew I'd seen it somewhere, but couldn't think where. Until suddenly it came to me, and I had to grab onto a pew to steady myself.

Gwyn Davis had worn a ring like that. It had belonged to his grandfather, he said, and he'd never taken it off, not even down the mine.

I wasn't the only one to recognise it either; just the first. Wish I had been sometimes, and then I could tell myself I'd imagined it.

But other people saw what I'd seen, and Gwyn's wife started having hysterics a minute or two later.

I walked away from them. Up through the chapel, towards the first Beast, the man- Beast, sat huddled against the wall with its dead, glazed eyes. I looked and studied it, trying to see if I could recognise anything about it.

And there was nothing in the face, but then I remembered that Dewi had a tattoo of a fish on his right shoulder. I remember how my fingers shook when I reached out to part the fur. It was all matted with blood. The shotguns had made a royal mess of the Beast and no mistake, nearly cut it in half. I remember hoping for a second that there'd just be a ragged wound where the tattoo had been. But there wasn't. The hair was very thick and it was very hard to see the skin beneath, but I didn't need to see everything. Just to see enough. And I did. I saw the fish's eye, the scales etched on the pallid skin in blue.

I stumbled away and collapsed into a pew. And then I was doing all I could not to weep—for my brother, and the thing that he'd become.

*

I looked for crime scene photos, but there weren't any. According to Ware's notes, Llewellyn had been unable to find any police reports pertaining to the deaths of Lawrence Gordon Newell or Gavin Powell, but it was a matter of record that both men had died on the same date. According to the company there'd been an accident down the pit, injuring some miners, including one Evan Pritchard.

Newell had gone down the mine to help, but been trapped by another roof fall. He'd been mortally injured and Powell had been called on to minister to him, but both men were killed when a final roof fall buried them.

Inventive, but at least it gave Newell a fictive hero's death, as he'd had in life. Assuming that was what had happened, of course; in the absence of other evidence, there was only Owen Lloyd's word to go by.

FROM WARE'S INTERVIEW WITH OWEN LLOYD, MARCH 1980:
(RW: Russell Ware, OL: Owen Lloyd)

OL: We burned the bodies—Gwyn's and Dewi's, I mean. They made up a story about Newell and Powell. Last bit of—what would they call it nowadays?—'damage limitation'. Not that it did any good. The village had been teetering on the brink anyway, and even with the Beasts dead, that last attack tipped it over. Assuming they *were* all dead. John Rees seemed pretty sure that the last of them, the one that'd been Tom Jones, had been dying. But there was always the chance it had recovered and was still lurking down the mine. And there was always Bert Williams at the back of people's minds. No-one had seen him since the Beasts got him, so what if he was one of them, too?

That was the biggest thing of all, of course: finding out who the Beasts really were. It was the last straw; none of us were going down that bloody mine again, not after that. I packed up and left the next day, and so did most everybody else within the fortnight. Not like the company was going to even try stopping us. Not now. Newell was dead, and the firm had troubles of its own, you know?

So the pit shut down, and that was the end of Maes Carnedd village. And those who'd seen what had happened? Well, we didn't talk about it. We'd be thought mad. And besides….

RW: Besides what?

OL: I've told you plenty, haven't I boyo?

RW: Yes, you have, but—

OL: So perhaps now you won't mind giving me an answer to something. What are you going to do with all of this?

RW: All what?

OL: All of this that I've told you. A book, was it?

RW: Yes, a book. About Mynydd Du.

OL: Give you some advice?

RW: Okay.

OL: Don't do it.

RW: What?

OL: The book. Forget about it. Bury it.

RW: What? But you just—

OL: I didn't want the truth to die with me, boyo, that's all. Maybe one or two other people still know what really happened at Maes Carnedd, but none of them are talking. Maybe I should have just kept my mouth shut, too. That might have been better all round, but it's done. But think about it. What did I tell you before, about Mynydd Du?

RW: That there's something there? Something alive?

OL: Yes, and what else? That it wants to be left alone. It tolerated the village for a long time, when there were just a few folk there and they didn't bother it, but when the mining started… that's why folk kept quiet for so long. They didn't want to draw its attention. And what you're doing—that might get the attention of whatever's up there. And you don't want that. You don't.

RW: I see.

OL: Don't go thinking I'm mad, boyo, not after all I've told you. Me, I'm an old man, and I'll soon be gone. That's why I'm talking, because I'll be beyond its reach soon enough. But you, you're a different story.

RW: You could be right.

OL: I am. Think on what I'm saying.

RW: I will. I promise you, I will.

*

Owen Lloyd died six months later, which was a good while longer than the doctors had expected him to last. He was two months short of his 103rd birthday.

Russell Ware, then forty-two years of age, had less than a year left to live.

PART 2

MARKLAND

4: THE LAST OF RUSSELL WARE

Russell Ware: West Indian/British journalist and science-fiction author. Born Kingston, Jamaica, 1938. Died near Bala, North Wales, 1981.

PUBLICATIONS:

Out of the Fire (1st novel: Mayflower, 1967)

The Wind Dancer (2nd novel: Sphere, 1970)

Weapons of Grass: The Great Short Fiction of Russell Ware (posthumous short story collection, Sphere, 1983)

UNPUBLISHED:

The Sand Ghosts (3rd novel: MS destroyed)

The Bala Triangle (non-fiction)

I. Sidonie Ware's Statement

Edited transcript of interview with Sidonie Ware:

In retrospect, there were a lot of warning signs. Russell was clearly struggling. There were financial problems: my own business was having a number of difficulties, and to make ends meet Russell had to take on a great deal of jobbing work—'hack work' he would have called it, to be honest. It brought in a trickle of money, but it left him very little time to concentrate on his real passion: his book on the Bala Triangle.

In addition, while I don't know all the details, I do know he was struggling to unearth more material for his book. Some aspect of the research... but I don't know what. He was very secretive about it. He always was, whenever he was working on something. Wouldn't even tell me about it. But I learned to recognise his moods. Even so, his behaviour became quite erratic—alarmingly so. There were some phone calls... I never learned who he was calling or what was discussed. He was becoming....

I'm sorry—it's painful to have to say this about him, even after all this time. He was becoming quite paranoid. Accused me more than once of going through his notes, or disclosing their contents to others. He almost struck me on two occasions.

For my own part, I tried to remain calm and persuade him to get help. You must remember that we were both quite traditionally-minded in these matters. A wife stayed by her husband through thick and thin. And in my view, Russell was... oh, I don't know what to call it. At the time, even to myself, I would have said he was under great strain, struggling to cope. Today we'd talk about depression, mental illness, but back then....

Anyway, it all came to a head over the Christmas and New Year of 1980. We spent the period with my family, and Russell was awkward throughout—silent, morose, drinking heavily. Certain members of my family had never been happy about my marrying a black man, and they didn't miss the opportunity to claim they'd been proven right. Between dealing with them and Russell, I was worn to a frazzle. I couldn't wait to get away. He was in a filthy mood—hungover and angry, because he'd certainly been aware of what those people were saying. And I wasn't in a much better frame of mind myself by then. When we got home we had a blazing row, and he retreated to his study and slammed the door. He didn't come out. I left sandwiches for lunch, and his evening meal outside the bedroom door, but they were untouched. He didn't come to bed.

When I woke up the next morning, Russell was gone. He'd left a note. It was rambling and incoherent. Apologising for hurting me, a mixture of rage, bitterness and self-pity about his failure as a writer. And a lot about the mountain—that was what he kept calling it, the mountain. Said it had come between us, destroyed our marriage, ruined him. And that he was going up there to settle matters once and for all.

What did I think he meant by that? To be honest, dear, I didn't think anything much. What was on my mind just then was that my husband appeared to have gone insane. I contacted the police, of course—I felt I had to, by then—but they weren't very sympathetic. He hadn't even been gone a day, after all.

Russell had taken the car, so I borrowed a friend's. And I drove up to North Wales. My first stop was Bala, as that was the nearest town to his 'triangle', but he hadn't been able to get a room there. Luckily when I asked about him, people remembered. It was a quiet time of year, after all.

I finally found him in Dolgellau. I don't know if you know the place. It's a market town, about twenty or so miles from Bala. He was in a hotel there. He wasn't particularly pleased to see me—I think it embarrassed him. We argued again, in his room. I wanted to know what he hoped to achieve, but he wouldn't say. Finally he stormed off, talking about showing me—showing everyone. And he drove off, and….

That was the last time I saw my husband alive. In fact, it was the last time I ever saw him at all. The coffin at the funeral was closed. The state he was in, you see. The condition of the body. I couldn't look at him.

Yes, he was found quite quickly, but—in the fall, he'd struck his face against rocks, which had disfigured him very badly. And I understood from Huw that the fish had… been at his face as well.

That's right, dear, Huw Llewellyn. I rang the local police after Russell drove off, but they were very like the police at home. He was an adult, and he'd driven off after an argument. If I'm honest, I think they wrote me off as a hysterical woman. Luckily I had Huw's telephone number and spoke to him, and he took me rather more seriously.

The search started the same day—the second of January. He enlisted a couple of local constables to help him. They searched around the clock. Huw telephoned me the next day, very early.

I remember it was barely light. This beautiful winter's morning. The sun was red, the sky was clear, there was this bare oak tree silhouetted against the sunrise. The Welsh landscape is hauntingly beautiful—you'll know that if you've ever been—but just then it was very stark, too. Austere. Bleak. And of course I knew, I just knew. I'd had this terrible dread all that night that I wouldn't see him again, that matters had come to some sort of head. I knew what the news would be. What had kept me up was another kind of uncertainty.

The past couple of years had been so difficult, so painful. I loved Russell dearly, and I'd never considered leaving him for more than a minute. I'd made my commitment to him and as far as I was concerned that was it, non-negotiable. Till death do we part, and so on. And I knew the loss would be terrible, that it would almost destroy me—but a part of me also knew that it would be like a weight lifted from me. And so when the call came and Huw told me that they'd found Russell's body, I was anguished—but I was relieved as well.

I collapsed shortly after getting the news. I hadn't slept that night, and the whole Christmas period—and before, if I'm honest—had been one long nightmare of frayed nerves and broken nights. I was very grateful for Huw's support at that time. At least he spared me the horrors of having to identify the body. He had some effects of Russell's, and just asked me to confirm they were his. He even helped make the funeral arrangements. A cremation. The service itself took place in Llanaber, which is a very beautiful churchyard on the coast. Very helpful, since due to my then-financial straits I'd have been hard-pressed to meet the funeral costs. Well. In the event, after the service, I returned home with Russell's ashes in an urn. I still have them, as you can see: there, on the mantelpiece.

Huw was a great support. I think he may have been a little in love with me, but with the best will in the world it would have been too early for me. And there was the distance to consider. And most of all, he was married. I think I had some high-minded idea of saving him from himself. They got divorced a couple of years later anyway. But as you know, I never remarried. There was no-one to replace Russell—and besides, I'd grown wary of relationships, after all the difficulties we'd had.

So instead, I buried myself in my work. My business recovered and became successful once more, as you can see. I moved house, let my contact with Huw Llewellyn tail off, and tried to only remember the good times with Russell. And that, I'm afraid, is all I can tell you.

II. The Fragments

I) From Russell Ware's notes for *The Bala Triangle*:

Area Surrounding Mynydd Du: The adjacent woodland is called Coed Capel—meaning 'the wood of the chapel' in Welsh. This suggests a link to the village. The lake's name, Llyn Daioni, means 'Lake of Goodness', while Capel Teg means 'the fair chapel'. It's possible these names are propitiatory, in the same way that fairies were traditionally referred to as the Good or Kind Folk; to speak ill of them was to invite their disfavour.

What happened to Capel Teg? The dig there was cut short by Britt Nordenstam's disappearance, but Professor Thurlow's team uncovered evidence of extensive fire damage, and the remains of weapons such as arrowheads and blade fragments—very out of place in a mediaeval farming village. It's hard not to conclude the community was destroyed by violence. But why? I still haven't been able to find any records of the village, or anything else that would shed light on what happened there.

The Coed Capel woodland is to the south-west of Mynydd Du. There are two other major woodlands in the mountain's immediate vicinity: Coed Lleidr, to the south-east, and Coed Dinas, to the north, just beyond Maes Carnedd. The last of these might be connected with another rumour I've been trying to trace. Some Roman remains were allegedly uncovered during early work on the Maes Carnedd mine. There might even have been a dig, or the beginnings of one. But so far I haven't been able to find anything about it.

There's more, much more, I'm sure of it. But the evidence is getting harder and harder to find….

*

Possible Explanations for Reported Phenomena:

One: It's all just coincidence. That's the least attractive one, of course, and for the purpose of my book it's completely useless, but I have to entertain it.

Two: There's some sort of toxic agent there, something that causes hallucinations and/or psychosis. Something in the water table, most likely. Drink the water, or perhaps even breathe the air under certain conditions, and it gets into your blood. Even a mild dose would leave the victim disoriented and confused—a recipe for disaster if, say, they were working on a mine or building site, which are dangerous to begin with. That would account for the accidents that plagued both the Hafan Deg executive village building site and the Maes Carnedd mine. It would also explain the disappearances. A hiker, passing too close, gets contaminated somewhere and wanders off into the woods, lost. And if there's a toxic agent present, they may well absorb more and more of it, so the problem gets worse. Finally the toxin builds to a fatal overdose, or else they die of exhaustion and exposure.

That would also explain certain aspects of Britt Nordenstam's disappearance—i.e. Craig Stowe's insistence that he saw the woods move and swallow her up, and his claim to have seen 'the dancers in the pines'. Although it *wouldn't* account for the preservation of the Nordenstam girl's body when she was found two years later.

It would also account for certain aspects of the Maes Carnedd business. Granted, my only information on what actually happened comes from one very old man, who could be lying or delusional. But assuming he's telling the truth as he *remembers* it, the 'Beast' could have been a human killer or killers, driven violently psychotic by the toxin. And the villagers could have seen the killers as something else, something other than human.

Three: There's some sort of radiological or electromagnetic activity in the area—caused by mineral deposits under Mynydd Du, perhaps—that interferes with brain function. Causes the same effects as the toxin (hallucinations, psychosis) but in a different way.

Four: This is the least likely explanation, but it's the one that would sell the most copies, of course. There's something there, around Mynydd Du. Something alive. A *genius loci*, a spirit of place....

*

II) FROM RUSSELL WARE'S PERSONAL DIARY:
6TH OCTOBER 1980
I feel as though I'm caught in a trap. This constant spiral of ill-luck. Perhaps I'm not meant to write about Mynydd Du. I keep telling myself that my fourth hypothesis about the place is the least likely, but that doesn't always help.

And there've been times when I've tried to break away from this project, to write something else. To write fiction again. How many times have I tried to write *The Sand Ghosts*, only to rip it up and destroy it? I've lost count. Whatever I do, I just can't make it work or come alive, and the same thing's happened every time I've tried to put together a new novel. Even short stories and novelettes are like pulling teeth.

I'm a writer. I *am*. It's what God put me on Earth to do; I've never doubted that for a moment. So why can't I write? Why can I only spend my time on this? I can't even be sure it'll make money now; it's fast looking like the kind of thing that would be too serious or scholarly to sell. Do I make it sensational, or important? Either way, I can't see how it can progress. Everything's a struggle. I used to love writing, used to bound to my notepads and typewriter every morning—now I dread it. I feel like the condemned man every time I go there now.

Why can't I write? Why can't I bloody *write*, you fucking bastard? Let me write a novel again, let me publish it, and I'll burn every note I've made and never mention you again.

But that's not enough for you, is it? Is it, Mynydd Du? Yes, I know, this is insane: I'm writing a letter to a mountain. But it seems to make sense. I don't want to believe it—I *don't* believe it—but more and more I feel it to be the truth. You're alive, and you're my enemy. You've felt me poking my nose in, haven't you? And now you've decided you're going to punish me for it. Letting me off with a warning wouldn't suit you, would it? Oh no, you want blood. You want your pound of flesh. You want to punish me fully for having the temerity to probe your dirty secrets, your wicked past.

How many lives, how many souls? Britt Nordenstam and Craig Stowe; Robert Thurlow, too, to all intents and purposes. Bill Lewis and all the men who died labouring on Hafan Deg—and what really happened to Harry Yelland?—and the miners at Maes Carnedd; the men killed by the Beast, or who became it. All the disappeared: John Rogers, Margaret Jones, Richard Herbert, little Katherine Owen and Rachel Morris—and those are just the ones we know about, aren't they? How many more, Black Mountain? How many more have you taken?

Well fuck you. You won't take me. You won't beat me. You won't. You won't. You won't.

*

18TH NOVEMBER 1980

Terrible nightmare last night. And not just last night. The last three—no, four—nights running, it's been the same. Exactly the same, every time.

The first couple of times, I just put it down to the stress and the strain of recent months. The money troubles, the arguments with Sidonie, and of course with this place that's obsessed me for so long. I struggled not to admit it the third time, although I think I knew by then what I'd have to do.

After last night, I've admitted defeat, so I'll set it down here. This is my dream.

It starts with Maes Carnedd. I'm standing among the ruins at dusk. There's a creaking noise; the pit-head gear's standing there again, the wheels turning. I turn around and the houses aren't ruined any more. They're whole, but dark. And then the doors open. All the doors open; they swing wide as one. Inside there's only darkness; inky-black, total. And then in that darkness, red eyes gleam.

I know that I've only got seconds before the owners of those red eyes come out, and I know I mustn't see them, so I turn and I run. I can see the mountain, but I never reach it. I run into woodland and no matter how I run I'm always circling the mountain.

As I run, I hear singing and chanting. It sounds religious somehow—but not in a way that comforts me. The opposite: I can't understand the words, can't even identify the language, but I know it's something terrible.

And I'm not alone in these woods. There are other people there too, winding their way endlessly round the mountain in a spiral. Some run. Some stagger blindly onwards, as if they're close to collapse but daren't stop.

And now and then, I glimpse the ones who dance. They're naked and pale and I can't see them properly, and I know that I don't want to. They're so pale they almost shine with it. I see them through the pines, among the trees.

Once, someone comes close to me. He's one of the ones stumbling through the woods, exhausted beyond exhaustion. His hands are stretched out ahead of him, feeling, fumbling for branches and trunks. I know him; I know that I know him from somewhere. And then he turns to look at me. Stowe: it's Craig Stowe. His eyes are bleeding. They've been bleeding for a long time. There's both fresh blood on his cheeks and black, crusted dried blood there, too. I can't tell if he's actually still got eyes, or if they're just holes.

Then something comes up through the woods. Water, gleaming in the moonlight—night's fallen as I've run. And beside it, there are these strange pill-shaped buildings with little windows around them, like portholes. Hafan Deg. It's Hafan Deg. And there are faces pressed up against the windows. I know who these people are. I recognise them from the files I've read. They're all the missing and the lost. Rachel Morris, John Rogers, Margaret Jones, Katherine Owen, Richard Herbert – even Craig Stowe has somehow managed to get inside one of the buildings. Even Britt Nordenstam. Her face is bloated up and tinged with blue, but she's alive. They all are. And they're screaming.

Things are coming through the woods at me, coming out of the lake, dancing through the pines. I daren't even look at them, and they're herding me towards Hafan Deg.

And as they do, a door swings open in one of the empty buildings, and the darkness inside rushes out to meet me.

*

2ND JANUARY, 1981 (2AM)

I can't take any more. I have reached breaking point. I don't know how I got through this last appalling Christmas and New Year. Sidonie and her bloody family....

Well, that's unfair on my wife. But I haven't shared this with her. I'm afraid of what it'll bring down on her if I do.

The nightmares won't stop. I have to drink myself stupid at night to have even a chance of avoiding them, and even that doesn't always work. In fact, it's working less and less often.

Mynydd Du is killing me. But my biggest fear is for my wife. If I tell her too much, she'll be at risk. Or—God, I've almost struck her on two occasions. I'm so afraid that I'll hurt her. I won't let that happen.

I can't fight it any longer. I'll take my camera and notepad, tape recorder... I'll even see if I can scrounge up some old jam jars. Perhaps it is just a case of something in the water, after all. If so—if I can make it, if I can get back—then I'll expose the whole thing at last. Otherwise if it wants me, it can have me.

I'm going now, before she wakes.

*

And that, except for the note he left for Sidonie, was the last thing Russell Ware ever wrote.

*

So, now I had some decisions to make. As it stood, Ware had given me enough material for three articles: Hafan Deg, Britt Nordenstam and Maes Carnedd. I might be able to spin the other disappearances into a fourth article—the Nordenstam case was weird enough to be one in itself—and maybe, *maybe*, I could pump up Sidonie's account of Ware's last days into something as well. Although that might take some careful discussion with Sidonie. I know some writers who'd have just said 'fuck it' and gone for it, but I liked Sidonie Ware. I'm too soft, I know.

But there were a few notes left. Nothing detailed, but making it pretty clear Ware thought there was more to tell. He'd certainly believed there was enough for a book, but he hadn't had the chance to dig deeper before he died. If I wanted the rest of the material, I was going to have to do the legwork.

Pros: If Ware had been right, I might actually manage to put a book together about Mynydd Du. If I could sell that, it would be a good-sized payday—enough to put me ahead for a while.

Cons: It was a gamble. Writing a full-length book would be a big commitment and would crowd out other work; work that wouldn't pay as much as a book might, but was at least certain and would help me pay the bills month to month.

In the end I decided it was worth a go. As well as Ware's own leads, I could look into whether any other weird shit had happened in the area since the '80s. And—with a little care and finesse—I could pump up what I had on Ware's death to make it part of the pattern.

In the end, I decided to give it six months, fitting the work in around any existing paying projects. If at the end of that I could see the makings of a saleable book, then all right. Otherwise, I'd abandon it.

Looking back, I was fooling myself with that last. I was already hooked. Just as Russell Ware had been.

III. HUW LLEWELLYN (I)

I made an FOI request to access the case file on Ware's death. I succeeded, but there wasn't much there. As it turned out, though, Ware's old Welsh police contact, Huw Llewellyn, was still alive—now in his seventies, and living at Harlech, on the Gwynedd coast.

It took a lot of persuasion, but he agreed to see me. So I went up to the Welsh coast and spent an afternoon with the old man, quizzing him about the events of the 2nd and 3rd of January 1981.

"Don't know what you expect to hear, boy," he said as I started recording. "It was more than thirty years ago. Doubt I can tell you much that wasn't in the file. At my age, you forget things."

Which I very quickly decided was complete bollocks. While Huw Llewellyn might be knocking on, I doubted he'd forgotten anything important in his life.

*

EDITED TRANSCRIPT OF 1ST INTERVIEW WITH HUW LLEWELLYN:

RM: Sidonie reported Russell missing, and his car was found—near Llandderfel, is that right?

HL: That's right. Near the river, as I recall.

RM: Okay. And then—

HL: Look, lad, I'll be straight with you. Russell Ware was a decent enough chap, but he got obsessed.

RM: With Mynydd Du?

HL: No, with his sister's underwear. Of course with bloody Mynydd Du. Now I told Ware enough times that he was chasing shadows. No, not chasing shadows. Chasing *nothing*. Old wives' tales and coincidences, that's all there ever was about the place. He had a good woman in that wife of his, and he damn near drove her away. Probably would have, if he hadn't died. Simple truth is, Mr Markland, Russell Ware went mad. Oh, I'm sure they'd have a hatful of fancy names for it nowadays, but that's what it boils down to. (HOLDS HIS HANDS UP TO HIS EYES LIKE BLINKERS.) He got so focussed on Mynydd Du he let everything else slip. And a man like him can't afford to do that. So his career fell apart, and his marriage was all set to go the same way. And he snapped. Now, I have no idea what exactly he expected to achieve by coming out to Dolgellau that day. It probably wasn't even anything you or I would call rational. But he went to those woods, and they can be a

85

treacherous place at the best of times. Easy to get lost in them, day or night, and there's old farmsteads and what-have-you dotted around in them—all with abandoned well-shafts, too. One of those gets overgrown, and the first you'll know about it is when you fall through. If the fall doesn't kill you, you've no chance of being found in time. Or probably being found at all. Those disappearances he was on about? That's what probably happened to most of them.

RM: But Russell Ware drowned, right?

HL: Course he bloody did. If you're exhausted and half bloody frozen to death—which he would have been, after blundering around those woods for hours on end—then it's very easy to put a foot wrong, see? That's what I'd say happened. He got lost in the woods, saw the water through the trees, and made for it. And he got there, too—came out just next to Hafan Deg. Probably thought he was home safe, but he slipped, or tripped—and in that state, once he fell in the lake he'd have had no chance. Banks are pretty sheer round that end, water would have been bloody freezing. He'd have been weighed down by his clothes and slowed down by the cold. Simple as that. No fancy explanations, no spooky stuff. Just an accident.

RM: So you started looking....

HL: We went up to Heol Capel farm, took the dirt track. We looked for Russell, shouted for him, but soon enough it was pitch dark and in the end I had to call the search off. Go off the path in Coed Capel at night and we'd be in the same boat as him.

RM: But didn't you have torches?

HL: Yes, but there's a limit to how much risk you want to take. I told you, there's a lot of hazards in those woods. We came back at first light and we found Russell in the water. Doctor reckoned he'd been dead for hours. Probably long before we'd got there the day before. Tragic, but as I've said more than once to you, it's very easy to come to grief in those woods. Didn't you ever wonder why folk give a pretty, quiet little lake like Llyn Daioni such a wide berth? Nothing to do with any stupid bloody curse, as I tried to tell Russell enough times. But he wanted it to be something more. Same as you do, I reckon. Anything else?

*

There wasn't; at least, not then. But as I typed up the interview in my hotel room, something didn't feel right. I couldn't put my finger on it, but something was off-key.

I re-read the interview notes over and over that night, and the sparse information in the case file. And then it leapt out at me.

There was one point in the transcript where Llewellyn actually cut me off, changing tack completely. The old bugger was in control of the conversation throughout—but at one point, and one alone, he shifted the topic from the one under discussion. It was when I talked about Ware's car.

I got my map of the area out. I'd already marked the key locations on it in biro. And after a moment, I saw what the old man hadn't wanted me to notice.

The next day, I went back to see Huw Llewellyn.

IV. HUW LLEWELLYN (II)

Transcript of 2ND interview with Huw Llewellyn:

(RM: Rob Markland, HL: Huw Llewellyn)

HL: So, what do you want now, boy? I've got better things to do than answer your bloody questions.

RM: I was reading the case file again last night.

HL: Congratulations. Me, I prefer Wilbur Smith. Bit of a better story that way, you know?

RM: I came across something.

HL: What do you want, a medal?

RM: There was a discrepancy.

HL: Ooooh, was there now? A discrepancy, was there? My god, the boy's a detective already. Bugger off, will you? I've got things to do.

RM: Ware's car was found on the B4402, south of Llanderfel, near the River Dee.

(PAUSE)

HL: So?

RM: That's over to the south-east of Mynydd Du. And there's several woodlands between it and the mountain: Coed Fronheulog, Earl's Wood, Coed Bryn-Banon and Coed Lleidr. But you and the others started looking over to the west, near Coed Capel, heading down to the lake. You basically came back in the morning and went straight to Russell Ware's body, even though the last trace of him was miles away on the opposite side of the Bala Triangle.

(LONG PAUSE)

HL: (SIGHS.) You know, for over thirty years I've been waiting for somebody to notice that. I suppose nobody really wanted to. All right. Sit down.

(SILENCE.)

HL: Yes, I lied about what happened. And not just me, but the officers who were with me that day as well. I persuaded them to, but if I'm honest, that wasn't difficult.

RM: I don't understand. What did you lie about?

HL: Finding Ware's body, of course. It was for Sidonie Ware's sake, I'll admit it. She was a fine woman—had to be, to stick with him through all of that—and I could tell when I met her that she was near the end of her rope. I didn't feel I had any right exposing her to any more of the madness that had taken her husband than she'd had to deal with already. When it comes to Mynydd Du, the less you know, the safer you are.

RM: What do you mean?

HL: She kept his notes, but she never read them, did she?

RM: No. She didn't.

HL: Well, there you go, then. Maybe you should think on that, boy. Why didn't she? Because she thought it might be catching. You might want to think about that, before you go further.

RM: You didn't find Ware's body in Llyn Daioni, then?

HL: You're not going to listen, are you?

RM: Did you?

HL: Fine, then. Have it your way. But it's on your head, boy. Understand?

RM: Yes.

HL: I don't think you do. But, all right. No, Mr Markland. We did not find Russell Ware's body in Llyn Daioni. In fact, we never found his body at all.

*

EDITED TRANSCRIPT OF 2ND INTERVIEW WITH HUW LLEWELLYN:

It didn't take us long to find Ware's car. Question was where he'd gone from there. Now, to my mind there really was only one place he'd be heading. Mynydd Du, of course. He was hardly going to potter down to Bala for a cup of tea after all that.

So we started searching in the vicinity of the car; this was myself and the two PCs I'd roped in from the station at Bala. Jones and Roberts, their names were. Roberts was about forty, as I recall—very tough, very experienced—while Jones was in his early twenties, only been on the job eighteen months or so.

If he was going to make for Mynydd Du, the quickest route would be through the woodlands you mentioned. Now why he was taking that route, and not a quicker and easier one—like the dirt-track through Coel Capel—that's beyond me. I've no more idea what was going through Ware's mind by that stage of the game than you do. In fact, I've probably got less. You're the one who's been reading all his notes.

We searched the whole area, but we paid particular attention to Coed Fronheulog, and it wasn't long before PC Jones found something. A scarf, hanging from a tree branch not far inside the wood. It had a nametag inside, like the ones parents put in kids' school clothes, with Ware's name on it. It was a habit either of his or Sidonie's, apparently, to do that. And there were signs someone had been that way recently.

So we made our way through the woods. We found a glove as well—again, with Ware's name in it. He made that part of finding him easy at least. Then we were out of Coed Fronheulog. Now the next wood to that—if you're making for Mynydd Du—is Earl's Wood. And then Coed Bryn-Banon. Well, we carried on. Found Ware's other glove in Earl's Wood, and his backpack in Coed Bryn-Banon. So it looked as if he was discarding stuff as he went. I mean, the scarf could have slipped off, I suppose. And as for gloves—I don't know about you, but I'm forever losing mine. Take them off to do some fiddly task, stick 'em in your pockets, and you can bet any money at least one of them'll fall out. But your backpack? He had a Thermos flask and a packed lunch in there. A Kendal Mint Cake, notebooks, the lot. He'd come prepared, that's what I mean. And by the look of it, he'd just thrown it away. I wouldn't call that the act of a man in his right mind.

That's how I was thinking at the time. He'd had a breakdown, flipped his lid, gone crackers, however you want to put it. So we needed to find him, but we needed to watch it as well, in case he turned violent. So I told the lads to watch out and be ready to defend themselves if necessary.

By then we were out of Coed Bryn-Banon. If there was any doubt which way he'd gone, it didn't last very long because there were only a hundred yards or so between it and the edge of Coed Lleidr, and I could see something hanging from one of the trees there.

Ware's body? Course not. Coed Lleidr's mostly pine wood. Try hanging yourself from one of those. Besides, if someone's planning on doing that, they usually go deeper into the wood to commit the deed. No-one around to try and stop you, and besides, you sometimes need to give yourself a bit of time if you're trying to do yourself in. Gear yourself up for it.

And anyway, I told you: we never found a body at all.

What was hanging from the tree was a light brown duffel coat. Which, according to Sidonie Ware, Russell had been wearing when he'd left his hotel in Dolgellau. It certainly wasn't a very promising trend. So we went up to Coed Lleidr.

God alone knew why Ware had gone in there. Coed Lleidr's a nasty bugger of a wood. Most of the paths are narrow, winding and badly overgrown. Very easy to get lost in there. God knows Ware could have found a way round it—but he'd gone straight in.

We managed to get in after him—he'd snapped quite a few twigs and branches to make a way through. And before long we found a footpath. Seemed likely he'd have followed it, so we went along it, deeper into Coed Lleidr. About ten minutes in, we found a jumper hanging from a branch. Ware's again, according to the nametag. Well, by then I was certain of what we were dealing with. He'd gone nutty, hadn't he? Had to have, stripping off in this weather. We found his shirt hanging up before we'd gone a lot further.

We shouted for him, but there was no answer. And more to the point, it was dusk. Less than half an hour and it'd be full dark, and that'd be no joke out here. But something else was starting to bother me, too.

We'd been walking twenty, twenty-five minutes, and as far as I could tell we were going in a straight line. Coed Lleidr's not that big a wood, Mr Markland. We should have come out the other side by then. I was about to tell the lads to turn back, before we got stuck in the middle of Coed Lleidr in the pitch black... and then the trail ran out. Just stopped dead. The pine trees were just like a wall in front of us. Just like.

I looked round to see if there was any sign where Russell could have gone, but there was nothing—and believe me, Mr Markland, he couldn't have gone off that path without leaving some mark, some trace, *something*. The three of us, we were all local, we all knew the land and we could all track a man or an animal. But there was nothing. It was like Russell had climbed a rope up into a helicopter from there.

I'd had enough, Mr Markland. I'd been certain there was nothing more to the whole business than Russell Ware finally going doolally, up till then. And I was still, ninety, ninety-five per cent sure. But all of a sudden—stood there at the end of the path in the middle of those woods, with the night coming down... all of a sudden, some of those stories and old wives' tales didn't seem quite as daft as they had.

So, I told Jones and Roberts we should turn back, resume the search later. And I'll tell you this for nothing, boy: neither one of them argued the toss. Not even Jones, and he was the original eager beaver. So around we turned and back we went, torches at the ready. Carried on walking, back the way we came, for about ten minutes.

And then—the trail stopped. Just the way it had when we were going the other way. And before you say it, no: there was no way we could have taken a wrong turning, because there *weren't* any turnings. It was just the one path, there was nothing branching off it, none of that. We were going back exactly the same way we'd come in, so there was no way this could have happened. But it had.

More than anything else, I concentrated on staying calm. Jones, funnily enough, was pretty level-headed, except he was looking at me in that 'What do we do now, Sarge?' kind of way. He was still young enough to have faith in his superior officers. It was Roberts I was worried about. He was looking badly frightened and was mumbling to himself. Praying, I think. He was a very religious sort, Roberts. And local enough that—well, I think he knew some of the stories about Mynydd Du and the area. I believe Coed Lleidr had some sort of bad reputation, as well. Same as Coed Capel does.

Yes, there's another woodland to the north—Coed Dinas—but I really wouldn't know about that, lad, for the simple reason that after this business I decided I didn't want to know anything about Russell Ware's bloody Bala Triangle, not then and not ever. You follow me? Now, can I tell this bloody story you're so determined to hear, or what?

I was trying to work out the next move, but my main priorities were keeping Roberts calm. I told him to call headquarters—we all had our radios with us—but all he got was static. Jones and I tried on ours, but we didn't have any luck, either.

That was bad enough, but then we heard movement in the trees. You know—twigs snapping, rustling sounds, that kind of thing. Someone was moving—definitely some*one*. It was too big to be an animal. I called out, "Russell?" but there was no answer. I tried "Hello?" and a few other phrases—English and Welsh—but there was still no response.

It came closer, and then moved around. Circled us. It was directly in front of us at one point. Only other sound I could hear was PC Roberts. Poor bastard was practically hyperventilating.

It got louder and louder as it went—you know the way a kid having a paddy will stamp around and slam doors? It was a bit like that. It *wanted* us to hear it, wanted us to know it was there and that it knew where we were. And then it stopped. A second later, Roberts screamed and bolted.

I looked round and I caught a glimpse of what he'd been looking at—this tall shape, standing right at the edge of the path, not much more than a shadow among the trees. I only caught a glimpse. It looked sort of wild and shaggy, but it vanished as soon as I shone the torch at it. I could hear it moving, though—around the path towards Roberts.

See, Roberts had thrown himself into the trees and was laying about him with his truncheon—trying to batter his way out, I'm guessing. Then he started screaming.

Jones and me grabbed hold of him and pulled him back. He'd lost his truncheon and his collar was ripped open and his face was bleeding. Looked like scratch marks of some kind. His coat sleeve was torn up too, and there were scratches on his arm as well. I heard whoever had gone for him crashing away through the trees—leaving us alone, at least for now.

"Jesus," he was saying, over and over again. "Jesus. Jesus."

"What's up? Roberts? Come on, snap out of it, man. What happened?"

"Attacked me," he said at last, near enough whimpering. "Jesus. Jesus. Would have had my bloody face off if you hadn't…."

All I could get out of him was that it'd looked like a werewolf. *A wolfman*, he kept saying, over and over.

Roberts was in shock, but he was able to walk. Jones was white as a sheet, but he was a good lad. He'd stay together, I reckoned, as long as I was giving him something to do.

There was no question of staying put—you guessed as much, I bet—so the only thing to do was to try and force a way out of the woods. I told Jones we must have lost the path in the gloom and we needed to find it again. I don't know if he believed that or not. I was doing my best to, of course. Kept lying to myself so's I didn't panic. But at the back of my head I had a little voice telling me, over and over, that we'd done no such thing.

There was a last gleam of light in the distance that we could just about make out. That had to be west, so I said we'd head towards that—hopefully get out of Coed Lleidr through the side.

We started forcing our way through the trees. Used our truncheons to batter a way through when necessary. I kept thinking that wasn't the best idea we'd ever had—nothing like drawing attention to ourselves, and... sounds stupid, I know, but I kept thinking that the wood itself wouldn't like us hurting it. Or maybe that doesn't sound stupid to you, Mr Markland. If you've followed Ware's trail this far, you might think that sounds about right.

I didn't know as much as he did, but I knew enough. Enough files and pictures had passed through my hands—too bloody many for my peace of mind. Especially after what Roberts had said he'd seen. I kept thinking of the Beast of Maes Carnedd. Last thing I wanted to imagine stalking us through the woods.

Not that I had to imagine much. I could hear twigs breaking and bushes rustling—sometimes beside us, sometimes to the side. I'd turn to look, flash my torch at it, but never see anything properly. Just a glimpse. A shadow. Always too fast, always ducking away just in time.

But that wasn't the worst of it. As we went, the singing started. Singing and chanting.

And before you ask, no, I have no idea who was doing it, or what they were chanting. Now and again I'd make out the odd word, but nothing I could name. It sounded like a little like a Latin Mass—I'd heard that once or twice—but the few words I could make out didn't sound like Latin. I didn't think so, anyway. I'm no expert. I couldn't even tell you where it was coming from. Sometimes it seemed to be from the left, sometimes the right; sometimes from behind us, and other times from up ahead. It was a chorus, a dozen voices at least.

Roberts had been quiet up till then—been like a sleepwalker, if you want to know the truth, just shuffling on, putting one foot in front of the other, wherever Jones and I told him—but now he started moaning again. Real fear. Don't think I ever heard dread quite like it in a human voice, except my brother when he was dying of cancer. He was very afraid towards the end. But anyway, that chanting spooked Roberts, spooked him badly. He started mumbling again. Praying, in Welsh—and he wasn't one for speaking Welsh, either, was Roberts. Oh, he *could* speak it, right enough, but he had airs and graces to an extent. Thought it was only fit for clod-hoppers and the like. Wanted to get ahead, work his way up. Still thought there was time to try for it after ten years in, but everyone except him could see that ship had sailed. They've made their mind up about you after that long.

Wasn't long before it was pitch dark. And that was when the real bloody nightmare started. All we had were our torches to see by, and I could see the beam on mine was already starting to fade. I told Jones to keep his and Roberts' switched off—if mine conked out, we'd have two more. But even though it was heavy going, I was sure we should have made it out by now. We couldn't stop at all, see—there was no space for it. Just had to keep pushing our way through the trees, over uneven ground, trying to see ahead. Nearly fell over half a dozen times. Roberts mumbling away, shambling along between us. And through all of this, there was that bloody chanting, singing, whatever the hell it was. On and on and on it damned well went.

It was like the Chinese water torture times three. Roberts moaning on, the chanting, and this non-stop staggering through the woods, trying not to get your eyes put out by branches, and your feet killing from the lumpy, rocky ground. Couldn't do anything about the last two, of course, so in the end it was Roberts I laid into.

I just snapped. Spun round, grabbed hold of him and started screaming "Shut up! Shut up! Shut up!" Shaking him, the way a dog shakes a rat.

But all he did was bawl his prayers the louder.

I wanted to kill him. I balled a fist and pulled it back to throw a punch, and do you know something, boy? I honestly think that if I'd landed one on him, I'd never have stopped. Just kept hitting him till he was dead. Maybe not even stopped then. I could hear Jones shouting "Sarge!" and trying to get at me to stop me, but he didn't have much hope, not with Roberts wedged in between me and him.

And then someone grabbed me from behind.

Two big hands went around my throat and squeezed. They weren't messing around: the thumbs and forefingers were digging into my windpipe and piling the pressure on. Jones' torch flared on and he started swinging with his truncheon—over my shoulder, at whoever, or *whatever*, was trying to choke me.

I felt the impact—it juddered through the hands on my throat. Horrible, bone-crushing jolts. Jones kept swinging with the truncheon. I could see Jones' face. He looked scared shitless, to be honest. But he had a good right arm, thank Christ. Another few seconds and those fingers would've crushed my windpipe like the cardboard tube off a toilet roll. But the grip broke and Jones pulled me clear, and over the roaring in my ears and the sound of me heaving for breath I could hear someone running away.

Roberts was huddled on the ground, whimpering. My torch was on the floor; I picked it up and Jones switched his off. He was white.

I could hardly speak after the throttling I'd had. We picked Roberts up between us and carried on.

But that chanting, that bloody chanting, didn't let up for a second. And I was tired and weakening—we all were, even Jones. I was starting to weave as I struggled through the trees. We should have been out of the woods by then, boy. I can't make that plain enough. But they never ended. And something moved in the trees around us. And Roberts was back to mumbling his prayers again. And that bloody, *bloody* chanting just went on and on and on.

Finally there was a clearing. Not much of one. A space a few feet square between trees, where the ground hummocked.

I said to Jones, "Let's stop a minute," because, well, God alone knew when we'd get another chance and we were all ready to drop.

We sat down. Roberts was rocking to and fro, mumbling. Jones still had Ware's backpack. He was wearing it, and he'd stuffed most of the items we'd found in there. But there was food—bars of mint cake, remember? He passed them round. Christ knows that was what we needed by then.

It's a wonder what a few minutes' rest and a bite to eat can do for you, boy. I'll tell you that for nothing. But I wasn't soft. I knew for a fact it would be the same story when we got up and carried on. All that the rest and the food had done was buy us a bit more time. Delay the inevitable. We'd get up, and we'd keep battling our way through the trees, and the chanting would go on and on, and our stalker would keep circling us. And it'd attack again. And again. Till, sooner or later, it got me or Jones—most likely me, because I was older and still shaky from the last attack—and then the rest of us. Roberts wouldn't stand a chance. It could save him till last.

We were done for. That was all I could think.

And I started talking out loud. Almost a prayer. Except that it wasn't to God. If there was any such person, He'd long forsaken this place. No, I was talking to the wood itself. Or maybe to the mountain. To whatever was in charge in this place; whoever ruled.

"Let us go," I said. "Just please let us go and we won't come back."

I could see Jones staring at me. His eyes were wide open and his mouth gaped, full of half-chewed mint cake. Not a pretty sight, I can tell you. I could guess what he was thinking: *Oh Christ, now the Sarge has gone mental, too.*

Roberts had stopped his muttering, and he was looking at me as well.

"We won't breathe a word of what we've seen," I said. I didn't give a toss how I looked and sounded. I didn't care if they thought I was mad. I just didn't want to die in this place. "We'll never say a word about Russell Ware, if that's what you want. We'll do whatever. Just please let us go."

I flopped back against the tree I was leaning against. I was spent, now. Didn't dare look at the others.

And that was when the chanting stopped. Just stopped dead, click.

I opened my eyes.

"Sarge?" said Roberts.

"Shh," said Jones. "Listen."

He'd heard it first—the youngest, with sharp ears. I listened, and then I heard it, too. Running water. Somewhere nearby, there was a brook or a stream. And if it flowed through the woods, then it might just flow out of them again.

We shone our torches and staggered through the trees. The sound of the stream got louder. Roberts was quiet by then; I was the one doing the praying, though I couldn't tell you who to.

I damn near fell into the stream—Roberts grabbed my arm in the nick of time. It wasn't a big stream, or deep, but the banks were three or four feet high.

I climbed down. I was getting right next to the water; I was going to follow it out of there, whatever tricks the wood wanted to play on us. I saw which way it was running, and pointed. The other two climbed down, and we started walking.

I'm not sure how long it was before I realised we were getting somewhere at last. But I could hear something in the distance—a car, on a road somewhere. I could even see the headlights flicker through the trees. Jones let out a whoop. He'd seen it, too.

And then Roberts grabbed my wrist, and Jones'. "Listen," he whispered.

Jones opened his mouth to speak, but I shushed him. I could hear it too, now. The chanting was gone, but there was the sound of something beating a path through the undergrowth near the stream. I looked up and caught a glimpse of it: a dim, blurred silhouette, human-like but bristling with what looked like fur.

"Move it!" I told them, and we ran, splashing through the water.

Up ahead, the trees were thinning out. I could see street-lights shining somewhere far off. From behind us there was a noise of slipping and sliding, loose stones rattling, and then a heavy splash. And then the splash of footsteps in the water, following us. Breaking into a run.

"Run!" yelled Jones, and we all did.

The trees were thick above and around us, and for a moment I thought it'd all been a last cruel joke by the woods, that they'd close in around us and cut us off and we'd never get out. But then the tree cover vanished and we burst out into open air, following the stream out of a little cleft or gully onto flat ground.

We scrambled away, scattering across the grass, and shone our torches back down the stream, looking for our stalker. But there was nothing. Just silence, and the trickle of the stream.

And it could have ended there. Oh Christ, if only it bloody had.

But then the chanting began again. As we staggered away from the stream, we saw a light shining in the woods. We could see it very clearly, because it was shining down a path — a long, straight, open path. It might even have been the one we'd entered the woods through, I don't know.

The light came from a fire. A big, bright bonfire in the middle of a clearing where there shouldn't have been any clearing, its flames shooting ten, twenty feet up into the air. And standing all around the fire were a bunch of people in pale-coloured robes. They were all hooded, so I couldn't have told you what sort of faces they had. To be honest, I'm far from sorry about that.

They were singing and chanting. And then they turned towards us, and they stopped. And there was such a silence then, broken only by the crackle of the flames.

"Sarge," whispered Jones.

"Quiet, lad," I whispered back.

But he kept tugging at my sleeve. *"Sarge."*

"Oh Christ," said Roberts.

And at last, I turned and looked.

He came creeping towards us, from where the stream flowed out of the woods. Our stalker. He was naked. His hair was a dirty, tangled mess, all streaked with grey. His finger and toe-nails were long and sharp. And he'd coated himself in mud, or maybe shit, I don't know. He stank badly enough. He was caked in some sort of dried filth anyway, and mixed in with it was grass and twigs and pine needles, so they bristled out from all over his body like fur.

He'd been a man, once, but I didn't know how long ago. He looked as if he'd been living wild in those woods for years, but he couldn't have been. Because I knew his face, even under the dirt and the madness on it, even though he looked about a hundred years old now.

You're going to make me say it, aren't you, boy? All right then, blast you, yes. It was Russell Ware. Or it had been. It was all that was left of the poor bastard.

He just stood there staring at us, and there was nothing—*nothing*—in his eyes. Nothing at all. No recognition, no hope or love or fear or even anger or hatred, just... nothingness. The firelight danced in his eyes and all we heard was the crackle of those flames. And the robed figures just stood there, watching.

And finally, that *thing* that once upon a time had been called Russell Ware turned that horrible, empty gaze away from us and it just... walked away. Up that path, towards that fire and those robed figures. All quiet and docile, like a dog that had been called back by its master. And it joined them—he joined them—before the fire, and turned and looked at us one last time.

And then the fire went out. Simple as that. And there was blackness. And when we shone our torches we saw the path, but no clearing. There was no clearing at all, just a bend where the path wound into the woods.

And that, Mr Markland, *that* was the last of Russell Ware.

As for the rest, you can probably fill in the blanks yourself, but I'll tell you anyway. May as well join the dots. The three of us swore one another to secrecy. We got roaring drunk in Dolgellau that night, and the next morning I called Sidonie and told her we'd found Russell's body in Llyn Daioni. She fell apart at the news, and that was probably the best thing. It made it a lot easier for me to cover things up.

The local medical examiner owed me a favour. He faked up a post-mortem report that listed the cause of death as drowning following a fall. Wrote it up that Ware had slipped and fallen into the lake, smashing his face on the rocks in the process, and that fish had had a good nibble on what was left.

We had Ware's belongings, the things we'd found in the woods. I gave them a few hours' soaking to complete the pretence, and then I went to Sidonie a few days later and she identified the effects as her husband's. Told her she didn't want to see the body, and that an open coffin just wasn't a good idea. And thank goodness, the state the poor woman was in, she went along with what I said. I was in dread that she'd demand to see him, like they always do on the telly. But she didn't. So on the day, we cremated a coffin full of hay and straw and old clothes. It was the best thing for her, and for everybody else.

As for the three of us—Roberts quit the force not long after, and last I heard he'd gone to live in Canada. No idea what became of him since. Jonesy did very well for himself. Senior officer down south, I believe. But if you ask him about Russell Ware, he'll deny ever having heard the name. Even pretended not to know who I was in subsequent years. Probably for the best.

And I think that's everything, Mr Markland. Are you happy now?

*

I didn't know exactly how much had happened the way Llewellyn remembered it, but clearly *something* had, to him and the other officers. Question was, what? The story wasn't exactly easy to corroborate: I couldn't trace Roberts, and I got a letter from Jones' secretary claiming he remembered nothing of 'a short-lived search for a missing man thirty years ago'.

That left me sitting up late one night, drinking whisky and looking out over the Quays, taking stock and trying to plan the next move. All right, there was no way of corroborating his story, but I'd no reason to think Llewellyn wasn't telling the truth as he remembered it.

If, as Ware had believed, something around Mynydd Du caused hallucinations and psychosis, it was no wonder Llewellyn and the others had got lost in the woods. They'd been disoriented and confused. As for Ware... whether they'd seen or hallucinated him, either way he probably wandered deep into Coed Lleidr and whatever's left of him is probably still in there, somewhere or other.

Ware was onto something, anyway, and it ended up costing him his life. For that reason alone, it was worth pressing on. And because there was something near Mynydd Du that needed to be investigated, and shown to the world.

And, coincidentally, it would make a great book.

I was certain as I'd never been before: I needed to continue Ware's work.

Decision made, I closed the file and went up to bed.

I dreamt of robed figures around a fire in the heart of an endless woodland, through which Russell Ware still—forever—ran.

5: THE HOUSE BY THE CEMETERY

FROM *THE HOUSE BY THE CEMETERY: WHEN A DREAM TURNS TO DUST* BY ROBIN JACKAMAN. PUBLISHED IN THE *GUARDIAN*, APRIL 1994:
"That bloody house has poisoned everything. It's not just that we'll be ruined financially. It's even poisoned our marriage."

Toby Ashington remembers that there was almost a full minute's silence after his mother, Marie, uttered those words. His whole life, his parents' marriage had always seemed rock-solid, one of the constants in his life.

"I don't think my mother knew she was going to say that until she said it," he tells me. "That's why she didn't say anything else."

Marie had telephoned her son on the morning of January 23rd, 1993, to wish him a happy twenty-fifth birthday. She was calling from Tŷ Mynwent, a rambling farmhouse not far from Bala in Gwynedd, North Wales.

"She sounded strained," Toby recalls. "So I asked her if everything was all right, and it all came pouring out."

Two years earlier, when Toby's younger sister Lucy had left home to get married, Marie and Toby's father, Ronald, had bought Tŷ Mynwent with the aim of converting it into a hotel using Ronald's redundancy money. A catalogue of misfortunes had conspired to wipe out the Ashingtons' savings, leaving them with a still half-renovated building, cancelled bookings and unhappy customers.

"I didn't know what to say," says Toby. "They were very money-conscious, very careful with money. I couldn't understand how they'd got into that state, and I know it must have been shameful for them. I told her I had a spare room at the flat and they were welcome to stay. Mum said not to be daft, they'd get through somehow. They always did."

Those were the last words Marie Ashington ever said to her son. Three weeks later, she was dead.

*

Having read everything of Ware's own studies, I'd started my own research. One by one, I crossed my opening moves off the checklist I'd roughed out: emailing the Archaeology Department at Manchester University regarding a) Professor Thurlow's abortive dig near Llyn Daioni in 1969, attempting to uncover the history of the mediaeval village that had stood there, and b) the reports of Roman remains near the abandoned gold mine at Maes Carnedd, and feeding key place names into a tool Ware could only have dreamed of back in the 1980s: an internet search engine.

In went Llyn Daioni, Maes Carnedd, Capel Teg, Coed Capel, Coed Lleidr, Coed Dinas—and, of course, Mynydd Du.

Out came...

Nothing.

Even the cases I'd already studied had left little or no trace on the internet: if it hadn't been for the corroboration from official documents and witness statements, I might well have wondered if Ware had invented them all.

Then I remembered how, by the time of Ware's death, there'd been four or five farms dotted around the Triangle, abandoned one by one in the years since. I typed one of them—Tŷ Mynwent—into Google, and up came Robin Jackaman's article.

I tried contacting Jackaman to discuss the case, but never heard back. It was always a long shot: Jackaman was a busy man, and a serious broadsheet journalist, not a paranormal bullshit-peddler. Even so, his article gave me a starting point, and Huw Llewellyn had (grudgingly) provided me with a police contact in the area: a Detective Inspector Jones. So I started digging deeper into Marie Ashington's death.

*

FROM *THE HOUSE BY THE CEMETERY: WHEN A DREAM TURNS TO DUST* BY ROBIN JACKAMAN:

Ronald Ashington had worked as a civil engineer for almost forty years when he was made redundant in 1991. Due to his length of service, he received a substantial redundancy payout. In addition, both he and his wife, Marie, had been saving assiduously for years.

Marie Ashington had retired two years earlier. Their children, Toby and Lucy, had both left home, and the mortgage on their house in Moseley, Birmingham, was paid in full. Suddenly, the couple—still attractive, healthy and full of energy—were free and financially independent.

"We can think of ourselves again for a change," Toby remembers his father saying. "And we can afford to go wherever we want to and do as we please."

At the time, his father's announcement made Toby laugh, reflecting as they did an almost boyish exuberance in a man of sixty-three. Now when he looks back on events, they sound like the words of a man tempting fate. Or perhaps, those of a man whose dreams far outstripped his ability to realise them. But Toby Ashington is adamant that any such impression is due only to hindsight.

"I can see how some people might think that something was already wrong with my father, even then," he says quietly, his eyes downcast. "But that's just not true. Dad was always... larger than life. Ebullient. I think that's the word for it. He was the life and soul of any party he went to. He was funny; he was..." Toby takes a deep breath, steeling himself against the flood of memories that comes sweeping in whenever he thinks of Ronald. "He was a good, loving father. And husband," he adds, almost defensively.

It's hardly surprising that any discussion of his father leaves Toby prey to such conflicting emotions. Ronald was well-liked by his former work colleagues and by the couple's acquaintances at the Rotary and Liberal Clubs. His wife's family adored him. Even his bank manager was a personal friend who testified to Ronald's financial probity and prudence, and family albums support his children's description of a caring father who doted on them and was devoted to his wife. All of which should guarantee a childhood filled with happy memories. And yet, for Toby—and perhaps for Lucy, too—they are now all tainted, contaminated, in the light of what came next.

"It shouldn't have turned out the way it did," Toby insists. "They were both smart, financially savvy people. This shouldn't have happened to them."

But it did. And the kindly, handsome, bright-eyed woman in the family photos is now dead. And her loving husband, the doting father in the same photographs, has been charged with her murder.

Like many natives of the West Midlands, the Ashingtons found Wales an easy and enjoyable holiday destination. Like many others before them, they had long cherished dreams of settling there. With Ronald's retirement, a new dream was born: that of opening a hotel in Wales.

Unlike many others, the Ashingtons were not drawn towards the coast. "Mum nearly drowned when she was a little girl," Toby explains. "Her family went out on a boat and she fell overboard. We usually went to the seaside as a family, but I don't think we'd have gone if it had been up to her."

And so the Ashingtons looked towards the Welsh countryside instead. The town of Bala drew their attention: it was well-equipped for the tourist trade due to the nearby attraction of its famous lake, and was well-placed for holidaymakers looking to explore North Wales.

When they found the farmhouse of Tŷ Mynwent, the Ashingtons thought their dream had come true. The big, rambling farmhouse, standing on high ground surrounded by pine woods, with clear streams and pools running nearby, seemed an ideal retreat from the cares and pressures of the outside world. Couples or families would be their stock-in-trade, spending an idyllic holiday with only hills, rivers and woodland to look on, with all needs catered for.

The house would be perfect, they told Toby, except for its name. They'd have to change it to something a little more in keeping with their image. Something in Welsh, of course, but different. Tŷ Mynwent, roughly translated, means 'the house by the cemetery'.

*

Weirdly, for the first time I felt like stopping just then, and not reading on; it all sounded depressingly familiar, having read Ware's files on Hafan Deg. I found pictures of the Ashingtons online: a happy middle-aged, middle-class couple. I already knew how the story ended. Did I really want to follow the ugly trail of failure and disillusionment that led there?

Not particularly, or so I told myself. I wasn't doing this for fun; I was doing it because there might be a book in it, and therefore money. But at the same time, morbid curiosity's a powerful thing— so yes, part of me, whether I liked it or not, *did* want to know. And so I carried on…

*

FROM *THE HOUSE BY THE CEMETERY: WHEN A DREAM TURNS TO DUST* BY ROBIN JACKAMAN:

The Ashingtons put their home in Birmingham on the market and ploughed their savings into buying up Tŷ Mynwent and its grounds. From the start it was clear it would be a big job: the best part of a decade's abandonment in the windy, rainswept Welsh countryside had left its mark. Half the slates were gone from the roof and there was water damage in the building—but nothing, it seemed, that couldn't be fixed. It would need extensive refurbishment and modernisation, and that was just the house itself. For the grounds, the Ashingtons planned open lawns with water features, indoor and outside pools, an extensive play area, a games room, a library. An extension would likely need to be built, and of the same construction.

Ambitious plans, even grandiose. But, insists Norman Barker, Ronald Ashington's feet were always planted firmly on the ground.

"I knew Ron for the best part of thirty years," says Norman, a small, thin man in his late fifties, as we sit in his back garden sipping tea. "And from the very start, even when he was quite a young man, I was always impressed with his ability to budget and even save on a very tight income."

Norman, as the manager of the Ashington's former local branch of TSB, can speak with authority on these issues. "We went through the plans they'd made for this project, and—yes, of course there was an element of risk. There always is in a venture like this. But they'd planned it all very carefully, and with the sale of their home in progress, it did seem very likely that they had a very comfortable margin—enough that, even if things didn't work out, they'd be able to walk away and start over."

This plainly isn't an easy conversation for Norman. His affection for the whole Ashington family is obvious. He appears in several pictures in the family album Toby Ashington showed me, and it's hard not to feel he blames himself to an extent, as if there were circumstances which he, if not they, should have foreseen.

So what, I ask him gently, does he think went wrong?

"Bad luck," he says. "That's the worst of it. I can't really call it anything else. Just the most appalling run of misfortune."

Both Norman Barker and Toby Ashington—biased though they both may be—are saying the same thing: that the Ashingtons' venture should have been a glorious success. But the problems started almost as soon as they set out to realise their dream.

Ronald bought up an old static caravan and set it up near the farmhouse as temporary living quarters, then hired builders to carry out repairs and refurbishments. And that was when the first hairline cracks began to appear in the Ashingtons' dream.

"Ronald hired a local building firm to carry out the work on Tŷ Mynwent," Norman explains. "Obviously, it was going to be a lot cheaper than engaging one of the firms he knew back in

Birmingham, but it did mean working with a comparatively unknown quantity. Again, though, both he and Marie had done their homework and carefully researched construction firms in the Bala area. They didn't just pull a bunch of cowboys out of a hat. Nonetheless...."

Nonetheless, the work done by the firm Ronald hired, Meredith and Jones, proved shoddy and unsatisfactory—dangerously so. Repointed stonework collapsed, wall insulation had to be torn out and replaced twice, and when the partially-built extension collapsed, Marie narrowly escaped being struck by one of the stone blocks.

John Meredith of Meredith and Owen declined to be interviewed, but his reputation in the area remains of a very high standing. So why was the quality of his work on Tŷ Mynwent so poor?

"I couldn't tell you," Norman says. "The only possible explanation that springs to mind is that... well, some of these small Welsh towns can be quite insular, and resent incomers from England coming in and buying up properties, especially for holiday use...." He trails off.

*

EDITED TRANSCRIPT OF DS WILLIAMS' INTERVIEW WITH JOHN MEREDITH, OF MEREDITH AND JONES BUILDING CONTRACTORS, 6TH FEBRUARY, 1993:

Look, I've already bloody told you about Tŷ bloody Mynwent, haven't I? I don't know what the hell went on up there.

Yes, I know what Ashington said. Shoddy, that's what he called my work. That's never been said about a job I've done, before or since. And no, nothing to do with the *Saisneg* moving in and buying up the place. I'm no bloody Nationalist; you know that. One man's money's as good as another.

And no, I didn't fancy his wife, and no, I wasn't trying to milk him for a bit extra for being an outsider. I've heard all the bloody cock-and-bull stories. All rubbish, absolute bloody rubbish. I got along fine with Ronald Ashington—to begin with, anyway.

What changed it? What do you bloody think changed it? He starts accusing me of the same load of old rubbish you've been reeling off. I've been in this business forty-five years, Robert Williams, and I have *never* overcharged a customer or done less than my absolute best. I take pride in what I damned well do, and I'm not some bloody cowboy.

All right. But I know what you're going to say. Facts are facts. Mr Ashington had a catalogue of complaints about the work we did. Documented them all in graphic detail. Even took pictures. I know, all right? You don't have to tell me.

What you want is some sort of explanation. Well, the flat truth of it is that I don't have one, Sergeant. I did the same work on Tŷ Mynwent as I would on any other property, and to the exact same standard. There shouldn't have been a problem. There shouldn't have been. And yet the lads and I'd do a job, then come back a couple of days later, and it would be falling apart.

No. No idea what was causing it. Only explanation I could think of at the time was that Mr Ashington was doing it himself, somehow. You know, waiting till we'd gone, then fiddling with the work. You get that sometimes—punters who want the work done but don't want to bloody well pay the full whack for it.

But he didn't strike me as a man putting on an act. And most importantly, I was there when the extension collapsed. I saw it go. And I still don't have any explanation for why it did. The wall—one second it was standing, straight and solid as you please and then the next it just... sagged, bowed, buckled and spilled itself. Crash. This great bloody lump flew at us, and it would have taken Mrs Ashington's head right off if her husband hadn't grabbed her and pulled her out of the way.

And yes, that was when he dismissed me. Then and there, on the spot. I mean, I could understand where he was coming from, how it might have looked, but it wasn't down to any fault by me or my lads. I said it then and I'm saying it now—we did a bloody good job.

And yes, damn right, that's why I was chasing him for payment. He owed me for the work we'd done. We'd done twenty grand's worth already. What was I supposed to do, just put it down to experience or something? That kind of money I can't write off. Especially as, if I did, I'd be good as admitting I'd done half a job. And that just wasn't going to happen.

And with the stuff that came later—the thefts, the subsidence, all of that—well, I was even more certain the problem wasn't me.

*

FROM *THE HOUSE BY THE CEMETERY: WHEN A DREAM TURNS TO DUST* BY ROBIN JACKAMAN:

After ordering John Meredith and his men off the site, Ronald Ashington engaged a succession of builders: first local men, and then a firm from his native Birmingham who had worked on his and Marie's old home. In all cases, he complained of the same problems. But now new ones emerged.

All the builders complained, in their turn, of thefts. Bags of cement, stacks of bricks and timbers all disappeared.

"Ronald's relations with local builders was never the most cordial," Norman Barker explains, "not after what happened with the first firm. They claimed he was pilfering their supplies and sabotaging their work to avoid paying the full price—much as John Meredith had, to begin with. Meanwhile, from Ronald's point of view, he was paying for work that wasn't getting done. So you had almost a perfect storm building up. Matters ended very acrimoniously with both the Welsh firms. I won't say that Ronald was blacklisted as such, but certainly word got out that he was a very difficult customer, that supplies had gone missing, and that there were problems getting payment from him for work done. That last, of course, was the kiss of death. No-one's going to work for you if you won't pay them."

At the time of Marie Ashington's death, Ronald Ashington was fighting no fewer than five separate civil actions, four of them with building firms trying to extract payment. These included Dinkman and Sons, the Birmingham-based firm Ashington had hired.

"We had the same problems as everyone else," says Trev Dinkman, a brawny, balding man in his fifties. His normally cheerful disposition deserts him when the subject of the Ashingtons is broached, but he speaks more in sorrow than in anger. "It was very difficult, because we'd worked for Ron before and he was a sound bloke. Friendly; very understanding if there were any delays, and on the occasions we'd done work for him here in Brum, he'd paid very promptly. But, to be honest, I was worried the minute we saw him up here. Or even before—I mean, when someone calls you in from a hundred miles away because they can't get along with the local firms, it's not a great sign."

I ask Trev what his first impressions were on arrival.

"Pretty shocked, to be honest. Place looked like a bombsite. Marie looked her usual self at first—she was always cheery and well-turned out. But closer, you could tell she was stressed. And Ron looked ruddy awful. He'd lost weight, hadn't shaved for a couple of days and his clothes were a mess. He stank, too. He was rattling on nineteen to the dozen about the locals trying to fiddle him. I don't mind saying my alarm bells were ringing, but he was an old client, so…"

Dinkman and Sons experienced the same pattern that the others had before them. Supplies went missing despite their best efforts to guard them, repairs fell apart and had to be redone, and Ronald Ashington began accusing them as he had the previous builders. And the relationship ended the same way: with angry words on both sides, and with Trev Dinkman taking Ronald to court to recover his costs.

Meanwhile, other problems had arisen. Cracks had appeared in a number of interior walls and the fireplace in the farm's living room was close to collapse. It was determined that some form of subsidence had taken place, despite a prior survey that had found no trace of such activity. This was the genesis of the fifth civil action, the one Ronald Ashington was embroiled in at the time of his arrest: he was suing the surveyor for professional negligence.

The Ashingtons had moved to Tŷ Mynwent in the autumn of 1991, aiming to have the house ready to open for the summer season. They'd already placed a number of advertisements for their hotel.

"Unrealistic? No, I don't think so," says Norman Barker. "I went over their plans with them. They'd done their homework, and it really should just have been a matter of getting the builders in. The house was structurally sound and in very good condition considering how long it had been unoccupied. It would have been hard work and it would have taken a substantial investment, but Ron and Marie were more than capable of both. But time and again, they found themselves back at square one."

In the event, the summer of 1992 arrived and the Tŷ Mynwent Hotel's doors stayed shut. Ronald Ashington tried to carry out repairs himself, but the problems continued.

*

EDITED TRANSCRIPT OF DS WILLIAMS' INTERVIEW WITH BRIAN REES, CHARTERED SURVEYOR, 7TH FEBRUARY, 1993.

(DSW: DS Williams, BR: Brian Rees)

DSW: What was your relationship with Ronald and Marie Ashington?

BR: Relationship? There was no relationship. I did some work for Ashington once. That's all.

DSW: But not very well.

BR: I beg your pardon?

DSW: Obviously you didn't do a very good job, Mr Rees.

BR: That is slander, Detective Sergeant!

DSW: It's only slander if it's false, Mr Rees. For the record, I am showing Mr Rees a copy of the survey report. Is this or is this not your signature on the report, Mr Rees?

(PAUSE)

BR: It appears to be my signature.

DSW: Is it or isn't it?

BR: I don't like your tone, Sergeant.

DSW: Well, I'm not particularly keen on murders, Mr Rees. They're a bugger to clean up after and the paperwork's a nightmare. That's what I'm dealing with here and I can do without you getting on your high horse every time I ask a question. So I will ask again, Mr Rees, yes or no, is this or is this not your signature on this survey report?

BR: Yes. It's mine.

DSW: There. That wasn't so hard, was it? Okay. I am going to quote from the survey report. 'There is no evidence of subsidence on the property and no mining activity has taken place in the vicinity of Tŷ Mynwent or its grounds. We conclude therefore that there is no risk to the property from subsidence.' That's from your report, yes?

BR: I know where you're going with this, Sergeant, and—

DSW: Yes or no, Mr Rees. I've got a lot of interviews to do on this case and I don't have all night. So the sooner you answer my questions the sooner we'll have this done and dusted and you can go home. Eh?

BR: Yes. That's the report I filed.

DSW: And provided a copy of to Ronald Ashington?

BR: That's correct.

DSW: So you stated quite categorically that there was no subsidence and no danger of subsidence at the property. Is that correct?

BR: Yes.

DSW: And just for the record, Mr Rees, are you currently involved in any civil court proceedings?

BR: I am.

DSW: Care to elaborate?

BR: Ronald Ashington was suing me for professional negligence.

DSW: Why was that?

BR: Is this necessary, Sergeant? You know as well as I do—

DSW: Just for the record, Mr Rees. Please.

(LONG PAUSE)

BR: All right. Mr Ashington was suing me because damage had occurred to the property due to....

(PAUSE)

DSW: Yes?

BR: Subsidence.

DSW: Quite extensive damage, isn't that so?

BR: Yes.

DSW: Damage that had caused considerable delays to the development of the property and considerable expense to Mr and Mrs Ashington, yes? And which ensured that Tŷ Mynwent wouldn't be able to open as a hotel in time for the summer season? Yes?

BR: Yes, Sergeant.

DSW: I can imagine you must be a bit relieved with how things have turned out.

BR: What did you say?

DSW: Well, Mrs Ashington's dead and Mr Ashington's been charged with her murder. That should pretty much kick the court case into the long grass, shouldn't it?

BR: What are you implying? Are you implying that— ?

DSW: Not implying anything, Mr Rees. Just stating the simple fact that what was looking to be a long and very expensive court case, with a great deal of negative publicity and damage to your reputation, is now very unlikely to proceed. Have to look at all the angles, don't I? You must admit that for some men, all that would be a very persuasive motive to commit murder.

BR: Detective Sergeant—Williams, isn't it? Let me make something very clear. Yes, there was a court case in the offing. But I would have fought it, and I would have won. Ronald Ashington was a madman. You have ample evidence of that, most notably in the mortuary. Five minutes on the witness stand would have been enough to discredit him without my barrister having to lift a finger. According to that man, everyone was out to get him: the world and his wife, and probably his dog, cat, guinea pig and bloody goldfish as well.

DSW: Nonetheless—

BR: Nonetheless, my survey, yes. You're absolutely right that it says there's no evidence or risk of subsidence. And likewise you're right when you say the case clearly proved to be otherwise. So, quite reasonably, you want an explanation.

DSW: Well, I'm glad we finally got that part sorted out. So? The explanation?

BR: Quite frankly, Detective Sergeant Williams, I don't have one.

(PAUSE)

DSW: Come again?

BR: Look, you're a layman, so I won't try and blind you with science. But I'll tell you this, Sergeant—you get any surveyor you like to come in and check my report, to sit down with me and go through what I did step by step, blow by blow, and I guarantee you that they will confirm I did everything possible to detect evidence of subsidence. They will confirm that had there been any threat of subsidence at the time of my survey, I would have found it. And yet, mere months later, there it is, as if the place had been built on top of a disused mine. Do you see? What happened at Tŷ Mynwent, I can't even begin to explain.

*

FROM *THE HOUSE BY THE CEMETERY: WHEN A DREAM TURNS TO DUST* BY ROBIN JACKAMAN:

The Ashingtons' problems worsened throughout the summer and autumn. Subsidence is a word dreaded by all homeowners: it's one of the costliest problems to remedy, and most insurance companies refuse to touch properties affected by it except at greatly increased premiums. The cost of Tŷ Mynwent was mounting all the time, and with the hotel unable to open, there was no income to defray it.

To make matters worse, it was clear they would have to hire another builder: the house would have to be underpinned to counteract the subsidence. Even leaving aside the costs, which would run easily into the thousands, there was the problem of finding a suitable firm. Ronald Ashington's reputation as a difficult customer was spreading.

"I don't think anybody in those circumstances could be blamed for feeling as if the whole world was against them," Norman Barker says. "Viewed from Ronald's point of view, he was being roundly stitched up—first by the builders, and now the surveyors."

It's certainly true that the Ashingtons suffered, as Norman says, a truly phenomenal run of bad luck. And that's just the problem: it would be naïve to buy a property for development, as the Ashingtons bought Tŷ Mynwent, and not expect some ill-fortune. But that the amount they experienced came about only by chance or coincidence strains belief. If we discount this, only two possibilities remain.

The first is that Ronald Ashington was, as he believed, the victim of a wide-ranging conspiracy—one conducted, perhaps, because he was an English 'incomer'. But, if so, the same conspiracy would have had to include his former friend and associate, the indisputably English Trev Dinkman. Even if we accept that Dinkman was somehow induced or intimidated into acting against the Ashingtons, the question remains as to why so much expense and effort would be expended against this particular couple.

One other alternative remains, of course. It seems increasingly likely that Ronald Ashington's defence will maintain that he killed his wife while insane. If that is indeed the case, the question arises of how long that insanity might have been building towards its tragic climax. Could Ashington have been, quite literally, the author of his own misfortune, deliberately sabotaging his own dream?

Norman Barker vehemently refutes the idea. "I knew Ron too well, for too long, to believe that. Everything was fine until they moved in there. Something happened, all right. Maybe there was some reason for everything that happened, but it wasn't to do with Ron." He shrugs. "Maybe some places are just unlucky."

Whatever the truth, there's no doubt that as summer became autumn, and autumn winter, Ronald Ashington's state of mind began to deteriorate.

"I spoke to him on the phone a few times," says Toby. "I wanted to come and visit, but they always had a reason for me not to. The place wasn't fit to put people up in—they were still living in that bloody caravan—but even when I said I'd put up in a hotel in Bala or wherever, they always talked me out of it. I think they didn't want me to see the place until it was ready."

I ask Toby if he noticed any change in his father during their phone conversations.

"Oh yes," he says. "He was normally a laugh a minute. Always cracking jokes. But they got fewer and fewer, and more strained-sounding, and by the end he wasn't making any at all. And he'd rant on about the people who'd done him over. I mean, he used to get angry sometimes—who doesn't? But he'd usually just dismiss someone with a few short words: 'bloody idiot', 'bloody crook'. That kind of thing. But here he'd be going on about people non-stop and how they were all out to get him... really bitter, and *helpless* somehow. Not like him at all. Dad always told us if something went wrong you picked yourself up and dusted yourself down and started again, and to always try to have a back-up plan or three in case things went wrong. But he was sounding like he didn't know what to do—except carry on what he was doing, even though it didn't seem to be working."

I ask him how Marie seemed to be handling the couple's problems.

"Mum just seemed her usual self. She was always stoical—talk about the power behind the throne. I mean, don't get me wrong, even she was getting run down by all that was going on. But she was bearing up better than he did."

As the winter began, Ronald Ashington sank deeper and deeper into bitterness and paranoia. It isn't always easy to be accepted in a small, rural community, but Ronald's attitude and increasingly aggressive behaviour did nothing to help.

*

INCIDENT REPORT BY POLICE CONSTABLE STEPHEN HUGHES, NOVEMBER 15TH, 1992:

I was on patrol in the area around Bala when I received a report of a disturbance in the bar of the White Lion Hotel. Arriving there, I found an altercation in progress between one Ronald Ashington of Tŷ Mynwent, and a group of several local men, including Tom Evans, of Evans Lloyd Construction.

Mr Evans has undertaken building work for Mr Ashington and subsequently been dismissed without payment. It is understood that court proceedings are in progress to recover the payment. Mr Ashington contends that Mr Evans deliberately carried out sub-standard work on his house either to extort more money from him or to force him to move out. It is understood that he has made similar allegations in respect of work carried out by other local builders.

Witnesses report that Mr Ashington entered the premises about twenty minutes prior to the incident in question, when he purchased a pint of beer and sat in a corner drinking on his own, in silence. Shortly before the incident, Mr Evans arrived and made several remarks in Mr Ashington's hearing to the effect that he expected to extract payment for the work done, and that if it forced Mr Ashington to vacate Tŷ Mynwent 'then so much the better'. At this point Mr Ashington became enraged and attacked Mr Evans.

Mr Ashington was also heard to make a number of derogatory references to local/Welsh people that angered a number of other drinkers in the pub and caused the incident to escalate to the point that the police were called.

Owing to provocation on the part of Mr Evans, no charges have been preferred against Mr Ashington at this time. I cautioned both parties to keep the peace. The landlord has barred Mr Ashington from the premises.

*

EDITED TRANSCRIPT OF DS WILLIAMS' INTERVIEW WITH JOHN MEREDITH, OF MEREDITH AND JONES BUILDING CONTRACTORS, 6TH FEBRUARY, 1993:

After Ashington dismissed me, I didn't have any further contact with him—none that I could help, anyway. I did my best to keep everything going through legal channels, if you see what I mean. I've got a business to run, doing work for customers who actually bloody pay for the work I do. I'd lost enough time and money due to Ronald Ashington. Decided I'd leave it to the experts from then on.

None that I could help, yes. There were a couple of occasions… well, only once where I could prove anything. I was in Dolgellau on a job when we crossed paths. Lord knows what he was there for. A drink, maybe. He'd been barred from every pub in Bala, so I'd heard. Anyway, we saw each other on the street. It was a very long, awkward moment, I don't mind telling you. He didn't say anything, and nor did I—I didn't have anything to say to the man. I got the impression he felt like saying something, but I could see him looking around. Yes, I'd heard about some of the filth that had been coming out of the man's mouth, and what it had got him. He'd obviously wised up a bit. But, I'll tell you, it wasn't just words, I think. Way he looked at me, I reckon he wanted to fly straight at me.

To be honest, it took me a moment to recognise him. Main thing was the sideburns. You know? He had long grey sideburns, almost down to his mouth. Very distinctive. That was what did it. But the man looked bloody dreadful. His eyes were all yellow and bloodshot, he'd lost God knows how much weight, and he looked dirty, scruffy. Dirt on his face, on his skin, his hands. I'd heard he was trying to do the work himself now.

But no, he didn't approach me, or say anything. Just glared at me in a way that could've peeled paint, then got in his car and drove off.

That was my last contact with Mr Ashington. The last that I could prove, I mean. Couple of days after I had my little run-in with Ashington over in Dol, someone put a brick through the windows at my yard, and took a pot-shot at my house with a twelve-bore.

I reported it to your lot, of course, and I know they had a word with him, but nobody could prove anything. But anyway, that was the last I saw of him. Given the way things turned out, I suppose I should count myself lucky, eh?

But on the other hand, if he'd messed me around a bit more, he might have been banged up a bit earlier in the bloody madhouse where he belongs. And that poor woman might still be alive. She was a nice lady, was Mrs Ashington. I was very sorry to hear about her.

*

FROM *THE HOUSE BY THE CEMETERY: WHEN A DREAM TURNS TO DUST* BY ROBIN JACKAMAN:

Toby Ashington heard little from his parents over the winter, apart from a brief phone conversation at Christmas. Indeed, the Ashingtons seemed to have lived an almost entirely reclusive existence from November on through to January. Evidence suggests they abandoned the static caravan, which was proving inadequate to the task of keeping them warm and sheltered, and moved into the house itself despite its condition. But beyond that it's purely a matter of conjecture.

What does appear to be indisputable is that Ronald Ashington's mental state continued to worsen. How Marie coped with the conditions they found themselves in is hard to tell; even in her final conversation with Toby there was, he says, a strong sense of reserve.

"Mum was like that," he explains, "and Dad, too. They were from that generation, you know? They didn't wear their hearts on their sleeves, they just gritted their teeth and got on with things and put a brave face on it. I think she shocked herself with how much she told me."

When she rang Toby, towards the end of January, Marie told him that in addition to their other financial woes, Ronald had taken out a number of large loans in an attempt to keep the project funded and to pay legal costs. Not only were the Ashingtons almost penniless, their life savings and the proceeds of the house sale all but gone, but they were now saddled with thousands of pounds worth of personal debt—more than they were ever likely to repay in their lifetimes.

"Dad could be very stubborn," says Toby. "He didn't like to give up on anything or admit defeat. But at the same time, he wasn't stupid. And Mum was normally good at not letting him go too far. I'm surprised he didn't give up sooner, if I'm honest—put the place up for sale and bugger off. They could have got themselves back on their feet. I'm sure they could."

But the Ashingtons didn't give up. Or at least, Ronald didn't.

"He was throwing good money after bad," says Toby. "He'd obviously decided the project had to work, no matter what. It was make or break."

Toby doesn't say it, but it's hard not to suspect he's thinking it: the coroner has placed Marie Ashington's time of death as no more than forty-eight hours after Toby's last conversation with her. Could Ronald Ashington have seen her revelations about their finances as an act of betrayal? We may never know.

Toby tried ringing Tŷ Mynwent a few days later, but the phone rang unanswered. He rang again over the days that followed, with increasing frequency as his concern for his parents deepened. On February 1st he rang again, to find the line had been disconnected.

"I'd been trying to convince myself I was worrying over nothing," he says, "but when that happened I knew someone had to do something, so I rang the police."

Did he suspect what the police would find, I ask him?

"No," he says emphatically. "Never in a million years. I was afraid they might have had an accident, or fallen ill. But that Dad would ever hurt Mum? No. She was the love of his life."

When police officers arrived at Tŷ Mynwent on the morning of 2nd February, 1993, it became clear immediately that something was wrong. The static caravan lay on its side, burnt out, and boards had been nailed across the house's doors and downstairs windows. The Ashingtons' Land Rover stood outside, its windscreen smashed and its tyres slashed to ribbons.

When there was no response to calls, the officers forced the front door open. The house was unlit and the carpet was sodden with what proved to be raw sewage from a downstairs toilet, which had backed up and overflowed. In the kitchen, they found dirty dishes piled high in the sink and the floor littered with empty food cans. They also found, wrapped in plastic bin liners, the body of Marie Ashington.

They searched the rest of the house, calling out Ronald Ashington's name, but received no response—until they reached the top floor of Tŷ Mynwent and, having found no sign of him, tried to enter the attic. The door was jammed. When they forced it open, they found Ronald Ashington—who promptly opened fire on them with a shotgun.

Fortunately, Ashington was exhausted, malnourished and had been living in near-total pitch darkness for several days, since the last of the candles he had brought with him had burned out (the attic window, like the others in the house, having been boarded up) and neither officer sustained any serious injury. They managed to overpower Mr Ashington as he tried to reload.

The shotgun used by Ronald Ashington is believed to be the same one responsible for the wounds that killed his wife, a fact that Toby Ashington still finds almost impossible to believe.

"I want to say it can't be him," he says. "I want to believe that someone else broke into the house and killed Mum, that Dad was hiding from them, but…" he shakes his head. Toby has only seen his father once since his arrest. "I don't know what I'd say to him," he tells me. "This is my dad. But at the same time, now he's the man who killed my mum."

Tŷ Mynwent has been repossessed by the Ashingtons' debtors: unsurprisingly, neither Toby nor his sister have any desire to contest that decision. They want no part of the property.

So far the farm's new owners have taken no action, and the house stands black and dismal against the pale sky, much as it did on the morning of February 2nd. The front door has been replaced, the boards remain over the windows, and the now-rusting hulk of the Land Rover squats in the front yard. And around it, the Welsh landscape Ronald and Marie Ashington loved so much spreads out. It's a beautiful view, but there's no-one there to see it.

*

The article ended with helpline numbers to call for debt assistance. At the time of writing, the case had been yet to go to trial, but of course by now it was all long over. Ronald Ashington was found unfit to plead, and was committed to Broadmoor.

*

FROM THE REPORT OF DETECTIVE SERGEANT IEUAN WILLIAMS, DATED 5TH FEBRUARY 1993:

Based on Mr Ashington's refusal to co-operate with our investigation, we have only been able to rely on circumstantial and forensic evidence, but have tentatively reconstructed the order of events.

There is no evidence whatever to indicate the presence of any third party at the scene, or that anybody other than Mr Ashington is responsible for his wife's death. His fingerprints are on the murder weapon and the expended cartridges found at the scene, and indeed he discharged the weapon at the arresting officers.

Why Mr Ashington killed his wife remains unknown, as he has refused to make any statement on the subject. But we have ample witness testimony to indicate an emerging pattern of violent and irrational behaviour on Mr Ashington's part over the months leading up to the murder.

There is no sign of a struggle, indicating that Mr Ashington either took his wife by surprise in the kitchen or forced her in there at gunpoint before killing her, which he did by firing both barrels of the shotgun into her chest at a range of not more than two feet.

Death was a result of shock and massive haemorrhaging, and would have occurred in no longer than two minutes after the initial injury.

Following his wife's death, Mr Ashington went outside and set fire to the static caravan (his fingerprints were found on two empty cans of petrol found nearby) before shooting out the Land Rover's tyres and windows with the shotgun. This done, he retrieved a large quantity of planking from one of the outbuildings, along with supplies of canned food, a tin opener, cutlery, a camping stove, a cigarette lighter, cooking matches, candles, electric torches, spare batteries, pillows, blankets, a sleeping bag, a camp-bed, a bucket, toilet paper, chalk, two screwdrivers, marker pens, paper and shotgun ammunition. (These items were listed on a bloodstained notepad in the kitchen; forensic evidence indicates that this was done following the murder, not before it.)

Once Mr Ashington had boarded up the doors and windows, he carried the other items up into the attic (it is believed this would have taken several trips) and shut himself inside, where he appears to have remained up until his discovery by Constables Games and Duffy.

The various inscriptions and drawings inside the attic are all very recent and are believed to have been drawn by Mr Ashington over the period between the murder and his arrest.

*

That was the end, at least, of the written part of the extract from Williams' report. But thanks to DI Jones, I also had several photographs showing the attic at Tŷ Mynwent in February 1993.

The attic was wide and long but low-ceilinged. I could see the camp-bed, with the bucket that had served as a toilet beside it. And I could see the sheets of paper stuck to the wall.

Ashington had been busy. When he'd run out of paper, he'd taken to drawing on the walls, or incising words or pictures into the wood or stone—with the screwdrivers, I guessed. There were a lot of drawings and lots of writing, but very little variation in them. The pictures were usually of a spiral, a huge eye, or a loose mask of some kind—something that covered the upper part of the face but left the mouth exposed. Almost like a hood that was allowed to hang down over the face, with holes cut for the eyes. As for the writing, there were three phrases that recurred: *THE WATCHERS BY THE LAKE. THE FIRE IN THE WOODS. THE DANCERS IN THE PINES.*

I looked at each phrase in turn. 'Watchers by the lake'—the workmen on the Hafan Deg site by Llyn Daioni reported that they constantly felt 'watched'. I tentatively guessed that phrase corresponded to the 'eye' image in the drawings.

If—*if*—that was right, then possibly each of the recurring images matched one of the recurring phrases. In which case, 'the fire in the woods' might be linked with the image of the masked face. When Russell Ware disappeared, Huw Llewellyn saw a fire burning in the woods, surrounded by robed, hooded figures. Was that what Ashington was trying to draw?

And finally, 'the dancers in the pines'. I knew I'd heard the phrase before, but I had to go digging back through my notes to find it. Craig Stowe had said it—those exact words—in reference to the disappearance of Britt Nordenstam.

So if the eye meant the watchers *and the mask meant* the fire, *then the spiral must mean* the dancers. *Which didn't seem to make sense, until I reread the interview with Stowe. He said that 'the pines coiled in on her and took her away'.*

A coil, a loop—a spiral.

Apart from those three phrases, Ashington had scored two other messages on the wall. One read THIS IS HOME NOW THIS IS HOME NOW I CAN STAY NOW THIS IS HOME. *Half a wall was covered by this one phrase, repeated over and over again, scratched in with one of the screwdrivers.*

Elsewhere, close to floor level, Ashington had scratched a single word, in weak, spidery capitals: *MARIE.*

*

Finally, there were papers from Broadmoor.

According to the notes, Ashington had remained largely mute while in custody. He was usually either catatonic or he was attempting to break out, usually with violence, and one state could give way to another at the drop of a hat. When violent, he was usually medicated heavily to keep him under control, and wouldn't have been capable of discussing his condition even if he'd been willing to. The rest of the time, he just wouldn't speak unless he had to. For the most part, the doctors had no success at all trying to draw him into conversation.

There were, however, two or three periods during his incarceration at Broadmoor when he was more lucid, almost rational, and on one of these occasions a doctor managed to interview him.

*

EXTRACT FROM SESSION #2 WITH PATIENT RONALD ASHINGTON, BY DR JOSEPH BLOOM:

(RA: Ronald Ashington, JB: Dr Bloom)

JB: Do you understand why you're here, Ronald?

RA: I shouldn't be.

JB: But do you understand why?

RA: Yeah.

JB: Go on.

RA: I was cheated, wasn't I?

JB: Cheated? How were you cheated?

RA: I'd done it. They said I'd be allowed to stay.

JB: Who said this?

(SILENCE.)

JB: Okay. Let's go back to your earlier statement. You said 'I'd done it'. Done what, specifically?

RA: You know what, Doctor Bloom. Don't let's mess around.

JB: I'm not trying to mess you around, Ronald. I just want to understand. Done *what?*

RA: Marie. Okay? You happy? Marie.

(LONG PAUSE.)

RA: (SIGHS) I killed Marie, okay? Is that what you wanted to hear? I killed my wife. I'm not stupid, or a bloody vegetable like some of the poor sods you've got in here. I know what I did, and I know why I did it.

JB: That's what I'd like to talk to you about.

RA: Why?

JB: In order to help you.

RA: Help me how, hm? You gonna let me go? Is that the idea? (PAUSE.) Go on, then, Doctor Bloom. Tell me that you're gonna let me out of this place if I talk to you. You can't, can you?

JB: Would you believe me if I did?

RA: (LAUGHS) No.

JB: Well, then. You're not a stupid man, Ronald.

RA: Mad, though.

JB: Do you think you're mad?

RA: Yeah, I do. (LAUGHS) That foxed you, didn't it? If I was *really* mad I wouldn't think of myself as mad, would I? But in the end it comes down to definitions.

JB: In what way?

RA: Well, to you, madness is believing in things that aren't true. No matter what. Delusions. Like a bloke who thinks he's Napoleon. No matter what you say or do, you're never gonna convince him that he isn't Napoleon, are you? But it's obvious that he isn't.

JB: Well, I don't think you'd find it worded quite that way in any psychiatric textbook, but—

RA: Cut the crap. You know what I mean.

JB: All right. So, according to you, I define madness as delusion. Right?

RA: Yeah.

JB: All right. It's a little more complicated than that, but let's go with that for now. What about your definition, then? How do you define mad?

RA: What you've got to understand, Doctor, is this. If I told you in detail everything that happened at the farm, everything I saw, you'd call me mad. You'd say it was a delusion, that I saw things that weren't there, heard voices that didn't exist. But it's not like that.

JB: What is it like?

RA: I'll tell you if you'll *STOP BLOODY INTERRUPTING ME*— sorry. Sorry. It's okay. I'm okay. All right. My definition of madness. I have experienced, I have *witnessed,* things, phenomena so… removed from the normal run of human experience that they have brought about a fundamental change in my understanding of the nature of reality. In how I… *interact* with the world. And with others. This places me at odds with the majority of people, and even with society as a whole. But this is not because of *illness*. Not because of chemicals in my brain or any stupid shit like that. It's because while I was up I saw and heard and understood things. And I can't carry on as I did before, as if the old things matter. Because they don't.

JB: What old things are those?

RA: Money. Conformity. Family. Marriage. All the sacred cows. They're meaningless. Compared to what's up there.

JB: At Tŷ Mynwent?

(PAUSE)

124

RA: In that area. Yes.

JB: So what *is* up there, Mr Ashington?

RA: God.

JB: God is up there?

RA: *A* god, anyway. But it's not the one you learn about in Sunday school, Dr Bloom. It's terrible. But it's beautiful, too. And if you can look on it and live, if you're worthy, it'll let you stay. To keep its place pure. We're all impure, but those of us who devote ourselves selflessly to the god can stay. And believe me, Dr Bloom, if you witness the god—and you would, if you were around Mynydd Du long enough—all you'd want to do is stay there and serve it. To be near it, that's all that matters. And the impure are jealous. That's why.

JB: Why what?

RA: They conspired against me. Not just the Taffs, even the people I'd known for years, like Trev. They were trying to drive me out. Of course, the god didn't want me to turn Tŷ Mynwent into a hotel. I see that now. Too many of the impure would have come in. But I was worthy of staying. And all those others, they were trying to drive me out.

JB: And what about Mrs Ashington, Ronald? What about Marie?

(PAUSE)

RA: I thought she was different. I truly did. My soulmate, Dr Bloom. That's what I thought she was. But in the end she wanted us to leave. Tried to make me leave. After all I'd done, all my work... and of course, then I understand why everything had gone so wrong. And I heard the god's voice. Offering me a covenant. A bargain. A deal.

JB: And what deal did you make with this god, Ronald?

RA: Don't patronise me, Dr Bloom.

JB: I didn't mean to sound patronising.

RA: Oh, I'm sure you didn't. But that's what you are. To you, I'm just another sorry delusional case. But I'm very different. I've passed through the holy fire, Dr Bloom. And I've been transfigured by that passage. The impure had to be driven forth. 'If thine eye offend thee, cut it out.' And then I could stay. I could stay and stay and stay.

JB: And that's why you killed your wife?

RA: It broke my heart, but it had to be done. It was the price. Now can I go back?

JB: To your room?

RA: Don't be a fool, Dr Bloom. You know where I mean. Tŷ Mynwent. I won't bother anybody. Just let me go back and I'll eke out my remaining days in the attic. Trap rabbits. Catch fish from the stream. No-one will know I was there, and I won't harm anyone. On my honour. You can do it, Dr Bloom. Surely you understand now.

JB: You know that's not an option, Ronald.

(SILENCE)

JB: Ronald?

RA: (SCREAMS)

(SOUNDS OF STRUGGLE. JB CRIES OUT IN PAIN. ORDERLIES PLACE RA UNDER RESTRAINT.)

JB: Get him out of here!

Transcript ends.

*

Ronald Ashington had one more lucid period, but he refused to co-operate with any attempts to interview him; he'd said all he had to say. He spent the rest of his life either catatonic or doped to the gills to stop his raging. Not that the rest of his life proved to be very long: he died in 1996, in Broadmoor, after suffering a massive heart attack in his cell.

Toby Ashington, like his sister Lucy, moved abroad following his father's death. I couldn't trace either of them for interview.

After my last attempt to trace Lucy Ashington had ended in failure, I sat there doodling on a notepad for a while. Then I sighed, went back to the Britt Nordenstam files, and looked for the names of the other farms in the Mynydd Du area. Heol Capel, Cairnfield Farm, The Roberts Farm and Plas Gwynedd. The next step would be to find out when they'd been abandoned—and how.

I turned back to my notepad to make a list. I stared at the page for a second, then tore it off, balled it up and threw it in the bin.

I'd just been scrawling at random, keeping my hand moving, just for something to do. I hadn't really looked at the pictures I'd drawn till now.

There were eyes there. There were faces—or were they masks? And there were spirals.

The watcher at the lake. The fire in the woods. The dancers in the pines.

Probably, it meant nothing. Christ, I'd been reading about this all afternoon: no wonder it was spilling out of my subconscious.

But I remembered Russell Ware. And, for the first time, I thought I might have glimpsed the shadow of what he feared.

6: THE MASTER OF THE HOUSE

At the time of Britt Nordenstam's disappearance in 1969, there were five working farms in the Bala Triangle: Heol Capel, Cairnfield Farm, Plas Gwynedd, Tŷ Mynwent and the Roberts Farm.

By the time her body was found two years later, Heol Capel, on the outskirts of the Coed Capel woodland near the lake, was up for sale. For whatever reason, the house never sold. The elderly couple who owned it left for parts unknown, and Heol Capel fell into decay.

Mynydd Du and its environs are littered with the remains of abandoned homes and settlements. The surviving farmsteads were more the exception than the rule, and within less than two decades of Britt Nordenstam's death, these too had been abandoned.

Cairnfield Farm—where Isaiah Milne and his family had been murdered in the early 1900s—was the next to go. The elderly widower who owned it fell ill and passed away in Dolgellau Hospital in 1974. The property was auctioned off at a fraction of its proper value, and ended up in the hands of a company who'd bought up the site of the long-abandoned mining village of Maes Carnedd. Maybe they intended to re-open the gold mine, but they went bust in 1979, and Cairnfield Farm was left to its ghosts.

By then the Roberts Farm had fallen, too. Faced with mounting debts, poor crops and sickly livestock, the family flitted in 1978, leaving anything they couldn't carry.

Plas Gwynedd and Tŷ Mynwent struggled on for several years after that. Ill-health forced Tŷ Mynwent's owner to put the house on the market in 1984, where it remained for nearly a decade before being bought by Ronald and Marie Ashington. I read on quickly; I didn't want to be reminded of the Ashingtons.

That, by 1988, left Plas Gwynedd: the last farm in the Bala Triangle, and the last habitation in the shadow of Mynydd Du.

Seven years after Russell Ware's own death—if it *had* been a death—in the woods of Coed Lleidr, Plas Gwynedd was home to three people: Gareth Puw, his wife Katharine, and their fifteen-year-old son, Aled. Aled was the youngest of the Puw's three children, but his elder siblings had already left home. His brother James had taken a job with a firm of estate agents in Prestatyn; Bronwyn Puw, meanwhile, was taking a degree in Drama in Aberystwyth

University. They had no interest in helping their parents run their farm, and nor did Aled.

None of this made Gareth Puw's disposition any sunnier. A family photograph showed a near-giant of a man: well over six feet in height, with massive shoulders, brawny arms, and a hard, unsmiling face beneath beetling brows and a mop of curly black hair. Gareth had a reputation for devout religiosity and a bitter hatred of modernity in all its forms, especially since his elder children had—in his view—deserted him. He was a stern authoritarian with decidedly biblical views of a woman's place and a child's duty. In both cases, they boiled down to pretty much the same thing: total obedience to him.

It was hard to imagine him being an easy man to live with—especially in the case of Aled Puw, who was a thin, pale boy with spiky black hair and who wore thick black sweaters. He clearly favoured his mother in looks, right down to the wide, dark eyes. Delicate, almost feminine in appearance, he wouldn't have been a son for a man like Gareth to feel pride in, and his mother would have been able to do little to protect him.

Plas Gwynedd was soon to follow the other farms. 1988 saw a chain of events that left the farmhouse standing empty, as it remains to this day: roofless, windowless, home only to animals and whatever else lies in the shadow of the Black Mountain.

*

DI Jones came through for me again, providing me with copies of police reports, interview transcripts and crime scene photographs, but they made up only a tiny part of the whole. The bulk of the story, which he also ensured I received a copy of, was in a diary kept by Aled Puw.

I: ALED PUW'S DIARY

1ST JANUARY

Happy New bloody Year. Miserable Christmas—just Mam, Dad and me. A card from Bronwyn; not even that from James. Dad killed the scraggiest of the geese for Christmas dinner. Lots of silence and glowering from Dad, and a few shouting matches. Well, him shouting and waving his fists, and me keeping out of punching range.

As usual, I can't do anything right. Bet he'd take me to market and sell me if he could. Buy another son. I wouldn't say no, either— might get a better family than this—if it wasn't for Mam, anyway. She does what she can, but she goes in fear of Dad, same as the rest of us. I don't blame James and Bronwyn for clearing out; it's what I'd do given half the chance. One more year, that's all. One more year and I'm old enough to go.

I'd go now if I could, but I know Dad. He'd be on to the police quick as that, probably say I'd thieved something too. James won't have me: he's living it up in Prestatyn (as much as anyone *can*, in Prestatyn) and now it's all suits and cars and overpriced haircuts and that for him. And girls, of course. Doesn't want his kid brother cramping his style, even if I was just hiding in the spare room listening to The Cure. Twat.

Bron would help me if she could—we were always close—but she's sharing a flat with three girls at Uni and working every spare hour so she can afford just to eat. She's nowhere to put me and couldn't afford to keep me, and at my age I couldn't get a job or even sign on. Even if she could put me up, I bet you any money Dad would kick up a fuss and find some way to get me back. No, I'm going to play it smart. Tough it out till I turn sixteen and then go. Soon as I'm old enough, soon as I've got what I need. Hell, it won't even be a year. Eleven months, now.

Only thing I don't like thinking about is Mam. I don't know what it'll do to her when I go. She'll be alone in the house with him. Talk about a fate worse than death. Still, she's been married to the bastard twenty-odd years so she's used to it. But then again, at least she had us three for most of the time. And soon I'll be gone. Aw Christ, I wish Mam was horrible sometimes, like Dad. Then I wouldn't feel bad about going. But she isn't. She looks after me when she can, and she got me this diary, and the fountain pen I'm writing in it with.

But I've got to go. I can't stay here—I'm not a farmer, and I'll go mad if I have to stay in the house with Dad much longer. That, or I think he might actually hurt me. He's spent my whole bloody life trying to beat and bully me into being the son he wants. I think he might finally be getting the message that I'm never going to be that. But what he'll do then, I don't know.

7ᵀᴴ MARCH

First beating of the year. Not counting the half-dozen kicks to the backside and clips round the ear I've had off the old bastard so far.

Maybe I should have said something sooner, but funnily enough I had a feeling Dad would decide to shoot the messenger if I told him. He's been worse than ever lately. Moody and quiet most of the time, but that just means we're walking on eggshells because he's there, simmering away, waiting for something to kick him off because it hasn't been done right.

Thing is, anyway, one of the meadows is getting overgrown. Not with weeds or anything like that—with pine saplings. God alone knows how. I've never seen the like before. I didn't think they could shoot up that fast, but over the last fortnight they've gone from little shoots to... well, maybe not quite big enough for a Christmas tree, but pretty close. And worst of all, I could see new ones sprouting up.

I know, I know—I should have pulled them up or something. But I've been that tired and back-broken: now I'm coming up to being a man, apparently I'm expected to do a man's job. Is he trying to squeeze all he can out of me before I go, is that it? Does he know I'm going to leave? Or is he trying to break me down, so that I won't?

So I was tired. And maybe I wanted to spite him.

And, all right, I'll admit it. There was something about the trees that made me not want to mess around with them. They made me nervous.

I know, stupid bloody thing to say. Dad would just nod his head and go, "You see? Bloody milksop, that boy." But it's true. There was something not right about them, especially the way they were growing, the speed of it.

I suppose I kept hoping I'd catch Dad in a halfway decent mood and then I could tell him, but I'm fucked if I can remember when his last good mood was. Truth be told, I'm wondering now if he's ever had one.

Anyway, he saw for himself today. That meadow's supposed to be my responsibility, but he sent me into Bala on an errand and while I was gone he must have seen. Barely in through the door I was, when he grabbed a handful of my hair and dragged me halfway across the kitchen, then sent me the rest of the way with the toe of his boot.

That was just the start of it, of course. He took the belt to me, all the time raving: "Are you blind, boy, or just stupid? How the hell could you let that happen, you lazy little slug? By God, while you're under my roof you'll do a day's work when I tell you, and you won't shirk!"

Mam managed to make him stop by begging and hanging onto him and getting between him and me, although she got slapped herself for her trouble. But at last he calmed down and told me to take an axe to the trees and burn them, or by God there'd be more of the same.

Christ alone knows how I managed to even lift the axe, the shape I was in, but I did somehow. I wanted to run back to the farmhouse and put the axe in him, the vicious old bastard. Split his head wide open with it. But I didn't. Afraid of him, maybe. Or maybe it's because bastard though he is, he's my father still. It takes something, I reckon, to kill your own blood like that. You have to have something, or lack it. And I don't, not yet.

I felt like a killer when I hacked down the trees, though. No, that's not right. I didn't like doing it, and I don't just mean because I was aching all over and throwing up. It's not the first time for either of those. No, what I mean is that when I put the axe to the trees, I felt as if I shouldn't be. Argh, that's no better. It was a *wrong thing*. I can't put it any better than that. Not like a sin, but like... like I'd thrown a stone at a big ugly dog, or called Dad a bad name. I've thought of doing that last enough times, God knows, but what's stopped me? Fear, that's what. Knowing that however much I want to do it, something terrible will happen if I do.

In Dad's case it's easy to guess what that would be—more of what I got today. With this, though, I can't say. No reason cutting down a few trees should be a danger. But that was the feeling I had.

Maybe it's because there's something unnatural about those trees, springing up so fast. Or maybe it's just because I got my head banged a few times and it sent me a bit funny.

I did it anyway. Imagined every tree was Dad. Hacked them down and burned them, and now he's happy. I'm joking, of course. That old bastard would be miserable no matter what happened.

I'm in bed now, and Mam's been in and out with tea and soup. I've soaked in a hot bath—he allowed me that much mercy, when I was done—but I'll be one big ache tomorrow morning.

MARCH 18TH

They're back. I told Dad soon as I saw them. It was the only thing I could think of to stave off another beating. He saw those trees get burned himself, with his own two eyes. No bloody way could this be, but it is.

New pine trees are growing—as tall as my hip already, *and they weren't there last night.* As it is, it's not two weeks since I chopped them down. But they're back, and there are actually more of them than ever.

Dad hit me, of course—but it was more of a token cuff. He won't believe that they grew up overnight, and I suppose I wouldn't either. Even he knows, though, that there's no way they should be there. They couldn't have grown back this quickly, spread so fast, but they have.

We both went to work on them this time, cutting and burning. We didn't speak much, but we passed a flask of tea back and forth, shared a pack of sandwiches from Mam, and we were almost companionable.

At the end of it, with the flames crackling away at the pines, he nodded and said "Good work, son," and walked off.

I hate him; I do. He's a tyrant and a bully and a bastard, and I don't want to care what he thinks of me. I wish I didn't. But I do. That's the first bit of praise he's given me in as long as I can remember, and it matters to me. I don't want it to, but it does.

2ND APRIL

I couldn't sleep last night. I sat up, reading, till I thought I was tired enough to nod off at last. And that was when it happened.

I switched off the bedside lamp, and I saw the light coming in through the window. First thing about it: it wasn't steady. It flickered and danced about, not like moon or starlight does. And it was the wrong colour. It was like firelight.

I went to the window and I looked out. The sky was all clouded up, so there wasn't a peep from the moon or the stars. The only light I could see was on the mountain.

Now, nobody goes up Mynydd Du, and I mean *nobody*. I've lived here my whole life, literally in its shadow, but I've never been up. Mam and Dad both forbade it, soon as I was old enough to get about, and you know something funny? God knows I've wanted to tell them both to get stuffed a few times—more Dad than Mam, of course—and I've done things just *because* I was told not to, but I've never done that. And I couldn't tell you why. I just never wanted to. Never thought it could be a good idea.

I suppose we could have had hikers or campers coming this way, and not seen them, but it doesn't seem too likely. Anything's possible, but I doubt it. And who the hell would want to camp on Mynydd Du?

Besides, this didn't look like a campfire. I couldn't be sure, because the whole mountain's so thickly wooded, but the fire looked huge to me, like the flames were shooting twenty or thirty feet up in the air, dancing in the silhouetted pines.

It burned and burned, and I don't know quite how long I spent looking at the thing, and then... then it just *went out*, like *that*. I didn't see it burning lower, none of that; one second it was flaming as bright and high as it had ever been, and then the next—gone, and everything was pitch-black again, and there was just the afterglow floating in my eyes where it had been.

I got to bed as soon as I could after that; I didn't want to be alone and awake in that big house, and besides, I knew I'd have to be up and doing soon enough. Be a hard enough day ahead without having had no sleep.

Mam's been out of sorts all day. Feeling sick and holding her side all the time. Could barely cook the evening meal. I offered to, but Dad clipped me round the ear and told me to stop trying to shirk.

5ᵀᴴ APRIL

Mam's still in a lot of pain. Dad's trying to act like it's nothing at all. "Women's troubles," he keeps calling it, saying it'll be past and gone in a couple of days. But Mam will have had those troubles before, and I've never seen her like this. She's grey in the face, and I can tell she's in so much pain. She's been taking painkillers, but I don't think they're doing much good.

I think she needs to see a doctor, but I don't think either her or Dad want to admit it. Dad doesn't want anything else to mess with the farm being run right, and Mam... I think Mam's afraid of what they might find.

One more night. I'm going to give it one more night, and then I'll tell them straight and I won't let up until she goes to see a doctor. Bad enough that I'm going to leave her alone with that bastard in five months' time; I'm not making things any worse than they have to be. I expect I'll get a bloody good clouting for my trouble, but I'm not going to give up on this: she's going to get herself looked at, come what may.

6ᵀᴴ APRIL

Well, I got a proper belting for it. My ribs are aching, I've a fat lip and I won't be able to see out of my left eye for a day or two till the swelling goes down. But in the end, I got my way. Dad's driven off with Mam now, so as a bonus, I've got the place to myself.

Going to read for a bit now—outside, where it's sunny. Might as well enjoy myself while I can.

LATER

They got back from the doctor's a couple of hours ago. Dad went storming through the house. I was in the kitchen and I nearly pissed myself—I though he was going to lay straight into me then and there. But instead he stomped right past me and went outside, got to work.

Mam was different, though. She's always quiet, but not like this. Plus she was white. And her eyes—she was just staring. Thousand-yard stare, I think they call it. Read it in a book somewhere.

She didn't even seem to see the kitchen table till she walked into it; then she fumbled around for a chair and sat down. I think she'd have fallen down if she'd had to stand much longer. And she just sat there, white and shaking.

"Cup of tea, Mam?" I asked her at last. Sounded like a bloody stupid thing to say, but what else was there? *Are you all right?* Blind man could bloody see she wasn't. Least this way I could do something for her.

She nodded, and I put the kettle on.

Finally I put the mug in front of her and sat at the table and said: "What's wrong, Mam?"

"The doctor," she said. "The doctor's referred me to the hospital at Dolgellau. For tests."

She didn't say what for, but I don't think she had to. Whatever it was, it couldn't be good.

2ND MAY

Cancer.

I've written that word on a sheet of paper, over and over, trying to get the feel of it, trying to get it to feel real. But I can't, somehow. Mam—cancer. No. My mind won't go there.

Dad's still working outside. He hasn't stopped. Maybe it's so he can't think. Wish I could stop thinking, too. Must be great to be a pig-ignorant bastard like him.

15TH JUNE

It's becoming a routine now. Mam goes to the hospital at Dol for chemotherapy. When she gets back she's weak and sick, and I look after her. Feed her, help her to the loo, cook the dinner.

Keeps me out of Dad's way, at least.

God Almighty, I hate this house. I can't wait to leave. But with Mam like this, how can I? What do I do, leave her alone with Dad when she's sick? It's like this bloody farm's determined to keep hold of me, sink its hooks in deep and not let go.

28TH JUNE

Some kind of blight hitting the crops. Dad going apeshit. I just tried to keep the hell out of his way. Got enough chores, in and out of the house, to keep me occupied.

Mam has to go into hospital next week. I hope she's going to be okay, and home soon. I know how selfish it sounds, but I don't want to be alone with Dad. It's hell. And I love Mam, of course. But most of all, I don't want to be alone with him.

4TH JULY

Independence Day, if you're a Yank. But I'm not, and there's no bloody independence here at Plas fucking Gwynedd.

Mam went into hospital today. Dad drove the three of us into Dol and we said goodbye to her. Drove all the way back to Bala in stony silence.

They said she'll be in hospital a week at least. A long week, on my own with *him*.

5ᵀᴴ JULY

Dad's drawn up a schedule for tending the crops, so they won't fail. God knows how we're supposed to fit looking after the sheep and the geese in around it, but there's no point trying to tell him. When he doesn't want to hear, he won't. I'd tell him to call me Cassandra, but he'd probably interpret that as a declaration of homosexuality and that would be it. Be lucky to escape with my life.

Maybe I'll tell him I'm gay the day I leave. I'm not—least I don't *think* I am—but it would be worth it to see the look on his face. Probably give him a heart attack. But I'll wait till I'm in a car or something and heading away, just to be safe.

Seriously though, the thing with the crops is weird. I don't know what's wrong with them. I've never seen anything like it. It isn't any insect or fungus I've ever known; they're just withering away. Maybe it's the soil. But he's poured fertiliser in there, and it's done nothing. We'll have to see. No prizes for guessing who'll catch hell if it goes wrong.

8ᵀᴴ JULY

Well, I was right. The bastard leathered me again. Everything he's planted is shrivelled up and dead. All my fault, of course. It had to be somebody's and there was nobody else he could take it out on.

I hate him. I hate him. I wish he was dead.

All alone in the house with him. I'm afraid of him. I've taken to locking my bedroom door in case he comes after me. It wouldn't be the first time I've been shaken awake in the middle of the night to take a beating. Hasn't happened in a while now, but with Mam not here anything goes.

November 15ᵗʰ, that's my birthday. Counting the days. When I get there, I'm out of here. I don't care what I have to do. It's only four months. The year's gone quick. I've got to make some plans. Get a job I can go to so I can live somewhere. I keep getting scared they'll find a reason not to give me any dole, or a flat or anything. Best if I can pay my way.

But I'll sleep in a bloody doorway before I spend one more night under this roof than I must.

Mam, though. What about Mam? I keep coming back to that. Leaving her alone in the house with *him*. But I can't live here. I can't.

20ᵀᴴ JULY

Another day. One of the better ones. Dad only barked at me twice and didn't lay a hand on me once. That's about as good as it gets.

Mam's home tomorrow, from the hospital. That's got to be good news, hasn't it? Dad says she'll be back on her feet in no time. Probably will be, if he's got anything to do with it. He'd take the whip to the risen Christ to get him back to work.

21ˢᵀ JULY

Oh God, Oh Jesus Christ. Oh Lord, please, I'm sorry for what I wrote last night, I didn't mean to blaspheme. Please take it back. Let me not have heard aright. Let the doctors have got the files mixed up. Let it all be a horrible joke, let me wake up in the morning and find I've dreamt today. Don't. Let. This. Be.

Mam —

Mam's come home to die.

You wouldn't have known it from Dad. He brought her home from Dol, helped her up to bed, barked at me to make her a cup of tea—even now, of course, he'd never lower himself to do that. Then he went outside and I saw him yomping off through the meadows.

I brought the tea up to Mam and... chattered. I don't know why. No-one had said anything about how she was. Maybe I suspected what they weren't saying, what Dad wasn't saying. If no-one said any different, she'd be all right.

But she didn't let me chatter too long. She reached out and put a thin hand on my wrist. God, she looks so thin, so tired, so pale. Ground down to a sliver by the life she's had. With him. By him.

"I've got to tell you something," she said. Her voice was down to a whisper: tired, weak.

"What is it, Mam?" I wanted to scream at her not to say it, not to make it real. But that's so bloody silly. Of course it's real already. Real inside her, growing and hurting her.

She knew, of course—knew Dad wouldn't have told me. He's a big man with his fists, but he can't face this. Shows him up for the coward he is.

The cancer's metastasised. That's the word the doctors have for it. In plain English or Welsh or any other language that means it's spread. It was in her breast. They've cut her breast off, for God's sake—but at least if it had just been there, she'd have been okay. But they found it too late and there are bits of it in other places now. Her liver, her pancreas. And they can't do anything about those.

So she told them she wanted to come home. Wouldn't take no for an answer. Probably the one time she's stood up and been counted, and for what? The right to die under his roof, with a bastard who can't even bear to be near her like this.

And still she won't hear a word against him. Telling me I'll understand when I'm older. That he's her husband—thick and thin, good and bad. And no, I don't bloody understand it. I don't bloody want to understand a thing like this.

26TH JULY

Four of the geese are dead. We don't know what. Nothing's got at them. Not even a feather out of place, but they're dead as mutton, every one. Dad's hung the bodies up in a shed, in case they're safe to eat.

"I'm not going to waste a good meal, boy," he told me when I tried to point out that mightn't be the best idea.

Well, good for him. If I'm lucky, the bastard will poison himself. I'm not touching any.

I said he should call the vet at least, but he doesn't want to. Doesn't like putting his hand in his pocket. Stingy sod.

27TH JULY

He called the vet in today.

When he got up this morning, three more geese were dead and two more looked close to it. The sick ones just lay stretched out on the ground, wings spread, as if they'd fallen out of the air in mid-flight. They breathed and blinked, but not much else, and there was no sign of an injury.

To put the tin lid on it, there was a dead sheep in the upper pasture, and three others lying stretched out, as if dead. Same story as the birds. They breathed, blinked from time to time, but that was all. The chickens all seem okay, though.

Mr Protheroe, the vet, got here early afternoon. By then another sheep had died, and both the sick geese, and Dad was in a foul mood. I got inside soon as I could to sit with Mam.

Dad was in a proper mood because Protheroe hadn't a clue what it was. At least he managed to persuade Dad not to eat any of the dead animals. Not that I mind Dad catching whatever they've got, but he'd force Mam to eat them even if I wouldn't.

Protheroe took a couple of the carcasses away for tests. Dad burned the rest. I shut the windows against the smoke's reek. I saw the flames flash and flicker and I thought about the fire on the mountain. And then I tried not to.

29TH JULY

By now, we've got a bit of a new routine going. Dad's doing pretty much all the farm work single-handed. I look after Mam, keep the house clean, and cook the meals. She's in no shape to do any of that, and someone needs to be close by her all the time.

Dad says he might hire someone to help him out, if he can afford it. Hope he can.

The worst thing (and it makes me sick to write this, makes me feel the worst, most selfish bastard of a son alive) is that I'm—or a part of me is—glad about Mam being sick. Not that I want her to be sick or to die, but... her being sick means *he* leaves me alone. It can't last, I know it can't, and I wish it would end with her being well again, but I know it won't. For now, though, just for now, I'm a little bit safer.

30TH JULY

The last goose died today. They've been dying off steadily since Protheroe's visit. It was waddling around the farm looking confused, as if he couldn't understand where everyone else had got to. He seemed healthy enough. But come daybreak he was going slowly, neck drooping. By mid-morning he was spread out on the ground, breathing and blinking and sod-all else, and by lunchtime he was gone.

It's going through the sheep like a dose of the salts as well. Half a dozen of them gone now. I know because Dad's heaped all the carcasses up in a shed. At least he's given up on trying to make us eat them, thank God.

I'm just keeping out of his way all I can (as if I don't anyway!). He's in a foul mood, even for him, and I could hear him before, cursing Mr Protheroe under his breath.

Mr Prothero turned up around teatime, just as Dad was dragging back another dead sheep he'd found. Not the best timing on his part (Mr Protheroe's, not Dad's). Especially given what he had to say.

I heard the whole thing; I was in Mam's room but I'd opened the window to let in some fresh air. The two of them were yattering away right under us.

The long and short of it was that Mr Protheroe hadn't a clue what had killed the geese or was killing the sheep. He'd had every test run that he could, but found nothing. No germs, no poisons. Nothing.

Next thing I heard was Dad bellowing at him, and then a near-scream from Mr Protheroe. I ran to the window and saw Mr Protheroe running like the clappers with Dad at his heels. I had to bite my hand so's I didn't laugh. I hate Dad because he's the High King of all Bastards, but seeing old Protheroe legging it like that wasn't half a sight. He's a tubby fellow, bandy-legged too, and I'd never have thought he'd go that fast.

Even when he got in his van and was driving off, Dad chased after him, even landed a kick on the thing's back panel and stood there shouting after him as he drove off. Well done, Dad. Doing your bit there to make sure nobody comes near us. What's next? Leprosy?

I don't expect we shall be seeing Mr Protheroe again.

31ST JULY

Dad wanted eggs for breakfast, so I got three out to fry for him. Knew something was wrong the minute I cracked the first one open—Christ, the stink of it, and the colour! The other two were just the same.

I threw them out and got three more. Checked the shells all careful-like, make sure there were no cracks. All fine. Until I tried to break them. Every one of them, stinking like sulphur and nearly green with decay.

I went through the rest of the eggs in the house: the same story, every time. Well, except for a couple. They'd been fertilised somehow, but the chicks inside them, if that's what they were—I've no idea what had happened to them. They didn't even look like birds.

Dad had to make do with some bacon we still had. I fried it up for him. He wasn't happy but he managed not to belt me. That's a good mood, for him.

1ST AUGUST
The hens have stopped laying.

8TH AUGUST
More dead sheep. The chickens seem healthy enough, but there still hasn't been one egg laid.

Dad burns the animal carcasses every day. He doesn't say anything about them, but there are other fires too, out in the meadows. I've seen him going out there with his axe and fork. I think the pine trees are growing back on our land.

Mam's very weak, and in a lot of pain. She's on morphine constantly, and she's lost two or three stone in weight over the past fortnight. Her teeth are yellow and her breath stinks and she says it won't be long now, and that I must look after my father. Look after him? What can I say to that? She's my mam and I love her and she's dying. How can I lie to her, but how can I promise her that? I can't bear this life as it is; without her, what am I going to do?

14TH AUGUST
The hens are gone; the rooster, too. All the chickens. Something got in. God knows what. Dad says a fox, but I've seen what foxes do, and this isn't it.

They were torn to pieces. Part-eaten, yes, but ripped apart. Wings torn off, legs, heads—guts everywhere. As much was left as eaten, and smeared and scattered about. I don't know what animal could have done it. I could almost think a madman had done it— some lunatic, lurking in the woods or on the mountain.

Almost, but I'm not bloody going to. It's lonely enough in this place when it gets dark, without thinking on *that.*

Dad fetched his shotgun and went out looking for the beast, whatever it was. There was a trail, blood and feathers, but he lost it in the woods at the foot of the mountain, near the mouth of a stream. Maybe an otter, he said. Maybe it went into the water and upstream, into the caves the streams run out of.

Doubt it, somehow. Otters go more for fish, don't they? I don't know. Weasels, stoats, something like that? I don't mind saying it's rattled me. Dad, too, I think. He hasn't said anything, but he hasn't put his shotgun away; it's been close at hand ever since he got back—on the floor, propped against his chair, wherever. He's gone to bed now, and I'm pretty sure he took it with him.

Dad with a gun. Now that's a cheery bloody thought.

27TH SEPTEMBER

No dead sheep today. God be praised, it's a bloody miracle.

Mam's very weak now; can't move, can barely speak. She looks like... I saw some pictures once, of concentration camps. The German ones. She looks like one of the poor bastards there. A skeleton. And her skin's gone yellow. I hardly recognise her anymore.

I don't think it's going to be long now.

The day's been horrible. Hot, close, clingy. The sky's clouding up. It's about teatime—a bit after five o'clock—and the sky's *black.* I've had to put the lights on. The air's so hot and thick that when you breathe it feels like you're being suffocated. My nose and mouth and throat all feel stuffed with wool.

Mam's breaths are slow and hoarse. Each one has this horrible laboured sound, as if just doing that is this huge wearying effort for her. Maybe it is. I just wish it would stop now. That she'd stop. This thing in the bed, it's not my mother anymore.

I'm going to have to tell Dad. He should know that it could be tonight. I'll probably catch a leathering if I wastes his time, but I'll catch a sight worse if he isn't with her when she goes.

I hate him, that hasn't changed, but—he must love her. He tries like hell to hide it, I know, but this is ripping him apart.

Jesus. Just had the loudest crack of thunder I've ever heard. It's going to be a hell of a storm.

28TH SEPTEMBER

Mam died last night. Or the early hours of this morning, rather. We were with her till the end, Dad and me. Now and again I put the kettle on, make some coffee to keep us awake. I didn't want to leave, didn't want to miss the moment she—

No. No. That sounds horrible. That sounds wrong. As if I was looking forward to it, *wanted* it. But I suppose I did, in a way. I mean, I wanted it to be over for her, didn't I? But that was for her sake, nothing else. Even with the morphine, she was in so much pain.

I didn't want to *not be there*. That's it. What I meant to write. I wanted to be with her when she went, not leaving her on her own. Or on her own with Dad.

He cried, you know. Tried not to let me see, even left the room a couple of times. Never for long, of course. He didn't want to miss the moment either.

I can't remember how many times I thought she was about to go. The pauses between breaths just stretched out and out, longer and longer almost every time. And all through it, the storm was raging.

I couldn't believe it. When something builds up like that and then breaks, you expect it to be over quickly. But this one didn't let up. The rain lashed down, and there was flash after flash of lightning, and the wind howled. Outside, it was black—no moon, no stars for the clouds. You couldn't see a thing except when the lightning went and picked everything out.

And that's how I saw them—that's how I knew even to look.

I got up at one point, went to the window. The air in the room was still hot and close, and the stink of it was awful. I opened the window a bit, just to let in a little air, but the wind's howl filled the room and swept rain into my face, so I pulled it shut again.

As I did, the lightning flashed, and I saw them.

From Mam's bedroom window, you see, you can see Mynydd Du up close. The woods aren't far from the house—a hundred yards or so, maybe. And of course they're thinner at the lower edge.

There were about a dozen people spread out in among the trees. All of them were robed and hooded—white robes.

I made some sort of sound; whatever it was, it brought Dad to the window beside me, pulling the curtain wide. For once he wasn't shouting at me, wasn't angry; he could tell, somehow, there was something he had to see. There was thunder, and then the lightning again, and they were still there. Dad saw them, too: I know because I heard the gasp he made seeing them.

The hoods they wore were a bit like the Ku Klux Klan's, except there was a hole at the bottom, leaving the mouth exposed. I don't know why. Never seen or heard of anything like it before. They didn't move, and I don't think they made any sounds. Although you'd have been hard put to hear anything over that storm.

None of them moved or stirred. The only motion was their robes, flapping and rippling in the wind and rain. The storm lashed them, but still they stood, and watched the house. Dad made a growling noise in his throat.

I remembered Mam and backed away from the window. Her breaths were stretching out further and further now. "Dad," I called.

He wheeled away from the window and came over, leaving the curtain open. Lightning flickered in the black square of the window, turned it white.

We were each knelt on either side of the bed. Dad's side was nearest the window, so he had his back to it. Mam was so thin by now that she barely even made a bump in the covers. Her hands lay on top of the quilt, and I took hold of one. Dad took the other and we stayed like that till my knees ached.

Long hoarse breaths, and pauses deepening between them. And then they stopped, just like that. No warning, rhyme or reason. She was just gone.

Her eyes were closed. There was spittle on her lips. I wiped them with a tissue.

I heard a sob rattle in Dad's throat. He took her hand in both of his, and bowed his head.

And behind him, a bright orange glow flared up.

Not lightning, this; it was the wrong colour, and it didn't die. I stood up, still holding Mam's hand.

I could see it all right. It was a fire: a big fire, twenty or thirty feet tall, burning high up on Black Mountain, among the pines.

Dad looked up at me, saw where I was staring, and turned to look. He stared at the fire, and then Mam's hand slipped from his and he ran to the window.

"Bastards!" he shouted, then ran out of the room. A minute later he went crashing down the stairs, cursing at the top of his voice. The front door slammed.

I knelt back down beside the bed, still holding Mam's hand. It wasn't right, leaving her alone. Outside, I could hear Dad shouting over the storm, but I couldn't make out the words.

I didn't feel anything. I was just numb. Maybe a little glad: she wasn't in any more pain.

A while later the door slammed, and I heard him thumping about downstairs. I sat with Mam until he crashed back upstairs and came into the room, hair wet and plastered to his face, breathing hard. "Leave us," he said. "Go."

I didn't want to let go of Mam's hand. I wanted to say that I had a right to stay too, but I knew not to argue with that tone of voice. So I went to my room and I just… lay there. I don't know how long for. In their bedroom I could hear Dad talking, sometimes shouting, but I could never make out what he said.

I went to sleep at some point. When I woke up it was still early. Dad was passed out in the chair beside the bed with an empty bottle nearby. I folded Mam's hands across her chest and pulled the sheet over her face, and then I went downstairs and rang the doctor.

I'm writing this while I wait for them to turn up. Expect Dad'll blow his top when they arrive. He'll say I've gone behind his back, it's up to him who gets invited up here and when—but sod him. It's hot weather and I'm not leaving Mam's body to be got at by the bloody flies. And anyway, he chased me away and stopped me mourning her, so why shouldn't he get the same?

7TH OCTOBER

We cremated Mam today. Had the service in the little church on the road out of Bala, next to the lake: it's where she married Dad. Wasn't a bad turnout, all things considered. Most of the mourners were Mam's relatives, of course.

Bronwyn and James both came down. There was a wake at the White Lion in Bala afterward. James wolfed half a dozen sandwiches and a half of lager and couldn't get away fast enough after that. Bronwyn offered to stay a few days but Dad turned her down flat. That made her start crying again. He was a bastard about her going off to college, and even with Mam dead he won't let it alone. Far as he was concerned Bron was supposed to have been spending her life cooking and cleaning and fixing and mending, so when she left she betrayed the family and disgraced herself, or us. One or the other, I'm not sure which.

He didn't say so, but it wouldn't surprise me if he blames Bron for Mam's death. Mam had to do all the housework on her own, and that wore her out so she got sick. Completely free of any bloody sense, of course, but that's Dad for you.

Bron gave me a hug before she went. Maybe she knew what was coming. Probably. I did, of course, and I was dreading it. Even though the wake was a bloody dreadful affair, I didn't want it to end. Because when it did, it's back here to Plas Gwynedd, where I'm alone with him.

I could feel the rage coming off him all the way back to the farm as he drove. He'd had a few, so he shouldn't have been behind the wheel, but good luck to the poor sod who tried talking him out of it. The anger off him was like the heat from a fire, and I knew it was only a matter of time.

We got into the house and stood in the hall. He turned and looked at me and I was all tensed up, to run or to fight; not that I'd have had much chance of either, not that close to him. But then he went into the front room and I heard the clink of glasses and the creak of springs as he sat down. I breathed out and went upstairs.

You know, I think I might even have started to believe it was going to be all right, that I'd been wrong, that all that rage would go somewhere else. Stupid, of course. See, that's the thing with Dad. Whenever he's angry, it's someone's fault. And it's never his.

Maybe he finally remembered how I called the doctor without asking him, how they all arrived when he was still passed out and he woke up all sudden and had to behave himself. He'd have felt humiliated by that, and he'd had to part with Mam before he was ready. All told, it was a miracle he hadn't clobbered me already.

I was actually in bed and drifting off when I heard his feet thundering up the stairs. I tried to tell myself he was running for the toilet—something, anything else—but I knew. I knew. Just couldn't do anything about it except lock the bedroom door. The next thing, he'd just kicked it down and then he was flailing at me with his fucking belt.

I hate him I hate him I hate hate hate hate hate the bastard. Father? He's no bloody father to me; I wish he were dead. I'll fucking laugh when he dies, the bastard. I'll piss on his grave.

But it's nearly time. I'm sixteen in November and I can bugger off and leave him to it. And whatever happens then, it's on his head. He's driven his own family to death or away from him. His bed. Let him lie in it. It can't come soon enough.

9TH OCTOBER

Back to the usual farm duties again, what there are of them. He's supposed to be buying in more chickens and geese, but no sign of them yet. My guess is that he's worried about what carried off the last lot.

Meanwhile, the sheep are still dying. We've lost more than half our flock already. But that's not all of it.

Those trees are back growing on our land. Worse than ever. Nearly half of one meadow's gone. I told him, of course. Knew there was a good chance of getting clouted, but the thought of seeing his bloody face! And I wasn't disappointed. He went apeshit. Lucky enough, he had something else to get angry at. So he ran off and came charging back with his axe and set about the trees. I had to join in, of course—there were too many of the bloody things for even him to tackle on his own.

There are more of them, though. A lot more. They're sprouting up in every field we've got, I reckon. With any luck, that'll wear him out so he'll be too knackered to get violent. At least for now.

13TH OCTOBER

Christ on crutches. He's finally gone completely raving bloody mad.

The trees keep sprouting up, you see. And you know, I've got to admit, that is bloody weird. They shouldn't be shooting up as fast as they are doing. If there's something in the soil that's making them grow like that, we'd get monster crops, and we're not.

But this? He reckons someone's trying to drive us off our land. Or some*thing*.

"Them up on the mountain," he said. "Whoever, whatever they are. Don't act like you don't know who I mean. You saw 'em, night your mother died."

Okay, they were real enough because I saw them like he says, and I don't mind saying they creeped the hell out of me when I did. But all they're going to turn out to be is a bunch of daft hippies or something like that, another bunch of sad bastards who reckon they're the Druids.

See, according to Dad *everything* that's gone wrong is down to them: Mam getting sick, the crops and the animals dying, the pines sprouting up on our land, it's all down to 'them on the mountain'. And he can't even say who they are.

"My Granda used to talk about them," he said. "'All this belongs to the mountain', he used to say, 'and we're just here on sufferance'. Looks like the bastards have changed their mind, and now they want it all themselves. But this is Puw land, boy, d'you hear? It's our land! Always has been! They'll not take it from us without a fight, by God! I'm the master of Plas Gwynedd, not them!"

Stuff like that, anyway. I'm just glad there's a lock on my bedroom door. Won't keep him out for long, of course, if he decides to come bashing his way in again, but I might have a few extra seconds. I reckon I could bale out of the window or something like that.

I was going to wait till my birthday before doing a runner but at this rate I might have to go before then, and hope for the best. He's not just a bastard now, he's a mental bastard, too.

14TH OCTOBER

Oh Holy Christ. It just gets better.

Today Dad presented me with the rota. Now not only do we have to divvy up the farm tasks and the housework between us—that part at least makes sense—we've also got daily prayer sessions. Yes. I kid you not, dear diary. Apparently Almighty God is being asked to take a part-time job at Plas Gwynedd.

I got my first taste of it today. Every hour or so is a 'lesson' from Dad, where he reads some whacking great chunks of the Bible—so far I think we got through most of Leviticus, half of Deuteronomy and the entire Book of Lamentations—reels off a sermon and finally leads the congregation (i.e. me) in prayer.

We're actually getting less done under this system than we did before, but according to him this is all okay because God will bless our endeavours and deliver us from evil. Which I'm assuming means that he'll stop the pines growing and the sheep dying. Good luck with that.

Of course, when it doesn't work, Dad will be off in one of his rages again. And when that happens....

There's only a month to go, but I'm going to be ready to leave at a minute's notice. I've been salting away any cash that comes my way—whenever he sends me shopping or on errands, I pocket as much change as I think I can get away with—but there isn't much. There's a little tent that I think he's forgotten about, though, and a small primus stove. I've pinched them and smuggling them up to my room: if nothing else, I can camp out for a bit. If it comes to that. And I'm starting to reckon it will.

OCTOBER 24TH
Ofuk
Cant se strait
Sick
O jesus I just pissed blood
Bastard
Bastards going to kill me

OCTOBER 25TH
Better. A bit.

He's leaving me be. For now anyway. Maybe he feels guilty. More likely he just knows a lost cause when he sees one. Normally he'd expect me do a full day's work even if I've just had the belting of my life, but he's not stupid. Whatever else he is.

Dad found my stash. I had the camping gear, the primus, a tin plate and a can opener, some tins from the pantry—and the money, of course. Worst of it is that I was about ready to go. I'd had a week of his 'work and prayer' method and it was enough.

Christ, I should have gone before. I *knew* something like this was coming. Just thought I'd see it in time, get away from it before I got anything this bad.

He went berserk. I mean literally. Smashed up my whole room. Tore down the bookshelves, ripped and trampled the books, burned half of them outside this morning and—oh, God, I thought he'd beaten me before? I thought—I honestly, honestly thought, not being dramatic or anything, I mean this literally—he was going to kill me, that he'd just keep punching and kicking and stomping until I was dead.

As it is, I'm dizzy if I try to stand up. I've thrown up half a dozen times and there's blood in my piss. I managed to get downstairs somehow, earlier on while he was outside, clinging onto the banister all the way down so I didn't fall. Thought I could call somebody. But the phone's gone, God knows where.

I won't be calling anyone, then, and I won't be going anywhere just yet. It'll be a few days before I'm in any state to move, always assuming he hasn't done any permanent damage. But as soon as I can, I'm going. I've got to. He was bad enough before, but next time—next time he really will kill me. I'm sure of it.

Going to have to try and find somewhere to hide this. If he *does* kill me, this is evidence. He might get rid of my body, and claim I've run off.

OCTOBER 27ᵀᴴ

Feverish yesterday, but it broke during the night. Finally starting to feel better.

The sheep are all dead. Dad was burning the last of them today. Then he went back to the fields. I managed to spy on him from one of the bedroom windows. Those bloody pines are everywhere now. Growing all over our land. He goes and shouts his prayers at them, and then it's the axe and fire, and it doesn't seem to be doing any good.

Heard a sort of whacking sound from his bedroom in the night. Crept out and peer in through the door. He's got this great big piece of knotted rope and he's thwacking himself on the back with it. All welts and blood.

He nearly caught me as well. He stiffened and grunted and started to turn. I managed to get back to my room and into bed and pretended to be asleep. Could hear him snuffling and panting outside like a big dog. He had the door open and was standing in it, just breathing. I was terrified, waiting for him to come at me. If he had, I don't know what I would have done. Too weak to fight him.

A day, maybe two, I'll be ready to run.

II: THE POLICE INTERVIEW

Aled Puw's diary ended there.

I was almost afraid to look at the rest of the bumf Jones had sent. I hesitated before reading it; having been in the poor kid's head all morning, I wasn't sure I wanted to read the coroner's report on how his father had ended up killing him. But as it turned out, it wasn't. The next document I saw was a police interview with Aled, and my first feeling was relief.

There were photographs of the boy in the file, though, and of the damage done to him. He was very thin, his ribs like slats. The bruises from the last beating were a few days old: they were purple, blue, yellow and green. There were cuts on his back from the belt. And scars.

The interview was dated 1st November, and took place at Dolgellau Hospital. Present were Detective Constable Jones and Detective Sergeant Williams (I wondered if it was the same man who'd investigated the aftermath of the Tŷ Mynwent murder five years later), Aled Puw, his sister Bronwyn, and their solicitor, a Mr Gwyn. Must have been pretty crowded in that interview room. But it was Aled who did most of the talking.

*

EDITED TRANSCRIPT OF INTERVIEW WITH ALED PUW:

So, I'd decided—soon as I could walk, I was going to leg it. I didn't have any money, but I just had to get out of there. I was terrified even waiting till I was well enough to go. He'd completely lost the plot by then.

I'd wanted to go for a couple of days, but I just didn't have the nerve for it, if you want the truth. Every time something creaked or rustled, I thought it was him coming to get me. The night before last, I—he came and stood in my bedroom door just staring at me. Must have been there nearly half an hour. Not talking, just glaring at me like it was all he could do not to go for me. And... and he had his shotgun with him.

That was it, see. I was more scared of staying than going. I had to get out, but at the same time I had a feeling he was waiting for me to try, and if he caught me—well, I'd be for it. So I decided I'd have to pick my moment.

That wasn't difficult because, see, while I'd been trying to get my nerve up, I'd been keeping track of what he was up to. Dad liked his habits. Liked there to be a rhythm, a—a pattern to his day. Now it'd *changed* a lot, but he had a new pattern now.

He'd got into a habit the past few days, with me out of action. All he cared about now was hacking those trees down. There weren't any crops left, and there weren't any animals to care for. It was just him against the mountain, or whatever it was he thought he was fighting. So he'd cut them down, pile them up, then set light to them when it got dark. Fire gave him light to keep working by, you see. I reckoned that was my best chance. He'd be less likely to see me, and he'd be tired.

Yes, this was last night. I hid the diary—just in case anything happened to me—and I just took what I stood up in. Didn't want to stop to take anything. All it would take would be Dad showing up at the wrong minute and seeing me, and that would be it. I'd wait till I thought he was all occupied, then get downstairs fast as I could and out through the front door. There's a track from our house down towards Bala. I just thought I'd run straight down it, get to the main road and that'd be it, away.

It got dark—sort of twilighty. I could hear the wood chopping, and then the fire started crackling. Dad was off round the side of the house, nearest the mountain. I could have done with him being farther off, but beggars can't be choosers and I wasn't staying another night.

I got to the top of the stairs and listened. I'd left a couple of windows open so I could hear better. The axe was chopping away, so I ran down the stairs to the front door.

Dad always had three locks on the door, but the keys were always hung up next to it and thank God, he hadn't changed that. It couldn't have taken me long to get them all undone, but it felt like ages. You know how it is—fingers all thumbs. I pulled the door open and it jarred—he'd put the chain on. I fumbled it loose and got outside.

First thing I realised was that I could hear the birds singing in an evening chorus. They were chirping good and loud. There were bats weaving back and forth in the trees down the track. But the only sound was the birds singing, and the crackling of the fire. The one thing I wanted to hear, and couldn't, was the axe.

I looked at the track, and all I wanted to do was just run down it full-tilt. I knew where I was going with it, straight to Bala and away from Plas Gwynedd and Dad. But if he'd heard, then he'd be coming round the front, and if he did....

And then I heard him: his boots, crunching in the ground. And then there was a *clack* noise. I knew what it was, straight off, 'cos I'd heard it a hundred times. It was his shotgun, snapping closed.

I backed away—he'd be here any second—and then ran around the other side of the house.

This was the east side of the house. Reason I'm saying that is so you can understand what I was doing—I was going for the woods, for Coed Lleidr.

Our land's sort of squeezed between Coed Lleidr and the woods at the foot of Mynydd Du; the actual land is mostly north of the farmhouse. Anyway, Coed Lleidr's pretty close—there's only a couple of fields between it and the house, and one of them was now completely overgrown with pine saplings. The other one was fallow, full of tall grass. It'd be harder going, getting through Coed Lleidr, but I had a better chance of losing Dad in there. And once I got through there, I'd be practically on the Bala road. Get a bus—I had a little bit of change left—or hitch-hike. I was going to head for Aber, Bron, and find you.

Anyway, I was halfway across the field when I heard Dad shout my name. I looked back and saw he had the gun at his shoulder, so I threw myself down. I heard the bang of it a second later.

I went crawling for the trees, and he fired off the second barrel. There was a swish and a rattle and the shot came tearing through the grass beside me. Something hit me in the wrist and I yelped out. One of the pellets.

But then I realised he'd fired both barrels and he'd have to reload, so I got up again and ran. Got in among the saplings and pushed through them to the woods proper. There's not much in the way of paths through Coed Lleidr, but there's trails, sort of. I knew I wanted to go east, so I sort of headed towards where it was darkest—I knew what sun there was would be in the west.

There was another blast, and more pellets smacked into the trees behind me. "Aled!" he was shouting. "Come here you little bastard!"

I kept going, but it was nearly pitch-dark by then, and what trails there were were getting harder and harder to follow. And then there was another shot and something hit me in the back. My back, my shoulder, my upper arm. And I lost my balance and I fell.

*

More pictures from the file: the little red wounds where pellets had embedded themselves in Aled Puw's flesh. Two in his right wrist. A dozen more around his right shoulder, shoulder-blade and upper arm.

*

EDITED TRANSCRIPT OF INTERVIEW WITH ALED PUW:

I was on the ground, in the bushes. I could hear him crashing towards me, hear him muttering God alone knows what. And I could hear him throwing the empty cartridges away, hear him reloading and snapping the gun shut again.

"Aled!" he shouted. "Where are you, you little bastard? It's time to come and take your punishment like a man!"

He was getting closer and closer. I didn't dare move in case he heard me. I just stayed still, hoping he'd miss me.

And then the fire happened.

I couldn't tell exactly where it came from. Somewhere to the north of us, I'm guessing, and closer in towards the house, because it backlit my Dad, looming there with the gun in his hands. I don't know if he saw me or not, because suddenly, there were these other people there—all in white robes, ducking back and forth through the trees. None of them were close enough or stayed still long enough for me to get a proper look at them, but I think their faces were covered. I think they were the same ones that—you'll know who I mean, if you've read my diary.

Well, Dad spun towards them and started shouting at them. I couldn't make everything out, but he was ranting about them trying to take his land and his home away from him.

"Well you won't!" he shouted. "I am the master of this house!"

He'd turned away from me by then. Between the fire crackling and the chanting—they were chanting something, I don't know what—there was a fair old racket going, so I started crawling off. He kept on shouting and ranting behind me, and then I heard the gun firing, again and again and again. He must have been taking them all on. Anyway, I got going and as soon I thought I could get away with it I ran like hell.

*

Aled Puw was trying to escape from Coed Lleidr, as the police officers who'd searched for Russell Ware had seven years earlier. For whatever reason, he found his way out far more easily: within fifteen minutes he was clear of the woodland and making his way through the others until he reached the B4402. He managed to find a farmhouse before collapsing from shock and blood loss due to the gunshot wounds he'd sustained. He was rushed to Dolgellau Hospital at about nine pm on October 31st, 1988.

Having identified him, the police went to Plas Gwynedd, to find the house standing empty.

DS Williams visited the boy at Dolgellau the following morning. Aled told him where his diary was hidden, and where he'd last seen his father. By the time DS Williams read the diary, the body of Gareth Puw had been found. Although he was surrounded by discharged shotgun shells, there was no mark of violence on him: as far as could be ascertained, he'd succumbed to a massive stroke.

By then, Aled's siblings had been notified. Bronwyn came to the hospital to attend him and to contact Gwyn, the solicitor the family had used on the rare occasions they'd needed one. That was when the interview had taken place.

No hint of the robed figures Aled had reported in the woods was found, nor any trace of the fire. DS Williams surmised they might have attempted to restrain Gareth Puw, only for him to become more outraged until the fatal haemorrhage was triggered. Most likely, the police concluded, they were a bunch of fairly harmless hippies—there was no evidence to suggest they'd caused the Puws any harm—but they were never traced.

*

Aled Puw moved to Abersytwyth, where his sister was studying. He found some work there, and later went to sixth-form college. Eventually they both moved out of the area and, despite extensive efforts, I was unable to trace them for interview.

Mr Gwyn, the solicitor, was unable to sell Plas Gwynedd at auction, and the property fell into disrepair; like so many other places around Mynydd Du. Like Hafan Deg, Maes Carnedd and Tŷ Mynwent, it remains deserted.

*

I put aside the last of the notes on Plas Gwynedd, trying not to think of fires burning in the woods, or white shapes moving through the trees in a dance.

The fire in the woods; the dancers in the pines.

I wondered what Gareth Puw had seen before he died.

And I wondered if Russell Ware had seen it, too.

7: A LAKE OF FIRE

I: THE MYSTERY OF CAPEL TEG

No-one had lived in the Bala Triangle area since the Ashington murder, so there were no more recent events to trace. Maybe if I chased DI Jones a little I'd find a few reports of lights or weird-looking animals in the woods, or maybe not. It might put a cherry on top of the finished product, but it wasn't what I needed now, to beef the material I'd collated so far into a full-length book.

No, for that I'd need to turn my attention to another area, one that had defeated Ware himself. I needed to dig further into Mynydd Du's past, and most of all the nature of the 'god' on the mountain.

The best clue I had there came from the Britt Nordenstam case. Before all work had been abruptly halted by her disappearance, never to be resumed, she'd been involved in a dig at a deserted mediaeval village site. As I said, DMVs are common enough in England and Scotland, but rare in Wales, especially in the north. Professor Thurlow's team, however, found evidence of settlement going back much further than the Middle Ages: in the area immediately around the rough plan of the village they'd sketched, they found artefacts dating back to pre-Roman Celtic times, possibly even the Neolithic era. But the village itself, Capel Teg (Fair Chapel), although Thurlow could find almost no record of it, had clearly existed in the Middle Ages—up until the late 1400s, or so he estimated.

The soil was thick with charcoal and ashes, and mixed in among them were arrowheads and sword and dagger fragments. The village had been razed and sacked, but by whom was unclear. Professor Thurlow had intended to investigate further to try and determine who might have been responsible, but subsequent events had obviously put a stop to that.

Russell Ware had tried to find out more about Capel Teg—or, more particularly, how and why it had been destroyed—but without success. In the main, he'd been given short shrift at Manchester University, where the Britt Nordenstam affair, less than ten years old at the time, was still something of a raw wound. What assistance he managed to get had come from one or two individual students. By the time I tried to pick up the trail, the wounds had by and large healed, but the trail was colder by a factor of over forty years.

But this was when I got lucky, and I hope a certain person won't mind when I say this was in more ways than one. I was fortunate enough to meet a student at the university by the name Laura Hines: like me, she was fascinated by the stories, and found them intriguing enough that she wanted to help—to satisfy her own curiosity as much as anything else, I think. She was a mature student, a few years younger than me, but still eager enough to help a stranger dig around in the archives in search of background information just for fun. And to join him for a curry after. But that's another story. Let's just say that whatever happens with this book, I'll still have cause to be grateful to Russell Ware.

Thurlow hadn't pulled the name Capel Teg out of a hat: somewhere, he'd found a document containing information about the place. It didn't take Laura long to discover where, either: Thurlow's papers had been bequeathed to the university, and archived after his death. Among them was a package from a colleague at John Moores University, Liverpool, and in *that* was a journal in the name of the Reverend Oscar Childwall, dated 1819. It came together with a written deposition, signed by the same man and dated early the following year.

II. THE JOURNAL

The Reverend Childwall had been working on a book about the folklore of Wales. There's a lot of it, and a number of them revolve around either God's punishment for such transgressions as working on a Sunday, or divine intervention of behalf of devout Christians against the forces of darkness. The Bishop of Chester, George Henry Law, had encouraged him in the endeavour, believing a stern lesson on the respective rewards of wickedness and virtue would be much in order in the turbulent and ungodly Regency period.

And so in October 1819, Oscar Childwall found himself on a coach to Dolgellau, carrying a letter of introduction to an elderly parson, one Tudor Gwilym, who'd made a particular study of local legends and tales of the supernatural and who would be able to provide authoritative accounts for Childwall's book.

Childwall himself viewed the trip with mixed feelings. He was a young man, devout but, as he put it, 'somewhat untested in my faith'. By his own admission, he wasn't immune to the temptations of this world. He enjoyed good food, good wine, and wasn't 'proof against a pretty leg and a comely eye' either. On the one hand, Bishop Law's support for his book suggests he was held in some regard by his superiors; he was spared the everyday cares of a parish priest and had the opportunity to travel. Having said that, Wales at that time of year was not the most hospitable of places, and there were times when the everyday cares of a parish priest seemed positively beguiling.

The coach from Chester had to contend with appalling roads and increasingly foul weather as it pressed deeper into Wales, details of which Childwall doesn't spare the reader, or the poor qualities of hostelries along the way: rancid food, surly landlords, unattractive serving-maids and flea-ridden bedding.

However, Childwall's journey seems to have been brightened by his travelling companion, one Sir Percy Chetwynd:

Sir Percy, he wrote in his journal for October 17th, *is but newly succeeded to the title, and has clearly been of somewhat wild life, but he speaks with thought and purpose of his plans when he takes possession of his father's estates. His father owns land in the vicinity of Dolkettley[4] and Sir Percy now goes to make an*

---

[4] Dolgellau, a town about twenty miles south-west of Bala.

inspection and to decide on the future disposition of these estates. He is a most welcome companion on this journey through the God-forsaken landscape, being of good humour and a ready wit. Indeed, we have much in common: both of us are younger sons of the nobility, raised with little expectation of a title. In Sir Percy's case, his elder brother perished by mischance, being thrown from his horse, and another brother was lost in the late wars against the French. Both having died without issue, Sir Percy has found himself abruptly raised to the peerage! I believe that much of his profane and blustering manner will pass with time, as it is but a show to conceal his inner misgivings regarding his fitness for the role. If the opportunity arises, I hope I shall have the chance to counsel him for the good.

The following night, however, the final entry in Childwall's journal shows that his travelling companion showed a less appealing side to his character.

*

Anger, indeed [wrote Childwall] *is an ill master of a man, together with being one of the Deadly Sins, and it is a defect Sir Percy will do well to learn to rule ere he grows older, I think. He is a man used to gaining his desire, and grows most ill-tempered on being balked of it. It was intended that we should reach Dolkettley tonight—and I confess, such would have been no less welcome to me than to him, for I too have had my fill of lice-ridden hostelries and the jarring of my bones on these confounded Welsh roads— but the weather has worsened to such a pitch that Idwal, our coachman, averred no man could safely steer a path through it. Sir Percy flew into a great rage at this and came near to offering the poor man violence until he was guided by me to soften his disposition. But Idwal remained steadfast, even at the offer of additional coin.*

On our arrival in the town of Bala, Sir Percy sought to induce other coachmen to proceed on to Dolkettley, but capacious though his purse may be, he was unable to prevail upon them. I remonstrated with the young lord, reminding him that his estates waited solely for him to take charge of them, and that a further night's delay would be no great harm. At length, Sir Percy was ruled by me and made heartfelt apology to the men he had so recently berated. It is my belief that he fears greatly appearing ineffectual or incompetent in his new title, and has still to differentiate between those misfortunes we endure owing to a lack of will to evade them, and those we must perforce tolerate. I will endeavour to teach Sir Percy the Serenity Prayer; while a Romish device, it is not wholly lacking in wisdom.

The crisis averted, our host served us a most acceptable stew of mutton, together with bread and cheese, and much good ale and mulled wine. Few delights equal those of a roaring fireplace and full belly when the wind howls outside and the rain falls apace!

Miracle of miracles, too, the bed in this hostelry is clean! And well-warmed, both without by a healthy fire and within by a copper pan. We have been fortunate indeed to find such lodgings in this wild country, and even Sir Percy was well mellowed in disposition. And so, to bed.

III. FORESTS OF THE NIGHT

That was the Reverend Childwall's journal, but as Laura had found, he'd had more to say: there was a deposition in his name, submitted as a statement to the magistrate's court at Dolgellau (or 'Dolkettley', as Childwall continues to call it), or rather a copy of it. Perhaps he was afraid the deposition wouldn't find its way into the court records, which indeed it doesn't seem to have; Laura Hines found no traces of it among contemporary court records, and the document she scanned for me to read was among Childwall's own papers.

Nonetheless, the document—in Childwall's distinctive ornate handwriting, although a lot of it's in a shakier and more spidery hand—leaves few details unspared, and picks up the events of the night of the 18th of October 1819 from where the diary left off—less than an hour, in fact, after Childwall wrote his final entry.

*

FROM REV. CHILDWALL'S STATEMENT:

...I made an entry in my journal regarding the day's events, then laid down my pen, put out the lamp and settled down to sleep, but no sooner, it seemed, had I closed my eyes than I was rudely awakened by a loud banging on the door.

With some spleen I answered, to find myself facing mine host—Mr Evans—and Idwal, the coachman. Both men were in a state of real alarm, and informed me that Sir Percy had left the inn, taking one of their horses. An ostler, who had proven admirably resistant to the allure of gold, was now groaning downstairs in the inn after his Lordship had gone near to knocking out his brains.

At night and in such weather—I can offer no reason as to why Sir Percy would behave in such a manner. Perhaps there was some aspect of his affairs at Dolkettley that he had not seen fit to confide in me, or perhaps he was merely wilful, as the young can be.

In any case, Mr Evans and the coachman appealed to me to aid them in their chase of Sir Percy, to find him and persuade him to return to the inn before the worst befell him. Much as I would have preferred my warm bed, Christian duty compelled me to go with them, and thus we saddled horses and rode in pursuit, soon gaining the road past the lake.

And this is where events began to take a more curious turn.

We discovered that the road had become blocked. A great slide of earth and rock and uprooted trees had fallen from the steep hillside above and landed in a tangled pile of snapped trunks and branches and semi-liqueous mud, that even the most skilled horseman could not have mounted.

There was, however, another route that presented itself to mine eyes: a narrow track that branched off the main road. It was a rocky way, with only a thin layer of soil turned to mud by the rain, but it bore hoofprints. This, clearly, was the route that Sir Percy had taken, hoping to find an alternative route to Dolkettley, or at least to rejoin the lake road beyond the point where it had been blocked.

If anything, Sir Percy's actions could only increase his danger. The track was narrow and winding, leading up high slopes and through heavy woodland. Any number of dangers might befall him—a fall, a lightning bolt, even highwaymen or footpads, should they venture out on so ugly a night. It was clear that he must be found and brought back to the inn, by force if needs be.

But here I found my task made more effortful, for I regret to state that both Mr Evans and Idwal flatly declined to follow. Neither would give a reason for this refusal, but both were steadfast in doing so. I could only conclude that they were afraid.

I do not say this lightly, for Idwal had always struck me as the very man for whom the word 'stalwart' might have been coined, and Evans, publican though he might be, is a sober and God-fearing sort of man. What they feared I could not tell, but I remembered the reason for my presence in Wales and felt, for the first time, a deep unease. It is easy to pour scorn on tales of witchcraft and the powers of darkness and all manner of other hobgoblinry when you are in your rooms in a populous city, surrounded by light, a fire, a good meal and convivial company—but you may rest assured, gentlemen, that such scepticism vanishes apace amid a forested wilderness, by night, in a thunderstorm.

If I am honest—and I feel I must be, having twitted the memories of these two men with what some will call cowardice—I myself had little stomach from the chase, and not purely due to a yearning for the warmth and comforts of the inn. I was sorely tempted to defer to their judgement as countrymen, and to agree that however youthful, foolish and headstrong he might be, Sir Percy was nonetheless a grown man who must risk reaping the reward of his own folly, especially if the alternative was to put the lives of others at risk.

I can only say that at the time I felt I could not in all good conscience take such a course, that my Christian duty must be the rescuing of this lost sheep, and so I declared to both men that if they would not assist me, I would continue the pursuit alone.

I am glad to state that they did not call my bluff, for to my shame I cannot be sure I would have been able to hold to the vow. In the event, I succeeded in shaming them into assistance. Idwal agreed to go with me, while Evans would return to the inn and raise a party of men to assist in the search.

We watched the innkeeper ride back towards Bala. I shall admit I had misgivings as to whether we would see him again, but Idwal assured me that neither Evans' nor his courage in these matters were to be doubted, the man having served with honour in the French Wars before coming home to take up management of the hostelry.

With that, we urged our horses up along the trail.

These were brave men, Gentlemen of the Court. I feel this must be stated. For their blood is on my head.

*

The trail had, according to Childwall, wound back through the hills – in fact, it had seemed to be leading back the way they had come, perhaps towards Llanderfel. Perhaps Sir Percy had given up his quest by then. Or perhaps not. They never established why he'd been so determined to get to Dolgellau.

*

FROM REV. CHILDWALL'S STATEMENT:

We then came to a junction at the path, and the marks of Sir Percy's horse could clearly be seen, making—most strangely, given his desire to reach Dolkettley, which lies west of Bala—to the *east* of the town. Whereupon the coachman Idwal let out a most grievous cry and implored me to abandon the pursuit.

"What?" I demanded. "Are you so lily-livered? We almost have him, man—he cannot be far ahead!"

But the coachman shook his head. "Too late," he cried. "He will be in Coyd Clayder now—" I reproduce the Welsh as closely as I can pronounce it "—and if he be there, then only God can help him."

165

I could not be any means induce the man to enlarge on the nature of the threat we faced, other than that it was a menace that would not yield to any weapon of mankind. Whereupon I reminded the coachman that I was a man of the cloth and that, therefore, the Lord would be with us if we were only of stout heart and strong faith.

It was plain that even in the face of this argument, Idwal was not convinced and fain would have had us return to the inn post-haste. The Methodist doctrine has gained much credence of late in the Principality, and the Welsh are now apt to look as askance at an Anglican prelate as they would at a Papist. Nonetheless, since I stood on my religious authority, he had no real way of refusing me, and we took the path for Coyd Clayder, where and whatsoever the place might be.

*

By 'Coyd Clayder', Childwall can only have meant Coed Lleidr, which meant 'the Robber's Wood' and stood to the east of Bala, south-east of Mynydd Du. It was the same wood where Russell Ware had come to grief, and through which Aled Puw had made his escape from his father. I wasn't surprised to see its name come up again. If there was one thing I was certain of, it was that a common thread of some kind connected all of Mynydd Du's tragedies and mysteries. In the interests of clarity, I've corrected Childwall's attempts at spelling Welsh place names from this point on.

*

FROM REV. CHILDWALL'S STATEMENT:
We rode along the track, and as we went the wind and rain seemed to abate somewhat, although when we realised the cause it was of little comfort. It was simply that the trees on either side had grown up so thickly, their branches interlocking, that even in autumn they formed a canopy that hid us quite from the outside world. Nonetheless, we each carried a lantern, and were able to see what lay ahead of us well enough.

The horse reared up before us with a maddened neighing, and my own mount reared too, startled. Idwal grabbed the bridle and steadied the beast, else I might have been thrown and come to harm, then dismounted and ran to the other frightened horse, catching its reins and quickly soothing it. After only the briefest of inspections, he turned to me, eyes wide with fright.

"It's the horse Sir Percy took, Reverend." He looked around at the trees, which heaved and thrashed at the blowing of the wind. "God have mercy upon him!"

Horse hooves clattered on the ground behind us, and it was with some relief that I discerned Evans and perhaps a dozen or so local men riding to our aid. I climbed down off my horse and inspected the area by lantern-light, soon finding a place where the undergrowth at the roadside had been trampled down and low-hanging branches snapped from the trees.

"None of your ghosts or hobgoblins did this, man," I cried. "Sir Percy has been taken by footpads. Will you stand by and see murder done? In God's name follow!"

I very quickly found a path winding through the woods, which showed signs of recent passage, and ran along it, a lantern in one hand and a heavy stick in the other. I could have wished for a pistol or musket, but I would make do, and I had a party of men at my back.

Although, as I swiftly realised, they had followed me into the woods less to rally to my banner than to entreat me to return. I turned to remonstrate with them, when a cry of alarm went up that the path back out of the woods had vanished, leaving the search party unable to escape. I scoffed at so ridiculous a notion—but when I pushed my way through the men to the rear of the group, I found it was all too true. Indeed, not only was the path gone but the trees' branches were meshed so tightly together as to form an impassable barrier.

There was no question of a mistake or an optical illusion. The path came to a dead end and try as we might, we could find no other way back through the trees. At last I understood that neither cowardice nor foolish superstition had made these men try to stop me following Sir Percy.

One of the men let out a cry and pointed. I turned and caught the briefest glimpse, through the meshing branches that lay alongside the path, of a figure in pale robes. I soon spied another, this one standing still and watching us. It wore a hood that covered the upper part of its face, leaving its mouth exposed. I could not clearly discern its eyes through the ragged holes cut for them, only their febrile glitter as they surveyed us.

"God save us now," whispered Idwal, as the trees rustled about us and more shapes in those strange, heathen robes inched closer to the path.

"What are they, in God's name?" I said.

"They are the folk of Capel Teg," gasped Idwal. "They seek our blood, maybe our souls—"

From behind us came a terrible scream and I whirled about, just in time to see the youngest of our party, a stable-lad called Thomas, seized and dragged bodily from the path by a pair of white-robed arms. The claw-like hands that gripped him were wizened and dark, almost blackened, as if badly burned.

The boy vanished from sight and his scream was cut off. We ran to the spot where he had been, but there was nothing to see—just a few pieces of vegetation, waving a little where they had been disturbed. The boy was gone. Peering through the trees, however, something else soon became visible: two, perhaps three, other white-robed forms.

Hell, according to Mr Hobbes, is truth seen too late; now I had not only trapped myself in the woods, but also these good men. Some looked at me in misery, others with a desperate plea for help in their eyes, and a few with overt hostility. It was this last, I must confess, that did most to spur me into action; while I did not know the land and might well lead them into some further blunder, if I did not seek some positive course to amend my first mistake I might not live long enough to make another.

"We can only press on," I said. "With God's help we may yet clear these woods."

"But this path leads towards Llyn Daioni," said Idwal. "And beside the lake lies Capel Teg itself."

"What other remedy is there?" I demanded. "You are all brave men—surely you would not simply stay here and wait to be seized by those horrors?"

As I'd hoped, my appeal to their bravery had the effect of galvanising Idwal, Evans and the others into action, and we pressed on along the path. White shapes flickered among the trees, at the periphery of my vision, but I was determined not to look.

By this point, I must admit, all thoughts of Sir Percy had left my mind. Already it seemed that at least one life had been lost on his account, and unless God was with us in this instance, many more would follow. I cursed myself roundly for my arrogance and folly in ignoring the men's warnings and placing us all in danger.

When another scream rang out from the rear, it was in my mind to ignore it and press on, knowing that whoever uttered the cry was likely lost to us already, but the outcry from the men behind me made me turn, too. It was immediately obvious what had so appalled them, and even to recall it now, in comparative safety, strikes me with utmost fear.

The path behind us that we had already covered was gone; as before, the trees themselves had closed tight behind us in an impenetrable barrier. But that was not the worst, nor even that the branches were still sliding through one another in an ever-tighter mesh. No, the worst of it was that another of the men—a farmer, I later learned, by the name of Glynn—had been caught between them, snared helplessly, and indeed now began to cry out in agony as the twigs and branches pierced his flesh.

Only his hands were free, thrust imploringly out from the snare that pinioned him, clutching frantically at the air. A brave soul or two ventured forward and gripped Glynn's hands, trying in vain to pull him free, but they fell back with cries of horror as more white robes appeared behind the trapped man, slipping through the interlocked trees as easily as smoke and reaching out for him with long, charred-looking hands. When they laid those hands upon him his screams grew more terrible still, and every one of us, to our shame, turned and fled down the path in abject terror.

I do not know how long we ran. I am told that Coed Lleidr is not a particularly large or deep wood, but the path we took wound crazily back and forth, and often the trees encroached on it to such an extent that to still make our way along it was a constant battle, with thorns and branches catching and tearing at our clothes and stabbing at our faces—one jagged twig missed my eye by less than an inch. More than once I struggled, caught in such a snare, and felt the purest terror that the woods had fastened round me as they had poor Glynn, and that I was lost.

But nevertheless, at length, somehow—by God's grace I doubt not—we fought our way free of the woods of Coed Lleidr and onto open ground. By now, we found, the storm had abated and the sky above cleared somewhat. The moon and stars glimmered above us, and went some way to revealing the landscape.

We were in a wide valley. To the north a high mountain rose, bristling with trees. To the south our way was blocked by more woodland, which seemed to be a continuation of Coed Lleidr, as if the forest itself like Birnam Wood in *Macbeth*) were in motion— and moving to outflank us.

To the west, perhaps a mile or two distant, a low hillside rose, again thickly wooded. Below it I thought I could see the glitter of water.

"Where is everyone?" I called.

Idwal and Evans staggered to my side; the others followed in their wake. A quick head count showed that all but two of us had made it out of the woods of Coed Lleidr.

"Where should we go now?" I asked Evans.

He pointed to the north. "There's a village in that direction, Maes Carnedd. If we can reach there we should be safe. Bala is closer, but to reach it we must pass through those woods—" he pointed westwards "—Coed Capel, and that will lead us by the shores of Llyn Daioni and Capel Teg itself. There are farmhouses closer to us, but I'll wager none of them would open their doors to us at this hour. Not when the Capel Teg folk are walking."

"Who are they? Where is Capel Teg?"

"It stood by Llyn Daioni at one time," said Idwal. "They were wicked folk who lived there, and they walk here still. They walk in Coed Capel, Coed Dinas and Coed Lleidr, they walk by Llyn Daioni, and—" here he pointed at the mountain I had seen "—they walk on Mynydd Du."

I could get no more from him or the others; they were not disposed to stay in that place, and I could hardly fault them for that. I knew, then, that I must give Sir Percy up for dead. Our fleeing had almost certainly doomed him, and yet it might be all we ourselves could do to survive the night.

We began making our way north, and then Evans let out a warning shout and pointed up ahead. Out of the darkness a line of figures appeared. They were thin and wore pale robes that whipped about them in the wind, their faces covered by hoods, and they were advancing on us.

These men, if men they were, had come from nowhere and were closing at speed. In less than a minute they would be upon us. Looking about us, we saw, behind us and to the south, more white shapes moving in the woods of Coed Lleidr. To fly in either direction was sheer madness.

And so we ran to the west, towards Llyn Daioni and Coed Capel. As we went, Idwal gasped out to me that if we could by any means win through Coed Capel, there was a lane running down the hill to the road past Bala Lake. But to do so, of course, we would have to chance those woods—woods which might well be as dangerous and treacherous as those of Coed Lleidr.

And of course there were other hazards we must pass. Ahead of us lay marshes, and Llyn Daioni, where I was warned the banks were steep and treacherous. Not to speak of Capel Teg itself.

As it had been in that awful struggle through the woods, it is hard to say with any certainty how long it took to cross that ground. Each step of the way, we were dogged by those dreadful pale-robed figures, running after us in total silence. The absence of any cries or shouts, other than those of our own party, was, in a way, the worst aspect of all.

"'Ware the marshes!" Evans cried, catching at my arm.

Seconds later we crashed through freezing stagnant water that came almost up to our knees, but I realised he'd drawn me aside from my original course so that I only passed through the outer edges of the marsh, rather than blundering into its depths.

Then we were on firmer ground again, a brief stretch of flat land before it rose towards the western woods. To our right, the steep-banked lake glittered. We drew clear of it, for a step too close to the edge would fling the unwary runner down into the chill deep waters, there to drown. Rescue would be near impossible, even without that horrible silent horde behind us.

I was running in a straight line, eyes fixed on the trees. My heart felt as if it might burst, but I did not dare slow down—sheer terror of what might befall me if I stopped kept me running far beyond the point at which I would have expected to collapse. Yet now Evans seized my arm again and pulled me once more to the side.

"What?" I managed to gasp—for, at first, I thought he had taken leave of his senses and begun dragging me towards the southern woods.

"Capel Teg," he gasped, "beside the lake. None go there and live!"

And as I looked to my side, I saw one of the men in our party had either forgotten this advice or ignored it. But as he crossed the patch Evans had warded me away from, the air above the bare ground began to shimmer as it will when the day is very hot. Shadows appeared in the very air, limned in the moonlight—the shadows of low houses, and what might have been a church or chapel. And here and there, pale silvery light broke out of them, where there might have been doors or windows.

The running man slowed to a halt, then cast a beseeching glance at me. To my shame, I ran on—for I knew by now, without telling, that the poor wretch was already beyond any human assistance.

Shadows came out from the shadows—shadows with the shapes of men, or something like men—and closed on the hapless man. I turned away before his last terrible scream rang out, only to be cut off.

And then, at last, we reached the edge of Coed Capel, and the path that wound up through it. I prayed to God—prayed and prayed, silently, breathlessly—that I would be spared and find the road to the village. The path seemed straight enough, but I knew that at any moment it might twist about or seal itself before or behind us in a meshing of branches. I could only think of how a cat toys with a trapped mouse—slowly, and with the deepest cruelty— and imagine the wood doing the same to us. I have not the least idea what awful demon dwells in the woods near Bala, only that it had pleased God, for whatever reason, to grant it power over the lives of whichever unhappy mortals strayed into its compass. I could only hope that we were now nearing the limits of that influence.

From up ahead I heard another cry, and my heart sank—but the cry was of rejoicing, not of despair. The men ahead of us had found the road to Bala.

At the top, I looked back and saw two things. Below, at the foot of the slope, the white-robed figures stood gazing up at us. But barely a dozen yards from the path, in the woods, a fire was burning.

I might have done no more than note these facts before joining the other men in flight, but then a sound came from the woods where the fire burned. There was a chanting, some incantation whose exact substance I was never able to decipher, although I heard several phrases which might have been some form of Latin. Here and there was a word of Welsh, perhaps—and for the rest, only God or the Devil would know what tongue that terrible chorus used. And above them rose another sound. A human voice, screaming in the most terrible torment.

I knew, of course, who it must be. The luckless Sir Percy, taken by the folk of Capel Teg, whoever or whatever they might be. In the state of terror we all inhabited, no-one could have blamed us had we fled. Fled as we had from the three men who had already fallen prey to the Capel Teg folk and their demonic master. I am not a brave man, nor have I ever claimed to be—and, please the Lord, I never shall be again, for my one instance of courage proved too costly by far to be repeated. For it was not I who paid for it, but others. Evans… Idwal….

I cried out to them that I must try to rescue Sir Percy from his assailants, and ran into the woods. The coachman and landlord followed hot upon my heels, though why I cannot say. Perhaps they, too, felt guilt over the men we had abandoned, or perhaps, as previously during that terrible night, they felt some need to protect me (as a man of the cloth) from the consequences of my own folly and refusal to listen. I cannot say.

Beyond that moment, I have little memory. Only brief, broken glimpses. A roaring fire, white robed figures. A naked, screaming Sir Percy, bound to an altar of stone. I remember closing with one of the robed figures, raining blows upon it to no effect that I could see. Its hands were brittle claws. And then one blow of mine dislodged its hood, and the face beneath—

But beyond that, nothing. I cannot picture that face distinctly. I try, but my mind always shies away from it at the last, and in my heart I am convinced that this is for the sake of my own sanity, for I believe that some things were not intended by God for Man to look upon.

I know only that I next found myself stumbling down the road to Bala, clutching one of the men who had run in after Idwal, Evans and I. Two others followed, bearing Sir Percy between them. All our clothing was torn—save Sir Percy, who had been stripped naked—and we were all scratched and bloody. I later found that the silver cross I wore about my neck was missing. It was recovered the following day, crushed and melted almost past recognition.

Four men had not joined our headlong rush into the woods; we caught up with them further down the mountainside. As for Evans and Idwal, and the other men who had accompanied us—neither I, nor to my knowledge any other mortal soul, was to see them again.

Beyond this, I can add little to the report of other witnesses and the observable facts of the case. It is true that no altar was found in the woods, but by the same token neither were the bodies of Evans, Idwal or the men lost with them. Sir Percy Chetwynd we brought, as purposed, back to the inn alive, but we might have been kinder had we left him behind: his hair had turned snow-white, and he was—and to my knowledge, remains—a hopeless madman.

I remain, sirs,

Your obedient servant,

Reverend Oscar Childwall, DD.

IV. THE CHAPEL IN THE WOODS

Neither Laura nor I were able to find out how Oscar Childwall's statement was received, but there *was* now some clue, however vague, to Capel Teg's origin and its fate. As it turned out, there was more to come.

Childwall had written to old Gwilym, the parson he'd been due to visit. He'd never made it to Dolgellau, having fallen gravely ill after his experience at Coed Capel—although compared to some, he'd got off lightly. Childwall's letter hadn't survived, but Gwilym's reply had.

It was written in a thin, wavery but very clear script—age might have weakened Gwilym's body, but his mental faculties were still sharp—and began with an inquiry after Childwall's health, together with a few recommendations towards the restoration of his well-being (rest, light exercise and a simple diet free of over-rich food and alcohol, together with prayer and Scriptural study) before addressing two main topics.

*

FROM PARSON GWILYM'S LETTER:

Firstly, my dear Reverend Childwall, you have no need to make apologies for our missed meeting, although it is true the presence of another man of some education and culture is a welcome rarity in my benighted parish. By your account you came near to incurring the most terrible spiritual harm, and the Lord's grace is certainly to be seen in your survival and that of your rash travelling companion. For the other men, we can only pray for God's mercy upon their souls.

Regarding the principal matter of your letter, you are quite correct—the story of Capel Teg and its inhabitants is indeed a part of the body of folklore I have amassed regarding the north of Wales. As is often the way in these parts, one encounters several different versions of the tale, with details such as the names of the protagonists, the precise location and the year varying widely. I have found thus far no fewer than five variants of the story. However, no fewer than three of these agree that the village of Capel Teg was situated beside Llyn Daioni.

Capel Teg, translated from the Welsh, means 'Fair Chapel'. However, Reverend Childwall, you will doubtless in the course of your studies thus far have encountered the tradition prevalent in many parts of England and Scotland, whereby those places or persons believed to have to do with the unseen world are referred to as 'good', 'fair', &c—not for any good quality of their own, but out of the belief that they might overhear should any ill be spoken of them. Hence 'the Good Folk', 'the Kind Folk', &c. This tradition also holds true in Wales—indeed, the Welsh version of the faeries are known as the Tylwyth Teg, or 'the Fair Folk'.

Capel Teg, it seems, was so named due to having a similar reputation. I will go further: it was held that beneath an outward veneer of Christian observance, the people of the village in fact practised another, far older faith. It is unclear which god or gods they may have made obeisance to. It would appear that while there was a chapel in the village itself, this was merely for show: the true place of worship for this community lay in the woods to the west—which, as you will have noted, Reverend Childwall, are known as Coed Capel—that is, 'the wood of the chapel'.

Their holy of holies, it seems, was the mountain that lay a mile or thereabouts to the north of the village: Mynydd Du, or 'Black Mountain'. They held it too sacred a spot to set foot upon, and supposedly no man who attempted to do so would ever return. In any case, Capel Teg and its inhabitants succeeded in preserving their religion for some centuries following the advent of the True Faith to these islands. They were a secluded and out of the way community, and it was generally considered a good rule that if left well alone they would respond in kind. The other side of this, of course, was that if they were *not* left alone—were they to be harassed or slighted in any wise at all—they made bad enemies indeed, since their vengeance might well take the form of a murrain upon crops, wasting illnesses that struck loved ones and livestock. You can imagine well enough, I would expect, Reverend. It was no different an arrangement than one sees with 'cunning' or 'wise' men and women up and down the land, albeit on a somewhat greater scale.

However, there was another crucial difference with Capel Teg that perhaps ensured the village would sooner or later doom itself. As you will yourself have learned by now, the majority of so-called witches and warlocks, if not charlatans or lunatics, are certainly not followers of the Devil. In the main they confine themselves to preparing remedies for minor ills from this herb or that root, and in some cases their knowledge is indeed efficacious.

The Capel Teg folk, however, were a different breed. To maintain the favour of the being they worshipped (which manifested itself in the usual manner of successful harvests, the birth of healthy children and the continuance of their way of life) required offerings more corporeal than simple prayer. To be plain, theirs was a religion of blood sacrifice, and for the most part the unhappy victims of these ceremonies must be their fellow human beings. As you will have further noted, the woods eastward of Llyn Daioni are known as Coed Lleidr, or the 'Robber's Wood'. They were so named because many travellers came to grief near them from what were thought to be roving bands of footpads. Although of course for many years this remained no more than rumour, as their victims simply never reached their destination, no-one could say for certainty where they had met their fate.

This state of affairs continued until—goes the legend—the day came when they chose the wrong victim.

Two of the three versions pertaining to Llyn Daioni place this incident late in the reign of King Richard III, i.e. 1484 or 1485. In all accounts, our protagonist is 'a great knight' who owned lands in the area; a widower, he sought a new wife and found one in what appears to have been an authentic love match.

Of the three versions of the legend centring on the vicinity of Bala, only one gives this knight a name: Guy FitzUrse. (However, two other accounts, while locating the action in different parts of Wales, agree upon the name—and so I hazard that this is indeed our man.) The same account names his bride-to-be as Eleanor Woodham of Chester, a young woman 'noted for her beauty, modesty, grace and her rich mane of auburn hair' from a family of approximately equal social standing to his own.

FitzUrse and Eleanor were betrothed, and the time came when she was sent, by coach and accompanied with retainers and guards, to be married to her lord. She crossed the Welsh border in safety but, as you will have guessed, she never reached her destination.

When she did not arrive, FitzUrse did not stand idle. He was a military commander of accomplishment and experience, who had served the Yorkist cause with distinction during the Wars of the Roses. Bands of his men combed the countryside, lest the bride's party had strayed from their route and come to harm; meanwhile, his seneschal, Hugo De Vere, led another band which meticulously traced the route Eleanor's party should have followed, working backwards toward the border. Along their way, the occupants of every town, village or farmstead they encountered—anywhere she and her retinue might have passed—were closely questioned.

In love FitzUrse may have been, but he was not naïve; he had no illusions regarding his betrothed's likely fate. That she and her escorts had met with foul play he did not doubt; each passing day without word strengthened his certainty that she was dead, and he had steeled himself to receive the heavy news. But sooner or later, he knew he would discover where Eleanor had last been seen, and then he would know where to look. If nothing else, he would ensure her remains received Christian burial, and he would avenge her death.

And indeed, ere long, De Vere and his men found a farmstead a few miles east of Bala whose occupants had seen Eleanor's coach and riders pass. As no-one in Bala itself had seen them, it was clear the party had met with misfortune between there and the farmstead. And of course—this shall not surprise you in the least, Reverend Childwall—what lay between the two points but Coed Lleidr, the robber's wood!

De Vere sent word to his master, who rode at once to meet him with some thirty or forty of his fiercest fighters. The folk of Capel Teg were feared in Bala, but Guy FitzUrse had not made so successful a career without being able to instil even greater terror when he chose to.

To make a long story short, it was not long before FitzUrse, De Vere and their men were riding towards Coed Lleidr, and not long after that before traces of a struggle were found. Eleanor's party had been well-defended, and the robbers had not taken their prize without a fight. The attackers had sought to hide all evidence of their crimes, but here was a broken blade, there an arrowhead, elsewhere a brooch or buckle. To experienced soldiers like FitzUrse and his men, these told their own story.

In those days, it seems, a road led through Coed Lleidr to Capel Teg. At least, all the accounts speak of the avenging lord and his party following it to the village. Perhaps its remains form the vestigial path you encountered; in any event FitzUrse and his men reached the village very soon after.

And like brigands themselves, they fell upon it in blood and fury. It was fortunate for those still in the village that they were few in number and that FitzUrse's bloodlust was tempered by his need to know his beloved's fate. With co-operation being their only chance of survival, their refusal to talk only made the knight fear the worst. After several killings, a frightened villager finally confessed: the captives, together with the bulk of the villagers, were at the chapel in the woods.

These were nearly the last words the informer ever spoke, for at once several of his fellows set upon him and would have killed him had the soldiers not prevented it. With the knight's sword at his throat, he told them where this chapel might be found. You will, I think, have been able to guess where this was.

Leaving their captives under armed guard at the village, FitzUrse and his men approached Coed Capel swiftly, but in stealth, fearing that any surviving captives might be put to death should the villagers be surprised. As they did, a low chanting began, and a fire flickered into life in the woods. Soon after, they heard screams of awful torment.

They reached the place in the woods where the fire burned; for long moments, they were rooted to the spot—but then the knight, with a terrible raging cry, led them into battle.

The scene described was something like this. In the middle of a large clearing among the woods there stood a firepit, and a stone altar. A great fire was already raging in the pit; the altar itself was foul with blood, both old and fresh.

The villagers filled the clearing, dressed in white robes. Also present were the last survivors of Eleanor's party. At a signal from—presumably—their priest or chief, one of these unhappy wretches was dragged to the altar and held down whilst worshippers armed with heavy stone knives practised atrocious acts upon him. The victim was mutilated, disembowelled and dismembered—his limbs cut off and his innards ravelled out, and more beyond this, such stuff as we would hesitate to inflict on the foulest of criminals. He was kept alive throughout, up until the final moment when his head was hacked from his shoulders. And throughout all this the robed figures continued to chant their dreadful liturgy.

With this awful catalogue completed, the unfortunate man's remains were cast into the fire, all except the head. This, it seems, was mounted upon a pole, which joined other poles planted around the perimeter of the clearing, each of which carried the head of a previous sacrifice, for the ravens to gorge their fill of what flesh remained.

And it was at this point at last, so the longest of the accounts tells us, that the spell was broken. The would-be rescuers had been frozen in appalled disbelief at the blasphemous spectacle before them, but now as they cast their eyes up towards the circle of grisly trophies above them, Guy FitzUrse spied a glint of reddish-gold or auburn hair, and realised that among the heads upon the poles, and therefore among the unhappy wretches who had suffered the direful ending he had just witnessed, was that of Eleanor Woodham.

It was this sight that ended his paralysis. A moment later, as he charged into the clearing with a berserk cry and his sword aloft, his men were also jolted into action. Any worshipper offering even token resistance was cut down where he stood; the rest were taken and marched back down to their village.

This might have seemed a merciful act on Guy FitzUrse's part, given what he had witnessed, but it was in fact no such thing. He had been prepared to learn of Eleanor's death, but not that she had died in so cruel and agonising a manner—to say nothing of the obscene rituals of which her murder had formed a part. He may well, by this point, have been completely unhinged by grief.

Whatever the case, FitzUrse and his men marched the remaining white-robed celebrants back to Capel Teg, where they and the other captive villagers were herded into their cottages and the false chapel with which they had sought to conceal their heathenry. At this point, on FitzUrse's orders, the village was set afire.

FitzUrse's vengeance was terrible, for no villager was spared—neither the aged nor babes in arms, male nor female, received mercy at his hands. His men surrounded the village, driving any who fought free of the burning houses back into the flames with their pikes. The flames soared into the night sky along with the screams of the dying, and were reflected in the still waters of Llyn Daioni so that it resembled the lake of fire spoken of in the Book of Revelations, in which the false prophet was to be tormented for eternity and where those not written in the Book of Life were thrown.

By the morning, Capel Teg was only blackened ruins, but Guy FitzUrse was still unsatisfied, and had his men knock the remains of the buildings down, until blackened ground and ashes were all that was left of the village and its inhabitants. He and his men then returned to the 'chapel in the woods', where the remains of the white robes' victims were gathered up to receive Christian rites of burial elsewhere (none of the legends, I fear, offer us any clue to where the heads—for there could have been little else remaining of the pagans' victims—may have been interred). The poles on which the heads had been mounted were broken and burned. The altar stone could not be uprooted as it appeared to have been shaped from the living rock, so FitzUrse ordered it hammered into dust.

In short, the knight set out to eradicate, to the best of his ability, any sign that Capel Teg and its people had ever existed. But still his fury was not satisfied, and he turned his gaze towards nearby Mynydd Du, the mountain that had formed the centre of their secret worship, and vowed to root out and destroy any vestiges of their evil faith—for he was, it seems, convinced that some of the white robes might have fled there for sanctuary.

In vain did his loyal seneschal entreat him to remain; in the end, FitzUrse and half his men set off for Mynydd Du, while De Vere and the remainder left with the bodies of the dead.

De Vere, it seems, returned to FitzUrse's castle, but the knight and the men he had taken with him were never to be seen again, nor was any trace of them found: proof, perhaps, of the villagers' beliefs about their sacred mountain. De Vere himself, it appears, was killed at the Battle of Bosworth shortly after, having taken the Yorkist part against the forces of Henry Tudor, but gave account of what had taken place before his death. To my sorrow, I have been unable to find any trace of this testament.

In any case, Reverend Childwall, such is the legend of Capel Teg. You can doubtless imagine without much difficulty the nature of the stories now surrounding the locality: to wit, that the malevolent spirits of the slain villagers still prowl their old haunts, seeking new sacrifices to their mountain god.

Other versions of the tale suggest a more earthly explanation— viz, that some members of the destroyed village took refuge on Mynydd Du, and their descendants, hiding their existence from the outer world, still lurk in Coed Lleidr for unwary travellers. More prosaically still, of course, it may be a case of common footpads using the old legend to deter the inquisitive.

However, this would not account for your own experiences in the woods, and it is a fact that those dwelling near Bala still take pains to avoid Coed Lleidr and Coed Capel, especially at night. Llyn Daioni they likewise give a wide berth, and as for Mynydd Du—you will not induce a Bala man to step foot there at any price! Well; if God wills it, we may know more in the fullness of time, but it is my belief that other, wiser heads than ours must discover the complete truth.

I will remember you in my prayers, Reverend Childwall, wishing you a speedy convalescence in both mind and body; and I hope you will grace my humble parish with your presence when you are recovered quite.

Yours in Christ,
Tudor Gwilym

V. THE LAST ENTRY

There was one more email from Laura, containing a final scanned page from Childwall's journal. Apparently it had been written at the back of the book, and was dated January 26th, 1820.

The bishop has enquired when I might continue collating material for his book. It was all I could do not to laugh, I confess. My dreams are unquiet, and my waking hours little better. The lives of seven men are on my conscience, their blood upon my head. I led them into danger and death. They followed only to keep me safe—and I lived where they, wiser than me, their counsel ignored, perished. There is only one way I may hope to know peace. I must atone. I must return.

*

Laura and I did a little further digging. It wasn't hard to corroborate Sir Percy Chetwynd's existence: he had succeeded to the title, but within a month of doing so had been committed to an asylum, where he died in 1823.

The Reverend Oscar Childwall's year of death was given as 1820, but with no exact date. He had set off for Wales again in February 1820, supposedly to visit Parson Gwilym, but never got there. Attempts to trace the coach he'd ridden in proved unsuccessful. Like Eleanor Woodham, he crossed the Welsh border and vanished; unlike Eleanor, there was no knight devoted to finding him at any cost.

The chances were, of course, that even if there had been they'd never have found him. If there was one thing I'd learned about the Black Mountain, it was that those who probed its secrets too deeply tended to pay a price for it. Russell Ware, Oscar Childwall....

And what about me? Wasn't I immersing myself in the lore and history of the Bala Triangle, just as Russell Ware had? Even against my better judgement? But I'd have felt foolish, if not hysterical, throwing in the towel at this stage.

And so I pushed this bundle aside, and reached for the next.

8: ANCIENT VOICES

I. THE GIVING OF NAMES

The more I went back over what I'd found so far, the more one thing sprang out at me: the significance of names where the Bala Triangle was concerned. Llyn Daioni, for example, literally meant 'the lake of goodness', but going off Gwilym's letter, I guessed it was used to propitiate anyone (or anything) that might be listening, much like the village's name of Capel Teg or 'fair chapel.'

But the other place names were a little more accurate. Coed Capel was 'the wood of the chapel', for instance. Stretching the definition of 'chapel' a little there, but still more or less accurate. Similarly, the woods to the east of the village, near the Bala road, were Coed Lleidr, or 'the robber's wood'; they'd been where the folk of Capel Teg would lie in wait for unwary travellers to take as human sacrifices.

Mynydd Du itself, of course, is 'Black Mountain'—no concerns about propitiation there. But when I looked at the map, another detail hit me: all these locations were concentrated in the south of the 'triangle'. What about the north?

Well, there was Maes Carnedd, of course, and one other notable feature: another woodland, covering hilly ground, known as 'Coed Dinas'.

Time to summon up Google Translate (and double-check, where necessary, with DI Jones). It didn't take long to get a result: Maes Carnedd meant 'the field of the cairn' (or possibly cairns), while Coed Dinas translated as 'the wood of the fort'. What fort? And by the same token, what cairn?

I went back to Russell Ware's notes again. And in the end, he'd found something.

II. Maes Carnedd Revisited

The only case Ware had studied in the north of the Triangle was that of the Beast of Maes Carnedd, and his main source for that was his interview with Owen Lloyd. I reread the transcript in full, looking for... well, I didn't really know what I was looking for, except that I'd hopefully recognise it when I found it.

For the most part Lloyd had stayed on topic, but now and then he'd rambled slightly, talking about his childhood, the events that had led his family to the mining village, or everyday life in Maes Carnedd itself. Nothing with any relevance to the story of the Beast, but Ware had nonetheless conscientiously typed it all up with everything else Lloyd had said. Those were the bits I was looking for now.

As I went, two excerpts in particular caught my attention. The first was Lloyd talking about the woods near the village—ie. Coed Dinas.

*

Edited transcript of Ware's interview with Owen Lloyd, March 1980:

Most of the time, you dig into a superstition, you'll find a rational explanation. Like, there were a lot of stories about Coed Dinas, but that didn't stop the adults from going into the woods. There was plenty of game there, see—rabbits, pheasants, and the like. Always handy if you wanted to get something for the pot. But, it kept the children out.

See, the woods weren't safe for children, were they? Lot of ruins in there—not sure what. Old farmhouses, maybe. But there were things like foundations, ditches, chunks of masonry and the like. Very old. Lot of it was overgrown. Even the adults had to be careful, and so the last thing you want is a bunch of young ones running round in there, falling down some bloody hole and doing themselves a mischief. Probably never find them again.

*

The second excerpt, a little later, came out of passage I'd skipped clean over the first time I'd read the interview, when Lloyd had been holding forth about the cottage's kitchen gardens.

*

Edited transcript of Ware's interview with Owen Lloyd, March 1980:

Stands to reason, doesn't it? Even the new cottages would have a bit of green out back—so it made a sight more sense to put it to good use. Grow a few spuds, turnips, carrots, what-have-you. Peas. Better than having to buy the things, eh? So you'd often see the wives and the kids out back, digging away. Right little cottage industry.

And you know, you never knew what you might find. There's gold in them there hills, and all that. Not that I ever dug any of *that* up in my garden, more's the pity, but you'd be surprised at some of the stuff that turned up. Old clay pipes, of course. You found a lot of those, but you'd get coins too, sometimes. Found an old guinea once, I did. Cleaned it all up and got a few bob for it. And of course, there was that little statue John Rees found.

Mm! Digging away in his garden and up it came. About so big— four, five inches. You could tell it was old—pretty chipped and worn, it was—but he cleaned it up and put it on the mantelpiece. Took it to Reverend Powell first, of course—been to university and everything, *he* had, very brainy sort—and he reckoned it was Roman, if you please.

III. The Emails

Roman remains. Coed Dinas. A Roman fort.

*

Email from Rob Markland to Laura Hines:

Want me to bring anything along tonight? Naan bread from Tesco's? Couple bottles of El Cheap Bastardo wine?

BTW, do you know anyone who's well-up on ancient British history, specifically Roman Britain? Looks like there might be some Roman remains near Mynydd Du—round Maes Carnedd, to be exact.

*

Email from Laura Hines to Rob Markland:

Try El Costa Packetto unless you want to be sleeping on the couch tonight, mister. Naan bread would be handy too.

As for the Roman stuff, you're in luck. Remember my friend Jess? Or to give her her full title these days, Jessica Frost Ph.D? Guess what her area of expertise is? I'll drop her an email. Meanwhile: WINE. ALL OF THE WINE.

*

Email to Laura Hines from Dr. Jessica Frost:

Re the site at Maes Carnedd/Coed Dinas, I'm afraid that the initial signs aren't encouraging. There are two sets of Roman remains at Bala itself, but so far I've been unable to find any information about another site in the vicinity.

Ironically, while the Romans occupied Wales and left a strong cultural influence, most of it—apart from some parts of the south-west—was never 'settled' in the way other parts of Roman Britain were. Any occupation was exactly that: a military occupation. Its location never lent itself to trade in the way the main Roman settlements in southern England did. So Roman remains in Wales tend to be those of military bases and marching camps. Of the two in Bala, one camp, I think, was built as a replacement for another— a larger base to replace a smaller one. I'm afraid it doesn't seem likely that there'd be another one only a few miles away. If Roman artefacts were found at Maes Carnedd, the chances are that they originally came from Bala—perhaps lost in an accident whilst being transported, or stolen. As for any ruins that may exist in Coed

Dinas—while I agree that the name implies some sort of military installation, it doesn't necessarily mean a Roman one, or that the existing ruins are of the 'fort' itself. Sorry! As you can imagine, I'd love to be involved in uncovering a previously-undiscovered Roman site.

*

EMAIL FROM LAURA HINES TO ROB MARKLAND:
Hey gorgeous,
Got something to brighten your day here. Jessica's been in touch—looks like she's found something after all! Have a read.

*

EMAIL FROM DR JESSICA FROST TO LAURA HINES:
Hi, Laura. I don't know if this has anything to do with what your fella was chasing, but it might—MIGHT—be connected.
I'm getting the document scanned (the Reprographics Department owes me a favour!) and will email it over later today or tomorrow. It doesn't quite come out and name names, but there are enough correspondences for it to be a strong possibility—it's set in the general area, geographical references are a match and (the clincher!) there's a mountain known as 'Black Mountain' by the natives. Plays a big part in the story, as you'll see.
Of course, it could all be a load of old nonsense—this Bulbus character doesn't sound like he'd have been above winding up the likes of Spero—and some of it's frankly unbelievable. But maybe there's a grain of truth in there somehow.

*

EMAIL FROM ROB MARKLAND TO LAURA HINES:
BULBUS?!

*

EMAIL FROM LAURA HINES TO ROB MARKLAND:
That's what she said. I emailed her to ask, but she just told me to wait and see.

V. THE LIFE OF GENERAL QUARTIUS

We didn't have to long to wait: Frost's email arrived that evening. In fact several emails did, each with several .jpeg files attached: scanned pages from *The Life of General Quartius*, by Lucius Aemilius Spero.

Jessica's first email gave us the background: Lucius Aemilius Spero had been a Roman historian ('not much of one, though,' she added). He'd been from a minor Roman family, and as was often the way, had needed a patron to advance himself. He'd found one in the form of a wealthy merchant: the son of an Army General who'd proven as successful in his career as his progenitor had in his.

Spero's first work came about because Quartius—his patron's father—was approaching his eightieth year, and his son had commissioned Spero to write a biography (or more accurately, 'hagiography') as a birthday gift. ('*This is Your Life*, Roman style,' Jessica commented.)

Luckily, many of the general's friends and comrades had been as lucky and long-lived as him, so Spero spent the months leading up to the birthday in conversation with them, building up both an overview of Quartius' career and a stack of telling anecdotes, all of which he'd strung together into what Frost called 'a historically unremarkable, but reasonably amusing book.'

General Quartius was amused anyway, and it set the scene for a comfortable if undistinguished career for Spero himself. So all ended happily enough for him.

*

EXTRACT FROM EMAIL, DR JESSICA FROST TO LAURA HINES, CC ROB MARKLAND:

...but here's the kicker. I'd come across the book before, but you can thank one of my Italian colleagues for this—Maria Seragna. Her whole field of expertise is minor historians and biographers like Spero. She's one of the few people around who actually know his work well, and she told me something I hadn't realised. Apparently, there were four chapters that Spero decided not *to include in the biography for various reasons. A couple of them were politically inexpedient (they cast people who were now very influential in a bad light) and another one, on reflection, would have actually been more embarrassing for the general than amusing*

(according to Maria, it was an account of an episode involving Quartius, a great deal of alcohol, and a number of whores of both sexes).

And then there was the fourth one. This came from the chap whose name your fella found so entertaining: Bulbus. He'd been an optio under Quartius' command—an NCO, basically.

According to Bulbus, this incident took place very early on in Quartius' career, 'in the first year of the Emperor Domitian's reign, shortly after the pacification of the Silures and Ordovices' (two of the tribes that inhabited modern-day Wales). The conquest of what is now Wales was completed around 78 AD, and Domitian became Emperor in 81 AD; that would put it around 81 or 82 AD, which tallies with what we know of Quartius' life. Spero was writing in 142 AD, and Quartius' age is given as twenty in the account. If he was eighty in 142 AD, that would pinpoint these events at 82 AD.

Anyway, Spero seems to have felt Bulbus was pulling his leg— although he also told his patron that if there was any truth in the story, it was best kept quiet, as the whole point was that the affair had been carefully hushed up. Bulbus, it seemed, was dying. He had a 'wasting illness', likely some form of cancer, and so he probably didn't care particularly about talking out of turn.

The suppressed chapters weren't published in Spero's lifetime, but they survived somehow. At least, long enough for the monks of the Dark Ages to copy them out and preserve them. Point is, they did finally see publication in 1929, in a small English-language edition. It's very rare, so we've been very lucky on two counts here. Firstly, Maria, being who she is, has a copy of the 1929 edition, and she knows it inside out. Secondly, you mentioned to me—and I mentioned to her—that 'Mynydd Du' means 'Black Mountain' in English. That's what jogged Maria's memory and sent her rooting through her books.

Anyway, she found the missing chapter, scanned it and sent it on, so now I've promised to splash out on a bottle of sixteen-year-old Lagavulin malt whisky to send her. Costs a bloody fortune, so if either you or Rob would like to chip in, all contributions would be gratefully received….

V. Bulbus' Tale

In 82 AD, Quartius was a young decurion—the equivalent of a lieutenant or thereabouts—and newly commissioned, at the age of twenty. Bulbus gives his own age as twenty-six, but having joined the Army almost ten years earlier he was already a tough, seasoned veteran while Quartius was still a novice.

Quartius arrived at Portus Dubris (Dover) and was posted first to Deva Victrix (modern-day Chester) and then to Segontium (Caernarfon) before finally being assigned to the command of a centurion called Virgilius, based at a marching camp in western Britain that lay at the northerly end of a large lake.

Jessica Frost believed that this referred to the marching camp at Llanfor, near Bala: the older of the two Roman bases found near the town. There was one at either end of the lake. The Llanfor camp was probably built around 77 or 78 AD; archaeologists believe that its role was taken over by the second, larger camp at Caer Gai. 'They haven't pinned down a conclusive date for the completion of the Caer Gai camp,' Frost wrote. 'Could be anywhere between 70 and 85 AD. That upper date—three years after these events—could be quite significant in the context of Bulbus' account. Or, of course, it could all be bullshit.'

*

Now this Virgilius [*writes Spero*] was not an officer greatly respected by his men. He owed his position purely to his family's wealth and influence, and was deficient in the virtues which attend sound leadership. He was often indecisive, relying excessively on his subordinates, and those decisions he made were often wrong. He was quick to anger, also, and to violence—and, having settled on a course of action, would often continue to pursue it long past the point at which wisdom and good sense would dictate a different path.

Indeed, upon Quartius' arrival, he witnessed a most unhappy demonstration of this latter flaw in the centurion's character. One which Bulbus, the former optio, can well attest to—as it was he whose unhappy duty it was to carry Virgilius' orders out.

*

'Spero,' according to Dr Frost, 'inserts encomia and panegyric freely throughout his text.' In other words, he stops telling the story on nearly every page to rhapsodise about how everything from Quartius' military decisions to his toilet habits proved his wisdom, valour and general awesomeness, almost as soon as he was out of nappies (or whatever the Roman equivalent might have been).

Spero is also long-winded—he never uses one word where fifteen will do—so I've tried to spare you the worst by summarising the rest of his account in plain English.

*

As Quartius approached the marching camp, he witnessed a crowd of about fifty people (native Britons, by their dress) being herded together by a group of Roman soldiers with javelins and swords, under the command of a lean, tough-looking optio a few years older than himself, but heavily scarred.

At a barked command from this man, the legionaries drew their swords and cut the Britons down. This was carried out with characteristic Roman efficiency; in little more than a minute, the men, women and children were dead.

"Optio," called Quartius, and the other man sheathed his sword and marched over. "Your name?"

"Bulbus, sir."

"What has happened here? I understood the tribes to have been pacified."

Bulbus grunted. "So did we, sir. But some sort of sabotage is being carried out on the new fort. Been going on for some time now. Centurion ordered us to execute some locals as a reprisal. Send a message to whoever's doing this."

"I see." Quartius looked at the heap of corpses. "And will it?"

Bulbus glanced to and fro, then looked at the young officer, sizing him up. "To be blunt, sir, we've done this twice before and it's had no visible effect."

"None at all? Speak frankly."

Quartius might have heard some stories about Virgilius already; he'd certainly learned the wisdom of listening to what the NCOs had to say, as Spero tells us. In several pages' worth of excruciating detail.

Bulbus grunted. "Well then, sir, to be frank, the only visible effect it's having is to make the natives restless."

"I see."

"Centurion Virgilius originally wanted us to crucify this latest lot," the optio said, "but in the end he decided cutting down enough trees would be too time-consuming. We're behind schedule as it is."

"Perhaps a wise decision, if what you say is true."

"The right decision, I think, sir, certainly."

Quartius nodded. "Thank you, Optio. I had best report to the centurion, I think."

Virgilius was little older than Quartius—probably younger than Bulbus, in fact—but already plump and balding. He strutted self-importantly around his tent, tapping at a map of the region.

"The current marching camp," Virgilius explained, "was only ever intended to be a temporary structure. Our task is to build a new, larger camp—a well-fortified one, to ensure the Pax Romana is kept."

"I understand, sir."

"Do you, Quartius? Do you? Good, then! We need good men here. Intelligent men. There's a distinct lack of them. In any case— the new fort will be to the north of the lake, near this mountain here." Tap-tap. "Black Mountain, the natives call it. Some superstition or other. It isn't practicable to build a fort on the mountain itself, but a lookout post can be established. Give a fine view of the area. Yes?"

"Yes, sir," Quartius answered, having decided diplomacy was the better part of valour for the time being.

"North of this Black Mountain," Virgilius went on, "is a wooded hill, which will serve our purposes admirably once cleared. There's a spring up there, as well.[5] It's perfect, perfect for our needs—the Empire's needs. The only problem is this campaign of sabotage."

Virgilius went on to explain the problem. Work on the fort was continually being frustrated. Foundations that had been dug had been filled in (or on one memorable occasion, flooded by someone diverting the stream that ran from the spring into them), stones

---

[5] This description appears to correspond to the location of modern-day Coed Dinas, which covers a small hill to the north of Mynydd Du, beside which lies the flat ground on which Maes Carnedd and the gold mine were built. SB

laid down had been uprooted and flung away, and there'd even been fires on the site. Again and again it had happened, making progress impossible. Work was proceeding at a grindingly slow pace, and Virgilius, as the officer in command, was held responsible.

"Hence the measures taken," the centurion said. "This land is but newly claimed for Rome; it appears some of these barbarians haven't yet learned their lesson and understood they are Romans now. Unfortunately, they have the advantage for the time being: we have scouts, but they are of the Demetae, not the Ordovices.[6] They are loyal to Rome—or so they say—but they can't hope to match these saboteurs for local knowledge."

"No, of course, sir. They have a definite advantage there."

"It's a matter of who the natives *fear* the most," said Virgilius. "The majority of the local population understand that continued resistance is futile. But they're afraid of this small yet violent minority. Afraid enough to keep silent, to hide and succour them. The time will come, of course, to induce by kindness rather than compel by fear. Of course it will. But for now, they must know who is the master. So as a matter of policy, you see, Quartius, we must be cruel now to be kind later. They have to fear us more than these rebels, so that they will betray them to us."

"Of course, sir," said Quartius. "It's a fine policy."

Virgilius squinted at him, suspecting mockery, then grunted. "But despite all this," he said, "*still* this sabotage continues."

Quartius studied the map. "Unfortunate, sir," he said. "It does appear to be the best location in the immediate area. There may be one or two alternatives, but none as good—"

"What alternatives may or may not exist is irrelevant," snapped Virgilius. "We are Romans, Quartius! We do not change our plans because of a few barbarians."

"I heard stories of an island, off the western coast," Quartius said, "some strange fanatical cult—the Druids, I believe they were called.[7] Could this be something of the same kind?"

---

[6] The two Celtic tribes which put up the greatest resistance to Roman domination in Wales were the Silures in the south and the Ordovices in the north. Of the other Welsh tribes, the Demetae, who lived in the south on the Gower Peninsula, were among the first to make their peace with Rome. SB

[7] According to Tacitus, the Druids inhabited the island known today as Anglesey, or Ynys Môn, where they practised bloody and barbaric rituals involving human sacrifice

Virgilius glowered; it was clear he didn't like junior officers who tried to be cleverer than their superiors (although it seems pretty clear, at least according to Spero—who wasn't exactly a disinterested party—that Quartius wouldn't have had to work too hard). "Decurion Quartius," he said, "while I appreciate your zeal, I would advise you to *listen*, for now, rather than speak. You're more likely to eventually have something to say."

Quartius' pride smarted at that, but he held his tongue. "I apologise, sir."

"Druids, indeed!" Virgilius laughed, at ease now he'd put the new man in his place. "Where would they hide themselves here?"

"This Black Mountain you speak of, perhaps?" said Quartius. "You said that the tribesfolk were superstitious about it—"

"Enough, Quartius! Get to your quarters. And try to get some rest." Virgilius grinned. "You're going to need your energy tonight. You'll be pleased to hear that I intend to put a stop to these actions once and for all. I'm stationing men in and around the site of the new fort—among the structures, in the woods—and if these barbarians try to attack tonight, they will have a surprise awaiting them! I'll be overseeing the matter personally, together with the other officers. Well, all the officers other than you, I'm afraid. Someone needs to remain here and ensure all is kept in order. Unfortunately that will be you, as I'll need experienced men for this task."

And, of course, it would remind the new officer, who thought himself so clever, who exactly was in charge. Or so Virgilius seemed to think.

*

And so Decurion Quartius was left cooling his heels at the marching camp while Virgilius and most of the company decamped to the woods and their surroundings. Once the various inspections had been made there was little for him to do; Virgilius had at least had the sense to leave some seasoned men back at the camp to ensure all ran smoothly. It wouldn't do to have something go badly wrong, after all, because there was no-one experienced enough to cope with a crisis. (Not that this was an issue where future General

---

before being wiped out by the Roman general Gnaeus Agricola. The accuracy of Tacitus' claims is still disputed; some dismiss them as anti-British propaganda. SB

Quartius was concerned, as Spero reminds us. And reminds us. And reminds us yet again.)

Eventually Quartius ventured out of his quarters and wandered around the camp. Hearing his name called, Quartius turned to see Bulbus and another man sitting round a fire, inviting him to join them. The optio introduced his companion as Caratacus, which caused Quartius to start—Caratacus having been the name of the Celtic leader under whose leadership the combined forces of the Silures and Ordovices had fought against Roman rule. But the name was just coincidence; this Caratacus was one of the legion's Demetae scouts, a lean, stolid man with long moustaches.

"Our new officer," Bulbus told Caratacus, "doesn't think the locals are behind our troubles."

Caratacus studied Quartius in silence. The decurion flushed, embarrassed. "I didn't say that. Maybe some sort of cult, like the Druids...." He trailed off.

"You are right," said Caratacus after a moment, in stiff, heavily-accented Latin. "The tribesfolk are not responsible for what is happening." He looked at Bulbus.

"Tell him," said the optio.

"It's the god," said Caratacus. "The god on the mountain."

"God?" said Quartius.

Bulbus explained that at no price would you get any of the local tribespeople to settle where the fortress was being built—or indeed, anywhere close to the Black Mountain. It was held to be the abode of a god, who brooked no intruders on its domain. There *had* been a settlement on the shores of a small lake to the south of the mountain, but that was destroyed by the Ordovices themselves decades earlier: supposedly the inhabitants had been given to the worship of the mountain god, a practice involving human sacrifice.[8]

"Do you believe in this?" said Quartius. "Gods, and demons?"

"No," said Bulbus. "But I don't *disbelieve* either, if you see what I mean."

"Could some of these devil-worshipping villagers still be hiding on the mountain, perhaps?" Quartius asked (demonstrating yet

---

[8] This description again tallies with the Bala Triangle's geography: the description of the lake corresponds to that of Llyn Daioni, and the village to the DMV site of Capel Teg. The Thurlow dig of 1969 found signs of habitation going back to the Neolithic era, although the site appears to have been depopulated by Roman times. If so, it must have been resettled prior to its final destruction by Guy FitzUrse c.1484-5. SB

again, Spero tells us, his wisdom and powers of reasoning). "Virgilius said it would be used as a lookout point, but has anyone been up there?"

"Funnily enough, no," said Bulbus. "No-one particularly fancies the job. It's not just the natives who don't like the look of the place."

"Then maybe that's it," said Quartius. "They'd have every reason not to want us here—and no loyalty to the locals or reason to care if they were being killed."

"Maybe," said Bulbus. But Caratacus shook his head.

"It's the god," he said again.

Quartius, at this stage, still believed his theory to be correct—in which case, what was needed was to send a force of fighting men to the mountain itself. And if his theory *was* correct, then Virgilius' approach was doomed: the killers on the mountain would be able to observe everything that took place. Either they would make no move—or if they had the strength for it, they would attack.

He put this to the other two. Caratacus simply shook his head, looking mournful, and said, once more: "It's the god."

Bulbus, on the other hand, scratched his jaw and nodded.

"Even the legions aren't invincible," he said, "especially not with a half-wit like Virgilius in charge." (He spoke frankly and without fear for, according to Spero, Quartius already had the gift of winning the common soldier's confidence, et cetera, et cetera. Listen, you only have to read about it. I had to wade through endless pages of this shit.) "Depends how many there are on the mountain, of course. Might only be a small band. But against a century or so of men? That could just be enough."

"Then surely we should do something?"

"Like what, sir? No disrespect, but you've only just got here. I doubt you could win over enough of the other officers and men to mutiny against Virgilius. Besides, most of the men are out there with him. If you wanted to go over his head, you'd have to ride to Segontium. And by the time you spoke to anyone it would be too late."

"Then what *do* we do?"

"I'm afraid there's only one thing we *can* do, sir, and that's wait and hope we're wrong."

*

Which they did. Wait, that is. But they weren't proven wrong. In the dead of night when the moon was high, there were screams and the sound of heavy fighting. There was no doubt a violent struggle was taking place. Finally there was just the screaming left: voices, wailing in agony, begging for death.

Mostly in Latin.

*

When dawn broke over the dark, wooded hills, there were perhaps thirty men left at the marching camp—and no sign of Virgilius or his men.

*

Quartius took charge, leaving a dozen men at the fort. Riders were to prepare for urgent despatch to Segontium and Deva Victrix to summon help. But first the construction site had to be investigated.

Quartius and around twenty men rode out to the wooded hill where Virgilius had decreed the new fort would stand. Among them were Bulbus, who rode at the young officer's side, and Caratacus, who, according to Bulbus, 'looked more than ever as if he wished he were back in the south with his own tribe'. As they rode past the still, small lake and the place where the old village had stood, he muttered some ancient pagan charm against evil.

They circled around the Black Mountain, which rose stark and sheer and awful before them. "Even in the dawn light," Bulbus told Spero, years later, "it looked black. No matter which angle you looked at it from, it always seemed in shadow."

Hence the name, presumably.

There was only silence as they neared the half-cleared hill. All that broke it was birdsong, but Bulbus had quickly realised that the loudest bird-calls of all weren't songs, but the cawing of crows. After that, there was no doubt what they'd find.

All Virgilius' men were either dead or missing. Some had been hacked down where they stood. Broken weapons lay scattered everywhere, but there was no sign of a single corpse that wasn't a legionary.

However, comparatively few men had actually died in battle. Most, it seemed, had lived long enough to die by torture. A few had been stretched on wooden frames before being burned and mutilated, but for the most part the men had all died the same way.

In the middle of the cleared ground was a heap of... no, not corpses. Body parts. Severed limbs, ravelled-out guts, livers, lungs and hearts, and the hollowed-out cages of the torsos. The whole heap had been soaked in oil and was ready to go up in flame at the slightest stray spark.

Only the heads were missing; not that anyone had to look far to find them. Around the heap of corpses were a host of thin twenty-foot stakes, driven into the ground—so many of them, Bulbus said, that it was almost as if the woods that had covered the hill had grown back overnight.

Crowning each stake was a human head, and on one stake—taller than the rest, still wearing his centurion's helmet—was that of Virgilius.

*

I didn't have to consult the previous bundle of notes to see the parallels between the deaths of Virgilius and his men and the sacrificial rituals practised by the people of Capel Teg. The only difference between what Bulbus described to Spero and the scenes that Guy FitzUrse and his men had witnessed in Coed Capel fourteen hundred years later, was that when the Capel Teg folk had dismembered and disembowelled their still-living victims, they'd burned their severed limbs and innards outright—throwing them into a sacrificial firepit, followed by the torsos, so that only the heads remained.

Perhaps that had been a later refinement, although the oil poured over the corpses didn't suggest that. Perhaps the killers had been scared away—but it was hard to imagine anything that could have done that, not after they'd just wiped out a detachment of Roman troops.

No: the killers had left the bodies as they had for one, very simple reason. To send a message.

*

Quartius sent a man back to the camp, with instructions to despatch the riders at once. Bulbus and the others were immediately put to work on the flat ground beside the hill to dig a mass grave, which included the unenviable task of bringing the heads down off the stakes. It might have been easier to burn them, but that would have been too much like an acknowledgement of the killers' triumph.

At last, by the afternoon, the dead were buried and a cairn raised over the burial place as a marker.[9] The men were sick and weary from handling dead flesh, swatting away the swarming flies and fending off the crows, but at last the task was done.

"We should return to the camp," said Caratacus. "It would not be good to be here when night comes."

Quartius couldn't argue with that, but there were still two or three hours of daylight left. Long enough for what he had decided. "We aren't heading back yet," he said. "There's something we need to do first."

"What, sir?" Bulbus asked.

In answer, Quartius pointed towards the Black Mountain. "We must go there."

"Are you mad?" Bulbus gestured wildly round. "Look what those madmen did to a force four times the size of ours!"

"I know," said Quartius calmly. "But think about it, Bulbus. What will the troops from Segontium do when the troops arrive here? Will they listen to a young decurion who only came here yesterday? Or even to you? You know what will happen. They'll do exactly what Virgilius did: take reprisals on the locals for a crime they haven't committed."

"Better them than us, sir," said Bulbus. He glanced sideways at Caratacus.

"And what will happen then? How will the natives react? Why did they surrender, Bulbus? To avoid further bloodshed. If they think they're going to be slaughtered anyway, they'll rise up against us again. Why wouldn't they, if they believe they have nothing to lose?"

"He's right," said a Nubian legionary called Afer. "And by the time the powers that be realise they're wrong it'll be too late. We'll have a full-scale war on our hands." He spat. "I've just had one of those, thank you very much. I was looking forward to a little peace and quiet. But sir—what can we do? There are hardly any of us left."

"We're not mounting a punitive expedition," said Quartius. "And we don't need to go far. What we *do* need is proof—proof we can

---

[9]   Although no trace of the cairn remains today, it presumably survived into comparatively recent times: the location corresponds to that of the abandoned village of Maes Carnedd, and it isn't unreasonable to guess this may have been the source of the name. SB

show the reinforcements from Rome when they come. Something that will show them it isn't the local tribespeople they need to punish."

There was considerably more in Spero's version of this scene—several pages' worth of 'inspired oratory' about the glory of Rome, the honour of the legion and the Empire, plus appeals to the legionaries' pride and courage. All designed to show Quartius' bravery, eloquence and leadership qualities, of course. In any case, to cut a long story short, he persuaded his men to follow him—even Caratacus, as Wales erupting into all-out warfare would be even worse news for him and other natives than for the troops who'd have to fight them.

The scout confirmed that the power of 'the god on the mountain' didn't extend far—'to this hill to the north, to the lake to the south, and to the woods to the east and west'. Quartius took that to mean that whatever guerrilla force they were facing wouldn't venture far from its base. The marching camp, sparsely staffed though it now was, should be safe. He hoped so, in any case.

By now, there was only an hour or two of daylight left. With no time to lose, Quartius led his men towards the Black Mountain.

*

Trees surrounded the base of the mountain and bristled all the way up its steep flanks. According to Bulbus, it became almost as dark as night the moment they stepped under the canopy of leaves and branches. Thick though the woods were, they were also silent. No bird sang; no animal bolted away from their approach.

'Even though Caratacus had told us that no-one lived on the mountain but the god,' Bulbus told Spero all those years later (*shivering, his eyes shadowed with memories of old fears*, the historian wrote) 'there was a path leading through the woods, and we followed it.'

For some time they walked in silence—far longer, it seemed to Bulbus, than it should have taken them to reach the lower slopes of the Black Mountain—and it was only when they stopped to inspect what appeared to be the footprints of some sort of strange animal on the path that the optio noticed that their party had grown smaller by three men. They called out the men's names, went back along the path to look for some sign of violence, but found only the men's shields, helmets and swords lying in the dirt.

Some of the remaining men were for falling back then and there, but Quartius refused to countenance such a course of action: they must find the evidence they sought, else the consequences would be worse and further-reaching than anything they might expect to find in the woods. That, with Bulbus' backing, was enough to persuade the men to push on, but the optio knew—and whispered to his officer as he went—that the argument was unlikely to prove effective again. As the darkness gathered, the trees grew higher and the foliage thicker, creaking and soughing gently, their leaves rustling as they did: it sounded like surreptitious movement, coming at once from all around them. The shadows were oppressive, with a growing sense of threat. And three of their number were already gone.

Then there was a shout from near the rear of the group: it was the Nubian, Afer. Another legionary, a young recruit called Livius, was stepping off the path into the trees. He'd already discarded his helmet and shield, and was moving to unfasten his scabbard as Afer ran after him and grabbed hold.

There was a shriek—an inhuman noise—and the Nubian was flung back across the path. His armour was slashed and splintered across the chest.

'It looked,' said Bulbus years later, 'as though three swords had struck him all at once—three parallel rents in his armour. It had been torn like paper, and so had the flesh and bone underneath. Jupiter's cock, you could see his lungs and lights, the poor bastard.'

And Livius? They ran after him into the woods with their swords drawn, for they'd glimpsed enough of him to know he was the one who'd savaged Afer, and the quiet, rather serious young man the other legionaries had so often teased good-naturedly was gone for good. Three soldiers outflanked him and barred his way into the woods; others, with Bulbus and Quartius among them, followed him so that he was, like a beast, at bay.

And when Livius turned, it was plain that this wasn't the only way in which he resembled a beast. His hands were webbed paws, from which sprouted claws as long and sharp as daggers. Bristles of coarse black hair had sprouted in clumps across his face, his mouth was lumpy and misshapen from the long, curved fangs it proved to contain, and his eyes glowed red. Even as they watched, his jaws were lengthening.

He bayed at them, 'like a wolf', said Bulbus, and then turned and flung himself on the men barring his path. Two of them went down outright; one collapsed with his belly ripped apart by a single swipe of those lethal talons, while another had his throat seized between the beast's jaws. His scream was cut off outright as his windpipe was crushed, and his body flew this way and that as the hunched, bristle-furred shape—half its armour shed now and its body almost entirely covered with hair—shook him as a dog would shake a rat before flinging him away.

'Then it bolted for the woods,' said Bulbus. 'I expect it reckoned on outpacing those of us behind it. And as for the third man in its way, I suppose it thought he'd either run or else it'd tear him apart. But he was an older legionary, an Iberian, I think, and he was a steady sort. That, and he had his javelin ready.'

The Livius-thing charged, howling, and the Iberian first crouched, then lunged forward, driving the javelin at the beast's belly. With the bulk of its armour cast off, its only defence against the *pilum* of the legions was the hide of its stomach—and tough and leathery though it was, it wasn't proof against cold steel.

'It screamed and howled,' said Bulbus. 'Seemed *angrier* than anything else. It actually forced the javelin deeper into its body—and out through its back—so that it could get at the Iberian. And when it did, it just caught hold of its head, with one hand, and *twisted*. The poor devil screamed once, and then—it tore its head clean off his shoulders, and flung it away.'

But the Iberian legionary had halted the beast for just long enough. By then the other men were upon it, and despite its strength it wasn't invulnerable.

'We cut it down,' said Bulbus, 'but it was a fight and a half. I collected two new scars from it, and two more men died before the thing did. We dragged it back to the path, the thing that had been Livius, and sent two men back out of the woods with the body. Here was proof, we thought—an hour before this had been one of us—a friend, to some of us there. And now....'

Quartius had been tempted to turn back there and then. They had their proof, after all. But Bulbus quickly sensed the young decurion wasn't yet satisfied.

"Quickly," he said. "A little further. Then we can go back."

Bulbus stared at the torn bodies of the dead legionaries. "With respect, sir—"

"There's something up ahead, Bulbus. I want to take a look. If I must, I'll go alone, and you can get the others out of here."

Bulbus admitted to Spero that he'd been tempted—there was no getting away from the threat that emanated from the woods—but such was the respect and admiration he had found for the young officer, even on short acquaintance, that he 'felt duty-bound to go with him'.

They ventured further up the path, which now sloped up onto the lower levels of the Black Mountain. They could see its high crags and faces loom and rear above them; they also saw a little dell, like a notch cut into the foot of the mountain, in which lay what appeared to be a shrine. There was a stone altar, which jutted up from the centre of a pit in the ground. An earth bank had been heaped up to make a causeway from the edge of the pit to the altar. On the altar stood a number of small idols. Around the edge of the pit were thin wooden stakes, with heads—now no more than skulls—mounted upon them.

To Bulbus it seemed clear that the shrine had been long-abandoned. The pit was thickly overgrown; many of the stakes had fallen down, or the skulls had fallen from their mounts. But the sides of the central altar were blackened with soot from fires. He'd no doubt, he told Spero, that this had been used for the same sacrifices they'd witnessed back at the fort.

Caratacus had begun to murmur in his own tongue—another incantation or prayer, Bulbus guessed. The optio, while holding little belief in the gods, was tempted to plead for intercession as well, making a mental promise to offer up multiple sacrifices to any deity that got him out of this hellish place alive and still sane. For now he looked up at the mountain, and no longer felt as though he were studying a feature of the landscape.

'I felt,' he told Spero, 'the way I'd once felt in Gaul, when I was a lad. I was on a march, and found myself desperate for the latrine—something that wouldn't wait, if you see what I mean. So I decided to risk slipping out of line and into the woods to relieve myself. It would only take a minute, while the optio's back was turned, and I might get away with it.

'So into the woods I went, and I did what I'd gone there to do. And then I turned around to slip back out again, and there it was. A huge black bear, crouching there and looking at me. Even on all fours, its face was almost level with mine. But then it reared up on its back legs, baring its great fangs and raising its bloody great claws—must have been nine feet tall—and it roared at me. The damned beast's breath nearly knocked me to the ground on the spot. It stank of carrion.

'It was a good job I'd already relieved myself, because if I hadn't, then I would have, if you see what I mean. I don't know how long we stood there like that, but in the end the bear just dropped back down onto all fours and slunk away through the trees. I ran back to rejoin the march. The optio caught me, of course, and I was on punishment duty for a fortnight after that, but I reckoned I'd got off lightly.

'Don't worry, historian—I may be old and dying, but I'm not rambling. There are moments that seem eternal, while they last, and those moments when I stood before the bear were among them. And in that time, I doubt I ever felt so small or helpless or insignificant. I was faced with something greater and more powerful than me by far, something whose territory I'd disturbed, something I'd offended. Something that could spare me and let me fly away like a frightened bird, or destroy me with a casual blow. A swat, almost, the way you'd kill a fly—depending on how it chose.

'That was how I felt when I faced the bear in the woods. And that, years later, was how I felt when I looked up at the mountain. We shouldn't have been there, but we were, and it had noticed us and we would live or die by its whim.'

But when Quartius strode along the earth bank to the altar, Bulbus followed, even though Caratacus cried out in terror and begged the Romans to leave the place, to fall back while there was still time.

The altar stone had once been a grey colour, according to Bulbus, but it was a rusty reddish-brown now, stained with generations of blood. There were half a dozen idols on it, small white things, carved (Bulbus thought) out of bone. Some depicted creatures halfway between beast and man; others were strange, smooth and featureless: roughly man-shaped, but sinuously bent and twisted as if they didn't have bones. 'They looked as if they were dancing,' Bulbus said.

Quartius picked up one of each idol, each time provoking fresh cries and lamentations from Caratacus. "Let's go," he said.

They turned and ran back across the earth bridge, and kept running after that; the other legionaries were at their heels, and the scout was leading the way. 'It wasn't even a retreat or a withdrawal,' Bulbus told Spero, 'we were running, and nothing more.'

The shrieks and howls came first from above; the optio looked up to see dark, black-furred shapes swinging through the trees. His first thought was that they were some breed of ape or monkey, though to the best of his knowledge Britannia had neither, but then he saw the red glow of their eyes and knew what they must be.

The first of the beasts fell from the trees and landed on Caratacus as he ran. He screamed, thrashed—and then was still, although his attacker wasn't. A severed arm flew out from under the bodies. Another beast landed in front of Bulbus and lunged at him; he caught it with a lucky blow to the neck that sheared its head from its shoulders.

Quartius shouted commands, rallied the men into formation, shields together. They charged, and the beasts crashed against the shield wall. There were screams. Two men fell. But then, at last, they were out of the woods and into the light.

Bulbus looked back. Red eyes gleamed among the trees. The beasts drew close to the edge of the woods. "We must get back to the camp," Bulbus gasped, but Quartius caught his arm.

"No," said the decurion. "We go north, to begin with. Trust me!"

'And I did,' Bulbus told Spero quite simply. 'We ran like blazes, with the legionaries who'd gone out first—the ones with the dead beast's body—leading the way. Those monsters ran out after us, howling, and I heard the screams from behind me as they pulled men down. I didn't dare look back. None of us did. There was nothing anyone could do—just hope that the officer knew what he was doing. As it turned out, he did, all right....'

Just when Bulbus was sure his heart must give out from the running, the howls from behind him stopped, abruptly cut off. He ran a little further, but ahead of him he saw Quartius look back and then slow to a halt, arms raised to signal Bulbus and the others to do the same.

'Of course,' Bulbus recalled grimly, 'by that point there weren't really any *others* left to speak of. I turned around and the beasts were gone, but so were nearly all the men who'd gone into the woods with us. Behind us, leading back towards the mountain, I could see broken swords and javelins, fallen helmets and shields, ripped-up earth and blood on the grass. But no men. I'd made it, and so had the decurion and the two legionaries who'd been carrying the dead beast—and yes, they'd brought that out to safety as well. But that was it.

'As soon as we could, we began walking. I understood what Quartius had done. He'd remembered what Caratacus had told us about the mountain god's power, and how far it extended. Going back to the camp by the quickest route would have taken us right past the mountain itself, and on through thick woodland where there might be more of the beasts. The way we'd gone was the quickest and most open to get clear of its influence. For all that, it was almost night now, and none of us wanted to be abroad at such an hour.'

*

The rest of Bulbus' story was quickly summarised. The four survivors returned to the marching camp with their gruesome evidence and took up defensive positions—although having seen what had happened at the unfinished fort, none of them were foolish enough to believe they'd hold out long should the beasts attack in earnest.

The remains of the beast they'd killed were preserved in a cask of wine, and was there to be presented to the reinforcements that arrived from Segontium a few days later, along with the idols from the shrine.

The survivors were in a bad way by the time the reinforcements arrived, and were quickly shipped back to Deva Victrix. They later learned that a larger-scale punitive expedition had been despatched to the Black Mountain. One man had returned, dying and mutilated, babbling of gods and monsters before he died. The planned fort was abandoned; a larger fort would be built, to replace the marching camp, but at a different location.[10]

The decision was made that no further action would be made in respect of Black Mountain. Bulbus, Quartius and the rest knew what that meant: Rome would ignore the mountain and pretend the incident never happened. Better that than to admit that the might of the Empire could be defeated without punishment.

'We were sworn to secrecy,' said Bulbus. 'If any of us talked, something bad would happen. Whereas if we did as we were told, it

---

[10] Most likely, the aforementioned fort at Caer Gai. SB

was all promotions and easy assignments—and opportunities for advancement, for the ambitious among us. And our young decurion was.'

It was best to keep quiet in any case, according to the old optio. Even now, he admitted to Spero, he dreamt of the Black Mountain, heard its ancient voice calling to him. And he knew that the general, over all the years they'd served together, did so, too. But if they stayed silent, and kept far away… well, so far it had left them both in comparative peace. And soon enough, Bulbus would be beyond the reach of whatever god dwelt on the mountain *and* of Rome, which was why he had no qualms about finally breaking his silence.

Spero, though, felt differently. Maybe a dream or two troubled him. Or more likely it was the combination of the story's outlandishness together with the fact that, if true, it was probably safest to maintain the silence Rome had ordered. Whatever the reason, Bulbus' account was among the chapters omitted from the published *Life of General Quartius*. But even so it had survived, providing another piece of the puzzle of the Bala Triangle.

The Watcher by the Lake, the Fire in the Woods, the Dancers in the Pines. And the god on the mountain. But still I had no real idea what was out there on Mynydd Du.

And there was only one way to know.

PART 3

BESTWICK

9: THE RED KEY

I. OLD FRIENDS

And this is where I come in.

'I', in this case, being Simon Bestwick. The author. The guy whose name is on the cover of this book.

Sorry to intrude, and I'm guessing this has probably thrown you out a bit. You thought you were reading a work of fiction, didn't you?

Sorry. You're not.

This is how I came to be involved.

*

It's funny how things connect, how little chance meetings turn out to have consequences all out of proportion to themselves. If my writing career had started a little differently—if I'd just sent the first stories I wrote elsewhere—I probably wouldn't be writing this at all.

Which wouldn't be a bad thing.

When I started writing in the late 1990s, I sent my first four short stories out to one of the small press magazines that burgeoned at the time. These magazines were labours of love, produced by dedicated fans in their backrooms and with a circulation of a few hundred readers. *Odyssey*, *Peeping Tom*, *Terror Tales*, *Saccade*… hard to believe that back then they'd seemed like giants, rather than the first steps along a very long road. But they were where any number of writers starting out in those days—Paul Finch and Tim Lebbon, for example—learned and honed their craft.

The mag was called *Unreal Dreams*, and the editor, Rick Bennett, was based only a couple of miles away from where I lived at the time with my parents. He accepted three of the stories I sent him almost by return of post (this was in the days before email, when snail mail was the only kind and the rattle of the letterbox in the morning was a source of mingled hope and dread as you scurried downstairs to see if you'd received acceptance or rejection letters) and also mentioned that the magazine needed an assistant editor; would I be interested?

Well, I was, although my editing tended to be confined to saying 'yes, we should publish this' or 'no, we shouldn't' and writing the letters for Rick. On the other hand, I first met my future wife, Cate, through it—so on reflection, no, I can't wish that part of my life had never happened.

Just the part where I met Rob Markland.

If I only hadn't gone to the Sisters of Mercy gig. In April 1997, they played the Apollo in Ardwick, Manchester. At the time they were probably my favourite band, so I was determined not to miss it. I also spent several hours stood out back in the pouring rain waiting for Andrew Eldritch (the lead singer, for the uninitiated) to emerge and sign a poster of the band. I got it, too (I still have the poster somewhere), along with a galloping chest infection from the soaking I received.

I wasn't the only one waiting; there were a few die-hards with more fanaticism than sense who decided they were going to get Eldritch's autograph no matter what, especially when they were soaked literally to the skin and could get no wetter. One of them was a tall, thin guy with long brown hair and granny glasses. Like me, he wasn't exactly a typical Goth, and we ended up talking.

"So what do you do?"

"I'm a writer," I said, choosing not to mention the insurance office I actually earned my wages in.

"Yeah? Me too. Kind of stuff do you write?"

"Horror mostly. Bit of sci-fi and crime."

"No way. That's me, too."

And he told me his name: Rob Markland.

We swapped phone numbers before going our separate ways, and got in touch the next day. Unlike me, Rob had his own place—a flat in Levenshulme—and invited me over to watch horror movies and weird, obscure foreign films. And to smoke weed, of course.

We hung out a lot that summer, after I quit my job in my first unsuccessful attempt to become a professional writer. He was a pretty quiet, self-contained guy—the complete opposite of me—but with a very dry sense of humour that often had me in fits.

After a great deal of persuasion, I managed to get him to show me some of his short stories. He was very hesitant about it. It was one of the few times I ever saw Rob look uncomfortable or self-conscious. He was compelled to write, and the idea of becoming a published author was one that had a lot of appeal for him, but at the same time he hated showing his work to others. I'm guessing he'd had bad experiences in the past, with ex-friends or family members he'd shared his work with.

As it turned out, his work was good, and it wasn't just me who thought so. He had about seven or eight acceptances from the small press of the time, including *Unreal Dreams*. We published his first story, 'Detonation Boulevard' (named after a Sisters of Mercy song, aptly enough) in our fourth issue, and I requested a story from him for my first solo editing project, *Oktobyr*, a sort of Halloween special that also contains the only known photo of Rob from that time.

Rob was very camera-shy, and that wasn't all. He shied away from writers' meets and conventions. That gave rise to rumours that he didn't actually exist, and that his stories were in fact collaborations between Rick Bennett and myself.

Rob dated Teresa, a friend of my then-girlfriend, for a few months in late 1998. It didn't end well; my girlfriend—not Cate, who I'd only corresponded with at this point, and wouldn't come on the scene till later—blamed Rob for everything and pressured me to cut my ties with him. In addition, he was writing less and less. He'd always produced work slowly—a story every month or two, if he was lucky—but not only were his tales getting few and far between, but their quality was slipping. In any case, the day of the small press magazines was ending, with the advent of the internet and POD publishing. The little magazines vanished one by one, and no new ones appeared to take their place.

Rob published a couple more stories through *Unreal Dreams* before that too folded, and after that, fell silent. Sometime in 1999 he gave up his Levenshulme flat and moved away without a forwarding address. And for over a decade, that was the last I heard of him.

*

So, that was Rob Markland, as far as I was concerned: someone I'd once known for a little while, who'd moved on to who-knew-where. Until one day in October 2013 when my telephone rang.

"Hello?"

"Can I speak to Mr Bestwick?"

"Speaking." I waited, thinking that this had better not be another bloody sales call.

"I'm calling you about—on behalf of… that is… do you know a gentleman by the name of Robert Markland?"

"No, I don't think so." Then a memory stirred. "Hang on. I used to know someone of that name, but it was years ago."

"Robert Markland," the voice said again.

"Tall, thin guy? Long hair?"

"Tall and thin, yes." A pause. "Look, Mr Bestwick, my name's Keith Atherton. I'm a doctor at Prestwich Hospital. The, er, the psychiatric wing."

"Right. Okay." I definitely didn't like the sound of this.

"Mr Markland's a patient here. He was admitted about a week ago and, well, he's said next to nothing. A couple of days ago he started speaking. He's been asking for you."

"Me?" I sat down. "Well… look, Doctor, perhaps I haven't made it clear. I haven't seen Rob in over ten years, and even then we weren't particularly close. Why would he—"

"I honestly don't know, Mr Bestwick, but the fact remains that he is, and it's the only sign of engagement with the real world that he's shown since his admission." Atherton sighed, then half-chuckled. "I'm just glad you're in the phone book. And that there aren't many Bestwicks in Manchester."

I had to laugh. "Yeah. God help you if I was called Smith. So, what is it I can do for you, Doctor?"

"As I said, he's been asking to see you. For whatever reason, it seems to be important to him. I'd like you to visit Robert, Mr Bestwick."

"Well, um… when would you…."

"Tonight, if you could."

"That's a bit difficult. I don't drive, you see, and…." Prestwich isn't actually that far from the part of Manchester I live in, but it's not the easiest to get to by public transport.

"If you get a taxi, I'll be more than happy to arrange reimbursement. My main concern's the patient right now. He's not dangerous, Mr Bestwick. I can assure you of that."

On that one, as it turned out, Dr Atherton was completely wrong. But neither of us was to know that at the time.

*

I don't know what I'd expected the place to look like—some looming Gothic edifice with screams echoing down the corridors—

but it looked like any other hospital, as it turned out. There were private rooms, and there was a day room; half a dozen people sat staring at the television like so many dishes of pudding, but that's hardly a symptom unique to mental illness; you'll see the same in any suburban living room on a weeknight.

I shouldn't joke about it. I've had my own run-ins with mental health issues over the years—four months off work with stress on one occasion, treatment for depression on another—so the last thing I should be doing is hanging on to any clichés. But I fear that loss of control, ending up unable to function, to tell what's real from what's not. Or indeed, ending up in the hands of lobotomy or drug-happy quacks who are out to turn me into a vegetable.

Not that Keith Atherton struck me as one of those. He was young—somewhere in his thirties, with thinning sandy hair and a nervous, hesitant manner, but he came across as a decent guy, genuinely concerned for his patients. That was a relief.

"What's actually happened to him?" I asked.

"To be honest, Mr Bestwick—"

"Simon."

"Simon, thanks—no-one's quite sure."

Keith went on to explain the circumstances of how Rob had come to be admitted. He'd been living in a flat in Salford Quays (if he'd left the Manchester area, he'd moved back) and earning a living as a freelance journalist. Which probably explained why he'd more or less dropped off the planet from my point of view; he'd long ago given up on fiction.

The first sign anything was wrong had been about ten days earlier, when he'd started bawling tuneless but very loud renditions of songs by the Cure at two o'clock in the morning. His neighbours had not been amused, especially when banging on the ceiling had no effect. Or, indeed, on his flat door. When the singing continued into the daylight hours, his voice growing hoarser and more strained, annoyance gave way to concern.

The superintendent let himself into Rob's flat after further banging on the door and bellowed requests for him to answer it were ignored. He took one look at the scene inside, then bolted back out, locked the door and dialled 999.

"He'd been like that for several days," Keith explained. "He'd urinated and defecated on the spot repeatedly. He'd only started making the noise when the stereo packed up."

Rob had been squatting naked in his living room, beside the stereo system. A pair of headphones were clamped to his head, and he'd blindfolded himself with pieces of a ripped-up shirt. He'd hacked off his hair with kitchen scissors, gashing his scalp in places. Clipped hair and nail parings were strewn all around him.

The stereo had been set to continuous play and the volume turned up to maximum—but a fuse had blown, so it couldn't drown out whatever it was he didn't want to hear.

"When they tried to take off the blindfold, he went berserk," said Keith. "In the end, they had to sedate him. He was no different when he came round. The only thing that's kept him calm is the blindfold. That and the music. We found a couple of MP3 players for him. Keep one recharging while he plays the other to death. Give him that and he's perfectly happy."

"But not very talkative, I'm guessing."

"Not at all. We've tried talking to him on the couple of occasions that we've managed to get the headphones off him. On a good day he can stand it for a few minutes, as long as we leave the blindfold on. And nothing – no joy. And then, the day before yesterday, we got something out of him." We'd been walking down the corridor; Keith stopped and turned and looked at me. It was a rather deliberately dramatic gesture, I thought.

"He said my name?" I asked.

"He did. Asked us to get hold of you, said that he wouldn't speak to anyone else. And the rest you know."

"I don't understand why. We haven't spoken in years."

"Well, he seems to have kept track of your career, Mr Bestwick. They found several of your books in his flat. Even a few old magazines with your stories in."

I wasn't sure whether to be flattered or creeped out. "So, how exactly do we do this?"

"Just go in and see him. He wants to talk to you. See what he's got to say. If we can get some idea of what his problem is, we might actually be able to work out some way to help him."

I hesitated. "You said he could be violent?"

"Not as long as no-one messes with his headphones. I'll be with you, and there'll be staff nearby, just in case. Please?"

Well, what would you have done? I'd always felt a nagging guilt over curtailing my friendship with Rob at my ex's insistence; I couldn't help but think I owed him something. "All right," I said.

*

The room was brightly lit, overlooking a garden. There was a bed, a chair, a small table with toiletries on it.

Rob sat on the chair. He wore soft clothes: jogging pants, a sweatshirt, and a pair of trainers that fastened with velcro. He was humming and rocking to and fro.

He must have chopped his hair right down to the scalp; a week later it was starting to grow back, but I could still see the scabbed gashes the scissors had made. He'd blindfolded himself with a piece of fabric – it looked like most of a t-shirt, folded two or three, maybe four times before being bound across his eyes, so not even a glimmer of light would get through. A pair of earbuds were jammed into place and secured in position with tape. The MP3 was playing at maximum volume; I could make out the tune before I'd even sat down. It sounded like Iron Maiden. A group Rob had always hated.

"Robert?" said Keith. "Rob?" He hung back as I shifted in the hard plastic chair opposite the patient, presumably so there'd be some illusion of privacy.

"Rob?" I said, still trying to match the thing in the chair in front of me with the guy I'd known back in the '90s.

Rob stopped rocking. After a moment, his fingers fumbled at the MP3 and it fell silent. His head twitched, as if listening. After a moment, he lifted a hand to his face. It shook.

He bit his lip, breathing quickly in and out through his nose, faster and faster as if in mounting panic, then pushed the blindfold up to expose his right eye, still squeezed tightly shut. The breathing stopped. Slowly the eye opened, squinting shut again against the light—it had been covered over for more than a week, after all. Then it opened again, bloodshot and roving, before it finally focused on me.

Rob let out a long breath, and then spoke. "Simon?" he said. His voice was cracked and gravelly, partly from disuse and partly from screaming, I guessed.

"It's me," I said.

Rob's exposed eye blinked. He licked his lips, then tugged the blindfold back into place. "Simon," he said again.

"Yeah. I'm here, mate. What the fuck happened to you?"

He didn't answer. Instead, his head started twitching again, and he sucked a hissing breath in through his teeth. "Oh, fuck," he said. "Oh fuck no, not again. Leave me alone. Leave me alone, you cunt."

He didn't seem to be talking to me, but his voice rose sharply.

"Rob," said Keith, moving forward.

Rob cringed in his chair like a whipped dog. "Sorry, Doctor," he said. "Sorry, sorry. Simon? Simon, you still there?"

"Yeah. Yeah, I'm right here, mate."

Rob's head kept twitching. He was flinching, as if from threats and blows. "Simon?" he said loudly.

"Yeah."

"Do you—can you hear me?" He was almost shouting now.

"Yes."

"Hello?" Now he *was* shouting.

Keith took a step forward, but I raised a hand. "Yes," I shouted back. "I can hear you."

He nodded, taking deep breaths. "Do you remember where we met, Simon? I mean the first time we met?"

"Yeah. You mean the—"

"Shh!" He put his finger to his lips, giggled nervously. "Walls have ears."

I glanced at Keith. He nodded, mouthed 'go on'.

"Okay, mate," I said. "I know the place you're talking about."

"Go there," he said. "Ask for Victoria."

"Victoria?"

"Victoria." He nodded. "She's got something for you."

"Rob, what—"

He sucked in air through his teeth again and fumbled with the MP3 player. Music thundered tinnily out again. "Victoria," he shouted over it. "Where we first met. Victoria."

"Rob. Rob?"

But he wasn't listening anymore, just rocking to and fro in his chair again, humming along with the music, and nothing neither I nor Keith could say or do would bring him out of it.

*

Keith walked me back to reception.

"So what's going to happen now?" I asked.

He shrugged. "We'll just keep trying, I suppose. He hasn't responded to any medication we've given him, but it's early days yet."

We stepped outside and he lit a cigarette. "There's been some sort of psychotic break, but the question is what caused it. We haven't found any traces of drugs that could have triggered this reaction, and there's no evidence of a physical trauma—a few bruises and scratches, but no serious head injury—so it's more likely to have been a psychological event of some kind. Without knowing what it was, though…."

"Okay," I said. "Well, I'll see if this Victoria can shed any light on things."

"You know where he was talking about?"

"Think so."

"Thanks. That's good of you."

"Least I can do."

Which of course wasn't true; the least I could do was nothing at all. And that's exactly what I should have done.

*

The Apollo is an old theatre that stands on the road from Manchester to Ardwick, one of the city's more rundown districts. It's a decent-sized Art Deco building and used mainly as a concert venue—one example, of course, being that Sisters of Mercy gig back in 1997. (It was also where I went to see my first ever gig, at the age of fifteen—a Belinda Carlisle concert, but we don't talk about that.)

I got off the bus across the road from the place and stood watching it for a while.

"Talk about cloak and fucking dagger," I muttered to myself.

I'd made a similar comment to Keith Atherton outside the hospital, but he'd just shrugged and taken a long pull on his cigarette. "Paranoia's very common in cases of psychosis," he'd told me. "He obviously thinks he's in some sort of danger and has to stay ahead of it somehow. Perhaps that's why he asked for you. You know him, but you haven't had much recent contact."

"We haven't had any."

"Exactly."

So here I was, wondering what I'd do if I turned out there was no-one called Victoria there. Or if there was, but she didn't know what I was talking about. Rob was psychotic, after all; any knowledge she might have could have been entirely in his head. She mightn't even know who he was.

Oh well. I'd have to bite the bullet, so I crossed over the road and went in through the doors.

A slim girl in her teens with bobbed black hair, china white skin and a silver nose stud was on the desk. "Hi," I said.

She flashed a brief false smile. "Help you?"

"Yeah. Do you have a Victoria working here?"

"What's it about?"

"Mate of mine—Rob—he's in hospital and told me to ask for her."

"Simon?" said a voice. I turned and saw a stocky, crop-haired woman in her forties coming towards me. I'd never seen her before in my life. She held out a hand. "I'm Victoria."

*

There was a greasy spoon down the road. I followed Victoria there and sipped a cup of coffee while she gnawed a bacon bap.

Before the Apollo, she'd worked at the Cornerhouse, Manchester's arthouse cinema, which was where she'd met Rob. They'd become good friends—strictly platonic ones, of course. "I'm a gold star dyke, me," she grinned.

The smile faded as I told her about Rob.

She couldn't tell me much. "Hadn't seen much of him, the last couple of months," she said. "He was really into something. Planning a book, he said."

"A book?"

"Non-fiction." She licked bacon grease off her fingers and reached for her mug of tea. "He'd been plugging away as a journo for yonks. I mean, he was bloody good, too. I'd been saying for years he should do a book. Collect some of his articles or something. But he said you had to be a bigger name to pull that one off. But he reckoned he'd found something."

"Any idea what?"

She shook her head. "When he was working on something, he didn't talk about it. It was like a superstition with him—if you talked about it, you jinxed it. That or some other fucker would hear about it and beat you to the punch."

"Right. So – any idea why he sent me to you?"

"Oh yeah. It'll be this." She dug a crumpled envelope out of her jeans pocket and handed it to me.

It was a small, plain envelope, the kind you'd send any old letter in, but there was something lumpy in it; it felt as if it was swaddled in bubble wrap. My name was written on the front of the envelope. Nothing else.

"Last time I saw him," Victoria said. "Couple of weeks ago. He comes round to mine, 'bout eleven o'clock at night. Lou wasn't happy. That's my girlfriend."

I nodded. "How did he seem?"

"To be honest, I thought he must have dropped acid or something. Maybe smoked way too much weed. He was all twitchy. Kept flinching and looking around him and over his shoulder and all that."

"Yeah. He's still doing it."

"Christ. Poor sod. Anyway, he gave me that –" she nodded at the envelope " – and told me to give it to you when you showed up."

"And this was a couple of weeks ago?"

"Yeah."

Around about the same time that he'd stripped naked and taken up permanent residence beside the stereo, then. "Probably meant to ring me or send an email or something, but flipped out first." I looked at the envelope, then at Victoria, then at the envelope again. "Fuck it," I said, and opened it.

Inside was—as I'd thought—a ball of bubble wrap, with a small hard object inside. The bubble wrap was held in place by sellotape. I picked at it ineffectually till Victoria handed me her Swiss Army knife, then cut through it with the scissors and unwrapped the ball. Inside was a small brass key, the handle coated in red plastic.

I held it up. "Any idea what this is for?"

Victoria shook her head. "Sorry."

I looked inside the envelope again. It wasn't quite empty; there was something else inside. A single folded sheet of notepaper. I opened it.

"What does it say?" Victoria asked.

I showed her. "Next step of the treasure hunt."

*

The leisure centre was in Salford Quays, near Rob's flat. Luckily it wasn't members only; I paid to get in and then headed straight for the changing rooms.

The Quays Leisure Centre. Locker 38. That was all the piece of notepaper had read. I took the red key out of my pocket and gripped it tight. Even though I wasn't actually doing anything wrong, I still felt like a criminal or a spy. Bloody Rob and his bloody cloak and dagger games.

I walked along the row of lockers till I found the one I was looking for, then put the key in the lock and turned it. The lock clicked and the door started to give. I held it in place; it was only now that it occurred to me to wonder what Rob might have stashed in it. Body parts? Guns? If it was anything like that, I'd ring the police and have done with it.

I let the locker door swing open. Inside was a carrier bag stuffed with papers. I manhandled it out, carefully; it was starting to split in places. As far as I could see from peering into the open bag, it was mostly occupied by two buff manila folders filled with scribbled notes, newspaper and magazine clippings, computer printouts and photocopied documents.

I glanced around, still feeling like a spy, then stuffed the bag into my rucksack, shut the locker and slipped outside.

*

Once I'd got home, I cleared a space on the kitchen table and put the kettle on.

I could just turn the papers over to Keith Atherton and let him try to puzzle it out, but Rob had meant the documents for me. Maybe there was something only I'd understand. Or maybe Keith was right: it was simply that Rob knew how to get hold of me, but I wasn't in his life anymore, so it made sense, in his paranoid world, to entrust me with the documents.

I was tempted to ring Keith then and there; at the same time, though, I was curious, especially as I'd been chasing back and forth across Manchester to find the damn thing.

In the end, I decided to take a quick look. If it was gibberish or made no sense, I'd wash my hands of it and pass it straight on to Keith.

Just a quick look. What harm could it do?

I sat down at the table with a cup of coffee to hand and eased out the bag's contents.

The less battered of the two folders had Rob's name and address scribbled in one corner. Most of the cover, though, was taken up by two words, printed in ballpoint and gone over again and again till they were thick and bold: *MYNYDD DU.*

I only know a little Welsh. My Dad comes from North Wales and used to speak it fluently, but having moved to England seldom had cause to use it. He'd talk Welsh with my grandmother occasionally, but less and less as the years went by. But I knew enough to decipher this one.

Mynydd was the Welsh word for mountain.

And *du*? *Du* meant… that was it. Black.

Black Mountain.

I opened the folder and began to read.

II. A CONSTABLE CALLS

I read over what Rob had put together over the next week or so, in between various temp jobs (which was how I was keeping body and soul together at the time); his own draft chapters, and the notes he'd inherited from Russell Ware.

All fascinating enough, I suppose, but when I'd got to the end of the last file—the one covering the Roman expedition to what is now Coed Dinas—I doubted I'd found anything of help. The last bundle of notes was read; Rob's work, and that of Russell Ware, had come to its end. And what was there to show for it? I didn't know. I still didn't really know what had caused Rob's breakdown, beyond his obsession with Mynydd Du. Laura Hines, I thought, might shed more light on the story—but perhaps I'd let Keith Atherton follow up on that.

It was all over, anyway, after ploughing through all the notes. I was relieved, but still felt a sense of loss that I was done with Mynydd Du.

At least, that was what I thought—but I was wrong. I was temping again the next day, and set off to work bright and early. When I got home that evening, there was a car parked outside my house, and a tall, athletic-looking young man in chinos, a blue shirt and a sports jacket got out.

"Mr Bestwick?" he said.

"Yeah."

He held up a warrant card. "Detective Constable Warren. Can you spare me a few minutes?"

"Um…." I was pretty sure I hadn't done anything illegal, but that never stops you feeling guilty, or racking your brains for something you might have done wrong. "Sure. What's… what can I help you with?"

"Could we step inside? Probably easier that way."

My stomach was knotted. "Sure," I said, and let us both in.

*

I put the kettle on; I felt in need of coffee and it seemed impolite not to offer the guest one. Plus which, it delayed the dread moment when we finally had to sit down and talk. But in the end, that moment came.

"So," I said, "what can I do for you?"

"Rob Markland," said Warren.

"Okay. What about him?"

"You know him?"

"Yes." I explained my background with Rob, and the Mynydd Du research.

"And you've got those documents here in the house?"

"Er, yeah. Do you need them?"

"Does the name Laura Hines mean anything to you, Mr Bestwick?"

"Yes, of course. Mature student at the university—she'd been helping Rob with some of his research. I think they were seeing each other, as well."

"Yes, that was our understanding. Did you ever meet her, Mr Bestwick?"

"No. As I said, I hadn't seen Rob in years. I only know of her through his notes."

"So you weren't aware that Miss Hines has been reported missing?"

"Missing? No." The knotted fear was back in my stomach, only now it was more like dread.

"She hasn't been seen in some weeks—by her tutors, her flatmate, her family, friends. We traced the last boyfriend anyone knew of her having, but he was abroad and only got back a few days ago. He said they'd split up a while back. One of the things that broke them up was a friend she'd made online who she was spending a lot of time working for and with."

"Rob?"

"Rob. The last time they spoke, she told her ex she and Mr Markland were now, as they say, an 'item'."

"Right."

"The last time anyone seems to have seen or heard of Miss Hines was about a month ago."

Shortly, I realised, before Rob had his breakdown, and I said as much.

"Yes. We managed to track Mr Markland down to his current abode, and Dr Atherton gave us your details. Turns out a couple of Mr Markland's friends are also missing. They'd been talking about a weekend away, camping—and never came back."

"You think it's linked to this? To Laura, and what's happened to Rob?"

"They were last seen about the same time as Miss Hines. You must admit, Mr Bestwick, it's quite a big coincidence."

"Yes, of course. I'm guessing you'll want Rob's notes on Mynydd Du?"

"I think that would be a pretty good idea, don't you?"

The two buff folders were next to my armchair. I folded them shut and presented them to DC Warren. "Is there anything else I can—"

"We'll be in touch, Mr Bestwick." He handed me his card. "Let me know if you remember anything else."

III. THE PACKAGE

And, of course, I *did* remember something, about an hour after he'd gone.

I am an untidy bastard, as Cate would be the first to tell you. At that time we weren't living together, so I had even less incentive to clear up after myself. Which was why, to my shame, after DC Warren had left, I remembered the bag they'd come in.

I'd found the papers packed into a carrier bag which in turn had been stuffed into a locker at a leisure centre near Rob's flat. I'd wrangled them out of the bag before it split apart and got them to a table so that papers wouldn't go cascading everywhere, but I had a distinct impression that the bag hadn't been quite empty. It might only have been a few last pieces of paper, but they might have helped piece together what had happened.

I pushed the sofa back and looked underneath—and yes, there it was, where it had been kicked under. When I picked it up—yes, there was something inside. There were a couple of pieces of paper, but there was something else, something bulkier.

I shook the contents out onto the kitchen table. A crumpled printout of an email, and a sealed, unmarked jiffy bag. It was lumpy; there were several solid, regular-shaped objects inside.

I knew the right thing to do was to leave it as it was and call Warren. But there was no guarantee they'd ever tell me what was in the bag—and after all, who knew? It might actually, finally, give me some answers.

I slit open the bag and slid out the contents.

They were:

A Dictaphone.

A digital camera.

A digital camcorder.

And a crumpled sheaf of scribbled-on A4 pages.

The printout was a last long exchange of messages between the lovers, following Jessica Frost's email. All that really mattered here were the last two, dated just over a fortnight before the police had broken down the door of Rob's flat.

*

EMAIL FROM LAURA HINES TO ROB MARKLAND:

You know what you—what we—need to do, really, don't you? There's only one thing we can do. We've got to go and take a look at the Bala Triangle for ourselves.

*

EMAIL FROM ROB MARKLAND TO LAURA HINES:

Yes. You're right. We've got to go to Mynydd Du. Let's do it.

10: THE WATCHER

I. BODY OF EVIDENCE

I badly wanted to see what the devices had on them; they might provide the final clues to what had happened. But by the same token, that might damage evidence. Instead I leafed through the A4 pages. Mostly they were lists of items that would be needed, in a neat, looped, feminine hand that I guessed had been Laura Hines'. Digital cameras, two. Digital camcorders, two. Dictaphones, two. Test-tubes and stoppers, fifty. Adhesive labels, filter masks… the list went on. There were other items as well, that caught my eye— Geiger counter, magnetometer—next to which, in brackets, the words *Glenn and Angela* appeared.

For what might have been the first time since picking up the Bala Triangle files, I resisted my sense of curiosity. It might be I'd never find out what had happened, but that was the way of it; I had the examples of both Russell Ware *and* Rob Markland to show where an obsession with Mynydd Du led.

Warren had left me his card. I sighed, picked up the phone, and dialled.

*

He'd threatened to show up at my place of work, but in the end he didn't turn up till after I'd got home. I heard his car door slam and saw him stomping, grim-faced, towards my door. Feeling like an errant schoolboy, I stuffed all the items back into the jiffy bag and went to let him in.

"Here," I said. "Only found them after you'd gone. They were—"

Warren, peering into the bag: "Did you open this?"

"I'm afraid I did. Sorry."

I braced myself for an explosion, but Warren just sighed. "Oh well," he said, "least you didn't cart it off to Cash Generator and flog it."

"I wouldn't have done *that*," I protested.

"Hm." He didn't look convinced. "Right, well. Thank you, Mr Bestwick."

I made to close the door, but Warren stuck out a hand. "Actually, Mr Bestwick, I'd like you to accompany me, if you would."

"Why?"

"Because I'm asking you to."

At some point Warren seemed to register that I wasn't (if I say so myself) a complete low-life, and that a polite request might get a better result than trying to frighten the crap out of me.

"Look, basically my boss wants to talk to you. We could plough through all of this stuff ourselves, cross-reference it with what you've told us and what we have—or we can go the quicker route. You're the nearest thing we've got to an authority on this subject. Please?"

I had the distinct feeling that there was more to this than I was being told, but in the end, I agreed.

II. The Expedition

I was right; there'd been developments since I'd seen Warren the night before. To be exact, it had been before he'd called on me, but GMP had only found out that evening, and Warren had only heard about it later.

I was kept waiting for half an hour before Warren came back and ushered me into an interview suite. A digital recorder was running on the table; so was a laptop.

"Yesterday afternoon," said Detective Inspector Nolan, a smooth-faced, dark-haired man who looked more like an office middle-manager than a police officer, "North Wales police found two abandoned vehicles on a road near Bala called Heol Capel." His eyes lingered on me, just to make sure I recognised the name. "They fed the registration numbers into the computer system— later, when they could be bothered—and one proved to be registered to Robert Markland. The other was registered in the name of an Angela Owusu-Lane. She and her husband Glenn Lane are also reported missing. They're both mature students at Manchester University, and known to be friends of Mr Markland. So, Mr Bestwick, tell me about this..." he almost smirked, but didn't quite "...Black Mountain."

So I did, as simply and undramatically as I could. I tried to keep the focus on Ware's theories, which Rob had later adopted. "Assuming that all the stuff that's happened—"

"*Allegedly* happened," said Nolan.

"—around Mynydd Du over the years aren't all just coincidences, Ware believed there was something there that affected the mind—caused hallucinations or psychosis. Something maybe in the water or the soil, most likely, or perhaps some sort of radiation or magnetic field." I drew his attention to the list Laura had drawn up. "That's probably why they wanted Angela and Glenn along—they could lay hands on equipment that would pick stuff up if the second theory was right. I'm guessing their background was physics or something like that?"

"They were both studying Advanced Physics—" Warren began, until a glare from Nolan shut him up.

"Go on," Nolan said.

"Well, meanwhile, Rob and Laura were bringing test tubes, presumably to take soil and water samples to check for whatever toxin they thought might be there. If you look at that last email between Laura and Rob, they agree they need to go up to Mynydd Du and check things out for themselves. Looks like that's what they did."

"And then what do you think happened, Mr Bestwick?"

"I really don't know." I almost called him *sir*, but stopped myself in time. I wasn't letting this tosspot intimidate me. "Maybe they were right about there being something there. They put filter masks down on their list—maybe they thought that would protect them, and maybe it didn't. I'm just guessing now, though," I added quickly. "I've got no more idea than you do."

"Hm," said Nolan, still staring at me. "Show him, Constable."

Warren produced a plastic evidence baggie, inside which lay another Dictaphone. When he turned it over, I saw a strip of dyno-tape (I hadn't even known you could still get the stuff) on the back marked LAURA HINES.

"The North Wales police eventually got their finger out," Nolan said, "and began something resembling a search. That is, they followed the footpath towards—" he squinted, grimaced "—towards the nearby lake—"

"Llyn Daioni?"

He glowered; from the corner of my eye, I thought I saw Warren suppress a smile. "The nearby lake," he repeated. "They found this near an abandoned structure there."

"Hafan Deg?"

"You're the authority here, Mr Bestwick, not me." It was Nolan's turn to smirk. "It was agreed we'd handle the investigation. With the co-operation of the North Wales Police, of course—"

I wondered how common that was, or if the Welsh constabulary had maybe heard enough stories about Mynydd Du to be happy with leaving an investigation there to someone else.

"—and so we had this driven over at speed. We had a listen to what was on it, too. Do you have the transcript, Constable?"

"Here, sir," said Warren, holding up a sheaf of papers.

"We also examined computers belonging to the mispers," said Nolan.

"Missing persons," Warren told me, helpfully.

Nolan gave him a look before carrying on. "We found emails," he said, "between Miss Hines and Mr Markland, essentially bearing out what you suggest, Mr Bestwick. They procured containers and other equipment for sampling soil and water, and presumably anything else that took their fancy, and then Mr Markland contacted Mr and Mrs Lane with a view to enlisting their help for this expedition. And he did, even to the extent of them managing to lay hands on some fairly expensive scientific equipment for the jaunt. To test this theory about radiation and magnetic fields. Seems he could be very persuasive." Nolan smirked. "But then, killers often are."

I got the distinct impression that Nolan was baiting me, probably for reasons best known to himself. I was tempted to say *Rob's no killer*, but I didn't. After all, I couldn't be sure of that. As it was, I couldn't be sure how the story ended. Even if there *had* been something on the mountain—something that had driven Rob to violent murder as it had others before him, like Ronald Ashington or the 'Beasts' of Maes Carnedd—he'd still be the one to pay for it.

Nolan held up some papers. "Printout of the last few emails," he said. "Miss Hines sounds less and less comfortable with the idea the closer it gets to the agreed date. Maybe she'd started believing Markland's crackpot ideas. Maybe she didn't fancy roughing it in the middle of sheep-shagger land when she could be whooping it up in Manchester."

The Welsh half of me growled a little at that one. I really wasn't warming to DCI Nolan at all; can't think why.

"Or," said Nolan silkily, "maybe it wasn't so much the location she had a problem with. After all, Wales can be quite nice, if you like that sort of thing. The wife and I spent a weekend in Rhyl once."

"You enjoyed yourselves?" I asked. He seemed to want an answer.

"Bloody horrible place," said Nolan. "Far as I'm concerned, they should bomb it into the sea."

Warren pinched the bridge of his nose, looking as though he wished one of us was elsewhere.

"But some people like it," Nolan went on. "Like you, Mr Bestwick, am I right?"

"Yes. Sorry, what are you trying to say?"

"Just an observation, Mr Bestwick. It takes all sorts to make a world. Even people who like Wales. Maybe Miss Hines was one of these. My point being that it mightn't have been where she was going that made her reluctant, but who'd she'd be alone there with."

"Rob? But you just said they weren't alone."

"Mr and Mrs Lane were friends of Markland's, not Miss Hines. For all she knew they were as batty as him." Nolan studied the papers. "This is the transcript of an exchange of messages between Miss Hines and Mr Markland on Facebook, two days before they set off. See what you think."

*

Transcript of Facebook messages exchanged between Rob Markland and Laura Hines:

LH: Are you sure it's safe for us to go there? If you're right and there IS something here, we'll be exposed to it, won't we?

RM: That's what the filter masks are for.

LH: What if it can get through a filter mask? Anyway, what if it IS some sort of energy field? The masks won't do a thing about that.

RM: In most of the cases we've looked at, stuff started happening to people who'd been there for a while.

Look at Hafan Deg—it was a construction project where they'd been there for days on end.

LH: Not all of them, though.

How long was Britt Nordenstam there?

Just the one night?

RM: We won't be staying the night. We'll be staying in Bala.

LH: What about Russell Ware?

RM: What about him?

Look, he'd made multiple visits over the years, but more importantly the man had a whole raft of psychological problems already.

Probably wouldn't have taken much to tip him over.

LH: But what about the police who followed him in?

They were hardly exposed any time at all.

RM: Jesus Christ, Laura. If you don't want to go then fine, just say so. I can manage okay with Glenn and Angela.

LH: Hey!

I never said that.

No need to rip my fucking head off.

[There is a delay of nearly two minutes before Rob's reply. Other responses in the conversation were much faster, almost instantaneous.]

RM: We've got a theory—a hypothesis, anyway—about this place, but the only way to test it is to GO there.

Sooner or later, we'll HAVE to.

Look, you know what our best defence is?

We already know what this place can do.

We're not looking for ghosts or goblins or fairies or werewolves or King Kong. If we see something weird, it'll be in our heads. AND WE WILL KNOW THAT.

If things start getting weird, we just get out of there.

We're not there to sightsee. We go in, take pictures, shoot footage, take samples, and then get out.

Laura?

LH: I get what you're saying. It's just—well, there's no two ways about it, are there? There are risks here.

RM: Yeah, maybe. But if you never take risks you'll never get anywhere, will you?

*

Nolan nodded to Warren. "Let's have a listen to what Mr Markland had to say for himself, shall we?"

Warren nodded back.

"I thought Rob wasn't speaking," I said.

"He isn't," said Nolan, "not now. But it looks like he had a fair bit to say for himself on his Dictaphone. Those items you so kindly provided? All those files have been copied to that laptop. Wonders of modern technology, eh? Okay, Dave. Let's have a listen."

*

EXTRACT FROM TRANSCRIPT OF ROB MARKLAND'S DICTAPHONE NOTES:

We're all packed and ready to go. I'll be glad of it. A few days in the Welsh countryside will do Laura some good. We've booked a week off after the weekend away. Once we're done at Mynydd Du, Glenn and Angela can head home and Laura and I—well, we'll see what she wants to do.

The coast, maybe. Maybe Barmouth? That guy I used to know was always on about the place. What was his name—writer, editor?

Bestwick, that's it—Simon Bestwick. Wonder what he's doing these days? Have to have a look. Google is your friend and all that.

[*Break in recording.*]

We're at the top of Heol Capel road, near the abandoned Heol Capel farmhouse—although if we hadn't known it was there, I doubt we'd ever have found it. The house and grounds are very heavily overgrown with trees and brambles—the buildings themselves are nearly covered in ivy. Trying to remember off the top of my head how long this place has been deserted for. Since the '70s, at least. Forty-odd years. Jesus. I feel old.

Okay, we're all ready. All present and correct. Rob Markland, glorious leader—that's me, by the way. [*Laughter and catcalling in background.*] Laura Hines, beautiful assistant—ow! And historian. Okay, and photographer. And cameraperson, and chief sample-taker. Angela Owusu-Lane, chief Geiger counter operator. All other instruments played by Glenn Lane.

Okay, below us is the footpath leading down through Coed Capel—Laura, can we get some photos? Thanks. This is interesting. Considering how no-one lives around here—or comes here, supposedly, if they can help it—the footpath seems pretty clear. You'd think it'd be badly overgrown, if not completely lost. Specially given the state of the farm nearby.

I know some urbex types checked Hafan Deg out—Christ, that was how I actually first found out about all this—but that was only a year or so back and no-one seemed to know about it beforehand. In fact, if I remember right, they'd only known it was there because one of them had seen Russell Ware's old article about the place. So even *that* wouldn't cause much traffic. Maybe some of the locals aren't above sneaking down here for a spot of fishing or rabbiting. I don't know.

Anyway, we're about to head down. Next stop is Hafan Deg, assuming it's not been knocked down or something. Would be just my luck. Probably get lynched by the rest of the team if it has. [*More laughter in background.*]

Okay, then. [*Rob's voice is suddenly serious. It occurs to me he may have been joking to allay his nerves.*] Off we go, then.

[*Break in recording.*]

III. THE FACES

"Photos," said Nolan.

Warren fiddled with the computer, bringing up the first images from the digital camera.

"This is Hafan Deg?" Nolan asked.

I studied them. "These aren't," I said, clicking my way through the first half-dozen, which showed a dirt track winding down through a tunnel of trees. "I'm guessing this is the path through Coed Capel. These, though—they're Hafan Deg, all right."

It was strange seeing it again. Rob's notes on Hafan Deg had been the first things I'd read in the Mynydd Du file—only a couple of weeks ago now, but it felt like years. The ESCAPE houses: round, pill-shaped structures, stacked one on top of the other. Many had broken windows and a couple had split open in places, but considering that, like Heol Capel Farm, they'd been abandoned for the better part of forty years, they were in pretty good shape. They weren't overgrown either, I realised; the area around them was thick with brambles, and tufts of bare shrubbery sprouted from the roofs of the houses, but that was all.

"Weird bloody things," said Warren.

"What was the story, again?" said Nolan.

I told him: "It was supposed to be an executive village—a weekend retreat for rich city types. The ESCAPE houses were supposed to be the home of the future. But there were accidents on site, things going wrong, and in the end the money ran out. They've been like this ever since."

Laura had taken shots of an ESCAPE house's interior. It was bare, with only the moulded fittings left. There was a toilet, minus its seat. And the windows. Each with a sort of misty, oval shape in the middle of it.

The next photos showed those pale blurs both from the inside and out. Then there was a succession of close-ups—different windows, but the same image.

"How the hell did *that* happen?" said Nolan.

"Glitch at the factory, I guess. No-one's sure."

Each blur had what looked like dark smudges for eyes and a mouth, completing the image of a screaming face. In the main the faces were vague, undefined, but the longer I looked at these close-ups the more sense I had that more detailed features were visible; that they formed a specific face, perhaps even a familiar one.

Nolan nodded to Warren. The pictures disappeared, and Rob's voice returned.

*

EXTRACT FROM TRANSCRIPT OF ROB MARKLAND'S DICTAPHONE NOTES:

Strange feeling, being here at last. Hafan Deg's probably the single most individual feature of the Bala Triangle. All the others are just ruins, abandoned buildings, bits of woodland. And a mountain, of course.

They're definitely creepy, these ruins. But that's all. I suppose I was expecting… something. Which might make me more liable to see stuff, but to be honest it's a bit of an anti-climax. Apart from those faces, of course. Christ, they're strange. Maybe I am a bit susceptible—for a minute there, I was looking at one of them and I kept thinking it looked like someone I know. Not sure who, though. Probably one of those things where the features are so vague you can imprint anything onto them.

Anyway, we've taken the first soil samples. Samples of dirt and accumulated rainwater from inside the house. Managed to get some water from the lake with a tin mug and a length of fishing line. Don't worry, it's a spare mug, brought specifically for the purpose—like the fishing line! No-one's drinking out of that, I can tell you. I knew we'd need some lake water, but I didn't want to take any chances—heard enough stories about Llyn Daioni and how easy it was to fall in and drown.

Anyway, from there we moved on to Capel Teg. Now that *was* a let-down. I've got to admit, I'd have gone straight past it if it hadn't been for Laura. She's the DMV expert—spotted traces of the old earthworks. Took some pictures, but you've really got to look hard and know what you're looking for.

We've taken soil samples here too, also water and silt from the nearby brook and the marsh. Angela and Glenn have been waving their Geiger counters and magnetometers about non-stop, but so far they've picked up nothing unusual.

Today I want to visit all the main sites around the mountain, all the ones we've found reports of. There's still Coed Lleidr to explore, but I think we need to tread carefully there. My guess is that whatever causes the hallucinations is pretty strong in the woods, and it's thick woodland, probably a struggle to find a way through at the best of times. Tomorrow maybe, or Sunday.

This means we've basically covered the main points south of Mynydd Du. Now we need to look to the north—there are Plas Gwynedd, Tŷ Mynwent and Maes Carnedd. All the places specifically mentioned as sites of some sort of... activity.

Tomorrow—probably—we'll look at the woodlands. The purpose of that will be twofold. Firstly, we'll be looking at the perimeter of the Triangle, specifically the points at which some of the people who've gone missing over the years would have crossed into it, assuming that's what they did. Secondly, we'll be trying to find the sites of the sacrificial temple in Coed Capel, and of the Roman fort in Coed Dinas. The third and final part of it will be Mynydd Du itself. I don't know how far we can hope to get up it— I'm not sure if it's ever been climbed—but we need to take samples there, too, and see if there's any weird magnetic or radiological activity. Personally, my money's on some kind of toxin; I'm keeping my eye out for any weird-looking mushrooms while I'm at it.

In the meantime, gloves and filter masks to be worn at all times. Hands to be cleaned with antiseptic wipes before touching food or water. And we keep a close eye on one another, for any signs of weird behaviour. Until we know what we're dealing with, I'd rather look paranoid and still be alive.

[*Break in recording.*]

*

There was another picture; a photograph of Mynydd Du. For the first time, a view of the Black Mountain itself.

I'd pictured something high and narrow, like a huge dark spire. The mountain was broader than I'd expected, more hunched; it put me in mind of a fist punching its way out of the ground, the summit resembling one knuckle pushing further ahead of the rest. Everything about it suggested something poised and ready to strike.

Ready, and waiting.

IV. NORTHWARD

EXTRACT FROM TRANSCRIPT OF ROB MARKLAND'S DICTAPHONE NOTES:

So here's our first stop on the northward trail, Plas Gwynedd. Very nearly missed it.

Not so different from what we saw at Heol Capel. Plas Gwynedd was built pretty close to Mynydd Du itself, and on the other side was the western edge of Coed Lleidr—most of the lands were stretched up to the north and south. The woods have sprung up since the place was abandoned—I think Aled Puw's diary talks about young trees shooting up on their land at a rate of knots, so they must have grown like Topsy with no-one there to cut them down.

I was hoping to keep clear of the woodlands—some of the worst episodes have happened in Coed Lleidr in particular. It could be there are some sort of fungi here, like magic mushrooms—maybe they're responsible for the hallucinations. I've been keeping my eye out for them anyway: more samples to take.

Anyway, we didn't have go far in to find Plas Gwynedd. To be honest, there's not much left of it.

[*Break in recording.*]

*

More photographs: they showed a roofless, windowless shell of a house surrounded by trees. Pines had grown up inside it, poking up through the emptiness where the roof used to be. Some scattered outbuildings, equally ruined, were dotted around.

A couple of shots from inside. Nothing there either; the floors had fallen in. The floor was a broken, tangled heap of rubble, earth, tree roots, brambles and ferns, choking everything. The woods must have closed in fast on Plas Gwynedd; I wondered how long it would take for the entire edifice to collapse.

The Dictaphone notes resumed.

*

EXTRACT FROM TRANSCRIPT OF ROB MARKLAND'S DICTAPHONE NOTES:

We've taken more samples. To be honest, there's not much else to do. Angela and Glenn took some readings, but they haven't found anything unusual.

[*Lowers voice.*] I'm starting to worry about Laura, though. She's already very on edge—she's said a couple of times she thinks we're being watched. I haven't felt anything, though, and neither have Angela or Glenn.

It could be that Laura's somehow more susceptible to whatever's here than the rest of us. Like the canary in the mine. If so, that could come in useful—give us some kind of idea of when to get out. Alternatively—and I'm more inclined to this—it could just be hysteria on her part.

[*Angry voice in background: 'Fuck off, Rob*—]

[*Break in recording.*]

[*Resumes:*]

Currently in Coed Dinas, inspecting what may be the ruins of the Roman fort. It's hard to tell. They could be anything. Laura might be able to tell me more, but she refused to come into the woods with us. We quarrelled before. Pretty embarrassing. I shouldn't have called her hysterical.

Coed Dinas covers a low hill, north of Mynydd Du and just to the north of Maes Carnedd. That makes sense. Logical place to build a fort is on high ground—if I remember right, Mynydd Du itself was unsuitable. There's a spring near the site as well—it disappears into the ground partway down the slope and emerges near the village ruins as the stream known as Nant Coch. The name means 'the red brook'; maybe that's related to the massacre of the Roman garrison. I can imagine the water would have run red back then.

Okay—we had to cut through more woodland, beyond Plas Gwynedd, to reach Maes Carnedd. Some of it's bloody thick. We almost needed to break out the torches.

Laura had a bad time in there. I don't think she's got any problems with claustrophobia or anything like that—she's never mentioned any, anyway—so either she's reacting to whatever energy field or toxin the area produces, or she's just handling the situation badly for whatever reason. I really can't tell. But none of the rest of us have had any issues. She could have some sort of hypersensitivity to it—past cases seem to show some people are affected more than others. I'm going to have to make a decision soon—more visits, probably. At the same time there's a lot to do, so cutting the day's work short just means more to do later. Either way, it's taking the pitcher to the well more often. I don't know what the bigger risk is.

Okay. Better recap. Forgot to do so back at Maes Carnedd. Basically, we made our way out through the woods—Coed Lleidr—

and emerged onto open ground about a mile south of the village ruins. Throughout that journey, Laura continued to report that we were being watched. Then she reported seeing a robed figure. Red robes, she said. That's unusual. Generally it's been white-robed figures. Glenn thought he may have seen something too. Or he might not. Angela and I saw nothing. We will have to be careful. But for now we're pressing on.

Laura wasn't happy with me. I'm a patronising sexist pig, apparently. Christ.

Anyway, we finally reached Maes Carnedd and took water and soil samples. There's precious little left there, either, but it's easier to get around than Plas Gwynedd.

Laura was convinced we were being watched there, as well. Wouldn't come into Coed Dinas with us. Flat-out refused. I already said that, didn't I? Chrissake. I could use her help here—I'll just have to make do with the photos.

[*Break in recording.*]

*

We clicked through the next set of pictures. Rob was right; there wasn't much left of Maes Carnedd. Most of the houses had collapsed into nests of nettles and bramble, cradled in a rim of mossed, lichenous stone. A few others were still standing—the walls, at least. Like Plas Gwynedd, they were hollow shells, only far less complete. The biggest difference was that the ground was clearer, with sparse grass stretched out between the plots of land where the houses had been.

The biggest single structure was the chapel where the Beast of Maes Carnedd's short but bloody reign had come to an end. Bare stone floors, no pews; everything stripped away. Even the stained-glass windows were gone. I looked at the photos for signs of old dried bloodstains, from where the beast—or more accurately, the Beasts—and their final victims had bled out, but the walls and floor were so dim and dirty I doubted I could have seen them if they *had* been there.

Of the mine, there was nothing left; it had long been filled in and sealed, and any trace overgrown.

As for Coed Dinas: there were hollows in the ground, stubs of masonry, just about visible when you lifted the concealing skeins of bramble and ivy. But as Rob admitted, they could be anything.

"And now," said Nolan, "it gets interesting." He pushed another sheaf of papers over to me.

"What's this?" I asked. I'd lost track of the various documents by this point.

"That," said Nolan, "is the transcript of what we found here." He held up Laura's Dictaphone. "Miss Hines seems to have made her first entry at about the same time as Mr Markland and the Lanes were in that bloody wood."

He put down the Dictaphone quickly. I realised he'd only been holding it up by one corner of its plastic baggie, between forefinger and thumb, as if he didn't like to touch it.

And in that moment I realised that Detective Chief Inspector Nolan was... afraid? Perhaps that wouldn't be the right word; I expect he'd have denied it flat-out if I'd suggested such a thing. But unsettled, uncomfortable, uneasy... he might have admitted to that. Try to rationalise it as he might, he *knew* that something had happened to Rob's party, something that wasn't covered at any police training college. Most likely that was why he gave me a hard time; he didn't really have anyone else to take it out on.

Nolan prodded the transcript. "Read it."

So I did.

*

EXTRACT FROM TRANSCRIPT OF LAURA HINES' DICTAPHONE NOTES:

This is Laura Hines—photographer, sample-taker, chauffeur and bed-warmer to Mr Rob bloody Markland, and fed up to the back fucking teeth, quite frankly.

Bloody hell. They say you see what people are really like under pressure. If there's anything to that, I might have to rethink this relationship when I get back home. I was going to talk to him about moving in together, too. Thank fuck I decided to wait till we'd got back off this little trip.

Patronising, insensitive wanker. Did everything but pat my head and say 'There, there, dear'. Okay. Okay. Deep breaths. No, sorry, I need to rant a bit more. Get it out of my system.

Less said about the other two the better. Glenn's a long streak of piss who hardly says a bloody word, and Angela swans around as if her shit doesn't stink like everyone else's. Looks at me like I'm something the cat forgot to bury. And—okay, okay. Enough, Laura.

All right. That's better. I was this close to fucking off and leaving them to it, but I'm not that petty. Besides, if something did happen to me out here, they'd never find me. And if I'm honest, I'm angry as hell with Rob just now, but it'll pass. And I'm worried about him. He's been so wound up about this place for so long—he's really on edge just now. That's why he kept talking over me, telling me I was hallucinating. That's how he's getting himself through. If he sees something bad, it's just this toxin or energy field or whatever he thinks it is.

Can't say I like being here on my own, but I was *not* going into those woods. There *was* someone in there with us. I saw them. Bright red robes, a hood. And I've felt watched pretty much since we got here—at Hafan Deg, at Plas Gwynedd, all through those woods. I could tell myself what Rob does, that it's all imaginary—but what if he's wrong? What then?

Okay. Maybe, just *maybe*, I could be hallucinating. I accept that. But maybe I'm *not*—and even if I *am*, Rob was going to pull us out at the first sign of trouble. He won't. He'll keep on insisting everything's fine.

One way to find out, I suppose. I switched the camcorder on while we were cutting through the woods. Pointed it straight at anything I saw, if it moved. All I have to do is play it back. If I'm tripping or something, it'll be blank.

It'll be blank. Course it'll be blank. Hope it is and I *am* just freaking out. I'll be bloody delighted.

Here we go.

[*Long pause.*]

Oh god. Oh god. Oh no. Oh god. Please.

[*Break in recording.*]

[*Recording resumes. Nearly a minute of silence, other than the sound of rapid, panicked breathing.*]

I'm not going to show this to Rob. It, they—whatever's watching us, it's waiting for us to panic. I know it is. It wants us to. Got to hold it together. Let Rob do whatever he's got to do.

After this we'll be heading back. Got maybe one place left to stop off at: Tŷ Mynwent. Maybe I can talk Rob into leaving that until tomorrow.

[*Pause.*]

Anyway, if I show it to Rob... what if none of the others see it? What if I'm still hallucinating? There could be nothing there. I only saw one before, in the woods. Now there are—no. It could all just be in my head. I've got to keep telling myself that. I *can't* go off on my own, not in here. It's suicide either way, whether I'm tripping or not. We've got to stick together. Must. Not. Panic.

[*Pause.*]

Oh God.

[*Break in recording.*]

*

"Show him," Nolan told Warren.

"Show me what?" I asked.

Warren went into another folder, one full of .wmv files. He selected the first of them, looked at Nolan, who nodded, and then at me. He swallowed, hard.

"This is what she saw," he said, and opened the file.

*

DESCRIPTION OF DIGITAL CAMCORDER FOOTAGE:

Shaky, jostling footage. Woodland—tall pine trees wheeling about the screen. Three people, seen from behind, wearing brightly-coloured cagoules and toting backpacks as they make their way along a thin worn trail through the trees. Who made that path? And then the camera's swinging away from the walkers, sweeping back and forth across the ranks of trees.

A gasp, close by.

Another voice—Rob's, probably—calls back from up the trail. "Laura? What's up now?"

"Nothing. Nothing. Just—nothing."

A long sigh—feminine, theatrical. The camera swings. A tall, *café-au-lait*-skinned woman turning to look back at the cameraperson, at Laura. Looking her up and down. Then a thin smirk, then turning away.

"Cow," Laura mutters, very softly. If Angela hears, she doesn't turn.

The camera turns again, sweeping back and forth across the trees once more, then stops. It zooms in.

The frame's still shaky, but there's no mistaking the shape that stands between the trees. And it stands out. Its long robes are the colour of blood, livid and sullen in the gloom. Otherwise, it's the same as the figures others have described in the woods around

244

Mynydd Du: a hood with holes for eyes and a bigger, ragged one for a mouth. Is that mouth smiling? It's hard to tell.

"Laura? Come on, love. What's bloody wrong?"

Two more figures, white-robed, move out into view behind it.

"Nothing," Laura says, and then she's heading after Rob and the rest. The camera's still rolling. So as it sweeps along the row of trees, it's easy—especially when Warren slows the playback down—to see the row of white-clad shapes that stand between the trees, watching. And as she brings it back to bear on the path and on the others, it's easy to see the ranks of them who stand on either side, watching these latest intruders of their domain.

*

"That'll do," Nolan said. Warren stopped the playback with fingers that perhaps—or it could have been my imagination—shook a little.

Even Nolan looked rattled. No smart comments now; no digs to make. He was pale, licking his lips. "I could use a coffee. Dave?"

"Yeah. Me too, sir."

"Well, you know where the kettle is. Mr Bestwick?"

"Please," I said.

"There's more," said Nolan, nodding at the computer screen. When Warren came back, Nolan nodded again, and the big man pressed PLAY.

V. As the Sun Goes Down

DESCRIPTION OF DIGITAL CAMCORDER FOOTAGE:
The woods footage cut to a new image: another big farmhouse, but in a better state than Plas Gwynedd had been. Its roof sagged and some of the slates had flaked away, but it was still there. Broken windows looked into empty rooms, but its floors hadn't collapsed like the other buildings'.

In the yard outside was the rusted hulk of a Land Rover, perched on bare wheel rims. A few perished, buckled twists of rubber remained where the tyres had been. The camera panned and found something else: a tangle of charred metal and melted plastic, tipped on its side and half-overgrown. It might once have been a caravan.

*

"Tŷ Mynwent," I said. "The House by the Cemetery."

"What cemetery?" asked Warren, pausing the footage.

I shook my head. "Dunno. Far as I know, there's no trace of one, or even any settlement nearby—apart from the house itself."

"Does it matter?" said Nolan. "Go on, Dave."

Warren started the film again.

*

DESCRIPTION OF DIGITAL CAMCORDER FOOTAGE:
The camera swept back and forth. It panned, and Angela Owusu-Lane appeared; a tall, thin man, face almost hidden by a mop of long, thick, unruly hair, crouched beside her. Glenn Lane, presumably. The hoods of their cagoules were pulled up; rain speckled the camera lens.

"Anything?" Rob called from out of shot. Glenn shook his head.

"Nothing," said Angela. In one hand she held a metal box with what looked like a microphone attached, which she waved about. The box let out a faint, staccato crackling. "All readings are normal. Nothing here that isn't consistent with normal background radiation."

"Okay, then. Let's get some samples, and then we're done."

The camera mic picked up Laura's sigh of relief.

A few more clips followed: the grounds of Tŷ Mynwent. It was a lot less overgrown than the other places. True, it had been abandoned later, but no more than five years after the next most recently occupied place, Plas Gwynedd. It at least meant that the open ground around the farmhouse was easier to cover. They took more soil samples, and water from the streams and pools.

And then.

*

DESCRIPTION OF DIGITAL CAMCORDER FOOTAGE (LATER):

"What the hell do you want to go in there for?"

"To look around."

"Looking for what, Rob? We've *got* all the samples we need. We don't even know it's safe in there."

"Looks in pretty good nick to me."

"On the outside, yeah. But we've no idea what it's like indoors. For Christ's sake, you can see the holes in the roof." Laura seemed to be holding the camera around chest level. At a guess, it was started accidentally. Rob was in the foreground on the right of the frame; the Lanes stood behind and to the left. All had their cagoules' hoods up. With the grey rain hissing down, it gave them a sinister look; for a moment I found myself wondering if Nolan mightn't have a point about Rob after all. Despite their stillness, I could sense the others' hostility towards Laura growing. Maybe whatever was responsible for Mynydd Du's death toll had claimed another victim in Laura Hines—but then what about the Lanes? Maybe they'd fled to avoid being arrested, while Rob, overcome with remorse, had suffered a breakdown?

"The floorboards could be rotted to hell—probably are. Never mind stairs, or ceiling joists. Do you want to end up with a broken leg out here? I mean, look at it, we've less than an hour till it gets dark—"

"All right, Laura, for fuck's sake just put a sock in it, okay?" Rob flipped back the hood, glaring at her. Glenn Lane's shoulders heaved up and down in a weary sigh; Angela shook her head. "Apart from anything else, there'll be plenty of fungal growth. Might just include our culprit. Okay? Tell you what—if you're scared, you can stay out here."

"Fuck off, Rob."

"What? I'm just saying you don't have to come in. I'll take the risk because I think it's worthwhile. Now just give me it. Laura— *give me the fucking camera*, will you?"

Rob had gone over to her; the picture turned into a blurred flurry as they wrestled over the camcorder. Finally the camera staggered backwards, and I got my first sight of Laura Hines: a full-figured woman in her thirties, with a round face I expect would have looked kind and sunny in other circumstances, framed with brown hair, now glaring at Rob.

"Bastard," she said.

"Just wait out here," said Rob's voice. "We'll be right out. Come on, guys."

The camera tracked along the floor, before Rob's voice muttered: "Fucksake, she's left it running—" and the picture cut out.

∗

We were all silent for a moment after that.

"I think that next Dictaphone note of hers comes straight after this," Warren said.

Nolan nodded. "Yeah. Yeah. If you just have a look, Mr Bestwick—"

I did.

∗

EXTRACT FROM TRANSCRIPT OF LAURA HINES' DICTAPHONE NOTES:

That's it. That is bloody *it*. You are fucking *dumped*, Markland. You rotten, selfish *arsehole*.

[*Sniffs angrily.*]

Okay. Just keep it together, Laura. Not much longer. Christ, I'll be glad to get out of here. And tomorrow—he can go back if he wants, but I'm not. Back to Manchester for me.

[*Deep breaths.*]

I hope I'm hallucinating. I really do. Still makes him a selfish prick, but at least—well, it's been affecting me, not the others. What was it he said? I'm the canary in the mine? Not stopped him ignoring me and pressing on. All the good intentions go out of the window once he's on the trail of something. Twat.

If I'm not, though… I keep seeing this figure. Just the one. The Red One. The camera footage seemed to show a bunch of them back in the woods, but maybe that was a hallucination, too. Or not. I should have showed him before. He'll just think I'm trying to get attention or something now. Unless there really is something there.

And I don't think I want to know that. Not now. Tomorrow, maybe, when we're out of here and having breakfast at the hotel and I can just say, 'Well, that was scary, good job I'm not going back'. But I don't think I can handle that right now. And I'm pretty sure I *know* Rob couldn't. As for the other two, I couldn't give a shit.

[*Break in recording.*]

*

"And meanwhile..." said Nolan. "Next clip, Dave."

Warren cued up the next piece of camcorder footage.

*

DESCRIPTION OF DIGITAL CAMCORDER FOOTAGE:

Dimness. Chinks of light here and there. Odd details: peeling paint, rotten wood, dirty stonework. A click, and then the beam of a torch.

"Jesus Christ," says a woman's voice. Angela.

The camera pans and tracks. The torch shines wherever it goes.

They're picking their way down the hallway of Tŷ Mynwent, crossing at last into the stone-flagged kitchen. The torch and camera pan round there too. And they find the same thing.

It's on the walls, the ceiling, the stone flags, the remains of the melamine kitchen counter. Every surface visible. It's been carved into them with a knife by the look of it; carefully, with absolute attention to detail.

Three phrases, and three symbols.

An eye. *The Watcher by the Lake*

A masked face, or perhaps one covered by a hood with holes for mouth and eyes: *The Fire in the Woods*.

And a spiral. *The Dancers in the Pines*.

"What the fuck?" says Angela. "What the bloody hell's this?"

"Ashington," says Rob. "Ronald Ashington."

"Who?"

"The last owner. The one who killed his wife here."

"Here in the house?"

"Here in the kitchen."

"Jesus, Rob."

"When they found him, he was hiding in the attic. He'd covered it with this." The camera waves around. "Those three phrases and those three symbols, over and over and over."

"All over the house?" a man's voice: Glenn.

"No. No. Just the attic."

"Who did this, then?"

"I don't know. Kids, maybe?"

"You think kids would come here?" says Angela. "And even if they did, they wouldn't do all this. It's everywhere. And it's *carved*. They didn't use spray-paint or marker pens, someone took time to carve this into every surface they could find. And anyway, *look*. It's the only thing anyone's written. Not one *Kilroy Was Ere* or *Tom and Jan 4 Ever* or *Dave Is Gay* or *Kelly Sucks D—*"

"I get the idea, Ange." The torch plays over the floor—and then whips up to the ceiling as a loud creak sounds above.

"The *fuck* was that?" says Glenn.

"Dunno. House settling, maybe."

Another creak, then another.

"That's not something settling," says Angela. "That's something moving."

"Animal, maybe," says Rob. "Foxes?"

The creaks become slow, steady thumps of something moving.

"Badgers?" says Rob weakly, and then the footsteps—that's the only thing they can be—are getting louder. They're coming down the stairs.

"We're going," says Rob.

"I bloody know that," says Angela; the camera swings to catch her and Glenn halfway to the front door.

"Don't say anything to Laura! She's terrified as it is."

"I wonder why," Angela throws back over her shoulder as they stumble outside.

Even with dusk approaching, the change from the darkness creates a flare that whites out the camera for a moment. Then a glimpse of Laura, staring at them.

Then the camera's pointing at the ground. Looks like Rob's forgotten to shut it off.

"Okay," he says, "We're going, and we're going now. Let's get back. South."

"Back the way we came?" Angela, I think.

"Where else?"

"We could head north," says Laura. "Up past Maes Carnedd—get out of the Triangle quicker."

"The cars are on the other side," snaps Angela.

"I know. But once we're clear, it's safer. We can work our way back round."

"We'll be hacking it through the woods," says Rob. "No way of getting clear without them. And we don't even know what's there. At least we know the way we came."

"Oh shit," says Laura. "Oh shit. *Shit.*"

"Whatever we do, can we just get on with it?" says Angela. "While it's still light?"

"Yeah," says Laura. "Okay. The way we came, then?"

"All right."

The camera's view bounces and skims over the ground.

*

"Christ," said Nolan. "Spin it on a bit, Dave."

The images sped up; when they returned to normal, the camera was swinging from side to side, across rows of trees.

*

DESCRIPTION OF DIGITAL CAMCORDER FOOTAGE:

Rob's voice, gasping, muttering:

"There's nothing there. There's no-one. No-one there. Nothing, no-one, no-one there."

Then just the gasping and the running.

"Spin on," Nolan said again.

Racing through the woods. Then it cut to black.

*

"There's not much more," Nolan said. "One more chunk of footage. Nothing else on Markland's Dictaphone. No more photos, either."

"Okay, then," I said at last. "Let's get on with it." I nodded to Warren. "I'm ready. Play it."

"Not yet," said Nolan. "There's one other thing first."

He pointed at Laura's transcript. "Didn't you notice? There's one more bit there."

And there was. I set aside the sheets I'd read and started on the last ones.

*

EXTRACT FROM TRANSCRIPT OF LAURA HINES' DICTAPHONE NOTES:

Fuck. Fuck.

This is Laura Hines. Oh God—Rob, quiet.

This is what happened to us. I'll try and sling this somewhere before—before the end. Someone should know.

We're—we're next to Llyn Daioni. Just a little bit past Capel Teg. Hafan Deg's just ahead of us. The ESCAPE houses, they're all—no, no, this can't be happening. I'm tripping out on something. Must be. This stuff can't be real. It can't be.

Okay. Okay. This is what happened. We ran back through the woods—we realised it was getting dark and we just wanted to get out. Get back to our cars. Drive away.

I could hear voices all the time when we were running. Chanting. Almost like a song. I just looked straight ahead the whole time. Eyes on the path. I knew if I looked off to the left or the right, they'd be in the trees.

We were all terrified by then, not just me. Even that cow Angela wasn't so high-and-mighty anymore. Not *as* scared, though. Rob, and me—we'd both read about the stuff that'd happened, and I'll tell you this, however crazy that stuff sounds when you're reading it in your flat with a bottle of wine handy, you believe it all when you're out here in the middle of this shit.

But we got out of the woods. Out of them. We thought we were okay. Just had to leg it round the lake, and then it was up the footpath to Heol Capel and the cars.

But even as we got to Llyn Daioni, we could see something was wrong.

There was light, shining out across the lake. It was coming from Hafan Deg. From the ESCAPE houses. I'd seen the state of them, there was no way anyone could've been living there. But there were lights on inside them. Funny-looking light—cold, bluish-coloured, like the glow from a TV, only brighter. And there were shadows moving in them, spilling out over the grass.

By then, the chanting was coming from everywhere. Coming from Coed Lleidr, which was the only other way we could have gone. We'd have to get past Hafan Deg to escape.

We made it past Capel Teg okay. Steered clear of the ruins, not that there was much to see—but I remember reading about someone who blundered through them and got taken by—by—Christ, I don't know what.

And we were nearly there, just a minute from the path up through the woods—then Rob tripped, and went flying.

[*In background, Rob's voice: 'Laura love, I'm sorry babe. I'm sorry.*]

It's okay sweetheart. It's okay. Twisted his ankle. Don't think it's broken. He might be able to walk [*Rob, in background: 'Yeah, I can now—let's get out of here*] but I don't know where we can go.

See, I stopped to help him—Christ knows he's driven me mad today, but he's still my fella. But Angela and Glenn, those *cunts*, they just kept legging it. I screamed at them to come back, but they wouldn't. Hightailed it up into the trees and left us behind.

But as it turned out, that might not have been a bad thing. Because when they ran up into the trees, there was this... I thought it was an explosion at first, maybe one of the cars going up. But it wasn't. It was a fire, up in the woods. Must have been a load of wood and stuff there, all soaked in petrol or god knows what, but up it went, *whoomf.* And then—then I could hear... screaming. Both of them, I think. And something—something else, an, an animal or something. Christ knows what.

I don't know what to do now. I don't know what to do. There's nowhere to go. There's—

Oh Christ.

One of the ESCAPE houses. One of the topmost ones. There's someone in there. I can see them, in the window. They're leaning down, watching us. They can see us. Robes. Hooded robes. That's all I can see. Now they're—

Rob. *Rob!* The camera. Get out the camera. Film it. Try and—

[*Recording ends.*]

*

I looked up.

"Done?" said Nolan. "Okay." He licked his lips. "Play it, Dave."

Warren opened the last .wmv file.

*

DESCRIPTION OF DIGITAL CAMCORDER FOOTAGE:
Darkness. Glowing windows.
LH: Oh Jesus. Jesus. Fuck. Fuck. Fuck.
RM: Oh no. Oh Laura I'm so sorry –
LH: There. Up there.

The camera zooms. We're looking at a stack of ESCAPE houses: red, yellow, purple, green. All of them are lit up from within. The windows, or the holes where the windows should have been, are aglow. In each one, silhouetted figures move back and forth.

All except one: the topmost one.

In there, the occupant is utterly still. It's standing in the window and leaning forward, just as Laura said. It's only visible in silhouette, so its face can't be seen—its outline suggests a robe and a hood, but I can't tell the colour.

On the soundtrack, over the scared whimpering of Rob and Laura, I can make out a low, rhythmic sound: a chanting. I can't make out the words.

The camera pans left, away from the ESCAPE houses, gazing up into another cluster of silhouettes: the black, bristling silhouettes of the trees, a huge spiky mass. And in among them, roaring up and rising clear of the treetops, a fire. Huge and brilliant and orange.

"Rob!" says Laura. *"Rob!"*

The camera jostles, then swings to the right again. It blurs, then refocuses. The topmost house reveals itself again; its silhouetted occupant is on the move, crossing the space to the door.

The door swings open, spilling light. The robed silhouette steps out onto the top of the staircase leading down the side of the stack. One hand on the rail, it descends.

The camera zooms in, and at last we can see the figure in more detail. It's the robes I've become familiar with—long and loose, reaching to the floor, and with that hood that covers the whole upper part of the face, leaving the mouth exposed, with two more holes for the eyes—but what's different is the colour. They're red; blood-red.

This one figure, with them every step of the way, but waiting here to reveal itself. *The Watcher at the Lake.*

Rob keeps the camera on the Watcher, closing to a head and shoulders shot as it advances. And then it stops.

A long silence. The chanting halts. An animal howls somewhere, then is silent. The only sound is a far-off crackle of flames.

And then the Watcher reaches up and flings back his hood.

Another frozen moment stretches out.

And then the chanting begins again, beasts howl and scream, a noise indistinguishable from the laughter that bays from the Watcher's throat as his mouth stretches wide.

And then he lunges forward, and the camera weaves, swings upwards—

And cuts to black.

*

"That's everything," said Nolan. "Christ, I need a fag."

"That man," I said at last.

"Which one?"

"The one at the end. The Watcher."

I used the name I'd given him before I realised I'd done it, but Nolan just nodded. "What about him? He look familiar to you?"

"Yes."

Nolan must have known he did; how could he not?

"Want another look?" he said, and motioned to Warren, who cued up the file again, and skimmed through it to the end, to the final moment before the Watcher howled his insane laugh and flung himself towards Laura and Rob. He froze the frame.

"Mr Bestwick," said Nolan, "can you identify this man?"

"Yeah," I said. "His name is, or was, Russell Ware. Born in 1938 and went missing, presumed dead, in Coed Lleidr in January 1981. That is exactly what he looked like in the last photos I've seen of him. And yes, I know that this was nearly thirty-five years ago. And no, I don't have any explanation for it."

*

There was a break. We went outside, drank coffee, smoked cigarettes. I gave up back in 2009, but just now and again I have one for old times' sake. Just one. I smoked three that night, one after the other.

We went back inside. The interview room again. More coffee. A long silence.

"There are still a lot of gaps, Mr Bestwick," said Nolan. "We don't know exactly what happened to Mr and Mrs Lane, or to Miss Hines. We don't know how Mr Markland got out of there and back home to Manchester. Or exactly what caused his breakdown. Other than something fairly traumatic, obviously. Whatever was going on there presumably qualifies, anyway. He made it back to Manchester, secreted all his notes on Myn—on Black Mountain, the Bala Triangle, in his locker at the leisure centre, and for whatever reason decided on you as his literary executor. Does that about cover it?"

"I'd say so," I told him.

"The North Wales police found the cars," Warren said. "Along with Laura Hines' Dictaphone—at a guess, she threw it some distance in the hope it'd be found even if she wasn't. But that's all. They've found nothing else. No sign of her or the other two."

"She seems to have been a nice woman," said Nolan. "Laura Hines."

I remembered the face I'd glimpsed, the emails and messages I'd read between her and Rob. "That was my impression too."

Nolan nodded. "My assessment is that she's most likely dead. Would you agree with that?"

After a bit, I nodded. "Yeah," I said. "I wish I didn't, but—yeah."

"God knows what chance we've got of ever finding a body. But... she's got family. Parents. A brother. And I spoke to them earlier today. Saw how this whole business has torn them apart. At the very least, Mr Bestwick—even if I can't bring them their daughter's killer—I'd at least like to try and bring them her body for a decent burial. Or cremation. Hardly any bugger gets buried these days, do they? But to do that," said Warren, "we need to find out what happened next."

I nodded. "And the only person who can tell you that is Rob. Have you tried interviewing him?"

"Tried," said Nolan. "Didn't we, Dave?"

"Yesterday and today," Warren said. "The second time we had a bit more luck. He didn't tell us anything, but he *did* speak to us."

A cold, horrible weight formed in my gut.

"He told us that there's only one person he'll speak to about it," Warren went on. "Guess who that is?"

I put my coffee down. I didn't think I could swallow it.

"We have Dr Atherton's agreement," said Nolan. "Will you help?"

I looked at him, then at Warren.

"Please?" said Nolan.

"Okay."

11: THE DANCERS IN THE PINES

I. THE LAST INTERVIEW

I sat in a corridor in Prestwich Psychiatric Hospital, holding a plastic cup of vendor coffee, waiting.

I wasn't alone. Sitting next to me was Dave Warren; the only sound in the corridor was the slow crackle as he squeezed and rolled his emptied cup between his hands.

There was a window behind me. Reinforced, just to be safe. Outside, it was night, and it was raining. When the wind blew, the streaming rain lashed the windows with a metallic noise, like chains.

A door opened and closed; I stood and offered my hand. "Keith."

"Simon." Dr Atherton shook it. "Constable."

Warren nodded.

"How is he?" I asked.

"There's been some improvement," said Atherton. "We've got him on a new drug regime. He's stopped hearing the voices, most of the time at least. He's generally lucid and able to have a rational conversation. I do have to say, though, that I have grave doubts about his being fit for a full-scale interrogation."

"That's not what we're here for, though," said Warren.

"That's the only reason I'm allowing it. That and an unconscionable amount of pressure from Chief Inspector Nolan. Be that as it may, he's ready." Atherton looked at me. "Are you sure you want to do this?"

"Not particularly," I said. But I went anyway.

*

I went into the room, sat across the table from him. "Hi Rob."

He blinked. "Simon."

"You look better."

That was stretching it a bit far. He wasn't rocking to and fro any more or deafening himself with rock music to blot out the voices in his head—the new drug regime had done that—but he looked half-asleep, eyes wandering, and his grey sweatshirt was spattered with food stains. They'd stopped the voices, but at what cost I didn't know.

"Thanks," he said. "So. You read the files, then?"

"Yeah. And the police showed me the tapes."

"Tapes?" he said.

"Camcorder footage. We could see who it was at the lake."

"Russell Ware," Rob whispered, so softly it was almost a breath.

"Yeah. We contacted Sidonie; she confirmed it was him. She doesn't know when it was taken."

He nodded. "That's fair. She's a nice lady."

"Yeah."

"So why are you here?"

"Why do you think? They want to know what happened next?"

"What—" Rob snorted. "What do you *think* happened next?"

"I don't know." I tried to keep the irritation out of my voice.

"I got out, they didn't. That's all. I mean, what else do you *need* to know?"

"You know what the police are like, Rob. Cross all the t's, dot all the i's."

"Nothing to do with curiosity on your part, then?"

I shrugged.

Rob glanced at the mirror that took up most of one wall. "I suppose they're watching all this, and recording it?"

There wasn't much I could do about that but shrug again, but he only smiled.

"Fine by me. Might actually do some good to talk about it now. Sorry."

"Sorry for what?"

"You'll see. So, you pieced things together up to the point that we encountered Russell?"

I nodded.

"All right. So what happened next was this."

II. Rob's Story

Transcript of statement by Rob Markland, Prestwich Psychiatric Hospital:

There'd been this chanting, coming from the woods and from Hafan Deg. It'd stopped when he came to us. Now it started up again, and there were these howling noises from the trees. Animals. Or something. And he sort of laughed, too, or—or howled. And he leapt at us, knocked the camera out of my hands, pinned me down.

Laura yelled something, but he just snarled at her and glared back down at me, into my eyes. I don't even like to think about what I saw in his, but I suppose I have to, now. They were animal eyes and they were human, all at once. A mad human's, because of what he'd seen—do you remember what Ronald Ashington told them after he'd killed his wife? *If you witness the god, all you'd want to do is stay there and serve it. To be near it, that's all that matters.*

His eyes were human, but they weren't; animal, but they weren't. I was so stupid, Si, so fucking stupid. Thought I had it all worked out, knew it all. I knew nothing. Talk about playing games on the motorway. Babes in the wood, that's what we were.

Ware had seen. He'd seen what was really here. And look what it had done to him. Same as it does to anyone who stays too long. This isn't something you can measure with test tubes and Geiger counters, or protect yourself against with suits and filter masks. This is something else, something terrible. Wonderful too, maybe, in its way. But it doesn't matter which you call it, because it's so much of each that looking at it will drive you mad. Mad the way Ashington was, and Ware.

He laughed at me. His breath stank. And then he climbed off me and he just turned around and went back up the steps into his ESCAPE house. Went inside, shut the door, and looked down at us.

I grabbed up the camcorder. God knows why. It had switched off and I didn't see a point in filming anything else. Laura got to me, took hold of me, shouting something I couldn't hear over the howling and the chanting. She got me on my feet.

And then somebody ran at us, screaming.

Laura and I grabbed at one another, but it was only Angela. She was shaking. There were cuts on her face and her jacket was ripped to shreds at the shoulder with blood coming through there too. She nearly fell; Laura caught and steadied her. "They got Glenn," she said, over and over. "Up in the trees. Monsters. Monsters. They got Glenn."

The chanting went on, low and relentless. Something about it had changed now; it felt like a threat. And something else; it was still low, but at the same time it seemed to be getting louder.

That was when I realised that it wasn't just coming from up ahead anymore. Coed Capel reached out to the side of us, and the chanting was coming from there. Far behind us was Coed Lleidr, and I could see fires burning there—and I could *feel*, as much as hear, the wash of sound coming out of it.

Angela was hanging onto Laura and sobbing. Shapes moved inside the ESCAPE houses, silhouetted against the broken windows. Splashing sounds came from the lake as we backed away—and from the marshes behind us as we neared those.

"Oh fuck," I heard Laura saying. "Oh fuck, fuck, fuckity-fuckity-*fuck*. What do we do?"

"We're going to die," whispered Angela, and started mumbling what I think may have been a prayer. I decided not to mention that death might well be the least of our worries, after seeing Ware.

"Rob?" Laura spoke through her teeth. "Come on, boyfriend, you're supposed to be the fucking expert here."

Well, what was I going to tell her? That I'd thought I was so bloody clever and hadn't been? I couldn't talk about hallucinations any more—hallucinations didn't do what Ware had done, hadn't killed Glenn and nearly killed Angela.

"Rob!" Laura shouted. "Come on, what do we *do*?"

Wait for it to kill us, if we're lucky, I nearly said, but didn't. "North," I said. "It's the only chance we've got. Never get through these woods." Even if it hadn't been for the chanting, I wouldn't have fancied trying to get through Coed Lleidr, not after reading what had happened to the others who'd gone in there—Oscar Childwall, Huw Llewellyn, Aled Puw. Aled and Llewellyn had made it out, just, but it had only been playing with Childwall, waiting to reel him back in. "Go north, past Coed Dinas. Get out that way, to the road. Only chance."

It wasn't much of a chance—and I know now, probably knew then, that it wasn't really any chance at all—but it seemed better than standing around waiting for the chop, especially as new howls were coming out of the woods. So the three of us turned and legged it. We could hear things splashing in the lake and in the marshes as we went around it. Finally we were clear of the lake and heading northward. Any chance of a brew, mate?

[*Break in transcript.*]

*

I had to laugh at that; Rob threw it in so casually, so matter-of-factly. I couldn't decide whether that was a part of his madness or if it was just something of the old Rob surfacing for a moment, maybe for the last time.

"I don't see why not," I said. "If Doctor Atherton doesn't have any objection."

Rob blinked and looked away at the mention of Atherton. He knew they were watching and listening, of course—Christ, he'd said so himself—but I think he'd blotted them out while he was talking to me. It was easier to tell a story like this when you thought it was one-on-one.

Keith stuck his head into the room. "Coffee?"

"Please," said Rob.

"Me too," I said.

We drank in silence. I studied Rob. He seemed quieter, stiller, except for little things. His free hand was shaking badly; his lips moved soundlessly between sips of coffee and when he closed his eyes they roved about under the lids as if in REM.

"You okay to carry on?" I asked him eventually.

He nodded fast, not looking at me, then took a deep breath. "Trouble was, really, there was no way to avoid going through at least some woodland. They'd grown thicker when you got near the mountain. But you probably know that if you've looked at the stuff I left you."

"Yeah," I said. "You had to go through woodland going there and back when you went to Maes Carnedd and Tŷ Mynwent. Was it the same on the other side of the mountain?"

He nodded again. "Those pines grow fast. Faster than they should. And for some reason, the woods always seem to be the most dangerous parts. Apart from the mountain itself. Obviously. Not that anywhere around there's safe. Anyway—"

*

TRANSCRIPT OF STATEMENT BY ROB MARKLAND, PRESTWICH PSYCHIATRIC HOSPITAL:

We went as fast as we could, which wasn't very. It was dark now, and we were all exhausted. My ankle was okay—no serious damage—but it was still giving me twinges as I went, which slowed me down. And Angela was in bad shape. She was bleeding and in pain, and—well, I don't exactly know what she'd seen happen to Glenn, but whatever it was, he was her husband and she knew he was dead or as good as. I don't know how she kept going at all, frankly. Some sort of autopilot.

Laura held her up and kept her going. Funny—Laura had been the most on edge of any of us about coming here, but out of us all she was keeping it together best. Good instincts, I suppose. She hadn't even liked Angela, I know. But that didn't matter now.

The chanting kept up as we went. I stopped and looked behind us a few times; never saw any sign of anyone following—they'd stick out a mile, in those white robes—but the chanting never seemed to fade. It was all around us, coming from everywhere and nowhere all at once. When we actually got to the woods it was nearly a relief. Nearly. Flailing our way through those branches and twigs was a nightmare. I still don't know how none of us lost an eye.

It was hard going. Harder going than it'd been before. Of course it was darker now, and more confused, with the panic and everything. But when we'd come through here before—and I'm sure of this—the paths through the woods had been easier to find. Now it was as if they'd vanished. I was having to fight for every foot of progress: bending or snapping branches out of the way or stepping over them, ducking under them. There was no chance of getting into any kind of easy rhythm. All we could do was battle through the thickets, obstacle by obstacle.

And then....

Well, this is where it starts to get a bit confusing. There's a bit of a gap here, you see. I remember the woods, and everything becoming a blur of twigs and branches. Couldn't see the wood for the trees, I guess! Ha. Anyway.

The next thing I remember is Laura hitting me and shouting my name. She was shouting to Angela too, but didn't seem to be getting much help. Laura was slapping at my face, punching at my shoulders. I grabbed her hands at the wrists and shouted at her to stop it. Calm down, I told her. It's the mountain. It's affecting you.

"Me?" she yelled back, nearly laughing. "Affected *me*? Look at where we *are*, for Christ's sake."

I started to ask her what she meant, and then I realised two things. The first was that we were on open ground, although there were trees up ahead, and when I looked around there was a bunch of them behind us. Angela was hanging back between us and the trees to the rear; she looked terrified.

And then I realised the other thing that was different.

The ground wasn't flat; we were on a slope, and a steep one. I looked up and the moon came out. It shone through the trees and it picked up outlines above me: cliffs and crags and slopes, and I'm sure I could see a couple of footpaths on them, although I don't see how there could have been. No-one I knew of had ever gone up Mynydd Du, after all. Definitely not regularly enough to leave footprints.

Mynydd Du, yeah; that's where we were. I don't know how. Well, I do, really, if I'm honest. It was that place. The mountain itself.

Oh come on, Simon. Don't look at me like that. You must have guessed. You didn't really still think it was all about hallucinogens, did you? Toxins in the water, weird energy fields? Load of bollocks. I was face to face with it that night and I knew it was nothing like that. There's something on the mountain, or *in* the mountain—I don't know which and I don't bloody care, it doesn't matter. Call it a devil, call it a god. Those are just words. Tags, something to call it to make it sound less. It doesn't really have a name. It just *is*. Whatever it is, that's where it lives, and it wants to be left alone. And if anyone disturbs it—well, it all depends what mood the god's in. Maybe it'll just toy with you a little, then let you go. Might just take you then and there. Or it might play you out, like a fish on a line—let you think you've got away, then reel you back in. When it gets its hooks in you, it *has* you. And I don't think you have to go there for it to do that. Just reading about it can be enough. Knowing too much.

Of course, you can get on the right side of it—like the villagers did at Capel Teg. It doesn't *need* sacrifices or anything, but they amused it. That's why it let people live by Llyn Daioni for so long. Amusement. After they were wiped out, it decided it couldn't be bothered to restock the pond. It just wanted to be on its own. And by and large, it's got what it wanted. Of course, there's always some clever bastard, time to time, thinks he knows better. Gareth Puw, Ronald Ashington, Guy FitzUrse, Centurion Gaius Lucius Virgilius. Russell Ware. And now me. I'm just the last in a long line of funny little insects who got too bothersome. I thought I'd got clear, but I think I... amused it. So it's played me, out like a fish.

But anyway. That's all stuff I realised later. I mean, I understood some of it then and there, but the rest... well, I've had plenty of time to work out just what a stupid little bastard I've been.

The thing was—I was sort of out of the trance I'd been in, but not all the way. Because I was still going up. Still trying to climb the mountain to whatever the hell was up at the summit. I couldn't stop.

Laura was slapping me, shaking me, pushing me, grabbing at me, trying to hold me back. "Help me!" she screamed down at Angela. "Don't just fucking stand there you cow, fucking help me!" But Angela just stood there staring up at us, then shuffled backward. And then shuffled backwards again.

"Angela!" Laura screamed.

"Fuck you!" Angela screamed back, then turned and ran, vanishing into the woods.

"Bitch!" Laura screamed after her, and that was enough for me; she was distracted, she let go of me, and I was off, sometimes walking and other times crawling on all fours, up the mountain to the trees above and whatever lay beyond them.

"No," Laura was shouting. She clutched at my belt. I kicked out at her and she yelped in pain. I don't understand why I did that. I loved Laura. I honestly did. I don't understand why I felt I had to keep climbing. All I know is that... it was my purpose. Something had happened along the way that made going up that mountain the most natural thing in the world. The only thing that mattered.

Perhaps it was—yes, the more I think about it the more I think it was. The singing. I thought I could hear singing. Not the chanting that had come out of the woods, but... song. Beautiful, beautiful song. No, I can't sing it for you. It's gone now. You never had that, Simon? A tune that's beautiful, you love it, but as soon as it stops playing it goes out of your head? Like that. I could just about hear it, but it faded in and out, as if the wind was taking bits of it away, or the singer was moving so that trees or crags got between me and some of the words. But I might be able to hear it properly, in its full glory, where I'd remember it and never forget. If, if I just climbed a little further.

Laura rugby-tackled me round the ankles and I went sprawling forward. I thrashed my legs free and kicked out, but she jumped aside before throwing herself on me and trying to pin me down. I screamed and flailed about like a kid having a tantrum. I hit her, Simon. Punched her in the face. Didn't stop her, though; she punched me right back.

The blow snapped my head round and it hit the rock. There was a bright flash; then nothing.

I don't know how much later it was when I came round. I didn't wake up all at once. It was in and out. I was lying on my front on cold stone and grass. I was cold, shivering, but I didn't want to get up. Too much work. So I closed my eyes and went away again. That repeated itself two or three times; finally I was shaking so hard from the cold I *had* to get up.

I looked around, but there was no sign of Laura, or Angela. I was on my own. I felt different, though: clearer-headed. Laura knocking me out might have broken the spell. But I could still hear the music.

I shouted for her, and Angela, but there was nothing. The wind was blowing hard, and it was beginning to rain.

I started up the mountain again. But it was different this time. I wasn't in the trance. I was going because I needed to find Laura. Angela too, if I could, but Laura most of all.

I kept climbing until the final band of pines sprouted in front of me. I fell on my knees, gasping, looked around—fucking hell, what a view. I could see Llyn Daioni below, and Hafan Deg, still all lit up. I could see the woods around the mountain, the fire burning at Coed Capel, and in Coed Dinas and Coed Lleidr too.

Further out in the distance I could see other lights—streetlights, electric lights, sodium vapour lights. The lights of the sane, rational twenty-first century, where there were no ghosts or gods, where the workmen who'd built Hafan Deg had died by tragic accidents and nothing more, where Britt Nordenstam was murdered by a jealous lover, a college tutor, a student, where the Beast of Maes Carnedd was just a madman on a killing spree and everything else imagination or Chinese whispers or superstition. Where Russell Ware had fallen in Llyn Daioni and drowned; where Ronald Ashington had gone mad from the failure of his dreams and gunned his wife down, where Gareth Puw had gone mad for the same reason and, maddened, had driven himself to the stroke that killed him. Where the stories of Oscar Childwall and General Quartius were just old wives' tales. Where Mynydd Du was just a mountain and the woods around it just woods.

I could see out to Bala, see the moon glimmer on the long wide lake. Even headlights moving along the lake road. So close but so far away. I felt I could almost have touched them. But 'almost' is a cruel word, isn't it Simon?

I was near the very top of Mynydd Du. As far as I knew, no-one had come this way in years—decades, centuries maybe. Maybe not ever. But there were paths, worn in the dirt, and you'd only have those if people were still passing back and forth.

But none of that mattered now. I'd climbed Mynydd Du. I'd conquered Black Mountain. I shouted for Laura again, but there was only the singing. But I thought—somewhere I thought I heard her voice, coming out of the woods.

I forced myself in among the pine trees. God knows how they grew there. The ground sloped up and it was uneven, rocky. I flashed my torch around. I glimpsed shapes among the trees, moving this way and that, but always in the corner of my eye—never there when I turned and looked.

The singing got louder, louder, louder. The ground levelled out. I was at the very top. And then light flashed through the trees—firelight. Something was burning on top of Mynydd Du.

I ran forward. I could see a path at last, and I followed it, winding through the trees. There was singing, there was fire, and there were shapes moving against the fire; silhouettes writhing, dancing, flinging their long, stretched shadows through the trees and across the firelit ground.

And then I realised, I remembered: dancers. There was that phrase that had kept coming up, again and again, in the story of Mynydd Du. Craig Stowe had claimed to have seen them the night Britt Nordenstam disappeared; Ronald Ashington had carved them into every wood, stone and metal surface of the attic at Tŷ Mynwent after he'd killed his wife. *The dancers in the pines.*

And one of the silhouettes up ahead—one of the dancers—I knew the shape of that body; I got into bed beside it at night and held it close.

I shouted but the singing was too loud now, I couldn't hear anything else. A few last steps, and then I burst through the trees and I could see.

There was a clearing, a huge clearing, in the woods on top of the mountain. And right in the centre of it was a hole, a big gaping one in the rock. The fire was burning down inside it, roaring up to kiss the starlit sky. There were poles stood around it, almost high as the trees, and there were skulls on them, and there were men and women in white robes and hoods and one in a red robe and hood, and there were the dancers, and I knew their faces.

I recognised Laura outright, of course. Her face had that earnest look it sometimes took on when she was in the middle of learning something new and important as she hopped from one foot to the next, moving her arms from one position to another. Earnest, but then sometimes that look would go and there'd be another expression on her face—lost, frightened, then terrified as she realised where she was, where she always would be, where she will be now, Simon—and her eyes would dart madly around. They found me once or twice. She tried to move her lips, to call out, but couldn't. And what could I have done? Nothing. I promise you that, Si. There was nothing I could have done to save her. It was already too late.

It didn't take me long to find Angela, all in the same boat. Glenn was there too—he was bloody and badly mauled, but still alive. Perhaps he always would be, now.

And then there were the rest.

The first I recognised was a gaunt man in filthy clothes. He had long, straggly hair held back with a sweatband, a scarred face that pulled his mouth askew, a crooked nose, and those teeth that weren't missing were yellowed. I knew I knew him, but not from where, not at first. And then it clicked. It was Craig Stowe. Remember him? They released him when they found out it couldn't have been him, but it was too late because he was fucked on drugs. Except that I think it was too late long before that. He'd seen, you see—glimpsed, anyway. Glimpsed something. He'd seen the god on the mountain reach out and take Britt. Why her? Maybe she could hear the call the clearest. Or perhaps because she was beautiful, because she shone, and it wanted her for itself. All the time after that he'd heard voices, the singing. That's why the drugs, I think. To make them go away.

As for Britt Nordenstam herself—I don't know how she got away from the mountain god, but she must have somehow. It killed her, of course, but at least she wasn't with the rest, condemned to dance and dance among the pines. But poor Craig Stowe, eh, Simon? In his way, he'd loved Britt and tried to save her—and this was his reward, and he didn't even have his beloved to keep him company, the poor bastard. Or maybe it was a comfort to know she *wasn't* there. Who knows?

And yes, I know what you're going to say—Craig Stowe vanished into thin air all the way back in 1979, when you and I had just started primary school, but here he was thirty-odd years later, looking no different. But then again, you saw the Watcher. You know who he was, or who he'd become.

How many did I see in that clearing? It looked like hundreds, but I can't be sure. I saw Roman soldiers and men in plate armour, I'm sure of it. And I saw all these others I recognised from the old files.

There was another gaunt man, but older, in his thirties. Except his hair was grey. But again I knew I knew the face, and so I did. His name was John Rogers; he was a Great War veteran who lived in Llangwm, and he disappeared on 5th October, 1932. After that they came thick and fast; the tall thin man with the white hair and Van Dyke beard was Richard Herbert, the amateur painter who'd set out to paint the Black Mountain in August 1948. The round-faced woman in her fifties with her hair in a bun was Margaret Jones, who walked out of her house in Ty-Nant one day in 1942 and was never seen again. A little blonde-haired girl—eight-year-old Katherine Owen from Llandrillo, who disappeared in February 1953.

And a small, blue-eyed woman with short black hair, wearing jeans and a red coat, a knapsack on her back: Rachel Morris, who vanished somewhere on the road between Bala and Sarnau just before Christmas in 1964. Twenty years old. She'd been struggling at college, trying to decide what to do, but the mountain god had taken that decision out of her hands. What do you think she'd be now, Simon, if she'd—I was going to say if she'd lived, but that's the worst of it, isn't it? She did live. She isn't dead. None of them are. But you've read the file. 1964—what's that now, nearly fifty years? She'd be seventy. Would she have married, had children? Grandchildren? Would she have stayed at University, changed subjects? Who knows what the world would have seen from her, from any of them? But the mountain decided otherwise and it took her, to dance for it forever among the pines.

I saw others, too—there were things that were half-beast and half-man, with glowing red eyes. I doubt I have to tell you what they were. You've read about the Beast of Maes Carnedd. I saw some men in what looked like nineteenth century clothes—most of them were rough-looking sorts, but one was a portly man in a dog-collar. Oscar Childwall, at a guess, and the men who were lost trying to help him rescue Sir Percy Chetwynd. And there were others, too. From every century. All of them. And every one of them, their eyes were the same. Apart from Laura and Angela and Glenn, who were new and still finding the steps of the dance. But all the others—there was a terrible kind of rapture in their eyes. That and the terror I could already see in Laura's.

And across the clearing from the fire, in the trees opposite, there were these others. I don't know what the fuck they were and I don't want to.

They looked like men—a little like men. But they weren't. They were white and pale and smooth and *boneless*, somehow. All they had in common with men was the general shape. They had no faces, no features of any kind. They just swayed and writhed and danced and *undulated* somehow, twining their bodies around the trees like snakes.

How long was I watching this for? No idea. Sorry. Not a clue. Was I falling back into the trance? I might have been. But then I saw something that snapped me out of it.

Beyond the fire, beyond the white dancers, something stirred: I heard the creak and snap of twigs and branches, heard the trees rustle as something moved and rose. Above the trees were the millions of stars, the Milky Way, like tiny jewels and the powdered dust of jewels scattered across the night, and then this great black *stain* rose from the treetops and began to blot them out.

The dancers turned their faces towards it and they moaned; I could hear them even over the singing. Ecstasy and torment. The great black mass of it kept rising. I could see no beginning to it or end, no shape, but if I looked long enough I might, and then I'd be fucked, game over. Somehow I knew that much, and somehow that was enough. Enough that I managed to turn around and weave back through the trees along the path.

I put my hands over my ears and sang and shouted as I went. Anything to blot that singing out, to stop it luring me back. I made it out of those woods, and then went scrambling and bawling down the mountain path, bawling out any tune I could think of at the top of my lungs because I needed my hands free to make my way down.

Somehow I managed to get down off the mountain and clear of those woods. And once I did, I ran to the north. Easy enough to do that—I was on the opposite side of Mynydd Du from Llyn Daioni and Hafan Deg and Capel Teg and all the rest, so I just put that damned mountain at my back and ran away from it as fast as I could. Nothing on earth would have got me to chance my luck going back through Coed Capel.

Right at the north end of the Bala Triangle, you see, just east of Maes Carnedd, there's a gap—a gap between the woods of Coed Dinas and the woods of Coed Lleidr. And I made for that.

It was a bloody nightmare, I tell you. I'd managed to keep hold of my torch, and the beam flashed and jolted across the ground as I ran. I kept thinking something was going to leap out at me, but nothing did. The scariest thing I saw on that run was a rabbit, I kid you not. Of course, the state I was in, I shat a brick as you can imagine.

But I just kept going. I fell a couple of times, then got up. I kept going, till I nearly ran full-tilt into a drystone wall. Beyond it was a little country lane.

I hopped over the wall. I was shaking, and my legs were killing me, but I didn't stop. I just got on the road and started walking. I didn't care which way it went, as long as it wasn't to Mynydd Du.

Finally I reached a village. Can't even remember the name of it, but I do remember they had a concrete bus shelter. I got my sleeping bag out of my rucksack and bedded down there.

I didn't sleep well. I bet that doesn't surprise you. I dreamt of the mountain, and the dancers. Laura. She was beckoning me to join her, and the others, and I wanted to. Thankfully, that was only in my head.

I woke early in the morning. There was mist everywhere and I was shivering. I ate a couple of bars of mint cake waiting for the bus to show. My car was back at Heol Capel, but I wasn't going back there. No – I could arrange to get the car towed, or something – fuck, I'd have left it there to rust rather than ever go near Mynydd Du again.

I got the first bus that showed up. Thank god I had some cash on me—enough, anyway. It ran to Barmouth. Looking back, I could have got one going the other way, to Wrexham, and that would have got me closer to home, but all that mattered right then was getting as far away from Mynydd Du as I could.

There was no-one else on the bus, so I huddled at the back, hugging my backpack to me and crying into it a couple of times. It was starting to hit home to me what had happened. Laura was gone. Glenn and Angela too, yes, and they'd been friends. But Laura was gone. That most of all. I loved her, Si. I said that, didn't I?

I finally got off at Barmouth. The day turned out quite bright. The sea shone blue and I could smell the fresh salty tang of it. People were walking their dogs on the beach. None of it seemed real, but it was.

All of a sudden, I was hungry. I went to a café and stuffed myself silly with a full English. But then I remembered the mountains. They're all around in Barmouth. It's right at the edge of the Snowdonia National Park. I didn't want to be near a Welsh mountain again, ever. So I went right to the train station and bought a ticket home. A single. One way. I was never coming back to Wales, not if I could help it.

I caught the train and stared at the back of the seat in front of me all the way home. Changed at Wolverhampton—Christ, I never thought I'd be happy to see *that* place. Then I caught one back to Manchester, and when I stepped off it, I could have kissed the ground.

For a day or so I really thought I'd got away with it. I knew at the back of my head there'd still be questions about Laura and the others and wondered how to deal with them, but whenever I tried to think about it my mind shied away from the topic.

But then I started hearing the voices again, the singing. It was calling me back. Demanding I return. On and on and on.

And I'd—see things. Never quite full-on, but close by. Corner-of-your-eye stuff again. Sometimes in white. Sometimes in red.

Think I told you, didn't I? Sometimes the mountain likes to play with its prey. Play out the line, let the fish run, then start reeling it in when it's off-guard and tired. I don't know how much of my getting away was luck, or down to Laura knocking me out, and how much was down to it toying with me. But now I could feel it calling me back.

It does that, most of all, because I know too much. No-one's pieced as much of it together as I have. But—and this is the big *but*—it's working at a distance. And I wondered, how many people are too many for it to handle? Two at once? Three? Four?

So I got all the notes in order, bagged them up, then stuck them in my locker at the leisure centre. And I left the key with Victoria. It was the best I could do. I didn't want the notes or the means to get them with me. I knew the mountain wanted me, but there was always the chance it would try and persuade me—or I'd persuade myself—that it might let me go, might spare me, if I destroyed Ware's notes and mine, anything that might point others towards the truth about Mynydd Du. Then there'd be just me, and if I could only convince it I'd keep quiet it might spare me.

I knew I might come to believe that if this went on long enough—and unless I killed myself it probably would—but I also knew it wouldn't be true. It wanted me and it'd have me.

But if two of us knew, the pull on us might be weakened. And that was when I thought of you, Si. If you could spread the word, get the whole thing published somehow, more people would know. And I'm betting it can't reel in hundreds, thousands of people.

I know there were loads of other people I could have gone to, maybe, but I wasn't thinking too straight. And we weren't close anymore, so—I didn't feel as bad about it as I would have about a good mate.

So—yeah. I can see from the look on your face that you get what I was about and you're not impressed. Well, I was up against it, mate. I didn't want to die, but most of all I didn't want to end up dancing away eternity in the fucking pine trees on Mynydd Du with Laura and the rest. I'm sorry about her, I even loved her, but I wasn't doing that for her. And stop acting like you would, like you're so fucking noble, because you're not.

Anyway. You want the rest of it or not? Aw come on, Si—Si!

Okay, okay. Thanks.

I only just made it back to my place after I left the key with Victoria. It was like the mountain knew what I had in mind, so it was cranking up the pressure. The song was so loud I could barely hear, and I couldn't see straight for shapes that appeared and disappeared at will.

Somehow I got up the stairs and into the house. It was all down to you now, Si, all I had to do was let you know.

I knew I had to do that. Just had to find a way. An email, Facebook, something—but I wasn't thinking straight, like I said. I couldn't think for the singing. So I got to the stereo, got the scissors and the headphones.

Yeah, I know – I hacked my hair and scattered it around me. Nail-clippings too. I'd read somewhere that was some sort of a charm. I needed all the help I could get. I ripped up my shirt and blindfolded myself so I wouldn't see, put the headphones on and played the loudest heavy metal I could find with the volume turned all the way up, so that I wouldn't hear.

I thought it would do, just for a while; thought the attack would let up and then I could go and get a message to you. But it never did let up. Every time I turned the sound down, the singing was back, louder than ever—if I shifted the blindfold, I could see the shapes, the dancers, the robed ones. And it became about blotting them out and holding on.

Then the stereo blew a gasket and I had to sing. All I could think of were some songs by the Cure. So I started singing them, over and over, till I was bellowing them out. Upset the neighbours, I believe. Which was all to the good. If they got someone round, if I could talk to someone, I could get a message to you.

I don't really remember much after that. Next thing I'm at all clear on, I was here. But the singing wouldn't let up. I got them to blindfold me and give me music – but first I got Keith to get in touch with you. And then you came here, and I told you about Victoria. And now here you are again, Simon.

That's everything, really. I'd like to be taken back to my room now, please. And Si—for whatever it's worth—I'm sorry.

III. THE COVER-UP

It had been a long night, and for my sins it didn't seem to be over yet. After Rob was ushered back to his room, Warren and I headed to Keith Atherton's office, where Nolan was waiting. At least Keith made his own coffee.

"Well," said Nolan, in greeting, "that was a fat lot of fucking use, wasn't it?"

I almost told him where to go, but remembered he could ensure I ended the night in a cell and was probably just pissed off enough to do it. "Hey, he talked."

"Nothing we could use, though."

"No."

Nolan slumped into a chair. "Take a pew, gents."

We did.

"For the record," said Nolan, "I have absolutely no idea what the fuck happened to those people. I'm not entirely sure I want to. But I can hardly put on a report that they were taken by some kind of… god, can I? Now, of course, there's always the possibility that this theory about some sort of toxin was right. It's in the ground, in the water, it seeps up into the air, you breathe it in and you go doolally. Nice idea. Given that we've only got Markland's word for what happened up there."

"But we don't," I said. "We've got Laura's Dictaphone. We've got the DVR footage."

"How do I know Markland didn't fake that ahead of time? You'd be surprised how far some people'll go to try and convince you of a cover story. He could have faked the video footage, right down to the date stamps, could have forced Laura to record her Dictaphone comments—"

"Oh come on—" I said.

"Well, what would you say if someone fed you a story like Markland's? Gods and monsters, dancers in the pines? What was it Sherlock Holmes used to say—eliminate what can't be true and whatever's left is your answer, however unlikely it sounds?"

"Something like that," I admitted.

"Right. So, come on, Simon. On the one hand, Markland killed the other three, after going to batshit crazy lengths to cover it up. Christ, I can even give you a motive: he was going to put a Bala

Triangle book of his own together and this was to try and convince people it was for real."

"You're not seriously saying—"

"Believe me, I've known people kill for madder reasons than that. So that's explanation number one. Explanation number two is that the mountain god reached out and got them all. Now out of those, which one do *you* think most folk would say was impossible?"

I had no answer to that.

"But anyway, back to the toxins. Nice idea. Only one problem. Complete bollocks. None of those soil and water samples made it out of the Triangle with him, but Keith here took blood and urine samples from Markland when he was admitted. They didn't find any toxic or foreign agent in them. But I did have the original samples rechecked and some new ones taken. After all, he's off his head so you'd think there'd still be something knocking around in his system. They checked and rechecked, looked for the most obscure, weird chemicals they could find on the books. But there's nothing. As for that other idea—an energy field or whatever it was—I'm reliably informed that it's complete bullshit too. Might have sounded half-convincing in the seventies, but not anymore." Nolan breathed out. "At least there won't be a trial, not the state he's in."

"So you're just going to... hush it up?"

"Who says there's anything to hush up, really? When you get down to it? At least, that's the line I'm gonna take, Simon. No offence, but—you write stories about shit like this, so maybe you're more used to it than I am. Me? I like things to make sense. More importantly, so do my superiors." Nolan sighed. "When you come down to it, anyway, if Markland *is* telling the truth—it's not as if there's anything we can do for Laura Hines, or for Glenn and Angela Lane, is there? And not much anyone can do for *him* either. Except keep him shut up somewhere safe, like here. Or Broadmoor."

"But—"

"That," said Nolan, "is how it's gonna be, okay? So I'd like to take this opportunity, Mr Bestwick, to thank you for helping us in this case. It's much appreciated. DC Warren will take you home now."

*

"You can see his point," Warren said later as we drove. "There's no way we could tell the truth about what happened."

I blinked at him. My eyes felt gritty; it was starting to get light. "So you believe it?"

"Course I bloody do. And so does Nolan. Trouble is, you're never going to convince the people we need to. So…" he shrugged. "And it's not gonna make much difference to Markland."

It did make me wonder, as he drove me home, how many events reported as sordid little crimes were really window-dressing for something else, something like this? A phrase of the occultist Montague Summers came back to me: *the monstrous things visible beneath the crust of our cracking civilisation.* It wasn't a pleasant thought.

"Best thing you can do," Warren said as we pulled up outside my house, "is to forget about this. Bala Triangle, Mynydd Du, Rob Markland—forget it all. Go back to your life, don't rock the boat. And that'll be that."

He offered his hand. "See you."

I shook his hand. "See you."

I got out of the car, went inside, up to bed and slept.

But I'd hear from him, and Nolan, again.

IV. THE LAST OF ROBERT MARKLAND

After my last interview with him, Rob Markland returned to his former near-catatonic state, listening non-stop to his music, covering his eyes and blotting out the world.

Two weeks after the interview, around the middle of November 2013, Rob escaped from Prestwich Psychiatric Hospital—they're still not sure how he managed it, but he did.

In his room, his bed had been neatly made and all his belongings tidily arranged, as if the room was about to be moved into.

On top of the coverlet was a single sheet of carefully folded white A4, with FAO DR KEITH ATHERTON printed on it in painstaking block capitals.

*

TEXT OF ROB MARKLAND'S LETTER:

Dear Dr Keith,

Sorry to be leaving you so soon, but the truth is I can't stay. Please don't take it personally.

Please do me one last favour and get back in touch with Simon Bestwick. Tell him that it didn't work. I can still hear the singing. The drugs don't work, as another song put it. Maybe if he'd published what I'd told him, written it up and got it printed, this wouldn't be happening, but he didn't and it is.

Now, you might be safe, doctor, you and him. And the police officers who were with me. That's four of you who all know about the place. As I think I might have said before, I don't know how well the mountain works at long range—especially not with people like Simon and you, who've learned about it second-hand. I don't know where the mountain's power stops and plain old human curiosity starts, I'm afraid.

You might be safe. Or you might not. If not, then I'm sorry. Truly. My only defence is that I was desperate and afraid and wanted very much to save my own skin. People make that out to be a very low reason for doing something, but the truth is it's a very strong motivation.

I've done my best to hold out, but I no longer can. I've been issued a clear invitation to the dance, and the host doesn't take no for an answer.

Remember: there is *something on that mountain, and it wants to be left alone. One way or the other, it ensures it is.*

If nothing happens to either of you, then forget everything I told you, and that you ever knew me. That really is the best advice that I can give. BUT, if the singing begins to bedevil you too, then the only suggestion I can make—the only thing that might *save you—is to spread word of Mynydd Du far and wide. Its power is vast but limited; it's omnipotent within the Bala Triangle, but outside it… outside the Triangle, if enough people know the truth, you might be safe. It's all I can offer, I'm afraid.*

Good luck and best wishes,
Rob Markland.

*

However Rob got out of Prestwich, he managed to avoid any kind of detection until the CCTV camera in a motorway services station caught him climbing aboard a truck. When the driver was identified, he admitted picking Rob up there and dropping him off in Chester.

Warren said it was possible Rob had ended up begging in Chester until he had some money. He might have caught a train from there, or hitched. No-one was sure.

What was certain was that the trail was next picked up in Wrexham, where Rob boarded the X94 bus from there to Barmouth. One way or another, he now had money; the driver remembered him buying his ticket, not least because he was a 'weird-looking bugger—all scruffy and dirty and acting odd'. When pressed for details, the driver had described Rob as constantly twitching and muttering to himself, and had been afraid he'd turn violent. As it turned out, he didn't, but the driver still breathed a sigh of relief when he got off the bus in Bala.

Of course; where else would he have got off?

In Bala, he bought a couple of bars of chocolate and a bottle of water and started walking west, in the direction of the lake. The proprietor of the Loch Café, situated at the end of the lake, remembered seeing him walk past, weaving and mumbling. She said she hadn't been sure whether to be alarmed or concerned at his appearance, and regretted not trying to help him. Apparently Warren told her that she'd done the best thing, as the escaped patient could be dangerous. I suppose Rob could have been at that stage, to anyone trying to stop him getting where he was going.

Robert Markland was never seen again.

After that he just walks up the lake road and to all intents and purposes out of existence, but I can guess where he went. He would have carried on till he found the overgrown, almost invisible turn-off and climbed up Heol Capel. For all I know, his car might still have been there; the ruins of Heol Capel farm would have been. But I doubt he stayed long.

Soon he would have been taking the footpath down through the woods of Coed Capel to come out by the ruins of Hafan Deg. He would have walked along the shores of Llyn Daioni and past what had once been the village of Capel Teg, squelched through the edges of the marsh beside the lake and then headed north, towards the pine-bristling silhouette that rose from the ground like a knotted fist of stone.

Towards Black Mountain, and a final rendezvous with his god.

AUTHOR'S AFTERWORD

I was given a copy of Rob's letter and told of what had happened, but it didn't hold my attention for very long. Towards the end of November 2013 a close friend of mine, Joel Lane, died very suddenly and unexpectedly. Any interest I might still have had in either Rob Markland or Mynydd Du was forgotten as I, and many of my fellow writers, grieved for an immensely talented author and a good man. The account you are now reading is dedicated to his memory.

But by early December, I was forced to think of Rob again, and Mynydd Du, because it was then that the singing began.

I heard it on and off for the first day or so. I was busy with temping work, and Manchester city centre was busy with the build-up to Christmas, so there were distractions. But by the second day, it had become a regular occurrence, and by the third day, there was no way I could dismiss it. It sounded like dozens, even hundreds of voices, male and female, singing in chorus. And no—I couldn't, even if I tried, describe the melody.

I tried to get in touch with the others—Keith Atherton, Dave Warren, DCI Nolan—but with no luck. Last I heard, Atherton and Warren were both off sick and no-one seemed to have a clue where Nolan had got to. I had a nasty feeling I could hazard a guess, and that the rest of us would be joining him in short order unless I did something quickly.

I knew what I needed to do, of course, because Rob had told me. I didn't want to put anyone else at risk, but... well, as Rob said himself, self-preservation is a powerful instinct. If this doesn't work, you'll be finding that out for yourself.

Getting a book published isn't exactly an instant process. I could self-publish, of course, but that's a hit and miss process in terms of readership. Then again, so are most forms of publishing.

There was an added complication—all I had were photocopies of Ware's notes, with no real provenance. The couple of non-fiction publishers I contacted made it clear they wanted to view the originals so that they could be authenticated, especially the photographic evidence, most of which wasn't of sufficient quality to be used in the book.

Unfortunately, when I contacted Sidonie Ware, she admitted that after learning what had happened to Rob, Laura and the others, she'd destroyed all her husband's notes pertaining to Mynydd Du and the Bala Triangle.

The only remaining option, then, was to publish the book as a fictional account. I didn't know if it would work, but by then I was pretty desperate, as I'd just started seeing things from the corner of my eye. White robes. And occasionally red ones.

I contacted a small press publisher I knew, and spun him a pitch. I had to try and sound calm, and make the proposal for a serial sound as convincing as I could. If he turned me down, what could I do? Back to the self-publishing option, presumably. I was already looking into that when he said yes.

I was glad of that, because it took most of the work off me; all I had to do now was tell the story. I had to try and do so as convincingly as possible; people had to believe it for this to work. But when I started – hell, the first chunk of it didn't even begin to cover Mynydd Du or its history. I delivered it, anyway, and the first instalment of Black Mountain went up on the publisher's website on the 18ᵗʰ December, 2013, as a free taster of what was to come.

And almost at once, the pressure eased.

The singing didn't entirely stop, and from time to time I'd still catch glimpses of things from the corner of my eye—but it was bearable. I could stand it; I could blank it out, I could resist.

I'd succeeded, I realised, in dividing the mountain's attention. A couple of weeks into January, the singing was getting worse again and the 'sights' as I called them had begun to rise in volume once more. But by then I'd completed the second instalment, and started to get into the story proper, revealing the first of Mynydd Du's stories.

The same happened in February. In March I sold my house in Manchester and moved to Liverpool with Cate. It had been on the cards for a while, and maybe I had some idea of confusing the god on the mountain by moving around. It delayed the next instalment, but since then I've managed to keep the episodes coming out pretty regularly, and it's helped. I've no idea how many people have read *Black Mountain*, but I owe every one of you a debt of thanks for keeping the beast at bay.

But now the story has reached its end; it only remains to be seen what happens. There are no further instalments now, no more words to spread. Perhaps now it will start to work on those who've read the serial to date, working itself up to claiming us *en masse*.

*

UPDATE: 3RD OCTOBER, 2021

I'd hoped that I'd left Mynydd Du behind me. Since October 2014, when the final instalment of *Black Mountain* was released, there'd been no further episodes.

In the past few weeks, however, it's begun again. I tried contacting some readers who I knew had followed the serial. Some refused to discuss the subject; one admitted to experiencing similar symptoms herself. Two were untraceable.

It seemed as though my worst fears were being confirmed; at that point, I retrieved the text of the serial and began revising it into a single volume. My one hope now is that I can place it with a mass-market publisher; hopefully then too many people will know the story for the mountain god to affect them all; if you believe it's a work of fiction, that might even be for the best. It might realise it's to its advantage to let the world think so, and so to leave me, and the others—including you—alone. Perhaps. I don't know how or if it thinks, or how well it understands us.

I hope that will be the outcome, anyway. But I could be wrong.

If that's the case, your best chance is to keep spreading the word. Draw others' attention to the Bala Triangle and Mynydd Du. Anything that might weaken its hold. And if that doesn't work... if you begin to glimpse shapes at the edges of your sight, if you hear far-off voices singing a tune you can never quite name....

Then—for what it's worth—I'm sorry.

Simon Bestwick
Swinton, December 2013 – Liverpool, October 2014.
Revised Wallasey, Wirral, 2019-2021.

"Described by Ramsey Campbell as "Among the most important writers of contemporary British horror," Simon Bestwick was born in the West Midlands and grew up in Manchester. Married to long-suffering fellow author Cate Gardner, he now lives on the Wirral, and dreams of moving to Wales.

He is the author of the novels *Tide of Souls*, *The Faceless and The Feast Of All Souls*, together with the 'Black Road' series of novels: *Hell's Ditch*, *Devil's Highway* and *Wolf's Hill*. The final Black Road novel, *Road's End*, is in preparation.

In addition, Bestwick has also penned the short story collections *A Hazy Shade Of Winter*, *Pictures Of The Dark*, *The Condemned* and *And Cannot Come Again*, the mini-collections *Singing Back The Dark* and *Nine Ghosts*, and the novellas *Angels Of The Silences*, *Breakwater*, *Roth-Steyr*, *A Different Kind Of Light* and *Devils Of London*.

Bestwick's short fiction has appeared in many venues including Horrified, Railroad Tales and Body Shocks fiction, and has been reprinted in *The Best Horror Of The Year*, *Best British Fantasy* and *The Best Of The Best Horror Of The Year*. His work has been shortlisted for the British Fantasy Award four times.

He loves books, music, walking, the woods, the sea and enjoys cooking. He posts new fiction every month at HTTPS://WWW.PATREON.COM/SIMONBESTWICK and still hasn't kicked his addictions to Pepsi Max or semicolons. He also has a blog at simon-bestwick.blogspot.com, but would rather have a dog."

Black Mountain

Simon Bestwick

WWW.INDEPENDENTLEGIONS.COM

Available Books in English

CROTA
by Owl Goingback
Novel – Hardcover Edition
September 2021

THE MOTHER WOUND
by Jess Landry
Collection – Paperback and eBook Edition
May 2021

THE FEVERISH STARS
by John Shirley
Collection – Paperback and eBook Edition
March 2021

HER LIFE MATTERS
by Alessandro Manzetti & Stefano Cardoselli
Graphic Novel – Paperback Edition
December 2020

UMBRIA
by Santiago Eximeno
Collection – Paperback and eBook Edition
December 2020

LOST TRIBE
by Gene O'Neill
Novel – Paperback and eBook Edition
October 2020

SHILOH
by Philip Fracassi
Novella – Paperback and eBook Edition
October 2020

ARTIFACTS
by Bruce Boston
Poetry Collection– Paperback and eBook Edition
July 2018

KNOWING WHEN TO DIE
by Mort Castle
Collection– Paperback and eBook Edition
June 2018

NARAKA
by Alessandro Manzetti
Novel– Paperback and eBook Edition
May 2018

A WINTER SLEEP
by Greg F. Gifune
Novel– Paperback and eBook Edition
April 2018

SPREE AND OTHER STORIES
by Lucy Taylor
Collection – Paperback and eBook Edition
February 2018

THE LIVING AND THE DEAD
by Greg F. Gifune
Novel – Paperback and eBook Edition
December 2017

TALKING IN THE DARK
by Dennis Etchison
Collection – eBook Edition
December 2017

THE BEAUTY OF DEATH 2 – DEATH BY WATER
edited by Alessandro Manzetti & Jodi Renee Lester
Anthology – Paperback and eBook Edition
November 2017

DREAMS THE RAGMAN
by Greg F. Gifune
Novella – Paperback and eBook Edition
November 2017

CHILDREN OF NO ONE
by Nicole Cushing
Novella – Paperback and eBook Edition
October 2017

THE RAIN DANCERS
by Greg F. Gifune
Novella – Paperback and eBook Edition
September 2017

THE WISH MECHANICS
by Daniel Braum
Collection – Paperback and eBook Edition
July 2017

THE ONE THAT COMES BEFORE
by Livia Llewellyn
Novella – Paperback and eBook Edition
May 2017

SELECTED STORIES
by Nate Southard
Collection – Paperback and eBook Edition
March 2017

THE CARP-FACED BOY AND OTHER TALES
by Thersa Matsuura
Collection – Paperback and eBook Edition
February 2017

DOCTOR BRITE
by Poppy Z. Brite
Collection – eBook Edition
December 2016

ALL AMERICAN HORROR OF THE 21ST CENTURY: THE FIRST
DECADE
edited by Mort Castle
Anthology – Paperback and eBook Edition
November 2016

BENEATH THE NIGHT
by Greg Gifune
Novel – Paperback and eBook Edition
October 2016

WHAT WE FOUND IN THE WOODS
by Shane McKenzie
Collection – eBook Edition
September 2016

THE HORROR SHOW
by Poppy Z. Brite
Collection – eBook Edition
August 2016

THE BEAUTY OF DEATH VOL. 1
Edited by Alessandro Manzetti
Anthology – eBook Edition
July 2016

SELECTED STORIES
by Edward Lee
Collection – eBook Edition
July 2016

USED STORIES
by Poppy Z. Brite
Collection – eBook Edition
June 2016

THE USHERS
by Edward Lee
Collection – eBook Edition
May 2016

THE CRYSTAL EMPIRE
by Poppy Z. Brite
Novella – eBook Edition
April 2016

SONGS FOR THE LOST
by Alexander Zelenyj
Collection – eBook Edition
April 2016

SELECTED STORIES
by Poppy Z. Brite
Collection – eBook Edition
February 2016

THE HITCHHIKING EFFECT
by Gene O'Neill
Collection – eBook Edition
February 2016

INDEPENDENT LEGIONS PUBLISHING
Via Virgilio, 10 – TRIESTE (ITALY)
+39 040 9776602
www.independentlegions.com
independent.legions@aol.com

Printed in Great Britain
by Amazon

72164536R00177